For Jill, my strongest supporter from day one.

Special thanks to Louis Lamb, Sarah Pinborough,
my agent John Jarrold, and the awesome team at Gollancz,
without whom none of this would have been possible.

ROBOTEER

ROBOTEER

ALEX LAMB

First published in Great Britain in 2015
by Gollancz
An imprint of the Orion Publishing Group
Carmelite House, 50 Victoria Embankment,
London EC4Y 0DZ
An Hachette UK Company

This edition published in Great Britain in 2016 by Gollancz

3 5 7 9 10 8 6 4 2

A CIP catalogue record for this book
is available from the British Library

ISBN 978 1 473 20609 0

Typeset at The Spartan Press Ltd,
Lymington, Hants

Printed and bound in Great Britain by
Clays Ltd, St Ives plc

The Orion Publishing Group's policy is to use papers that are natural, renewable and recyclable products and made from wood grown in sustainable forests. The logging and manufacturing processes are expected to conform to the environmental regulations of the country of origin.

www.alexlamb.com
www.orionbooks.co.uk
www.gollancz.co.uk

1: BATTLE AT MEMBURI

1.1: WILL

Will Kuno-Monet was teaching lifter trucks to hunt when the scramble klaxon sounded. He stopped the ten-ton machines mid-stalk and listened, his body taut. The moment everyone had been expecting for days had finally come. The Earthers were attacking.

He ordered the trucks to their action stations, opened his eyes and yanked back his bunk curtain. His shipmates were already propelling themselves out of their beds and shouting as they hurtled towards the door of the cramped dorm chamber.

'Move! Move! Move!'

'Don't block the hatch!'

Will hurriedly unclipped and followed suit.

Outside, the snakeway was a torrent of figures in silver-green one-piece uniforms. Crew darted like fleeing fish, passing each other on the cramped zero-g bends with millimetres to spare. Will hurled himself into the throng, narrowly missing a couple of engineers.

Ten seconds and two levels later, Will reached the immersion room – a cramped cubic space made of cream-coloured plastic filled with elastic webbing and combat-bags. He clawed his way through the maze of cables to his place at the far end, past the seven other roboteers who were busily sealing themselves in.

Will thrust himself into the bag with trembling hands and let the gel-sac shape itself around his body. He rammed the fat-contact against his neck and tucked his arms inside before the fluid could lock solid. At Will's mental command, the ultra-high-bandwidth cable started sending. The battle status presented itself to him as fully formed thoughts, each tinted by the crisp, owlish flavour of the *Phoenix*'s central command SAP.

There were six Earther ships in tight hexagonal formation. Will saw them as bright-red arrows in a schematic representation of local space, zeroing in on the green circle that was their target – the antimatter factory near the star itself. The Earthers appeared to be making a direct bid for it. The *Phoenix* was instructed to maintain its position.

Strategic analysis showed that the force was far too light to be the predicted primary assault. The Earther ships had small gravity-distortion footprints, suggesting light gunships, probably Jesus Class. No match for the three huge Galatean cruisers guarding the facility. Their approach was almost certainly a feint of some kind. The real attack would come later, when attention was diverted.

Will saw the cruisers as green chevrons whipping across the system to intercept. Galatean ships had a strong speed advantage in-system as their more sophisticated engines performed far better in dirty space. Given the dreadful lag on optical comms, they'd probably engaged the enemy already.

The battle status clear in his mind, Will checked in with his expert – Franz Assimer-Leung, the ship's tactical assault coordinator. His vision connected to the camera above Franz's combat-bag, which became Will's eyes. Franz's blocky, furrowed face appeared before him.

'Reporting for duty, sir,' said Will. The fat-contact relayed the words he thought directly to the speaker bud implanted in Franz's ear.

Franz busily scanned the contents of his visor, readying his Self-Aware Programs, fingers flying across the console on his lap. 'Check,' said Franz. 'Stay ready, Will. I want you sharp on this one. No wandering off.'

Will couldn't help bristling slightly. He'd never *wandered off* during a battle, whatever that was supposed to mean. 'Yes, sir.'

Franz was clearly busy so Will turned his attention outwards, looking for the battle through the ship's long-range sensors. At this distance there was nothing to see but X-ray flickering, barely visible so close to the star's glare. With the filters turned up this high, the rest of the sky was bottomless black.

Will's mind churned. He could barely stand the anxiety of waiting to see what the Earthers would try. This battle was likely to determine the course of the war.

Memburi had been Earth's primary fuelling station on the straight-line path between the home system and Galatea – before the Galateans had captured it. If the Earthers didn't retake it, it would be almost impossible for them to wage war against their former colony, and easy for Galatea to strike back if they tried. On the other hand, if the Earthers did claim it, they'd be well placed to attempt another invasion, and Earth had no shortage of lives to waste in trying.

Will's train of thought was broken by a sudden nervous laugh. He glanced across at Gordon Inchaya-Brun, the roboteer for ship defence who hung in the bag next to his. Gordon was a large, well-intentioned youth who'd only been with the Fleet for a year. This was his first big battle.

'They dragged us in here just so we could wait?' muttered Gordon. His eyes were screwed tight shut.

Will knew Gordon wasn't talking to anyone in particular but the distraction was welcome. It beat staring into space and doing nothing.

'I guess so,' he said.

Gordon's soft blue eyes opened in surprise at the reply. Like the rest of the *Phoenix*'s roboteers, he treated Will with a mixture of wariness and awe. There were eight of them in all, one handler for each of the mighty ship's eight different software subsystems, and Will was definitely the odd one out. He didn't think like the others.

'But don't worry,' Will added. 'Space battles don't last long.'

Gordon gave him an anxious smile. 'That's what I'm worried about.'

Gordon's fears were well grounded. Today they would live or die with the *Phoenix*. There was no way off a starship when you were surrounded in every direction by kilometres of the most hideously irradiated machinery humanity had ever devised. You either left the battle with working engines or you fried.

A sudden flare drew Will's attention back to the view from the sensors. The distant battle was looking unusually bright. It winked at him. Will eyed it uneasily. If the Earther ships were on a suicide run, they might be self-detonating about now. And meanwhile, the next wave of the attack might come from any direction. His heart was in his mouth as they waited.

1.2: IRA

Captain Ira Baron-Lecke of the Galatean starship *Ariel* watched the battle from a few thousand kilometres beyond the combat zone. It was probably too close, but still a lot further away than he wanted to be. The disrupter cloud made it impossible for them to get any nearer.

He lay back in his crash couch, hands wrapped tight around the control-handles. Through his visor's standard display, the warring ships resembled flashing points of hard white light on a black background. At full magnification, however, he could make out their true shape. Each ship looked like a dull metallic egg covered with tiny umbrellas. Blue-white light crackled from the spokes, coating the vessels with sheens of spastic luminescence.

Ira did not like what he saw. The Earthers had come in too light – just a ring of six small ships, hemmed in by three immense Galatean cruisers. And they'd stopped short of their objective, as if taunting the Galateans to come out and meet them. They were up to something.

'Amy, give me an update.'

Though he and Amy, his first officer, occupied opposite bunks in the *Ariel*'s tiny main cabin, Ira used his subvocal throat-mike instead of speaking out loud. The *Ariel* was a soft-combat ship. Given the physical conditions it had to operate under, battle orders were never trusted to ordinary speech.

'No change,' Amy replied. 'The Earthers are using juice like it's going out of style. They haven't launched any gravity shields, just disrupter buoys. Central Command is convinced it's a suicide.'

Ira frowned. A disrupter buoy's single job was to fill the

surrounding space with ionic crap that made it impossible for your enemy to use warp. It was an important tool in warfare, but one used sparingly. Disrupters trapped you just as certainly as they trapped your enemy. Yet each one of those little Earther ships had come in carrying enough of them to freeze an armada. He watched the buoys buzzing around their parent ships like swarms of angry bees around a hive. It seemed like a profligate amount of hardware to waste. Furthermore, the battle was getting awfully bright.

'What are they doing down there? Attacking with g-rays?'

'Looks like it,' said Amy.

Ira shook his head. Scout-ship g-rays against battle cruisers. That was like coming at macrodozers with sharpened sticks.

A g-ray was nothing more than a gamma-ray laser, and it was only as good as the amount of power you put behind it. If your adversary could push the same amount of juice through his Casimir-buffers, there was no point firing. You just ended up charging his fusion cells for him. But the Earthers knew that. They couldn't possibly hope to summon more power than the cruisers, not even if they concentrated all their fire on a single target.

'They're insane,' he muttered.

'I'm not so sure,' said Amy. 'Those g-rays are *very* hard. The Earthers must have routed main-engine power to their arrays.'

Clearly the Earthers' tactic was to try to freeze out their opponents' gravity weapons and force them into an energy battle. It was just one more reason to believe that the Earthers didn't intend to go home. They hadn't exactly left themselves an escape route.

Ira still didn't like it. Even suicide squads launched gravity shields. Instinct told him to pull back, just in case. He keyed open the channel to his assault expert on the bunk below him.

'John, find any plans yet? I want to know what these bastards think they're doing.'

There was a pause.

'Uh, hang on.'

John was deep in his work with Doug, the ship's roboteer. Together they were gutting the enemy vessels' computer systems of their secrets with the help of the *Ariel*'s little fleet of specialised drones.

'Wait!' said John. 'Doug, go back. I think that's it.' He muttered to himself, then laughed out loud. 'Ha! Yes! We've got data, Captain, and plenty of it.'

Amy's voice chimed in. 'Uh-oh, John – I think you triggered an alarm.' She flagged a visual pointer in Ira's display.

The Earthers had fired a volley of pursuit drones directly at the *Ariel*. Fortunately, they were climbing out through the massive disrupter cloud, which meant they couldn't use warp. Forced to limp along on fusion torches, they presented no immediate threat. It would take them whole minutes to arrive.

'I see them,' said John. 'Prepping countermeasures.'

While John wrestled with the flow of information coursing between the ships, Ira turned his attention back to the battle with the cruisers. He had to be ready to make his move.

The Earthers had all but completely snared the Galateans' torpedoes, he noticed, drawing the battle out to a grindingly slow sub-light exchange. Nevertheless, they were still outgunned. It was only a matter of time before they died. As soon as the Earthers ran out of antimatter, their supercharged buffers would drop, and no number of disrupters could save them. However, the seconds kept ticking by and Ira found himself still anxiously waiting. His unease steadily deepened. For a suicide squad, those ships were taking a hell of a long time to die.

The Galateans kept battering away at them, but the Earthers didn't seem to be flagging. It was the Galatean attacks that appeared to be slowing. They simply weren't equipped for long battles. Nobody was.

'Something's wrong,' said Amy. 'I'm not seeing any degradation in the Earthers' disrupter cloud. It's just getting bigger.'

She sent him an ion filter of the battle scene. It showed the ragged hole the Earthers had carved in the local flow, like a filthy black smear on the rainbow of space.

'At this rate, it'll reach us in two hundred seconds,' she added.

If that happened, the *Ariel* would be stuck – and effectively dead. The one thing a soft-combat ship could never afford to do was hit a disrupter cloud. Only heavy, powerful ships could endure a disrupter fight and the *Ariel* was neither. It survived on speed and stealth.

Ira opened his hotline to Admiral Bryant-Leys aboard the *Aslan*, the cruiser leading the Galatean assault. 'Sir, we've got problems. That cloud is going to hit any minute now. Requesting permission to get clear.' He watched the cloud grow during the agonising seconds it took for the admiral's reply to reach him.

'Accepted,' said the admiral. 'Do what you have to, Ira.'

Ira keyed the channel to his crew. 'Okay, everybody, we're pulling back. Rachel, I want full warp.'

'Rails greased and ready.'

'Doug,' he told his roboteer. 'Brace yourself.'

Ira pressed the ignition stud on his joystick. An invisible hand slammed him into his couch as the gravity engines kicked on. They started moving away, but far too slowly. From cold, the trigger field needed time to build strength. The hammer beats of the engine were slow and intermittent.

'Ira!' said Amy. 'Look out!'

Ira saw what was happening but there was nothing he could do. The Earthers had turned the full might of their disrupters against the *Ariel*.

As quickly as they came, the brutal tugs of the gravity engines faded and vanished. They were stuck like a bug in amber. Whatever secrets John had unearthed, the Earthers were clearly very keen that the *Ariel* didn't leave with them.

'Rachel!' Ira snapped. 'Full power to the fusion torches!'

'Done.'

Ira turned on the power. Once again he was slammed into his couch, but this time it was merely conventional acceleration. Ira made his way up and out of the cloud at a creeping two-point-five gees. He cursed himself as he watched their progress. The minutes to drone-intercept didn't look so long and comfortable any more. Drones could accelerate as fast as they liked. They didn't have human cargo to worry about.

He never should have let himself be caught. He should have moved position without asking the admiral first. Adherence to protocol might have just killed them.

'Those drones are closing, Ira,' said Amy.

'I can see that.'

The drones slid effortlessly into targeting range and opened fire with their g-rays. Fierce crackling filled the tiny cabin as the buffers struggled to compensate.

Ira flinched in surprise. 'Shit!'

'I told you those rays were hard,' said Amy.

Ira yanked the joystick. The ship went into a gut-wrenching turn. 'Rachel, damage report.'

'Thirty per cent of our secondary buffers just blew,' his engineer replied.

Ira winced. Drones with that kind of power were unheard of. Another hit like that could finish them. Only one primary buffer had to fail for their fragile habitat core to be scoured with radiation.

'I want all the power we can spare going through those buffers,' he ordered.

'It already is,' said Rachel.

How could a single drone put more power into a laser than his ship's engines?

He keyed his roboteer. 'Doug?'

'Repairs in progress, Captain. We'll be good as new in no time.'

Even though synthesised direct at Ira's implant, Doug's voice still sounded strangled. Doug didn't do well in heavy gees. He was the only one on board not bred for the rigours of spaceflight.

'John, I want countermeasures,' said Ira.

'Launching now.'

'John, I need to know what I'm looking at. I want tactical profiles on these things. I want weapons specs.'

'Ira!' Amy squawked.

Ira banked hard and hurled on the power as another drone lined up to fire. It felt like a freight train had landed on his chest. Stars skittered across his vision. Someone whimpered on a lower bunk.

'Amy, how long till we're out of this cloud?' Ira gasped, relying on the throat-mike to turn his wheezing into words.

'Eighteen more seconds. I see another drone charging—'

Ira flipped the ship again and almost blacked out as the anvil of gravity crashed into him.

'Ten, nine, eight—' breathed Amy.

'Rachel?' said Ira.

'Ready.'

Ira kept the ship turning as he brought the gravity engines back online. This time, he meant to hit the edge of the cloud running.

'Three, two, one,' said Amy. 'We're clear!'

Ira engaged warp. For an awful second, the thrust from the fusion torches combined with the pull of the gravity engines. It felt like his organs were fighting to escape through his back. Then the torch died and they were away.

The drones shrank to dots behind them.

1.3: WILL

Captain Beaumont-Klein's voice rang in Will's ears.

'Brace for warp.' For the last ten minutes, Will had ached for the waiting to end. Now he wished it could have lasted a little longer. His combat-bag jolted as the *Phoenix*'s engines kicked in. As the growl of the drive filled the ship, a burst of fresh orders from Central Command unfolded in his head like a spiritual revelation.

Something had gone wrong. The ships guarding the antimatter factory were in deep trouble. Pictures of the battle scene flashed up to fill his field of vision. The disrupter cloud was the biggest he'd ever seen, its ragged ends stretching for tens of thousands of kilometres, like a dark scarf blown in a slow-motion wind. Will experienced a cold rush of fear.

All three cruisers were in danger. The *Baloo* wasn't responding, the *Walrus* was losing power and the *Aslan* was under heavy fire. And they were all deep inside that cloud. It was a catastrophe, and it had somehow been wrought by those six little ships.

The *Phoenix* closed rapidly on the battle, cutting in-system to get as near as it could without hitting the cloud. Then it turned and ploughed straight in, fusion torches at full burn. Will's combat-bag threw him sideways. Captain Klein was taking them in to rescue the trapped cruisers.

As soon as it was within targeting range, the *Phoenix* came under assault. G-rays raked the mighty ship's buffers. The vessel automatically fired off its gravity shields. Will called up a distortion map and watched the tiny drones race away. Each shield was visible as a hard little pucker in the loose weave of space. It was a shield's job to draw fire towards itself and away from the ship it guarded, but their fields softened and shrank almost as soon as they were launched. The enemy buoys had manoeuvred to turn their fire-cones upon them.

'Will?' said Franz.

'Here, sir.'

'We're taking out those disrupters. Here's your template.'

A SAP model immediately downloaded. It looked like a cartoon schematic of some fabulously complex clockwork machine. Shining recall trees hung off the core-cycle, laden with the SAP's memories, each one a brightly coloured block bristling with spiky semantic tags.

'It should compensate for the enemy evasives,' Franz told him. 'Now go!'

Will pressed the model to his mind like a mask. He could feel the SAP's cunning, its eagerness to hunt. With a sweep of one virtual arm, he created sixty-four copies of the program, injected their client modules into the *Phoenix*'s waiting torpedoes and fired. Then he tethered his perceptions to the lead torpedo and flew out with it into the dark.

This was the job he'd been bred to do: to manage, train and guide SAPs from the inside. In physical terms, his mind was just talking to the ship's server substrate. The servers talked to the comms array, and the array ferried orders to the torpedoes via bursts of laser light. But to Will, the effect was seamless.

He stared through unblinking electronic eyes and raced across the aching void of space. As the torpedo, he hungered to join with the disrupters hanging ahead of him in an embrace of spectacular death.

The disrupters hovered like a shoal of fat fish and then scattered as Will plunged into their midst. Will twisted and snagged the closest. They exploded together in a blast of fusion flame.

Will swapped his viewpoint to another torpedo. The disrupters boosted desperately away from him, trying to manoeuvre out of range without losing their hold on the pinned cruisers. Will ripped after them, his kamikaze brethren beside him. He picked his target and dived on it. The disrupter couldn't move fast enough. G-ray blasts from the ships below tried to spear him as he closed for the kill, but it was no use. Will was the shark and the disrupter the sluggish whale. Impact was ecstasy.

His perspective jumped again, to a new pursuit. Forests of g-ray blasts erupted on all sides. He slalomed between them, his digital senses far faster than the old-fashioned targeting programs on the enemy ships.

Suddenly, a ball of white-hot flame ignited next to him. One of his kind was hit. Will cursed. It was bad news to lose a torpedo so soon.

On impulse, he pulled back to re-examine the attack pattern. As expected, he still had enough torpedoes to kill every disrupter, and each of his torpedoes was more than a match for the Earther defences. So why did he suddenly feel worried?

Then he saw it. It was subtle – something only Will's specialist eye for a pattern would recognise. The fight no longer had an ordinary shoal-and-shark dynamic. Franz hadn't compensated for the increased power of the g-ray defences. Even glancing hits were reducing Will's numbers. The enemy beams would thin out his torpedoes too soon. That meant there would still be enough disrupters left to shower their poison onto the trapped starships. They wouldn't be able to free the *Aslan* – or themselves.

Will needed a way to make fewer torpedoes go further. He stared desperately out at the staccato blasts of radiation that were ruining his assault and cursed. Then an idea struck him. If those g-rays were a risk to him, surely they were to the disrupters as well. Was there some way he could turn that fact to his advantage? The answer was *yes*, but the SAPs would need to be sheepdogs, not sharks.

He spurred his lead torpedo on alone and ducked back to his home node where the SAP model hung before him. A blizzard of flashing colour-coded markers picked out the active thought-chunks of each weapon he had left.

Will chased along the stony tunnels of his mind to his private chambers. He grabbed a handful of memory-chunks for playground games and flicked back to the running model. Without pausing for a seizure check, he slammed his chunks onto a fresh branch of the model's primary tree and started hooking up instinct keys as fast as he could. With luck, this old game of his would bind to Franz's carefully structured pursuit tactics and give them exactly what they needed.

An angry shout filled his sensorium, almost breaking his concentration. 'Will! What in Gal's name are you doing?' It was Franz.

Under battle conditions, SAP design was Franz's job. Will wasn't supposed to touch them.

'Leave my SAP alone and get back out there!' Franz roared.

Will didn't listen. He couldn't stop now or the torpedoes would hit the new memories and stall. He frantically hooked up the last few links.

'Stop!' yelled the expert. 'Do you want to get us all killed?'

Will heard Franz open a channel to the captain.

'Sir, we have an emergency. My roboteer's gone rogue!'

Will connected the last strand and leapt back into the head of the lead torpedo. It was coursing through a barrage of enemy fire, hungrily chasing a fleeing disrupter. Will triggered the new memories.

It wasn't a clean patch, but it worked. He felt an abrupt surge of incongruous joy as the missile changed its mind about its intentions in mid-swerve. Rather than heading straight for the buoy, it veered at the last moment, forcing the disrupter to bank hard towards another of its kind. The buoys crashed, erupting in a blast of white-hot ions.

Will's heart soared, despite the furious bellowing from the captain he could hear in the back of his head.

'Monet! What the hell is going on?'

Will watched with glee as his torpedoes shepherded the disrupters into each other, and into their own ships' g-ray fire. Like most Earther machines, the buoys were gratifyingly stupid, designed to follow basic instructions from an unmodified human operator. They had no idea how to respond to being played with. Captain Klein fell silent as he witnessed the sudden rash of disrupter deaths.

However, while Will had started thinning the disrupter cloud nicely, his sensors showed him that the *Phoenix* was taking a beating. Secondary buffers were at sixty per cent and falling, and Gordon was having trouble fending off the enemy's barrage of fire. Will took a copy of the new template branch and passed it to him. With luck, the same thought patterns used in reverse would help to lead enemy drones away from the *Phoenix*.

By the time Will was back behind the eyes of his lead missile, the *Aslan*'s engines were powering up again. The *Baloo* and *Walrus* looked dead, but under the circumstances saving one ship out of three wasn't bad.

The Earthers made a last desperate attempt to ensnare the flagship again, but their buoys were spread in a hopeless sprawl. Five seconds later, the *Aslan* had warped out. Will heard cheers somewhere in the background. The *Phoenix*'s engines started to charge.

Will sent his remaining torpedoes on death dives towards the enemy ships just before the expected order came.

'Ready for warp!'

In the next second, the battle was a flaring dot in the distance behind them.

Will allowed himself a moment to exhale. He could hear the other roboteers laughing and whooping all around him. With pride and relief still coursing through him, he linked to Franz. Franz's face was beet-red and wide-eyed.

'I'm sorry, sir,' said Will, 'but I saw a problem with your pattern and had to improvise.'

For a moment, Franz just stared. 'You disobeyed a direct order.' His voice was cold.

Will's spirits fell. 'Yes, sir.'

Then the captain's voice came online. 'Mr Kuno-Monet.'

Will winced at the tone.

'You're damned lucky we got out of that alive,' said Klein. 'You jeopardised the entire ship, and the *Aslan*, too.'

'Captain, I—' Will started.

'What were you thinking – hot-patching in the middle of a firefight? And with private files, too. The whole volley could have seized.'

'I'm sorry, Captain,' said Will. 'There was a flaw in the attack pattern—'

'The pattern was fine,' snapped Franz.

Of course, Franz hadn't even checked. He was too confident of his own genius, and of Will's inferiority, to bother.

'The only thing flawed in that attack—'

Will cut the expert off before he could embarrass himself further.

'Sir, you failed to compensate for the g-ray barrage intensity. Had I left your pattern active, torpedo attrition would have run seventeen per cent higher than your prediction. We'd all be dead.'

Franz stared speechless into his cabin camera.

'I will of course prepare a combat simulation for you to explain my actions,' Will added.

The captain sighed. 'Franz, prepare a report,' he said tiredly. 'And Will, I want to see a full memory log.'

'Captain—' said Franz.

'Enough!' barked Klein. 'I don't want to hear another word about it till we're back in port.' The communication channel closed.

Will was dumped back into his home node, where the combat SAP was still winking. He ripped the fat-contact off his neck and sagged back in exhaustion.

1.4: IRA

Ira skipped clear of the Memburi system into the blissfully clean space between the stars. He locked in the autopilot, flicked up his visor and breathed a sigh of relief.

He looked down into the *Ariel*'s cramped main cabin. 'Everyone okay?'

Amy was already at the bottom bunk with Rachel beside her. That wasn't good. Crew only left their bunks under heavy warp in an emergency. Something bad must have happened. For a moment, Ira's heart went into free fall despite the shuddering tug of warp gravity.

'Amy?' he said.

She looked up at him, her face unreadable. 'Doug's dead.'

Ira blinked in disbelief. Something crumpled deep inside him. 'How dead? Can we use coma?'

His question sounded weak even as it left his mouth. Amy would have tried that already.

She shook her head. 'Sorry. It's too late for that.'

Ira struggled for words. 'That last turn,' he said stupidly. It had felt bad, but not that bad. 'How tight was it?'

'Fifteen gees,' she replied quietly.

Ira covered his mouth with his hand. Most roboteers were effectively unmodified when it came to dogfights. They just didn't have the stamina for it, not even with a muscle-tank to help them. Ira stared down at the corpse floating in the gel-filled box at the bottom of the cabin. Doug might have been a roboteer, but Ira had counted him as a friend. And now Ira had killed him.

'Hey,' said John, breaking the airless silence. 'I hate to be the one to point this out, but this isn't exactly a good time for grieving. I've just been looking at that enemy data and it's serious stuff. They're going to come after it for sure, and we haven't taken any evasives yet. We should get going – otherwise Doug won't be the only dead person in this cabin.'

Ira exhaled and shut his eyes. Part of him was grateful for the distraction, delivered as it was in John's usual tactless terms.

'All right, everybody,' he said. 'Get back to your seats. We'll have to deal with this later. We're going home.'

2: NEW ROLES

2.1: GUSTAV

While the dignitaries standing around him talked politics, Gustav stared out of the window. It was easy to be distracted by the view. All he had to do was let his concentration wander from the overfed face in front of him to the three-storey pane of bulletproof glass several metres beyond it. And from where he stood, in the primary antechamber of the Prophet's palace at Bogotá, the vista was compelling, if not exactly pleasant.

The antechamber looked out past the palace's bone-coloured tiers over the manicured miles of gardens to the slums beyond. In the distance, where once proud forest had stood, prote-farms now sprawled, a chequerboard of dirty brown and sickly yellow squares. The sky was an angry sulphurous grey. It wasn't that the scenery differed particularly from the rest of what Earth had to offer, but from the palace you could see that much more of it. It appalled Gustav that, even on the Prophet's very doorstep, the world still showed so few signs of recovering from the Terror Century.

While the dignitaries droned on, Gustav quietly adjusted his position to look into the antechamber itself, a view far preferable to the desolation outside. The antechamber, one of many, was a snow-white New Gothic fantasy. Vast columns like frozen waterfalls of milk met at a vaulted ceiling far overhead, and the floor was bright and smooth like a sheet of ice. It reflected the courtiers standing around in small groups, making impressionistic butterflies with their brightly coloured robes. Their muted conversations echoed off the glacial walls.

More importantly, Gustav now had a view of the enormous doors he'd shortly have to walk through. They led to the throne room of His Honesty the Prophet – the spiritual ruler of all Earth.

'So what do you think, General?' one of the dignitaries asked him.

Gustav had enjoyed no peace since he arrived. Everyone wanted to be seen to talk with him before he received his holy commendation.

The man who'd spoken had small, fat hands sticking out from the voluminous folds of his bright-orange robe. He waved them when he talked, like little pink balloons.

Gustav tried for a polite smile. 'I'm sorry, what was that again?'

'I said, what do you think? Is the education of females permissible under dogma?'

A skeletal man draped in moss-green fabric pointed a bony digit at the speaker. 'But that's *not* the question,' he said. 'We're only talking about the Following here, not the Leading classes. I have no issue with the girls of Leading families receiving an education. That harms no one.'

Gustav remembered. The Prophet had recently passed a dictate expressly forbidding the female children of Following families from receiving education. A few of the Kingdom's many subsect leaders had launched a doomed attempt to appeal the decision.

'I'm a scientist, I'm afraid, gentlemen,' Gustav said mildly. 'I try not to get involved in political matters.' *Or not the immediate ones, at least*, he thought. Gustav had dedicated his life to building a better future. He had long since given up on the present.

'But General...' said a voice from the back of the group. This new voice belonged to a man dressed in the white gown of a High Church disciple. He was handsome in a slightly soft, florid kind of way. Only his eyes and the point of his nose were hard. He wore his dark hair oiled back. 'Even the most reserved among us have a moral instinct, wouldn't you say? And as a *scientist*, education must be a topic dear to your heart.' His smile was filled with small, even teeth. 'You have women on your team, don't you? I'd be interested to hear your gut reaction on the subject.'

Gustav regarded the disciple warily. The man had hovered at

the back of almost every group Gustav had met that morning, yet this was the first time he'd actually opened his mouth. In doing so, he'd managed to justify practically every suspicion Gustav had entertained about him.

The fact that Gustav employed female scientists was supposed to be a secret, simply because everything about Gustav's work was secret. This conversation would have to be brought to an end, and quickly.

'I'm sorry, but my training encourages me to avoid gut reactions,' Gustav said with a hard smile. 'In my experience, they're a poor substitute for data.'

The disciple refused to be dissuaded. 'Really,' he said airily. 'We in the High Church see things differently. We consider the moral instinct to be a vital guide in decision-making. A kind of spiritual compass, if you like.' He looked around at the others, as if confident of their agreement.

'Then let me ask you a question,' said Gustav. 'Which do you think poses a greater security risk to the Kingdom – cycle-game or FROF-b command encryption? I assure you that is a topic of urgent interest in Military Intelligence circles at the moment.' Gustav waved his hand generously. 'I don't need an informed response, just a gut reaction.' He crooked an eyebrow and waited.

The disciple frowned. His cheeks turned a ruddy colour. Some of the dignitaries chuckled. Before the disciple could muster a suitable reply, a voice boomed down from the antechamber's lofty heights.

'General Gustav Ulanu. You may approach the Prophet.'

All across the great chamber, conversation died to silence.

Gustav inhaled. It was time. He bowed to the dignitaries. 'If you'll excuse me.'

He turned and walked with measured steps across the immense floor to the white portal that was swinging open to admit him.

How ironic it was. Most people would have given their lives to win a commendation from the Prophet, yet Gustav felt nothing but foreboding. Admiral Konrad Tang was the man who should have been there instead of him. Tang was the man who'd commanded the Memburi attack force. He was the one who'd successfully secured the system in the name of Earth two weeks previously. He was the public face of their project in all matters. So why would the Prophet choose to bestow such a visible honour on Gustav? Particularly given that Gustav had been purposefully dragging his heels for the last six months. A caution would be more in order than a commendation.

He stepped into the throne room and stopped. A raised dais like a stepped pyramid stood before him, lit by a single shaft of artificial sunlight that shone down from yet another vaulted ceiling. It illuminated the enormous seat in which sat the greatest socio-political genius of recent history: His Honesty the Prophet Pyotr Sanchez.

Sanchez was the man who'd answered the crucial question of their age: *How do you unite the warring factions of a world that has been locked in violence for generations?* His answer: by directing their attention towards a common enemy. The enemy he'd chosen was a good one, too: the capitalists who'd fled the world with as much money as they could carry when the ecology turned bad.

The organisation Sanchez had founded, the Church of Truism, was a masterpiece of administrative science. It was part pyramid scheme, part army and part cult. There was room in it for every human ideology that existed, so long as it was prepared to support his cause and recognise his ultimate authority. Sanchez had truly changed the world.

The Prophet's features were barely visible at this distance, just an oval of tea-coloured skin for a face above a snowdrift of robes, but he sat at the apex of an impressive tableaux. On the step just below him stood Ramon the First, the King of the Nation of Man and formal leader of Earth's military government. Ramon wore a gown covered from neck to toe with intricate heraldic symbols in the midnight-blue and gold of the Medellins – the favoured subsect he led. Beneath the king stood the Prophet's favoured courtiers, arrayed in all their ludicrous finery, looking towards the door – watching Gustav's approach.

Gustav knelt. For a few seconds, nothing happened. Then hidden speakers amplified the Prophet's hoarse rattle to a Titan's boom.

'You may approach, my child.'

Keeping his eyes carefully downcast, Gustav rose. He gathered the folds of his cumbersome robe of dark Reconsiderist brown and started the climb to the top of the pyramid. A sensation of profound unease grew in the pit of Gustav's stomach as he ascended. He ignored it. The feeling was not his own, but rather the result of a bombardment of tailored infrasonics. It was well known that Sanchez had the best psycho-architectural consultants the planet could provide. The watching courtiers, the incredible opulence and the grand flight of stairs ahead of him were all intended to create a feeling of awe and reverence. The two emotions they created in Gustav, however, were annoyance and suspicion.

Gustav reached the step below the king and knelt again. The step was fractionally too narrow to manage this comfortably. It drew one's attention to how easy it would be to fall backwards, away from the throne, and shame oneself irretrievably in the process.

The king spoke. 'Your Honesty, may I present to you General Gustav Ulanu. It was his work that made the liberation of Memburi possible.'

His voice was rich and round, just as a king's should be, and Gustav could read nothing from it. He knew the king would prefer to see a Medellin do his job, but Gustav doubted that any of the Medellins' pitiful scientific ranks could do what he did, even if they were given the chance.

The role of king was another of Sanchez's inspired inventions. By allowing the rulers of each faction that joined his church to retain power over their own people, Sanchez had created a highly volatile government. Many of the movements that had become Truist subsects were still fiercely acquisitive and held long-running grudges against each other. Sanchez had stopped them from knifing him in the back and taking power for themselves by giving the tangible reins of power to someone else. At the same time, he'd managed to make himself an indispensable symbol of authority for all.

Which meant Ramon was expendable, and he knew it. His voice carried far less weight than he would have liked.

'You may look upon me, General,' said the Prophet. His amplified words boomed around the throne room.

Gustav stared up into the walnut-wrinkled face. Sanchez was so old now. He'd finally lost the shock of white hair that had once been his trademark feature, but his eyes were still keenly attentive, and dark like bottomless pools.

'I commend you on your work, General,' Sanchez croaked. 'You have put a flaming sword in the hands of our crusaders. The forces of evil are driven back and the age of unity draws closer. God sees your efforts and is pleased.' He paused to wheeze. 'That is why he has instructed me to grant you personal subsect rights over twelve and one half per cent of the Sin-World Galatea upon successful conclusion of this crusade.'

There were gasps throughout the room. For a moment, Gustav couldn't believe what he'd heard. A grant like that represented a massive fortune – it would secure his family for generations, if he ever chose to have one. He struggled to keep the surprise out of his eyes. It was a long time since he'd been caught off guard this way.

A brief sideways glance at the round, jowled face of the king told Gustav that Ramon wasn't thrilled by the Prophet's generosity, but he wasn't surprised either. Gustav quickly returned his gaze to the Prophet.

Sanchez's face crumpled like a brown paper bag as he bestowed on Gustav a benevolent smile. His eyes, though, remained as hard as lumps of jet.

'I have heard the stories of your endeavours, General,' he said.

Gustav's ears pricked up. He didn't like the sound of that.

'The difficulties your research has presented you with. The *long* months of study it has taken for you to devise this great weapon for us. Now, at last, we have proven its value in battle. Soon, your great work will be done.'

Gustav held his breath. Sanchez had chosen his words carefully. Without sharing the news with the rest of the court, he had made it very clear that he knew Gustav had been delaying the attack on Galatea.

Why the gift, then?

'I have pondered your great sacrifice to the holy cause,' said Sanchez, 'and decided that there is something I can do to aid you in your final efforts. I have assigned Disciple Rodriguez from my own staff to act as your assistant.'

In other words, he was being handed a spy. Gustav's face stiffened.

'Disciple Rodriguez, you may approach.'

As soon as the Prophet said his name, Gustav could guess who it was going to be. He glanced to his side as someone in a white gown stepped up and knelt beside him. It was the man from the antechamber. For the briefest instant, they locked gazes. Rodriguez's eyes shone with something like victory.

It occurred to Gustav then why he'd received this sudden fortune. He was being bought off. The Prophet had finally decided to bring the whole unpredictable business of the suntap within the reach of the High Church. The realisation appalled him.

If the High Church imagined that any amount of *money* would be enough to make him simply hand over the project, they'd have to think again. He wasn't going to make it easy for them.

'You may speak,' said the Prophet.

Gustav kept his voice carefully neutral. 'Your Honesty, I have no words adequate to express the gratitude I feel. I desire only to do God's work. I pray that I can make worthy use of these unexpected gifts.'

The Prophet regarded him inscrutably for a moment, reading the implications behind his words. He might have been old, but his wits were still razor sharp. 'As do I, my child,' he said with a wry smile. 'You may leave, and take my blessings with you.'

Gustav stood and backed carefully down the stairs, struggling with the clumsy robe and seething all the while. The disciple matched his descent with practised ease, step for awkward step.

As soon as they reached the antechamber, Rodriguez turned on him with a triumphant grin. He bowed his respects to Gustav a little too quickly to be convincing.

'General,' he crooned. 'I'm honoured to be working with you. I'm looking forward to a close and highly beneficial relationship.'

Gustav kept his face still. He said nothing until his silence made Rodriguez's smile falter. 'Indeed,' he replied at last. He curved his mouth into a humourless grin and looked Rodriguez up and down. 'Welcome to the team. Now let's go and mingle, shall we? I'm sure half the court is dying to speak with us.'

Gustav had no appetite for the socialising that followed. Rodriguez hovered relentlessly by his side like some kind of pet or parasite. It was all Gustav could do not to let his fury show.

The real question was how the Prophet had learned of his delay. Gustav felt sure he knew the answer. It had to be Tang. In his eagerness to begin the full military phase of the operation, he'd sold Gustav out.

Tang was a fool.

Gustav was relieved when a white-liveried data valet approached him, his visor winking.

'General, sir. Your presence is requested by Lord Oswald Khan for a private audience.'

Gustav exhaled. Oswald was his ally at court. Maybe he could do something about this intolerable situation.

'I will attend him immediately,' Gustav replied. 'Gentlemen, I apologise.' He nodded his respects to the new batch of courtiers surrounding him and set off.

Rodriguez started to follow, but the valet stopped him in his tracks.

'I'm sorry, sir,' he told the disciple nervously. 'Only the general was invited.'

Rodriguez glowered angrily for a moment before he could paste an expression of nonchalance over his features. 'Of course,' he said lightly. 'I shall be here, General, if you need me.'

Gustav arched one eyebrow, then turned and walked quickly towards the exit.

The valet hurried to match his leggy pace. 'He's waiting for you in the Reconsiderist apartment, sir,' he explained. 'Room four-four-eight-three. The Fern Garden.'

Gustav nodded. He'd already guessed his destination.

The valet signalled the door open and Gustav stepped into the executive lift. He tried to compose his thoughts as he ascended. Oswald was the only person Gustav knew with the political power and skill to get Rodriguez dropped from the project. There was reason enough to think he could – Oswald was the man who'd created Reconsiderism. Gustav respected his political ability almost as much as he respected the Prophet's. For the longest time, Earth's Muslim population had been losing out to Truism. Islam specifically dictated that Mohammed was God's last prophet. Thus Muslims could not join the Truist cause, and so were excluded from the military and economic reforms sweeping the world. Reconsiderism had offered a way out of that economic trap. It claimed that God had seen the Terror Century and, in disgust, had changed his mind. He had given mankind one more prophet because they had strayed so far from the path of righteousness.

Oswald had converted Gustav to his new subsect in the slums of Sophia while the Pomak Riots raged all around them. He'd won Gustav over with a solemn promise that his movement would retain the proudest traditions of Islamic culture. To Gustav that meant vigorous rational debate, a strict adherence to law and no compromise over interference from outsiders.

So far Oswald had been as good as his word, even to the extent that Reconsiderism had become the Truist church's unofficial scientific division. Gustav hoped Oswald could stick to it now.

The lift reached its destination. Gustav strode out into the brown-and-white-tiled Reconsiderist apartment and down the hallway to the Fern Garden. He pushed through the old-fashioned revolving door into the sweltering air on the other side.

The Fern Garden was a greenhouse of sorts set at the corner of the great tiered palace. It was full of large fronded plants, most of which had been extinct on Earth for over a generation. New specimens had been brought back from Mars after the crusade. Not entirely accidentally, the Fern Garden's sprinklers and steam machines played havoc with surveillance equipment. Quirks in the room's construction also made wireless comms almost impossible. It was private, and the Reconsiderists kept it that way.

Gustav followed the narrow stone path, took the stepping stones over the artificial brook and found Oswald by the far window, looking out. Oswald was a tall man with nut-brown skin and a ring of white curly hair around his balding head. He turned as Gustav approached and smiled a little wistfully. His face would not have looked out of place on some ancient Ethiopian king.

Gustav bowed. 'My Lord.'

'It's okay,' said Oswald. 'We're alone.'

Gustav relaxed a little. He and Oswald had remained close ever since that day in Sophia, despite the different directions in which their work had taken them. As close, at least, as Gustav ever let his allies get.

He got straight to the point. 'I want that snowboy off my team.'

Oswald winced at Gustav's language and slowly shook his head. 'I'm sorry, old friend. I did my best, but Sanchez was adamant. He's determined to shut you down. Rodriguez is going with you to make a feasibility assessment.'

Gustav experienced a moment of horrible bewilderment. 'What do you mean, *shut me down*?'

'I mean it's over, Gus. Sanchez wants to close the Relic Project.'

The words took a few moments to sink in. 'He can't,' Gustav blurted.

'Unfortunately, he can.'

Gustav fixed Oswald with a stare. 'Doesn't he get it? You can't keep something like the Relic secret for ever. Sooner or later, someone's going to find out.'

Oswald nodded. 'I know, but the High Church doesn't see it that way. It frightens them, Sanchez most of all.' He spread his hands in a gesture of appeasement. 'Had it not been for Galatea, I doubt they'd have let us get this far. It was only because they needed the suntap.'

Gustav grimaced. Trying to bury the Relic was a crime against science. But more importantly, it was politically stupid. Sanchez had made the problem for himself years ago when he dismissed the possibility of extraterrestrial life on theological grounds. He'd decided at the very dawn of Truism that with so many conflicting religions to unite, no mere text would be strong enough to sit at the centre of his new faith. There could be no Bible or Koran because people would always prefer the books they already had to what he could give them. So he'd declared the human genome itself to be the living embodiment of God's word.

Unfortunately, that meant many of the Prophet's arguments hinged upon the idea of mankind's superiority among God's creations. Revealing the discovery of an ancient and highly advanced alien civilisation would cause an outcry in the Following, even if that civilisation was long since dead. In Gustav's opinion, a justification for the Relic's existence needed to be seeded slowly, carefully and soon.

'Maybe I'll have to give them an incentive to see sense,' said Gustav.

Oswald regarded him sadly and sighed. He clearly knew exactly what Gustav meant. Several times in the past they'd talked about leaking the news to the public in a controlled way, spun so as to minimise the unrest while also spurring the church into action.

'They'd kill you.'

Gustav shrugged. 'Perhaps. If they were rash. I could make it very expensive for them.'

Oswald laid a hand on Gustav's shoulder. 'Gus, listen. If the truth comes out now, the crusade will grind to a halt.'

Gustav smiled dryly. 'I doubt that.'

'And there is your problem, my friend,' said Oswald sadly. 'You've been away from Earth too long, hiding in your secret laboratory.'

'Meaning what, exactly?'

Oswald pressed his palms together and looked down. 'While you have been gone, the Prophet has become... unwell.'

Gustav peered at him. There had been no news of this. But then, of course, there wouldn't be.

'His doctors tell us he doesn't have long to live,' Oswald continued. 'I believe this is why he's decided to end the suntap project now. He doesn't have the strength to lead the people through such a big change to dogma, and he doesn't trust those who follow him to do any better. So he'd rather not have it happen at all.'

Gustav could guess the consequences of leaking the Relic's existence at such a bad time. With the High Church weakened, some subsect or other would break the truce and the entire crusade would go on hold while Earth's factions vied for power. In the worst case, they could collapse back into civil war. In the meantime, the Galateans would regroup. They might even try to liberate the other colonies. The chances of Earth mounting a viable second crusade would be poor.

Oswald nodded as he saw realisation dawn in Gustav's eyes. 'That's right. If you decide to speak out, you must be ready to live in a future in which the Kingdom exists beside Galatea. Perhaps even trades with them.'

That option was intolerable. It spoke of a future in which there were a dozen planets of poor, unmodified humans and a single barely populated world of the genius rich. The cycle of inequality that had oppressed Gustav's people for generations would repeat itself. Earth would be back where it started: poor and exploited. In other words, in exactly the situation that had caused the Terror Century in the first place.

'So you see, my friend,' said Oswald, 'you find yourself in a powerful position. The Prophet knows that, which is precisely why he's been so generous. Your next move could shape the course of the war.'

Gustav shook his head. 'You exaggerate.'

'I'm afraid I'm deadly serious. I beg you, bide your time, because hope is not lost. There is a way out of this.'

Gustav folded his arms. 'I'm listening.'

Oswald leaned close. 'Two nights ago, the Prophet promised me in private that he would act on Rodriguez's counsel, regardless of what he found. This could be made to work in our favour. Disciple Rodriguez is not a clever man. The Prophet trusts him for his faith and doggedness, but he's also greedy for influence and fearful of his credibility. If you can convince him that it's in his best interest to see our point of view, the Prophet will have no choice but to accept his word. The project will be saved.'

'He's High Church,' Gustav pointed out. 'We can't bribe him.'

'True, but there are other ways to make an ally. He must be made to see that it is in his political interests to keep the project open. Make him realise where he would stand if the project was closed down and word still leaked out.

'If you succeed,' Oswald added, 'I will do the rest. For the last six months, my people have been working on a report outlining how to spin the Relic to the Following as a miracle. So far, Sanchez has refused to read it. With Rodriguez's recommendation, he will have to. The speeches are already written. The press reports are ready to go.'

Gustav pulled a bitter face. He could feel the shackles of

compromise clanking shut around his wrists. He sighed and rubbed his eyes.

'You know me, Oz,' he muttered. 'I'm no diplomat.'

Oswald shrugged. 'What can I say? If I could send myself out there, I would. But it has to be you. It's your project.'

'All right.' Gustav looked away.

Oswald touched his shoulder. 'Thank you.'

Gustav looked out at the filthy sky. 'I'll tell you now, though, my people won't like this. The moment they see that white robe, they'll smell trouble. They won't want to cooperate.'

'Then make them understand how lucky they are,' said Oswald. 'Sanchez's other option was group termination. I told him it would be cheaper to buy you and your people off than kill you. I reminded him of just how badly he needs the support of the scientific community right now. If your people are careful, they could come out of this with an estate each and still get to finish their work.'

Oswald gave Gustav's shoulder a friendly squeeze. 'And now you should head downstairs or people will start to wonder where you are. Let them see you,' he said as he stepped back. 'And try to look happy. We can't have you appear ungrateful for the Prophet's gifts.'

Gustav laughed darkly. It was a dangerous game they were playing, but he could see no other choice. Earth simply couldn't afford to let a planet of genetic racists thrive and prosper. And to defeat them they needed a united church, at least for the time being.

He bowed his respects and turned to go.

'Good luck,' said Oswald. 'You'll be in my prayers.'

Gustav nodded and headed back the way he'd come – towards the lift, Rodriguez's eager company and another round of unwelcome congratulations.

2.2: WILL

Will took the overground transit to the headquarters of the Fleet's Roboteering Division. The car was empty except for him, though it had enough bright-yellow ergonomically designed seats for fifty. That was normal on Galatea. Will had never seen one full.

It was the first time he'd been home for weeks and his eyes hungrily sucked in the sights. Beyond the train window, a plain of butter-coloured scree stretched away under a deep-blue sky. Laid out in perfectly straight rows as far as the horizon were circular pools of steaming turquoise water tended by black-furred robots. They hadn't existed last time he came this way. The pools no doubt constituted another desperate attempt by the Terraforming Corps to prevent the nascent Galatean ecology from collapsing back on itself.

The rows made hazy diffraction patterns as the train carried Will soundlessly past them. They were also a welcome distraction from his anxiety about his upcoming review session.

He'd only been home for a day. He hadn't expected the Fleet to call on him so soon. Evidently they were taking the matter very seriously.

The return flight hadn't gone well. Franz filed a public report declaring that with adequate roboteer supervision, his SAP would have cleared the disrupters – a statement that was false but hard to completely disprove. After that he hadn't spoken to Will again.

Captain Klein had refused to comment on the matter and Will hadn't heard a thing from him since he filed his memory log. It had made for an uncomfortable week. Today he'd learn what the captain had to say, and he wasn't looking forward to it.

The problem was that Will had knowingly disobeyed a direct order. While the Galatean Fleet was the most relaxed and pro-initiative fighting force in human history, it still considered an order something sacred. Even if the Fleet condoned Will's actions, as he felt sure they would, some kind of formal reprimand was still on the cards.

Will bristled at the injustice of it. If he lost this position it would be his third transfer. No captain was likely to take him on after that. He'd be reduced to loading work on the evacuation arks – forced to flee with children and grandparents while the Earthers massed to destroy everything he cared about. He didn't think he could stand that.

The abuses other colonies had suffered were common knowledge on Galatea. Wholesale slaughter had followed Earther invasion. The genetically modified were 'purged' as abominations. Most were burned alive by marauding gangs of barely disciplined Earther troops. Will wasn't about to run away while that happened to his home.

He shifted uncomfortably in his seat and started counting in binary on his fingers, from zero to one thousand and twenty-three and back down again. It was something he often did when he was nervous.

Finally the transit began to slow as it slid through a region of gleaming pipes and pylons and onwards into the town of Resilience. Like most Galatean towns, Resilience was essentially a trench roofed over by a long, low bubble of impact-resistant plastic. Will passed rows of tiered apartments, their broad public balconies floored with modified grass. Furniture and possessions littered the open spaces so haphazardly that it was impossible to tell where one person's home ended and the next began.

There was a sense of the disposable about the place, common to all Galatea's habitats, as if the inhabitants expected to leave tomorrow and never look back. It was written in the collapsible screens and the unpainted walls. Will saw nothing of value that couldn't be folded or boxed and taken away at a moment's notice.

What else would you expect from a population who could never tell when the next emergency would arrive? There was always some kind of crisis going on, and the war was just the most recent in a long, long line of them. People joked that at least the war wasn't a home-grown catastrophe. Galatea's abortive terraforming attempt had afforded plenty of those.

The transit cruised gently into the station. This was it – time to face the music. Will rose and stood at the door as the car slid to a halt.

'Is this your stop?' asked the transit eagerly, sending the message direct to Will's sensorium. 'Is this where you asked me to let you off?'

The transit knew the answer already, of course. It just wanted to talk. Like a lot of public SAPs, it relished the rare opportunity for direct electronic contact with a roboteer. Usually, Will obliged. Today, however, he wasn't really in the mood.

'Yes, thank you,' Will messaged back and stepped quickly out into the warm, artificial breeze.

From the station platform it was a short walk to headquarters through the carefully tended gardens that covered the trench floor. Will followed the twisting path between the exotic cacti and succulents that were intended to one day brave the surface, then ascended the broad stone steps of the headquarters building and entered the open-fronted lobby. As he crossed the huge swathe of polished yellow sandstone, the two janitor robots cleaning it called their greetings to him. They looked like big, furry beetles.

'Hello, Handler Will! Hello, Handler Will! Will you make us play again? We like to play!'

Will sent them the electronic equivalent of a smile. 'Later.'

He checked in with the building's reception SAP in the lift on the way up.

'Welcome back, Will,' it said. Its messages were polite and sounded in his mind like crisply spoken English in a soft, female voice. 'Commander Rees-Noyes is busy with a call at the moment. He will be with you shortly. Will you wait in the rec?'

Will sighed. 'I suppose so.'

The lift slid to a halt and dropped him off. The rec, more formally known as the Roboteers' Recreational Environment, was a large sandstone room open to a balcony along one side. Gold light filtered in from the reflector mirrors high on the opposite trench wall. It cast mottled patterns across the thick purple spray-on carpet.

A dozen or so roboteers were present, all dressed in crumpled Fleet-issue ship-suits. A few sat on their own, but most were gathered in a ring with fat-contacts running from neck to neck like thick, white noodles.

To an outsider, the scene would have looked like something from a mental ward. The roboteers either sat motionless as stones or rocked slowly back and forth. None of them spoke, though a couple hummed tunelessly to music only they could hear. They made no attempt at eye contact. To Will, however, the room was alive with talk from the moment he entered. His sensorium was bombarded with messages demanding memories.

'What happened?'

'Franz is a bastard!'
'Where are your logs?'
'Tell us everything!'
It was the typical roboteer welcome. They'd probably followed his progress from the moment he entered the building, and in that time downloaded all the official reports about his recent activities. Roboteer culture was like that: earnest, honest, inquisitive and completely lacking in the social niceties they spent so long training into SAPs. Politeness would have served little purpose. They'd all been inside each other's heads dozens of times.

Will had known the request would come. Roboteers always wanted to hear exciting news of their own kind, so he'd prepared an edited subset of his experiences on the flight down and stored it in the Fleet database. In the personal node of his mind, he summoned the picture-book icon representing the address and dropped it in his public directory. He imagined the directory as a room open on one side to a trench lawn, like the one he grew up playing on.

'Here's everything I have,' he broadcast to the room, and watched the picture-book pages flutter as greedy minds hit it for downloads.

Will walked across the rec and sat near the window, where he could look down onto Resilience's quiet streets. A couple sauntered past below, trailed by a bumbling carrybot covered in yellow tact-fur.

'Join our game,' someone sent.

The message came with a memory chunk attached. It unfolded in his head to reveal some kind of chess variant in which each piece devised its own strategy and all pieces moved simultaneously. In an instant, Will knew all the rules.

The players were operating as joined minds, hence the cables. All roboteers had wireless contact with Galatea's pervasivenet, but for sharing entire mental states only cables would do.

'The sides are uneven,' the roboteers told him. 'We want your help.'

'No thanks,' Will replied. He had no desire to subsume himself into some chess-playing gestalt right now.

The others sent him the mental equivalent of a sorry smile and returned their attention to the game. They hadn't really expected him to join. Most roboteers thought Will was strange. For the most part, he found them obsessive. Will had simply never been that much into roboteer culture. There was something cloying and poignant about it – it managed to be oppressively intimate and emotionally distant at the same time. But then, telepathy wasn't really a natural state for human beings.

It didn't help that roboteers' minds were genetically tweaked to fit the consciousness profiles of the SAPs they handled. The first Roboteers had been born fully autistic. Even now, many retained traces of that condition. Consequently, the normal roboteer conception of friendship was close cooperation over some kind of project. Only a rare few like Will completely escaped the siren song of autistic thought patterns. He preferred the company of his friends in the mainstream community and tried to ignore the experiential gap that would always lie between them.

He gazed out across the trench and worried about what the commander would say. He thought about the speech he'd make to defend his actions. He'd done what he felt was right. Wasn't that what the Fleet all about: intelligently interpreting the requests of your superiors?

The room's silence was broken occasionally by sudden outbursts of synchronised laughter from the game players. They subsided as quickly as they began and served only to scatter Will's thoughts. Close proximity to other handlers often did that. Their presence made him wonder at the hubris of his own culture. Galatea had created a whole community who could never be a part of normal human society. How had they managed to justify that act to themselves? He knew the answer even as he framed the question: they'd been desperate.

Twenty-five years ago, Galatean scientists had discovered the Ng-Black heating limit. Put simply, it showed that any molecular building technology above a certain power would melt itself down into proteins and slag before it could do anything useful. At a stroke, it put an end to humanity's dream of a nanotech future, and to Galatea's greatest hope: that nano would solve their terraforming problem.

And they did have a problem. Upon arrival, the early Galateans had kicked off a process of environmental change they could not now afford to stop. Hard experience had shown that doing so would bring about a time of world-scouring storms as the atmosphere lurched back to its former inert state. The Galateans would have to evacuate their entire planet.

Thus they'd been forced to turn to that familiar, robust technology which had enabled the human diaspora in the first place: robotics. The problem was that robots were large and clumsy, and now they were required in vast numbers. Galatea had needed to find a way to coordinate the work of thousands of machines engaged in the most complex and precarious engineering project in human history. It was work normal humans simply couldn't do, so they bred new people to do it for them – people like Will.

In their schooling, roboteers were encouraged to think of themselves as the saviours of the planet. In Will's experience, that wasn't how they were treated. The one prejudice it had proved hardest to root out of a society was the one towards people whose social skills were limited. For his entire life, he'd felt boxed in by that prejudice. People always treated him differently from the moment they learned he was a roboteer. It didn't matter that he was quite capable of operating in mainstream society. Their speech slowed down anyway. The volume increased. They assumed they knew better than him because his modifications were state-funded, while theirs were private. Franz was a perfect example.

Finally, the building pinged him. 'Commander Rees-Noyes is ready to see you.'

Will's stomach tightened as he stood and marched over to the lift. Thirty anxious seconds later, it deposited him at the commander's office.

The office was a huge, barren space that filled the top floor of the building. In one corner stood a lonely-looking desk with a work console and old-fashioned bookcase. At the other end brooded a conference table beneath which chairs were neatly tucked away. Between them lay a vast expanse of gold-patterned carpet.

The only other items were the pair of soft brown armchairs out on the balcony. In one of them sat Robert Rees-Noyes – or Bob, as he liked the roboteers to call him. Bob was a huge bear of a man who always wore the same clothes: shorts and a pale-green T-shirt bearing a Fleet emblem. He smiled often and insisted on informality. Today, however, his smile was absent.

'Come on in, Will. Take a seat,' he said, standing as he gestured towards the remaining empty armchair.

Will steeled himself and set off across the carpet ocean.

Despite his casual demeanour, Bob was not a man to take lightly. Part military officer and part psychiatrist, Bob ran everything in the Fleet that concerned roboteers. His parents had modded him for empathy and recall, and Bob had built on those talents by acquiring an encyclopaedic knowledge of both neuroscience and the history of roboteering. Like most of Galatea's middle class, he was brilliant.

Will reached the balcony and shook Bob's outstretched hand. He couldn't help glancing sideways, though, over the edge. Bob had a fantastic view. The tiered gardens below looked like paddy fields out of some Old World period-drama.

'Sit, Will, sit,' said Bob.

Will let himself settle into the chair. It was absurdly comfortable. Someone, somewhere on Galatea, was a genius at chair design.

Bob sat down opposite him and steepled his hands. 'All right, let's get down to business. From what I hear, you disobeyed your expert and tampered with a combat SAP during a live firefight. Is that true?'

Will stiffened. 'Yes, sir.'

Bob waved one hand. 'I don't want to hear any *sirs* in here. This is between you and me, okay?'

Will nodded reluctantly.

'Suffice it to say,' rumbled Bob, 'Combat Expert Leung is pretty pissed off at you. He's filed a complaint and has been grousing about it since he landed. He says he can't work with you. *Won't* work with you again, in fact. He says that if you had fears about the SAP, you should have raised them with him rather than attempting to fix the problem yourself.'

Will frowned. When was he supposed to have done that? By the time he'd spotted the problem, they were in the middle of a battle.

'Your captain isn't much happier,' Bob added. 'Regulations force him to note that you disobeyed orders, but mostly he doesn't want to have anything to do with you or the whole issue any more.'

'I know it sounds bad,' said Will. 'But—'

Bob held up a warning hand. 'Let me finish. Then we'll talk.' He glanced down at his lap. 'You see, the flip side of all this is that the model you filed with your memory log bears out your decision. You probably saved the lives of everyone aboard both the *Phoenix* and the *Aslan*, including Admiral Bryant. He's seen your model, and he's personally asked that the Fleet go easy on you.'

Bob let the words hang there for a minute while Will took them in. The admiral had got involved! Will had no idea that word of his actions had spread so far. His spirits began to lift. Then Bob sighed.

'Why did you sign up for the Fleet, Will?' he asked gently.

Will's unease returned instantly. 'Because I want to help fight the Earthers, of course,' he replied, blushing as he said it.

It wasn't quite the whole truth. Will had also joined up because he hated his life. He'd been bred for the terraforming effort. That meant working on an endless supply of ecological alerts. It meant leisure hours spent in roboteer-only dormitories and whole days playing over memory logs from people whose minds he didn't fit. It had been safe, controlled and oppressive beyond words.

His childhood dream was to be a starship captain. But as he'd repeatedly been told, that wasn't a job for a roboteer. Even if he had the necessary empathy and leadership skills, his special talents were too urgently required at home.

But Will had never given up the dream. In his spare time, he focused his talents on creating smarter, more creative SAPs. If he couldn't become a captain the ordinary way, he reasoned, maybe he could create a good enough artificial crew for a ship that would only need a roboteer to pilot it.

Before his ambitious dream had borne fruit, the war began and the employment laws changed. Aged just twenty at the time, Will had signed up straight away, much to his parents' distress. Five years later, roboteers were still no closer to becoming captains, but at least he was out of terraforming.

Bob shook his head. 'You're the most high-functioning roboteer I've ever met, Will. But you're also the most stubborn. From all three ships you've worked on, the reports on your performance have been exactly the same: excellent work, doesn't obey orders.'

'I obey orders,' Will retorted. 'Just not bad ones.'

'See?' said Bob. 'There you go again! Don't you see how unreliable this attitude makes you look? You got through this one by the skin of your teeth. You should have told Franz what you were doing, at the very least. Ideally, you should have flashed a message to the captain, too. It would have saved a lot of panic. If your action hadn't proven necessary, your career would be over.'

'But it *was* necessary,' said Will.

Bob nodded. 'I know. And the truth is, you did great. You were put in a very difficult position and you made the right call.' He shrugged. 'As it is, Expert Leung is going to face a personal inquiry and in all likelihood be reposted to Oort defence.'

Will was surprised by the news. He'd never intended to hurt Franz, no matter how much he disliked the man.

'You, however,' said Bob, 'aren't going to face any kind of disciplinary action. The Fleet isn't in the habit of punishing good decisions. However, we do still have a problem.' He steepled his hands again and looked at Will over the top of them. 'We can't leave you on the *Phoenix*. So we'll have to repost you, too.'

Will's insides tightened.

'Don't worry,' Bob added quickly. 'It's a promotion… of sorts. I'm transferring you to the *Ariel*.'

Will blinked. 'The *Ariel*?'

Bob nodded solemnly.

Will couldn't believe his luck. The *Ariel* was famous. It was a Mosquito-Class starship – one of the Fleet's best soft-combat vessels, and certainly its fastest. The crew were all high-flyers and the captain had a reputation for brilliance. Everyone had heard of Captain Baron. The Fleet common rooms abounded with legends of his exploits. It was a dream job.

'They need a new roboteer,' Bob explained, 'and quite frankly, you're the only qualified man we have available. But from your psych profile, you could be an excellent fit. With such a small crew, they need someone who can take spontaneous action. Someone who isn't afraid to think up solutions to unfamiliar problems.'

Will had never dared hope that he might achieve such a posting. It was about as high up in the Fleet as a roboteer could expect to get.

'But I warn you,' said Bob, 'this is *not* like the jobs you've had before. You'll be the only roboteer on board. That means you'll be responsible for handling every SAP they have. And there's no room for insubordination on that ship. If you break the rules again, it'll be in a very high-stakes game. You'll be out of the Fleet for good, if there's still such a thing around when you get back. Furthermore, your micromachines will have to be updated.'

Will barely cared. There was always a risk when they tampered with the machines that laid down the nerve tracks to a roboteer's neural interface. But what difference did one more operation make compared to the risk of being fried alive by a g-ray?

Bob peered at him. 'So, what do you think? Has the Fleet handled your case fairly?'

Will nodded quickly. 'Yes, sir! I mean Bob. Thank you. I don't know what to say.'

'Then don't say anything.' Bob pressed his hands against his knees. 'Well, you've got plenty to do,' he said sombrely, 'so I won't keep you.'

He ushered a stunned Will back toward the lift. 'The building will give you access to the confidential information you'll need, including memory logs. It'll also tell you when and where to report. You've only got twenty-four hours of leave now, I'm afraid, then you'll have to go directly to the surgery for overnight servicing. The *Ariel* is heading straight out on a new mission.'

Will's head reeled.

Bob gently guided him into through the doorway and waved farewell. 'Good luck. You'll need it.'

The last thing Will saw before the lift door shut was the commander's earnest, oddly worried face silhouetted by the gold light reflected from the wall of the trench.

3: DEPARTURE

3.1: IRA

Half an hour before his scheduled departure, Ira took the lift up to the exit lounge. The lounge lay near the Fleet station's hub, so with every level he climbed, Ira lost gravity. The short journey always unsettled him for some reason and today the feeling was the worst it had ever been. But then, the lounge was where he was due to meet his crew, and his new roboteer.

Ira stood with his arms folded, staring straight ahead into the beige impact padding of the lift chamber. Rachel stood beside him. Though he didn't meet her eye, he knew the look she'd be giving him. It was the look that told him he needed to get his act together.

'It really wasn't your fault,' she said for the fiftieth time.

'I know,' he replied quickly. 'Really, I'm fine.'

They both knew that wasn't true. The three days since they'd hit port had been hard. Ira had barely stopped working the entire time. First had come the debriefing. That had turned into a strategy meeting. By the time they were done with strategy, he'd barely had time to grab a little sleep before attending Doug's memorial ceremony to give the eulogy.

Telling the life story of a man he'd killed himself was one of the hardest things Ira had ever done, and he'd felt like someone was moving a knife around in his gut the whole time. He kept looking up into the hollow eyes of Doug's parents and flinching.

'My crew is my family,' he'd told the assembled mourners. How true it was. Yet he found himself unable to meet their eyes.

In the past when Ira had been in pain like this, he'd always turned to the same easy solution: get back out there. Usually he couldn't wait for the next mission to start. The *Ariel* was his own little world – somewhere to be busy, where he had no choice but to focus on the moment.

This time it was different. To his surprise and dismay, Ira had discovered that he was reluctant to go back into space. The reason was simple: two more fragile lives had just been pushed into his care.

One of them would be the Fleet weapons specialist, Hugo Bessler-Vartian. Ira had met Hugo a couple of times before. He was brilliant, if more than a little conceited. Ira wouldn't have picked him for the job, but he was the best in his field and, more importantly, he'd volunteered.

There was a warning marker in Hugo's file – apparently Hugo's emotional-stability index wasn't all that high. But Ira wasn't particularly worried about him. Dealing with fragile personalities was part of his job. Every crewmember on a Mosquito-Class starship had to be at the cutting edge of their chosen field. There was no room for extra staff, or for underperformance. Those kinds of intellects invariably came with quirks – often severe ones, which meant that traditional military discipline simply didn't work aboard soft-combat ships. Ira had spent years functioning as both military leader and group therapist. Personality problems he could deal with.

Ira's biggest concern was always stamina, and on that count Hugo wasn't a problem. He'd received surgical gravity tolerance enhancements before the war. They weren't as effective as genetic mods, but Ira knew first hand that the man had spent plenty of time in space. He was solid enough, even though he wasn't from a Fleet family.

It was the other new person who worried him more – the one who'd just been added to his permanent crew. Ira only had a single requirement in mind for Doug's replacement when he called Bob at the Handler Farm: high gravity tolerance.

'There aren't any left,' Bob told him. 'You have to understand, most of these people were bred for civil engineering, not spaceflight. Only six roboteers ever received high-gee mods, and they all have places aboard other soft-combat ships.'

'Then get me one of them,' Ira demanded. 'This mission has an *aleph one* rating, goddamn it!'

'I can't. They're all out of port.'

'Then get me one with surgical augs.'

'There aren't any,' said Bob gently.

'Listen. I'm headed deep into the shit this time. It doesn't get any deeper. And if I don't find someone who can take high-gee, they'll be dead before I come home.'

'Ira, please, try to understand. The division is badly short-staffed. The losses of *Baloo* and *Walrus* hit us hard. There's only one qualified candidate we can offer you, but I promise, he's excellent. He practically pulled *Phoenix* and *Aslan* out of the fire single-handed. He's gifted.'

'Can he take a ten-gee turn?'

Bob stammered his answer. 'I . . . I don't know.'

'Then why the hell should I care how gifted he is?'

'I'm sorry, but he's all there is. Take it up with Bryant if you have to, but I promise you, he'll say the same.'

And Bryant had. So it didn't matter what Ira thought of this Will Kuno-Monet. He was stuck with him, at least for the time being. Since then, Ira hadn't even looked over the new man's profile. He was afraid to.

Rachel touched him lightly on the arm. It was an unusually gentle gesture from her – a measure of her concern. 'I'm sure he'll be fine,' she said.

She could guess what he was thinking, but then he hadn't exactly hidden it well. He gave her a brief smile intended to look reassuring. She didn't buy it. Her pale-blue eyes winced in concern.

Thankfully, the lift doors opened at that moment. Ira bounced out and headed down the bland space-station corridor. 'Might as well get it over with,' he muttered to himself.

Rachel followed.

The lounge door snapped open at his brisk advance. He marched into the grey-panelled room and clapped eyes on the young man sitting there alone, perched on the edge of one of the chairs. He was tall and thin, at least six foot, with a fresh face and a mop of mouse-brown hair that looked as if it had never seen a comb.

He was clearly lost in a recall trance. His eyes were screwed tight shut and he was swaying from side to side, making a soft keening sound. Ira was lost for words. So this was the material he was supposed to work with? The boy looked barely out of Fleet School. His bones were thin enough to be snapped on the first tight turn. Ira could feel the grim responsibility for the boy's life settling onto him already, and they hadn't even left port yet. He stared imploringly at Rachel.

'Give him a chance,' she told him. 'He might be tougher than he looks.' She stepped forward to rouse the roboteer.

Ira didn't know what to say. It wasn't as if he had a choice.

3.2: WILL

As he swapped madly between tasks, Will took a second to glance out through the *Ariel*'s sensors. Set against the dark, roiling mass of disrupter cloud, the hard white lights of drone torches crawled menacingly towards him. The *Ariel* had just minutes to get out before the Earther munitions caught up with them.

'We have another C-buffer breakdown in panel one-one-eight!' Rachel shouted.

Will leapt into the head of the closest repair truck. Gears screamed as it accelerated away down the curving track towards the damage site, its hard little mind alight with worry. He'd only just sent it on its way when John started madly flashing messages at him.

'Is that countermeasure template loaded? I need that SAP online *now*!'

Will hurriedly loaded the pattern, running a desperate virtual eye over the massive memory trees as he did so. The SAP was a twisted thing, a typical John creation, full of sly trickery and outright brilliance. He copied it and hurled it out into the void. There was no time to give it a proper check.

Without warning, there came a lurch and rib-crushing pressure. The soft enclosure of Will's muscle-tank became a fist, squeezing him to death. He whimpered as every inch of him cried out in pain. Finally, the pressure released, but even as he gasped for breath, Amy blurted orders in his ear.

'Habitat core gravity compensation is slipping. We need three shifters up there now.'

Will leapt into the mind of the lead shifter idling in its bay. It unlocked with an eager snap, but Will got no further with its orders as the terrible pressure came again.

Pain drove out thought. The sympathetically linked shifter crashed against the back of its bay as it shared his suffering, hydraulic arms flailing. Will could feel his bones grinding against each other and snapping as his skull distorted like an eggshell in a vice.

'We need gravity compensation now!' urged Amy.

'Prepare engine double-checks for immediate warp engagement,' said Rachel.

Will could do nothing about their requests – it was enough of a challenge to keep from blacking out. Just when he believed the pressure couldn't get any worse, it did.

This time it was beyond his ability to endure. He was an ant trapped between the thumb and forefinger of a callous god. He felt himself dying. He tried to cry out, but he couldn't breathe, let alone scream.

Someone tapped him on the shoulder.

His eyes flicked open. He found himself sitting in the lounge again, sweating. His body was wound as tight as the field on a fusion bottle. He looked up to see who'd touched him and met a woman's eyes. She was dark and pretty, with a heart-shaped face and eyebrows that met in the middle. Will knew her immediately even though it was the first time they'd ever met. It was Rachel. She looked just as Doug had remembered her. Lovely Rachel, who sang in her bunk and had the loudest laugh on the ship. She was smiling at him, though her eyes held something of a nervous appeal.

Will already knew about Rachel's work on starships and admired it. He'd been looking forward to talking to her. Now he couldn't think of a single thing to say.

'Uh, hello,' he managed. 'Ma'am,' he added quickly, as Rachel outranked him by several grades. He stood and found himself towering over her. She couldn't have been taller than five foot. She was 'born to fly', as they said in the Fleet, though she managed to make the Fleet-family body style look curvaceous rather than stocky. Will flattened down his hair and gave her an awkward Fleet salute. He did his best to stand straight and be smaller at the same time.

Then he caught sight of the man standing behind her. It was Captain Baron. The captain was about the same height as Rachel but looked as broad as he did tall, with a skull shaped like a bullet and a hugely muscled torso too big for his green one-piece uniform.

For a moment, Will was thrilled. Then he noticed how the captain was eyeing him with a dark, unhappy expression. Will shifted uneasily. In most of the inherited memories Will had of the captain, he'd been smiling. Will's spirits faltered. He'd managed to make himself look like a handler freak already, in his very first meeting with his new commanding officer. He cursed himself. He shouldn't have arrived so early, and he ought to have resisted the urge to play Doug's last sequence one more time.

He'd spent all his spare time since the reassignment going through Doug's memories. It was never easy to feel strong emotions through memory logs, but Will had played the battle sequence nine times. More than any other clip, he thought it gave him an insight into what his new shipmates must be feeling. Anything that might help him know them had to be worth trying, he reasoned, even if it meant experiencing the death of his predecessor. But it was starting to look like he'd taken that theory too far.

'Are you okay?' Rachel asked.

'Uh, yes,' said Will. 'Yes, I'm fine.'

He winced. Rachel was looking at him like a stranger, which of course he was to her. Yet Will could remember working with her for years, or parts of those years, at any rate. He'd listened to her rant about her father, the admiral. He'd watched her cry. He'd lost to her at poker dozens of times, and won occasionally by sneaking a look at her cards through the cabin cameras behind her.

But he knew from hard experience that if he started treating her like the old friend he felt she was, it would only distress her. That was part of the burden of being a roboteer. He had to pretend not to know too much, at least for a while, anyway.

'I was just accessing a log,' he babbled. 'That's why I might have looked a little strange.'

She smiled wryly. 'I guessed. I'm Rachel Allesandro-Bock,

engineering officer.' She held out a broad, well-muscled hand for him to shake. He shook it as firmly as he dared.

'Of course,' he said.

'And may I introduce Captain Baron-Lecke?'

Will turned his gaze back to the captain. Baron looked him up and down, and then pushed his face into an unconvincing expression of warmth.

'Hi, Will,' he said. 'Please, call me Ira.' He took Will's hand and folded his gigantic digits around it in an embrace of almost pointed delicacy.

'It's a pleasure to meet you, sir,' said Will. 'An honour. I've read all your reports. Well, not actually read them as such. Just memorised them. But I'm sure you could have guessed that.' He realised he was running off at the mouth and stopped abruptly. He tried for a winning smile.

'That's good,' said Ira politely. 'An excellent start.'

He clapped Will on the shoulder so gently that he barely felt it. Will wanted badly to tell the captain that he knew how he must be grieving. He understood how close Ira and Doug had been. But he couldn't think of a way to say it that didn't presume some kind of familiarity.

'I'm very grateful for this opportunity, sir ... Ira,' was the best he could come up with. He tried again. 'I know I have big boots to fill, and I'm going to do my best.'

'Thank you, Will. I don't doubt it,' Ira replied blandly. 'Otherwise they wouldn't have picked you to be here today, would they?' He gave Will an opaque smile.

At that moment, Amy and John stepped through the door, sparing them further awkwardness.

Amy was in her forties with a round, motherly face. She had kind eyes, hair in plaits and the same indestructible body plan as Rachel and Ira. John was a little taller and thinner than the others, with side-swept blond hair and the face of a cartoon action hero.

'Will,' said Ira. 'This is Amy McKlusky-Ritter and John Jack Forrester-Klasse. Amy runs nav and medicine. John here is our pet spy. He runs weapons. Guys, I'd like you to meet Will Kuno-Monet, Handler Div's finest. He's fresh out of the same firefight as us, where he managed to single-handedly rescue two battle-cruisers *and* save the life of Admiral Bryant.'

Amy and John nodded their appreciation of his achievements. Will blushed from ear to ear.

'Farmer Bob has shown me some of his work and I can tell you, it's first rate, really first rate,' said Ira, nodding earnestly. To Will's ears, it sounded unpleasantly as if the captain was trying to convince himself.

Amy took one of Will's hands in both of hers and grasped it warmly, almost like a hug. 'Welcome to the *Ariel*,' she said. It's good to have you aboard.'

'Thanks,' said Will, starting to unwind a little.

Then it was John's turn. The assault officer winked and squeezed Will's fingers just a little too hard. 'Your first time in soft combat?'

Will nodded.

'Don't be fooled by the name,' said John with a sinister grin. 'There's nothing soft about it.'

Will's uncertainty returned. He watched the crew greet each other and felt like a lonely giant at a dinner party for dwarves. It didn't take a genius to see that he was the odd one out in this crowd. They were all from prestigious space-going families that had provided them with the finest spaceflight modifications Galatean science could provide. Those mods gave them countless advantages in shipboard life. They had reinforced arteries that could pump blood in the absence of heart function. They lay on couches during high-gee manoeuvres while normal people had to be suspended in special gel-filled muscle-tanks. Zero-gee environments were as natural to them as walking. They were also academically brilliant. Every member of the crew except Will had published important papers in their chosen fields.

In contrast, Will's parents were as poor as Galateans got. They'd only been granted a child licence because they'd volunteered for the roboteer project. With the exception of the quirky mix he'd inherited naturally through his parents' own alterations, Will's mods had been selected and provided by the state.

So what? No matter his humble origins, he'd still been chosen for this team. He had a right to be here.

He was urgently reminding himself of this when someone walked into the room who didn't feature in any of his memories.

'Greetings, all! Hope I'm not too late.'

The voice belonged to another stout man, though he didn't look superhuman like the rest of the crew. He was middle-aged with thin, reddish hair and highly animated eyes in a pasty face. He grinned broadly.

'Not at all,' said Ira. 'Folks, I'd like you to meet Dr Hugo Bessler-Vartian from Fleet Research. He'll be our passenger on this cruise. But don't worry, he'll be working as hard as the rest of us. Hugo, meet Rachel, Amy, John and our other new man, Will.'

Hugo introduced himself with earnest vigour.

'Amy, it's a pleasure.'

'John! The cryptographer! I read your work on counter-shells. Brilliant.'

He lingered for a moment on Rachel's hand. 'Rachel. Lovely to meet you. Are you the same Rachel who cracked the four-buffer problem? You are! I'm honoured.'

He turned at last to Will. 'Hello, Will! I heard about your clever trick out there at Memburi. Well done.' He slapped Will on the shoulder.

Will smiled back wordlessly. He knew nothing about Hugo. He framed a memory request to the station so that he could respond in kind, but by the time it fired, Ira was talking again.

'Well, ladies and gentlemen, we're all here now and I'm afraid time is of the essence. So if you'll just follow me, we'll get started.'

The captain led them over to the airlock on the far side of the room. Will tagged along behind the others, his stomach fluttering nervously. He was really going to board the *Ariel*. He was heading into space with these people. It had all happened so fast that it felt vaguely unreal. He'd barely had time to tell his family and friends.

It felt strange, too, boarding a ship without knowing where it was going. But that was how it worked in soft combat. The missions were top secret. The briefings happened on board.

The airlock opened to reveal a docking pod – a chamber shaped like an octagonal box laid on its side. It was lined with plush Fleet-green carpet. Foam handles stuck out from the floor, walls and ceiling, and little oval screens were set in each surface like pretend windows. In actual fact, the pod was lined with several metres of radiation shielding.

'Everybody grab a handle, please,' said Ira as Will stepped in.

The door closed and the pod began to slowly lift towards the middle of the station, shedding gravity as it went.

Will clutched his handle and floated. The rest of the crew chatted as if nothing were happening while the pod lost its spin and accelerated out along the docking spar.

Through the nearest screen, Will watched the ships pass. Without exception, they were huge. Even the *Ariel*, the smallest of the lot, was over a kilometre long. Most, like the *Phoenix*, were many times larger. They resembled petite grey worlds covered with forests of spikes. These were the collapsed field inducers, or 'brollies' as the engineers called them. During warp, they unfurled to envelop the ships in swathes of gravity. The hulls themselves were littered with scars and pocks the size of trench apartments – souvenirs of battle.

The pod turned off the main docking spar and followed the rail that led out towards the *Ariel*. It slid along the track between the mighty trunks of the inducers and down past the hull's grey metal horizon to the interior below.

Stripped of an outside view to show, the screens provided a diagrammatic impression of their position within the starship instead. The crew descended through the exo- and mesohulls, with their networks of tunnels where the robots lived and worked. They passed the outer Casimir-buffers and entered the narrow aperture in the lead shell of the endohull that led to the tiny command kernel at the centre of the ship. Finally the pod docked softly against the airlock. After a brief pause while the safety mechanisms disengaged, the door hissed open. The *Ariel*'s main cabin lay beyond.

Like all Galatean starships, the interior was decorated with cream-coloured crash padding and smelled as if someone had just mown their lawn nearby. Will had expected that. What he hadn't expected, not even with Doug's memories to help him, was the size. The cabin was about three metres wide and five high. Three vertically stacked bunks stood on either side of the entrance, filling most of the space except for a narrow channel down the centre. A coffin-shaped tank stuck out of the floor, half-blocking access to the couches at the bottom. It pretty much filled all of the space there would have been to stand in if the ship had gravity.

Will had known the dimensions in advance, so why did the room look so much smaller than Doug remembered it? To his dismay, he realised Doug must have been significantly shorter than him. He'd never thought to check. He tried not to let his disappointment at the size of the space show. After all, this was where he'd be living for months at a time, with five other people. He might as well get used to it.

'There you go,' said Ira. 'Your new home.' He pointed to the bunks allotted to Hugo and Will. They were the bottom two, of course, on the floor.

'Because we've got Hugo here, we've had to move the tank,' Ira explained. 'It'll be a bit more crowded than usual, I'm afraid. But don't worry, folks – it's not meant to be a long mission.'

The hatch closed, sealing them in and Will's chest constricted with sudden claustrophobia. Couldn't they have made the cabin just a little bit bigger?

The answer, of course, was *no*. Much of the machinery on a starship existed for one reason: to shield the area intended for human passengers. Make that space larger and the size of ship required to protect it grew disproportionately. Soft-combat ships were always made as compact as possible.

Ira gestured to the hatch situated in the main cabin's ceiling. 'This way first, ladies and gents.'

Will knew from Doug's memories that there were only three other chambers on the *Ariel*: a multi-gee toilet, a wash-space that doubled as a privacy chamber, and a gym with retractable mountings that could also be used as a meeting room or refectory. This hatch led to the gym/meeting room, which – unsurprisingly – was also oppressively cramped. They had just enough room to float in a circle, as if they were standing.

'Welcome aboard, everybody,' said Ira, surveying his crew. 'If you'll bear with me for a few minutes, I'll explain why you're here and why your leave was cut short.' He pulled a display tablet down out of the ceiling. It floated between them like a table. The panel flickered into life, displaying the green and silver Galatean Fleet logo. 'I don't have to tell you that by the time we got out of Memburi, it was pretty clear that the Earthers had some kind of new weapon. Something we don't have. That's a first. In the whole history of this stupid war, we've always been technologically ahead.'

It was true. Will knew that had it just been down to science, the Galateans would have won the war the same year it started. The problem was, Galatea only had a few tens of thousands of people to fight with. Earth had billions. The Galateans made up that shortfall with robots and smarts. But even with genius on their side, they could only do so much against such overwhelming numbers.

'This defeat presents a serious problem,' Ira told them. 'Earth has a direct route to our front door again, and enough firepower to finish us off. Needless to say, we can't allow them to keep that advantage.' He scanned the room, his dark eyes meeting every face in turn. 'If we can't find some kind of defence against their new g-rays before they send an invasion force, the war is over.'

He clapped his beefy hands together. 'And that's where we come in. As you know, on our last mission we liberated some data from their ships before they started shooting at us. It turns out that those ships didn't come from one of the Earther Fleet-bases we know about.' He clicked his fingers and the panel brought up a navigational map of the human galactic shell – the onion-skin layer of galaxy accessible with warp drive. 'They came from here,' he said, and pointed to a star off to the left of the Earthers' main traffic routes. 'It's one of the old Pioneer stars.'

The Pioneers had been a community of space traders before the war who'd taken it upon themselves to extend the frontiers of human space. They could have been great allies to the Galateans, Will thought, if they'd had enough warning. Unfortunately, the Pioneers were too few, and too spread out, to mount a defence when the crusades began. The Earthers had invaded and occupied their barely populated star systems within a matter of weeks.

'The Earther charts list it under a Pioneer name as Zuni-Dehel,' said Ira. 'We think they're using it as a weapons-development facility. Either that or they've taken over something the Pioneers themselves were working on. We're going there to take a look.'

He reached out and touched the panel. 'We'll be flying around the edge of Earther space, like this.' He drew a line and their route lit up. 'It's a long way around, I'm afraid, but we'll be making it fast. We have to get there and back before the nano hits the fan-o here at home. That means two fuelling stops. The first will be here, at Saint Andrews. The second is here, at Li-Delamir. With luck, it'll be a relatively straight recon job. We go in. We make a soft incursion. We get out. We'll be looking for *anything* that might enable us to mount a defence or a counter-attack against those new ships of theirs.'

Ira gestured at the nodding scientist on his right. 'Hugo's coming along to give us a hand. He's the Fleet's number-one energy systems specialist, so he'll know what to look for. But he's not just a theory man. Hugo worked for several years on Fleet prototypes. He's spent plenty of time in space, and he knows how to pull his weight aboard a starship.'

Ira paused for a moment. 'I'm going to be straight with you, people. This won't be easy.' He clicked again to reveal Central Command's risk assessment for the trip. 'This mission takes us into the thick of the enemy, to the very place where the concentration of that new firepower we saw is likely to be at its strongest. The security will be as tight as a trench-seal. We'll have to be on our guard and doing our best work. Because if we don't succeed... Well, we'll all be looking for a new place to live.'

He grinned, revealing a broad spread of perfectly even teeth. It was a dark kind of humour. If they lost the war, finding somewhere to live was likely to be the least of their problems.

Will stared down at the assessment and tried to appear as relaxed as the others. The threat indicators for the mission were nightmarish, into the red right across the board. However, no one else around the table looked remotely fazed, so Will hid the fear that churned inside him. These people were clearly used to dealing with situations far more precarious than the ones he usually encountered.

'Any questions?' asked the captain.

John stuck up a lazy hand. 'Any clues in the rest of that data about what we're looking for?'

Ira glanced at Hugo. 'You want to answer that one?'

Hugo nodded. 'I've been working on it since you got back, and we think we've found something – a new program in their soft core with rather heavy encryption on it. As far as we can tell, it's a monitoring harness for some kind of energy source. Presumably the energy source that was powering the attacks, given that it feeds directly into their main supply conduits. But there's no code in the core governing the source itself. In fact, there's no data about it anywhere in the enemy systems. It appears to be a sealed unit.'

Hugo's eyes gleamed with enthusiasm as he talked. Will had no doubt the man was used to giving lectures. Ira didn't look thrilled that Hugo had launched into a full explanation, but Hugo seemed oblivious.

'The source only appears to take three instructions,' the scientist said. 'On, adjust power level, and off. The energy source takes a map of the local space as the only parameter on its ignition sequence. And there's nothing for refuelling or maintenance.'

Hugo made this last point with one eyebrow crooked, as if to underline the mystery. Will had to admit that it sounded weird, and he was no energy specialist.

'No refuelling?' said Rachel. 'That's impossible. The energy has to be coming from somewhere.'

Hugo nodded eagerly. 'Certainly it does. Thus far, we've come up with two possibilities. Firstly, that the source unit is disposable. It's created with a certain amount of power and runs down over time.'

'But in that case, what's the map for?' Rachel asked.

'Exactly,' said Hugo. 'The second theory is that they have some way to pipe energy in from elsewhere, and the map acts as a frame of reference. Perhaps there's another ship outside the system.'

Amy frowned. 'But how would they do that? Some kind of particle beam?'

'Nothing showed up on our scans,' said Hugo. 'Seems unlikely, doesn't it? And their use of disrupters would appear to rule out curvon technology. So it's a mystery. Something totally new.'

Will had never seen a man look so hungry for knowledge. Hugo was about to start up again, but Ira beat him to it.

'And that's exactly why we're going, folks: to find out. I'd like to take this particular discussion offline. There'll be plenty of time to puzzle over it on the flight out and I'm sure our guest will furnish you with any extra details you desire. Meanwhile, are there any other questions before we begin?'

Will could think of nothing to say. The prospect of waltzing straight into the enemy's most secret base had temporarily robbed him of his curiosity.

The captain nodded, pleased. 'Okay, good. In that case, take your places, people. We're heading out.'

The crew floated back down to their bunks. Will dragged himself to the bottom-right couch and slid through the narrow gap between the muscle-tank and the bed above. The tank's side was open so that he could slide in quickly, in the event of a firefight. As the only member of the crew lacking the mods to keep him alive during high-gee turns, only he needed one.

He clipped himself into the webbing and listened to the sounds of people adjusting themselves above him. The bunk's ceiling and bulkhead wall both doubled as display screens and were currently showing him a view of a Galatean lichen field and a bottomless blue sky. No doubt it was supposed to look homey and familiar, to compensate for the pitiful space he was supposed to inhabit, but it was far from convincing. Will's claustrophobia returned, stronger than ever. He fought the feeling down and connected the retractable fat-contact to his neck.

The *Ariel*'s systems appeared abruptly in his sensorium as new corridors leading off his central stone-walled home node. His anxiety eased a little. At least he was able to escape into software. The others couldn't even do that.

'Everybody ready?' asked Ira.

Will reached out into the *Ariel*'s mental corridors, summoning his systems status. It appeared before him like a great field where a crop of green LEDs was growing, not one red in sight. Everything was in order.

The crew called out 'check' in turn, Will last of all.

'In that case,' said the captain, 'let's get to work.'

Will could just make out Ira's voice in quiet conversation with station control. Then the order came direct to his sensorium.

'Rachel, ready the torches, minimum power.'

'Torches ready.'

As the *Ariel* slid out of dock, Will swapped his eyes for those of the ship's external sensors and watched the vast mass of the Fleet station slowly pull away. The curve of Galatea was a soft, blotchy brown beneath them, dotted with thin scraps of white cloud.

Ira guided them away from the station and fired the torches up to cruise power. Will felt the tug on his body as the ship accelerated. It took the better part of an hour at a steady one-point-five gees for them to reach a safe exit distance, at which point Ira turned off the torches and spoke again.

'Rachel, how's the juice looking?'

'Nice and hot, sir.'

'Buffers engaged?'

'Buffers running at cruise charge,' she said.

'Deploy the brollies.'

All over the ship, the gigantic inducers slowly spread their vanes. It took them several minutes to reach full extension.

'Brollies deployed.'

'Grease the rails,' said the captain.

Rachel ignited the trigger field – a cloud of exotic heavy particles cooked up with help from the ship's fusion cores.

'Rails greased.'

Through the sensors, Will watched lightning course between the inducers, coating the ship with blue-white radiance. The inducer-vanes tilted, creating a long, tapered oval of flickering light that stretched away from the ship in front and behind.

'Ready for warp, ladies and gentlemen,' said Ira.

Will braced himself.

In the next instant he was slammed into his couch as the first matter/antimatter volley collided with the trigger field. Outside the ship, the local curvon flow was coaxed into giving up its spatial potential. The space ahead of the ship shrank suddenly while the space behind expanded and the *Ariel* leapt forward.

Two seconds later, the kick came again. And then again, quicker and fiercer. The further they travelled from Galatea's delicate gravity well, the more juice they could safely use. The thuds of the engine blurred together into a growl that reverberated through the cabin walls. They were on their way.

4: IN FLIGHT

4.1: GUSTAV

The captain of Gustav's personal starship engaged warp two light-seconds out from Earth and set them cruising at a comfortable point-nine gees. With the manoeuvre concluded, Gustav retired gratefully to his cabin. He was on his way back to his private realm at last, away from the poverty and politics of Earth after one of the most tedious weeks of his life. Now, perhaps, he could finally get some peace.

He locked the cabin door, sat down in one of the inflatable armchairs and pulled out the tablet on which he kept the suntap schematics. For over a year now, Gustav had pondered them in his spare time. Though they remained as opaque as when he'd first examined them, he found that concentrating on the inscrutable design served to calm and focus his mind. He lived in hope that one day, if he stared at its workings for long enough, he'd actually solve the riddle of the alien device.

For what had to be the five-thousandth time, Gustav turned to the blueprint for the gravitic generator, the most tangled and tortuous component in the entire assembly. He traced energy pathways through the familiar design and waited for peace to come. It didn't. His mind refused to settle on the details. Instead, he found himself dwelling on the events of the last few days.

Thinking about the suntap only reminded him that the Prophet had made it impossible for him to delay any longer. He would have to deliver to Tang the stockpile of finished units that he'd so long denied existed. Thus the Kingdom would go to war relying on a weapon they still didn't understand, and whose behaviour they could not predict. What if all the devices they built stopped working in the middle of the invasion? No one would have the first idea how to fix them.

Tang had undoubtedly been responsible for that folly. The man didn't appear to have any interest in the research-and-development process. He just wanted his ships. Gustav dearly wished he could have been given someone cautious and reasonable to work with, but political reality didn't work that way. The Reconsiderists had few potential admirals, and handing responsibility for the new Fleet to a different subsect would have weakened their position immeasurably. Tang was the best bet at the time. Now Gustav wondered if he'd have been better off recruiting from the damned Medellins.

No doubt the good admiral would be delighted to learn that his project leader had been saddled with a High Church spy. Gustav muttered curses under his breath. He would have to do something about Rodriguez soon, though the thought repelled him. The right time to start was probably now, while Rodriguez was still forming his opinions. With a grunt of frustration, Gustav stabbed the intercom button on his tablet.

'Sir,' said the ship's captain.

'Send Rodriguez to my cabin. Immediately.'

'Yes, sir.'

Gustav sank back into his chair and scowled at the wall until he heard a knock at the door. He took a deep breath and tried to will himself into a diplomatic frame of mind.

'Come in,' he called.

Rodriguez opened the hatch and stepped through. He was dressed in an all-white ship-suit. The changes in gravity they'd experienced since leaving Earth didn't appear to have affected his slick hair at all.

Gustav nodded to him. 'Father.'

Rodriguez returned the gesture with pious deliberation. 'You asked to see me,' he said, one eyebrow tilted in mild curiosity.

'Yes, I'd like to talk.' Gustav gestured at the empty chair opposite.

Rodriguez lowered himself into it like a large cat settling. 'Certainly. What would you like to talk about?'

'You, for the most part,' said Gustav. 'If you're to function as my assistant, it will be necessary for us to know a little about each other.'

'Of course,' said Rodriguez. His tone suggested otherwise. 'What would you like to know?'

Gustav steeled himself. There was no point wasting time. 'To begin with, your opinion of the Relic.'

Rodriguez's eyebrow tilted a little further. 'In what context?'

'Well . .' started Gustav. He struggled for a way to start. 'The origin of the Relic is still very ambiguous. There's nothing explicit in its structure or function that proves it's the work of an alien species.'

This was one of the ideas Oswald had raised in the report he'd sent Gustav as ammunition for this very moment. Gustav felt slightly dirty repeating it – it wasn't something he believed. However, drawing the disciple out had to be the best place to start.

'I'm interested to know,' he continued, 'whether you believe it to be the work of an alien civilisation or a message from God, as I've heard some people suggest?'

Rodriguez gave him a small, plump-lipped smile. 'Both,' he said.

It wasn't the reply Gustav had expected to hear. 'How do you manage that?'

'Science is how we know the mind of God, General,' Rodriguez replied with amusement. 'Your prayer attendance record may be poor, but surely you must have heard that? It's one of the Primary Teachings.'

Gustav refused to be baited. 'I'm not sure I follow.'

'Truism is not a backward faith,' said the disciple. He was clearly enjoying himself. 'If evidence suggests that the Relic is of alien origin, then we of the Leading must work on that basis.'

Gustav's brow furrowed. 'But doesn't the Prophet also say that mankind is unique? That we're God's greatest creation, unequalled in the universe?'

'He does. But being unique and being alone are not the same thing.' Rodriguez twisted a hand in the air to illustrate and smirked. 'The fact that mankind has universal primacy does not preclude the existence of extraterrestrial life. We would be foolish to deny the existence of dogs, say, simply because we have never set eyes on one.'

'I see,' said Gustav. He'd assumed the man would refuse to acknowledge the origin of the Relic flat out on theological grounds. And from the expression on his soft face, Rodriguez clearly took delight in defying that expectation. Perhaps he was not so much of a fool as Gustav had first supposed.

'Yet the builders of the Relic must have been highly advanced,' he ventured. 'By the Prophet's own teachings, does that not imply they knew more of the mind of God than we do? How do you reconcile that with the idea of human greatness?'

'Greatness requires more than scientific knowledge,' replied the disciple smoothly. 'It also requires faith. The Relic-makers did not have Truism, therefore greatness was never possible for them.'

In other words, 'greatness' meant whatever the Prophet wanted it to. It was typical High Church hypocrisy, but it was also perhaps something Gustav could use.

'That's very interesting,' he said. 'A subtle point. Tell me, how would you go about clarifying an idea like that to the Following?'

Rodriguez's smile dropped a notch. 'I wouldn't. As a member of the Leading, it is our job to spare the Following from the doubt engendered by subtle thinking. As the Prophet says, simplicity is stability. That which you cannot tell a child, do not tell a mob.'

Gustav sat back nodding, quietly annoyed. This was not a point he could openly debate without sounding like a heretic. To believe that people should know as much as their leaders was to invite accusations of being a democrat and a capitalist. The greatest lesson of the last century had been that knowledge without responsibility was a recipe for disaster. That was how terrorists were made.

He tried a different tack. 'But how can you possibly prevent the Following from finding out about the Relic? It's not going away. And if the people must never know, doesn't that leave the situation vulnerable to misinterpretation when they discover the truth? Worse still, what if they discover that the church has kept the truth from them?'

Rodriguez shrugged. 'Nothing in God's universe is free. This is the price that comes with the gift of the suntap. The Leading must exercise vigilance, and self-discipline.' He regarded Gustav levelly with small, gleaming eyes. 'Let us not play games here, General,' he said. 'I'm sure Lord Khan told you my real reason for joining this mission. I am here to determine the answer to exactly that question – how is the secret of the Relic best kept?'

Gustav folded his arms. 'Your honesty is commendable, Father. Let me in turn tell you that, frankly, I do not see what question there is to answer. The Relic is a world-sized artefact. It cannot be hidden any better than it always has been. It cannot be guarded any more securely than it already is.'

Rodriguez smiled cryptically. 'Surely that is a matter of conjecture.'

'Is it?' Gustav demanded. 'We have used the best strategic models the Kingdom has created. Increase the defences and you increase the chances of it being discovered.'

Rodriguez waved a placatory hand. 'I admit that the Reconsiderists have done an excellent job. I doubt any other subsect could have done better.'

'Then why close the project?'

Rodriguez's expression became guarded. 'There are many reasons.'

'Such as?'

'For a start, a string of miracles coming from a single lab would eventually raise questions. And there are radical factions among the Leading that would use such a discovery to further their own political aims.'

'What string of miracles?' Gustav asked tersely. 'So far we've extracted only one blueprint.'

The schematic for the suntap was still the most coherent piece of information they'd received from the Relic, and that was within the first week of contact. Since then, there had been a whole lot of nonsense and plenty of repeated data. Gustav, however, was still a long way from giving up.

'If there are to be no more miracles, then why keep the project open?' Rodriguez retorted.

'To better protect the church, of course. If there's one Relic, there could be thousands out there, waiting to be discovered. Surely it's preferable to be better informed of the potential risks.'

Rodriguez shifted uncomfortably in his chair, his expression clouding. 'If the protection of the church is really your primary goal, then you shouldn't mind if the head of the church takes over.'

'Except that the church has already put its best scientific men in charge. If the church wishes to understand the Relic, why replace them with people who know less? I'm forced to assume that the church intends something else.' And it would be something stupid, without a doubt.

The disciple's nostrils flared. He glared out from the depths of his armchair like a cornered boar. 'Your talk of other Relics is meaningless,' he said coldly. 'A known threat is more significant than an infinity of hypothetical ones.'

Gustav's brow crunched in confusion. 'What's that supposed to mean?'

'It means you would protect the church by leaving it constantly open to the threat of destabilisation.'

Gustav laughed mirthlessly. 'No more open than it would be under High Church control.'

Rodriguez shook his head. 'There may be options that your blinkered research has not allowed you to consider.'

'Like what?' said Gustav, exasperated. 'Whatever you do, that Relic is still going to be there.'

Rodriguez only glared at him, tight-lipped and sullen. It took Gustav a moment to work out what the expression meant. When he did, he was stunned.

'You're going to try to destroy it...' he said breathlessly.

Rodriguez glowered at him, clearly furious that he'd been pushed into divulging more than he'd wanted to. 'We're appraising *all* the options.'

Gustav sank back into his seat and put his hand to his forehead. 'That's the stupidest thing I've ever heard.'

'No stupider than risking the future of the church,' snapped the disciple.

'But it's a *planet*,' said Gustav. 'I regret to inform you, but the Kingdom doesn't yet have the power to destroy a planet.'

'You underestimate us,' Rodriguez muttered. 'A dangerous mistake.'

'Then enlighten me!' Gustav exclaimed. 'Impress me with the High Church's secret powers.'

There was a long silence, during which Rodriguez stared at him hatefully.

'I'm not going to discuss this further,' he said at last. 'I'm under oath on the subject. But think on this: we both wear the wrong clothes, you and I. You are a scientist who dresses like a soldier.' He let his contempt for the idea drip from his voice. 'But before I donned the robe for God, I *was* a soldier.'

If that was true, Gustav thought, it must have been a long time ago. Rodriguez had let all traces of hardness slide from his body.

'I am not ignorant of military matters,' the disciple added. 'You'd be wise not to forget that.'

Gustav wasn't impressed. 'Did your keen military mind consider the idea that you might be declaring war on a vastly superior alien species?'

'I think that's unlikely.'

'Really? Why? As far as we can tell, the Relic has survived for millions of years. Its surface is *smooth*. There are no craters on it. Not one! How did it manage that without defences?' Gustav demanded. 'We don't even know how it communicates with the probes we put on its surface. Yet you assume—'

'There will be no retaliation,' Rodriguez snapped.

Gustav leaned forward again, fixing the man with his gaze. 'What makes you so damned sure?'

Rodriguez stood abruptly. 'Because God would not give us the sword to smite our enemies only to have it break our faith!'

Gustav squinted in incomprehension. 'I'm sorry?'

'You think it a coincidence that we are handed so powerful a weapon in our darkest hour?' Rodriguez sneered. 'That we are handed such a moral dilemma *now*, in this way, at this critical time? Your so-called rationalism makes you naïve, General. We are being tested.'

Gustav's skin grew cold as he looked into Rodriguez's burning eyes.

'We should take what we need from God and no more,' the disciple went on. 'Any other course is intellectual avarice, pure and simple – a *sin* of the first order.'

It took Gustav a moment to find the words. 'You can't really believe that,' he breathed.

Rodriguez pulled his shoulders back and looked at Gustav down the length of his pointed nose. 'I cannot believe you don't. Your lack of faith disgusts me, General.'

Gustav stood to face the shorter man. 'We can't risk the future of the human race on the basis of a guess,' he said. 'That's insane.'

'Firstly,' Rodriguez growled, 'it is not a guess. And secondly, *you* don't have to. That's *my* job. Now if you'll excuse me, I think it's time for my afternoon prayers.'

He walked over to the door. Gustav could only stare.

Rodriguez paused on his way out through the hatch and looked back. 'I'm a reasonable man,' he said bitterly. 'I suggest that you might want to collect data supporting your claim that the Relic is too dangerous to destroy. I'll be happy to read it, and include it in my report to the Prophet.' With that, he smiled acidly and left, slamming the door after him.

Gustav paced up and down the narrow strip of clear space in the middle of the room. The sheer hubris of trying to *destroy* the Relic. It beggared belief. The single greatest discovery in the history of mankind and Rodriguez called it avarice.

He ground a fist into his palm. If that was what they stood for, then the High Church couldn't be allowed to determine the shape of the future any more than the Galateans. He should have leaked the truth while he had the chance.

As he turned to pace again, his eye caught on the holster clipped to his cabin wall. In it was his executive's automatic, the only lethal weapon inside the ship. It was designed to kill without damaging valuable equipment in the unlikely case of a mutiny.

Though Gustav had been forced to kill many times on Earth, he had never done so on one of his own ships. It was a point of pride. Nevertheless, a question came unbidden to his mind. Would he kill to protect the Relic if it came to that? He discovered it was a question he didn't want to answer.

4.2: WILL

Will twisted his head slowly by three hundred and sixty degrees, examining the grey-streaked wall of the antimatter-dispersion pipe through which he climbed. Sure enough, there was yet another crack. He groaned.

'One more,' he told Rachel.

The flaw would be far too small for human eyes to see – it was just a few molecules wide – but Will wasn't looking through human eyes. His senses were tethered to a worm-like pipe-cleaner robot nine centimetres long.

He flicked his perspective to the closest repair spider. In an instant, his world went from claustrophobic to vertiginous. Now he was clinging to a rail that ran up through an apparently bottomless network of struts and girders. The pipe hung vertically in front of him, clad in striped superconductor rings from which a tangle of power and monitor cables trailed.

Will accelerated up the rail till he was outside the faulty segment. He extended two arms to seize the pipe and another two to disconnect the power couplings. He yanked each one open with an angry snap. The problem was that the delicate inner lining of the pipes was under constant gravitational shear this close to the exohull. And with the *Ariel* working its engines flat out, that lining had to be repaired every time the ship docked to refuel.

Any crack left untended long enough to reach critical size would cause the microscopic bullets of antimatter to veer off their magnetically determined path. That meant having the single most destructive substance known to man spraying into your mesohull at near lightspeed, which wasn't exactly desirable. But despite its importance, it was dull, exhausting work, and Will had been at it for six hours straight.

The repairs had begun the moment they'd arrived at St Andrews, their first fuelling star, and were scheduled to finish the moment the tanks were full. The *Ariel* was leaving immediately, and the pipes would once again be coursing with power. That left Will about one hour to finish everything.

It would have been a lot a lot easier if he wasn't so tired, but tired was all Will had felt for the whole week since they'd left home. Ira had seen to that. On the first shift-end out from Galatea, Ira had surprised Will by instructing him to sleep in his muscle-tank.

'We'll have to build you up a bit,' Ira told him. 'I need you in the best cardiovascular shape possible by the time we reach our target.'

Will had never used a muscle-tank before and thought the idea a little strange. However, he was keen to show willing. It had been unnerving, sliding into that box of warm, sticky gel for the first time. Worse still was the sensation of the hundreds of tiny needles pricking his skin. Fortunately, he hadn't needed to tolerate the sensation for long. The tank knocked him out cold.

By the time he'd woken, Will ached as if he'd been in the gym for all eight hours. On the other hand, the striking increase in his strength from just one night's exposure had pleased him immensely. The first moment of real worry hit at the end of that next work shift, when Ira instructed him to sleep in the tank again. In fact, to sleep there every rest period till they reached Zuni-Dehel.

Now, with a full week of tank treatment behind him, Will could barely concentrate. His chest felt as if it was on fire the whole time. He was sure that if he did as Ira wished, he'd be completely unfit for duty by the time they reached enemy lines. That said, he wasn't about to get himself thrown off the most famous ship in the Fleet just because *the great Ira Baron* had decided to haze him. He'd see the orders through, even if it killed him.

Will ripped the old section of pipe away and shoved a new one into place. The repair spider flinched from the harsh treatment. Will knew he was hurting the robot's delicate limbs by working so fast but he was too exhausted to care. He rotated his arc-bonding arms to the front and welded in the new section.

As soon as the joint was finished, Will threw himself back into the mind of the pipe cleaner. It started with surprise at his sudden intrusion into its thoughts as Will dragged it up over the still-cooling joints to inspect the mend.

'Bright!' the pipe cleaner wailed as its lidless camera eyes passed the heated wall. There were no flaws to be seen. The new section was safe.

'Done,' he announced.

He flipped his mind back to the repair-survey node, a virtual space that he'd decorated like the command room of an Old World railway network, complete with beige plastic and fake wood trim. A huge display board filling one wall showed the ship's convoluted system of dispersion pipes laid out like tracks. Small electric lights indicated the progress of the other cleaners. To his immense relief, they had all now reached their stations and were showing green. There were no more flaws. Maybe Ira would let him rest for the last hour before they set off again. True rest – the thought of it was incredibly seductive.

'That's it,' he told Rachel. 'They're all finished.' He leaned back in his digital approximation of an office chair.

'Already?' came Rachel's reply.

Her avatar appeared on the seat beside him. The avatar was a model of Rachel that Will had assembled for himself. He'd made it out of footage from his memory logs, along with a live-feed of her face from her bunk camera. It looked like her, and most of the time it moved like her, too. Will had spent what few scraps of spare time he'd had compiling heuristics to mimic her physical behaviour. He hadn't told her yet that he'd built this replica of her in his private world. He wasn't sure what she'd think, and he didn't want to lose it. It made him feel less lonely.

One of the consequences of Ira's enforced regime was that Will hadn't yet taken part in any of the ship's social life. With his every minute spent either working or unconscious in the tank, he was missing out on the ship's banter – the conversation that kept them close. He often heard the others laughing in the background of his sensorium while he struggled to keep the ship's robotic population in order. Sometimes they sat together and ate meals while he slept or toiled. Will felt even more like an outsider than he had on the *Phoenix*.

Rachel was the only person he'd really got to talk to so far, and that was only because they'd been working together. Though their conversations were limited to topics like accelerator coils and magnetic sluice-gates, he'd rapidly come to appreciate why Doug had held her in such high regard. She was patient and smart in a no-nonsense kind of way. She'd taken plenty of time to familiarise him with the quirks of the *Ariel*'s architecture and listened attentively to his every stupid question. He felt more grateful to her than he cared to express.

With the avatar, his time with Rachel became more than just a dialogue through a camera window. It was as if she was actually in the metaphor space with him. And, admittedly, she was also pleasing to look at.

'I'm impressed,' she said. Her eyes darted from side to side as she checked the schematics in her visor, breaking the illusion of her presence for a moment.

She couldn't see Will's display board any more than she could see him sitting in the chair next to her. It gave her the disturbing appearance of someone partially blind, but Will didn't care.

'Have you dry-run them yet?' she asked.

'Didn't need to. I made tight-scans as I was going along.'

Rachel looked uncomfortable at that. 'I think we'd better, just to be certain, don't you?'

Will sighed. 'Sure.'

He sounded more snappish than he'd intended, but the mere thought of conducting another round of tests was draining. He slouched forwards in his chair and started mustering the presence of mind he'd need to reconfigure the test-suite again.

'It's okay,' said Rachel quietly. 'I can tell you're wiped. Why don't I do it?'

Will glanced up at her avatar. It wasn't her job, plus she lacked the mods to do the work directly. It would take her three times as long as it would him. Not to mention the fact that she had plenty of her own work to do overseeing the refuelling. On the other hand, it meant rest. Who was he to stop her if she wanted to volunteer?

'Are you sure?' he asked.

Rachel nodded. 'Of course. Why don't you unplug for a while and take a nap.' She sounded obscurely guilty. 'I should think you probably need one.'

It wasn't procedure, but it was appallingly tempting.

'Ira's still in conference with the Andrewsian defence minister,' she reminded him. 'He won't be out of the privacy room till it's time to go.'

She was right. Though the people of St Andrews were very minor allies, they managed to take up a lot of time with diplomatic chatter.

'Thanks,' he said at last with a sheepish smile. 'I really appreciate it.'

He turned his attention back to the real world and gasped with relief as he yanked the fat-contact from his neck. He stretched against his bunk and stared blissfully up at the blue sky of the ceiling. His body relaxed properly for the first time in days. Within seconds, he was asleep.

He was woken after what felt like minutes by a deafening alarm splitting the cabin air. He jerked into motion, reflexively grabbing the slide-bar on the muscle-tank.

'What's that?' he blurted. 'What happened?'

His sentiments were echoed a split second later by Ira barrelling through the hatch from the privacy chamber like a human torpedo.

'What the *hell* is going on?' he boomed.

The sound of the alarm died.

'It's okay!' Rachel said quickly. 'Everything's under control. Will, could I get you back in here for a second, please?'

'Why is he *out*?' Ira demanded. The captain yanked himself over to float beside Rachel's bunk, his face flushed with anger. 'What're you doing? What subsystem are you on?'

Will hastily reconnected his fat-contact. The moment he hit the repair-survey node, he could guess what the problem was from the cluster of flaring red lights on the board. A quick check of his active SAP stable confirmed his suspicion. His last pipe cleaner, made nervous by the cooling welds around it, had failed to return home when its survey was complete. The heat of the pipe was still above its default safety threshold, thus it couldn't retrace its steps without external instructions from Will. So, like all dim-witted machines, it had sat there quietly and waited for new orders. Thus, when Rachel started injecting a cool test plasma into the pipes, the presence of the cleaner had come up looking like a critical blockage, hence the alarms.

Will grabbed hold of the cleaner's mind and sent it scurrying back to its service alcove as fast as it could go. Before it got there, Ira's command icon appeared in the control room, denoting his presence in the system. It took the captain just seconds to spot what was going on.

'Monet!' he roared.

The sound was decidedly real, and close by. Will turned back to the real world to see the captain's beet-coloured face glaring at him over the muscle-tank.

Ira thrust his data visor up over his head. 'What in *fuck's* name were you doing unplugged while one of your repair robots was still active? And why do I find Ms Bock here running your tests for you? Do you know what *duty shift* means, Mr Monet?'

'It's my fault, sir,' said Rachel. 'I told him to unplug. And I was the one who injected plasma into the pipe while there was still a robot inside.'

'Quiet!' Ira ordered and turned his attention back to Will. 'What were you thinking? Do you have any idea what would've happened if we'd started up the pulse guns with that thing still stuck in there?'

And with sickly clarity, Will did. An antimatter bullet colliding with the cleaner would blow a hole in the hull large enough to drive a macrodozer through. In all probability, they wouldn't have time to realise their mistake before they died.

'In case you hadn't noticed, Monet, this ship only has six people on it,' the captain snarled. 'That means everyone has to pull their weight. And if you're going to make slack-ass mistakes like disconnecting on the job, I might as well leave you here with the fucking Andrewsians. Because I'd rather have Rachel and Hugo cover your job around the clock till the end of the mission than leave my ship in the hands of a second-rate shift-dodger. Do you understand me?'

'Yes, sir,' said Will, his face burning.

'And I don't care if someone told you that you could unplug or not,' he added, with a furious glance in Rachel's direction. 'Your duties on this ship are outlined very clearly in your transfer contract. Or do you need a refresher course in Fleet discipline?'

'No, sir.'

'From now on, I want to see that noodle on your neck at all times, in-tank or out, unless I *explicitly* give you permission to take it off.'

Will pressed his lips together hard. Ira might as well chain him to his bunk. What he needed was more rest, not less.

'Do you get me?' Ira demanded.

'Yes, sir,' said Will stiffly.

'Then finish those repairs. I want them double-checked, with a full report on my stack before we leave system.'

Ira shoved himself away towards the privacy room. With a grimace of frustration, Will re-immersed himself in the repair node and began running the last batch of tests all over again.

4.3: IRA

Ira dragged himself through the hatch, cursing. He was furious, but mostly with himself. He should have pushed back harder on Bryant about the new roboteer. It was clear Will couldn't take the pace. He had been deadly serious when he'd suggested leaving Will behind. Having no roboteer on the ship was better than risking a clumsy one. And St Andrews was desperate for technical help. He had half a mind to call the defence minister back and offer him a deal, then and there.

The tiny colony was one of Galatea's three remaining allies. The only reason the Earthers hadn't bothered to invade it yet was because the victory spoils wouldn't cover the invasion cost. Everyone down there was trying to build shelters to hide in for the inevitable day when the crusade arrived. Not that shelters would do them a shred of good.

Ira was about to press the close stud when Amy darted through the hatch after him. The lines on her round face were set hard. She slapped the door stud for him, sealing them in, and fixed him with a stern expression.

'Ira, what's going on? This isn't like you.'

'What's not like me?'

Amy snorted. 'What do you think? The way you're treating Will! You can't expect him to undergo a full metabolic enhancement and still be on top of his duties. It's crazy! You're pushing him way too hard.'

Ira folded his arms. 'You think so? Well, those Earthers are going to push him a hell of a lot harder than I am. All I'm trying to do is keep him alive.'

'How?' Amy snapped. 'By pumping his heart so full of drugs that he can barely move? That's bullshit, Ira, and you know it.'

Ira bristled. He took a lot from Amy. She'd been his friend for years and he valued her advice, but this was the first time he could remember her criticising his leadership decisions to his face. It amazed him that she didn't understand.

'If we have to take another turn like the one that killed Doug—'

She cut him off. '*If!* We haven't even got there yet, Ira. We have no idea what we're going to find.'

Ira set his jaw. 'We have to be prepared for that eventuality.'

'Do we? In case you hadn't noticed, this isn't a pitched battle we're walking into. It's a stealth raid. I think this has a lot more to do with your guilt problem than his gravity tolerance.'

'Call my problem whatever you like. It doesn't change the fact that we're about to walk into the very place where that disrupter attack was dreamed up. And if I have to face it again, I'm going to do everything in my power to make sure that my crew get out of there alive. *All of them.*' He shook his head. 'You seem to think I haven't been keeping an eye on Will. I have. I have a visor window open showing his bio-vitals twenty-four seven. I know what I'm doing.'

Amy sighed. 'Do you? Then how come we just faced down a possible pipe blast? If what you say is true, then you're as much to blame for that little fiasco as he was. Why not talk to him for once. Let him settle in. Make him *want* to work for you. He'll be ready a lot sooner if you start treating him like a human being.'

Ira's chest tightened. The last thing he wanted to do now was get chummy with Will.

'At least that way we won't kill ourselves in some stupid blunder before we arrive,' Amy added. 'Please, Ira. For all our sakes.'

Ira looked away. 'Sorry. I can't. The mission has to come first.'

Amy gasped in frustration. 'Fine! I didn't want to have to say this, but in case you've forgotten, I also operate as ship's doctor on this crate. When it comes to the welfare of the crew, what I say goes. So you'll dial it back and give that lad some downtime, and that's an order. Do you hear me?' she demanded, her tone a mocking approximation of Ira's.

Ira glowered at her and nodded. 'I hope you know what you're doing.'

'You can be damn sure of it,' she replied and stabbed the stud again.

She pushed herself out, leaving Ira alone in the chamber. He slammed the wall with his hand.

4.4: WILL

With St Andrews safely behind them, Will took refuge in the one task that afforded him any satisfaction in his new life: metaphor tagging.

A quick scan of the *Ariel*'s software map found him a node he hadn't worked on yet – a secondary resource-allocation system in the life-support domain. He followed the link and entered a room where the walls were still white and bare, the doorways empty rectangular holes.

The room's only defining feature was a huge portrait of a woman Will had never met at one end. She had a narrow, closed-mouthed smile and hair pulled back tightly in a bun. There was no furniture, just a few notebooks and brightly coloured polyhedra scattered across the floor. Will shook his head. Doug might have had a gleaming service record, but he wasn't a very imaginative man.

With a wild sweep of his arm, Will began his work. The notebooks and shapes jumped up into the air and landed in orderly rows. He stabbed a virtual finger at the wall.

'Casino!' he ordered.

The surface turned to red velvet and shaped itself like the bulkhead of an Old World cruise liner. Roulette wheels and craps tables extruded from the floor.

'And you can go,' he told the woman in the painting. He clicked his fingers and the painting vanished in a satisfying burst of flame. He strode about, pointing at the books and shapes, telling them what to become. 'Card deck! Chip pile! Croupier!'

Associating strong visual metaphors with software systems gave a roboteer rapid, intuitive navigation of a ship's systems. Will preferred to use vivid historical settings. They made for powerful moods, which cut jump times. He'd long since learned that the more like a real place a metaphor was, the more efficiently his mind could handle it. So he bothered with the little details like chairs and windows.

His own personal software was modelled on his childhood home in the trench town of Endurance. He knew it intimately. But the *Ariel* was a different matter. Many of the metaphor tags there were still based on Doug's experiences. It wasn't strictly necessary for Will to retag every single subsystem, but it was one of the tasks Ira had given him to do, and so he was doing it. And besides, ripping out all evidence of Doug from the ship had become a kind of therapy. Doug, who'd stared bravely into the jaws of death. Doug, who'd got along with Ira just fine.

'Hey!' Rachel's avatar appeared beside him as she opened a channel to talk. 'You busy?'

Was he ever anything but? Will managed to resist the urge to reply with a bitter quip.

'No more than usual,' he replied quietly.

'I want to apologise,' she said. 'It clearly wasn't your fault that alarm went off. It was mine. I should have checked the SAP stable before I started.'

Will shook his head. 'No, it was my fault. I pushed that cleaner too hard. That's why it stalled. I was mistreating my robots, and there's no excuse for that.'

'Not as badly as Ira's mistreating you,' she retorted. 'That's the other thing I want to say. I think you're doing great and that he's being a shit.'

Will raised his eyebrows. 'I hope you're subvocalising.'

She grinned and shook her head. 'No. I took my privacy hour early so I could talk with you.' Her face grew serious again. 'Ira's always a bit tough on new recruits, but this time he's taking it too far. He never treated any of us the way he's treating you. The rest of us can see what he's doing and it's starting to get embarrassing.'

Will was touched and surprised that Rachel had decided to take the time out to talk to him, but she was only confirming what he already knew: Ira had it in for him. In all Doug's memories of the captain, he'd treated his crew more like a family than a military team. Discipline on the *Ariel* was incredibly elastic, but the ship worked because Ira inspired an almost fanatical loyalty in his crew, despite their profound personal differences. The model *father-to-the-crew* couldn't have been further from the Ira Will had seen so far. Which led him to a single painful conclusion: there was nothing he could do that would make the captain happy.

'I don't think it's anything personal,' said Rachel. 'My guess is he's still messed up over Doug. But that's no excuse – he's supposed to be a professional.'

Perhaps it *was* about Doug, but Will had his doubts. Ira might have just taken a look at his career record and decided he didn't want Will on his ship.

'It's great, the way you're handling it,' she said. 'I wish I had that kind of restraint. If I were in your shoes I think I'd have popped him one back there when he made his little speech.'

Will found himself smiling. Punching Ira would probably have broken his hand. The man gave the impression of being made out of something a lot harder than flesh.

'When Amy followed him, I think that's what she had in mind, too,' Rachel added. 'My guess is they had a row, because they were both a bit red-faced, after.'

Will sat down on one of the casino chairs. 'I had no idea she did that,' he said quietly. He was surprised how much it meant to him.

He knew Amy through Doug, of course, but had barely talked to her, so he could hardly expect her to know him. For days now, Will had wanted to tell her that he liked the way she whistled in her bunk, even though Hugo appeared to find it annoying, and that her impersonation of Admiral Bryant was hilarious. However, there'd never been the time.

'Is she in trouble over it?'

Rachel laughed. 'Far from it. Ira may be the captain, but don't be fooled – Amy has a lot of clout on this ship. She's a force to be reckoned with. I don't think Ira would dare discipline her even if he wanted to. Those two are about as close as you can get to being married without actually sleeping together.' She shrugged quickly. 'Anyway, you're working, and I didn't mean to interrupt you. But if you ever want to talk more or need any kind of help, just let me know. And if necessary, I'll talk to Amy on your behalf. Who knows – one of these days I might even get the emergency VR rig out of storage. Then you could show me around that private world of yours.' A self-conscious smile played across her mouth. 'It must get lonely always being on your own.'

A warm, almost painful feeling spread through Will's chest. He'd never had a visitor in his metaphor spaces except other roboteers. No one had shown an interest before.

'Thanks,' he said. 'That would be great. I'd like that.'

She glanced away from the camera awkwardly. 'Well, see you in the cabin.'

'Yes.'

Her avatar winked out.

Will sat on the chair in the casino for some time after that, doing nothing and feeling better than he had in weeks.

5: SPYING

5.1: IRA

One week on from their second fuelling stop, the *Ariel* reached its insertion point – the place where its flight path crossed the time-compensated sensor boundary of their target star. From now on, the *Ariel* would have to be invisible.

Ira turned off the warp engines, silencing their rumble. Now they were floating weightless and undetected, just outside the realm of their enemies.

Through his visor, Ira could see Zuni-Dehel ahead of them, little more than a bright point of light. His enemies were still invisibly minute at this distance. No telescope ever built would have been able to see them. However, that didn't mean the *Ariel* was safe. Far from it. Simply flying this close would eventually give them away.

The problem for soft-combat ships like the *Ariel* was that ordinary warp bursts sent out flashes of hard radiation that could be seen for millions of kilometres. Entering an enemy star system undetected, therefore, required concealing the ship's approach by turning off normal warp engines long before it arrived at its destination. That way, by the time the tell-tale winking of the warp bursts reached your foe, you were already gone. Thus your choice of insertion point was determined by how long you intended to hang around. Ira was giving them three weeks.

'Rachel, prepare for stealth drive.'

'Sir.'

'Amy, I want a full-resolution scan of our destination.'

'Telescope drones are already away.'

Ira had felt a change in the mood of his crew over the last few days. Everyone was a little curt and impatient and there was less chatter between the bunks. The cabin air felt charged with some unexpressed emotion. Ira knew the mood well. It was the mood of people going into battle.

Only Hugo appeared to be unaffected. If anything, he was excited. Ira would have been troubled by that attitude in a member of his permanent crew, but in a passenger he chalked it up to a lack of front-line experience.

He'd watched Hugo over the last few weeks and felt he had the measure of the man. Hugo was pompous, abrasive and had the kind of arrogance of which only those bred for mental superiority were capable. People like Hugo invariably considered themselves supermen and leading them required a patient, delicate hand. But on balance, Ira had met a lot worse.

Far more importantly, with respect to the mission, Will had started to adapt. Though it rankled for Ira to admit it to himself, his old friend Amy had been right. The handler's performance had come on leaps and bounds since he started getting extra rest. He'd opened up to the crew, too. Ira just hoped they hadn't bought his cooperation at the price of his life.

On a whim, Ira leaned out from his bunk. 'Will,' he called.

The handler's head appeared in the gap between his muscle-tank and the lower bunk. 'Sir?'

How earnest he looked. How keen to please. 'You stay near that tank over the next few days, okay?' said Ira. 'I don't want you getting caught out if we need to do some fancy flying.'

Will nodded and smiled. 'Don't worry, sir. I promise.'

'Good,' said Ira gruffly, and ducked his head away before Will could catch the vulnerability he knew must be showing in his eyes. Ira still hadn't been able to bring himself to engage Will in conversation. Perhaps in a week or two.

'Scan complete,' said Amy. 'Drones retrieved.'

Ira buried himself in the output, looking over what little of their destination they could see. Two gas giants were clearly visible along with what looked like a broad asteroid belt just inside the orbit of the inner one. There were no solid planets in evidence, which made the belt the most likely site of enemy activity. So that was where they'd head.

'Will, how's our albedo looking?' he asked.

'Nice and low, sir. I have hull crawlers on it now. By the time they're done, we'll be black as space.'

'Good.'

Ira watched the last preparations through his visor. Then, when everything was ready, he gave the order. 'Strap down, everybody. We're going in.'

He waited for Will to be fully sealed into his muscle-tank before proceeding.

'Rachel, ready the torches.'

'Torches ready, sir.'

'Then here we go.'

Ira braced himself as the ship ramped its conventional acceleration to four gees. He couldn't resist glancing at the window in the bottom-left corner of his visor that showed Will's vital signs. They looked fine. Excellent, in fact. Ira smiled to himself. He'd done some good, at least.

For the next hour and a half, Ira did nothing but increase the *Ariel*'s conventional velocity. A careful pilot could drop out of warp with the same reference frame he went in with, and Ira wanted to arrive travelling fast with respect to the target star. He needed enough speed to slip past his enemies unnoticed, but not so much that it became hard to dump the surveillance drones as they passed. Eventually, the time came for the next step.

'Grease the rails,' he ordered.

He watched the engine-profile graphs jump as Rachel turned up the heat. Somewhere over his head, lead nuclei in the accelerators were being smashed together at a fantastic rate, and their exotic by-products pumped out to form the secondary field.

'Rails greased,' said Rachel.

Ira opened a window to view the ship's exterior. The brollies were now at full extent and humming with power. This time, though, the space around them glowed a dull, shimmering red. The *Ariel* was using its tau-chargers.

The tau-charger was one of Galatea's most impressive wartime innovations. While they made their way into the Zuni-Dehel system, energy released by warp would emerge as pseudo-stable particle pairs instead of g-rays. Their arrival should only be visible much later, as a slow, continuous stream of antimatter annihilation.

The bad news was that the chargers were a huge drain on the engines. The gravity profile they created was also flat and unstable. Ira used them sparingly.

'Ready for warp,' he told the crew and pressed the firing stud.

The first bump was softer than usual, almost syrupy. With uncharacteristic sluggishness, the engines climbed from a *whumping* sound to a gentle hum. As the space around them filled with flickering light, Ira swapped to a tactical model of the surrounding space. The small reddish sun hanging before them slid closer.

Gruelling hours passed during which there was nothing his people could do but man the sensor arrays and hope. Without doubt, the area would be primed with Oort drones. If one spotted them, chances were it would intercept at full warp. They wouldn't see it until it hit. And unfortunately, even in a small system like Zuni it took the better part of a day to make a stealth insertion.

As the tau-charged engines carried them ever closer, their emissions became more obvious. The field generators had to struggle to compensate for the grime of hot ions that filled in-system space.

They finally reached their closest safe distance.

'Preparing to drop warp,' said Ira. 'Dropping warp in six, five, four, three, two, one...'

He snapped off the gravity drive. Everyone exhaled as the *Ariel* became just one more small dark body in a whole star system of small dark bodies. Ira grinned to himself. They were in. That was always the second hardest part of every mission. The only thing trickier was leaving, and that was days away.

He turned back to the external sensors and received his first uninterrupted view of the system interior. They'd emerged just as intended, above the ecliptic, a little beyond the orbit of the Zuni's inner gas giant. The asteroid belt hung somewhere ahead of him.

'All right, Amy, let's have a look around.'

'Aye aye, Captain.'

A window in his visor showed him the output from Amy's telescope array. Little by little, a full-resolution target diagram emerged. Ira's skin crawled as dark patches resolved from fuzz to unmistakable definition. There were gasps from other bunks.

'Oh my God,' whispered Rachel.

Floating at the edge of the belt was an armada, a fat crescent of ships, small Jesus Class vessels like the six that had attacked Memburi. Only here there were nearly three hundred, more than twice as many as the entire Galatean Fleet.

In his most pessimistic estimates, Ira had thought he might find fifty. His people's hopes of raising an adequate defence suddenly looked thin indeed.

At the leading end of the crescent hung a small industrial complex consisting of a factory asteroid, two habitat rings, an antimatter plant and the filigree frameworks of at least four construction bays. Inside them, yet more starships were being assembled. It was a veritable hive of industry.

Ira's guts churned. The ships could only be intended for one target. They were looking at Galatea's death sentence.

'So many,' mumbled Amy.

For a while, the crew were quiet, absorbing the reality of what lay before them. Then, at last, Will spoke.

'They must be almost ready to attack.'

His voice was little more than a whisper, as if what they said aboard the *Ariel* might be heard outside as they slipped invisibly by.

'They're more than ready,' said John darkly. 'The question is: why haven't they attacked yet?'

Ira could feel the mood aboard his ship changing. People were growing afraid. He didn't want that.

'I have a better question,' he said, injecting as much vigour into his voice as he could muster. 'How did they manage to build all this without us noticing? I thought we broke crusade security.'

'We did,' said John. 'This fleet must be running out of a different subsect. A separate group with its own codes.'

'That still doesn't explain how they managed this,' Ira insisted. 'There must have been traffic to and from this place – arms shipments, crews, habitat parts. How come we didn't spot it?'

'I'm not so sure there would have been traffic,' said Rachel. 'Look at the size of that factory. It seems big next to the ships, but it's tiny compared to the Fleet yards back home. It would take ages to build a fleet that size with a factory that small. It must have been running at full tilt for several years. They've been planning this for a long time – almost since the start of the war. My guess is that any traffic's been slow and intermittent. Not so heavy that it'd register to our intelligence SAPs.'

'Then whoever runs this joint is a damn sight more cunning than most Earthers,' John remarked. 'And more patient, too. It's almost impressive.'

'If Rachel's right, it may be good news for us,' said Amy. 'Those ships might still be empty. I can't imagine that crews have been living aboard such small ships for months or years, just waiting. They'd have to be billeted somewhere else.'

She was right, Ira realised with relief. 'Good point,' he said. 'That might buy the home world a little time.'

Hugo spoke up. 'But if this fleet has been here for months, they must have had the new energy technology even longer.' He sounded appalled by the idea. 'Why didn't they use it sooner? It doesn't make any sense. I mean, with that kind of firepower, why haven't they slaughtered us already? They needn't have lost Memburi in the first place.'

Ira wasn't impressed by Hugo's choice of words. The man seemed personally insulted by the Earthers' strategy, as if they'd done it to spite him.

'Maybe they knew we'd come looking,' Ira suggested. 'They wanted to be sure of overwhelming force before they let us know it existed.'

'But where are the spin-off technologies?' Hugo demanded. 'Where are their trial runs? We spend the entire war convinced we're technologically in the lead. Then, at the last minute, they bring out a fully mature stand-alone technology that we can't even guess the theory for! Furthermore, we discover that they've probably had this edge for years and never bothered to use it. I don't buy it. It stinks.'

Ira could hear the others shifting in their bunks. Hugo had a good point, but it didn't help morale to dwell upon the thought that the

Earthers could have kicked their asses years ago and simply hadn't bothered.

'Then let's stop speculating and start investigating,' he told them. 'John, Will, I want you to get to work tapping their comms. Amy, find us an orbit that'll let us keep an eye on all this without being seen. Rachel and Hugo, I want both of you to take a closer look at the installation. Maybe some of those answers are right in front of us.'

There was a chorus of *ayes* as his crew set about their assigned tasks. Ira continued to stare hard at the crescent of ships looming in his visor. Part of him urgently wanted to turn around and get home as fast as he could. At least that way the evacuation arks parked in orbit around Galatea would have a chance of getting away before this armada turned up. But they'd come to listen, so listen they would. If this fleet hadn't left already, maybe that meant there was still some way to beat them.

5.2: WILL

Will sat in the virtual room he'd created for his soft-assault node and watched propaganda broadcasts from the Earther fleet.

'Rebuilding on the planet Drexler,' said the screen in front of him. An image appeared of joyful crowds dressed in rags leaping up and down in the streets of a rubble-strewn city. 'Liberated from the yoke of their former capitalist government, the people of Drexler are enjoying a free expression of faith for the first time in a century! All across this world, top subsects are lending a hand, bringing eager new members to the Following.'

The image swapped to a huge white building with a blue and gold dome set in a perfect lawn. 'Here, for instance, in the struggling tent-town of Kroto, the Medellins have contributed a brand-new church.' The screen showed a florid man in long blue and gold robes. The words at the bottom of the screen identified him as Igor Shanhuan, the new Medellin cardinal for Kroto.

'When the people here realised that their immortal place in heaven was determined by how soon they converted and to whom, it was amazing how quickly they came to their senses,' said Shanhuan. 'They're not bad people. They've just been kept away from the Lord's truth for a long time, and I can tell you, they're glad to finally hear it.'

A gaunt local in rags with wild eyes added his testimony. 'I cry when I think of how lucky we are,' he told the camera with tearful earnestness. 'When I look back at the life I used to lead, it disgusts me. I was lost. The whole planet was lost. My only regret was that we resisted the Kingdom for so long.'

The look in the Drexlerian's eyes gave Will the shivers. He'd seen broadcasts from Drexler from before the war. It had been a peaceful place with well-fed, rational people – one of the most successful of the Fifteen Colonies.

Will changed channel.

'The Kingdom makes astounding progress against the Sin-World Galatea!' said the screen. 'In a breathtaking victory this month, a special task force led by the Reconsiderist subsect saw off four Gallie battle cruisers and paved the way for the final push against the last major colony still violating human unity. However, sources in the crusade say there's still a lot of work to be done.'

A square-jawed man with bushy eyebrows, apparently named Captain Huen Gupta, faced the camera. 'We can expect a hard fight from Galatea,' said Gupta solemnly. 'What people don't understand is that the Gallies aren't like other colonists we've faced. They're genetic fascists, which means that for generations, they've subjected their own children to outrageous mutations in the hope of creating some kind of master race. By most measures, they're not even sane.

'They've come so far from God's truth that they'd rather kill us all than accept his justice. They've got so much hate in their hearts that I wouldn't be surprised if they kept fighting down to the last woman and child. Once the Kingdom takes up guardianship there, an extensive renormalisation process will be necessary.'

He looked supremely sorry about it.

'Scary, isn't it?' said John.

Will jumped. John's avatar had appeared next to him. John had acquired the disturbing habit of appearing unannounced in Will's metaphor space since they started working together a week ago. Will had been astonished the first time it happened and leapt halfway across the room in shock. He hadn't known that John could build avatars, let alone access his private realm. John had laughed for a long time.

In retrospect, the idea of data protection was a little silly when you were sharing a ship with one of Galatea's finest hackers. Now Will barely flinched, though John's creepy sense of humour still left him uneasy.

He nodded in agreement. It *was* scary. That ominous word *re-normalisation* still rang in his ears.

John created a chair for his avatar to sit down on, brushed some fictitious dust off it and took a seat. He manipulated the puppet version of himself with an almost roboteer-like deftness.

'You know, you really ought to get this place cleaned up,' he said with a grin. It was a subtle way of reminding Will that, unlike Rachel, he could see everything Will had made.

John's remark referred to the metaphor Will had chosen for the soft-assault node. He'd based it on an archaic wiretap-room he'd once seen in a flat-screen movie. Grey-brown sunlight slanted in through a window with slatted blinds drawn. To one side of him was a desk covered in bulky listening equipment complete with magnetic tape reels and oscilloscopes. On the other was the bank of cathode-ray screens Will was watching. The rest of the room was dusty and bare.

Will had spent most of the last week in there. During that time, he'd acquired a lot of respect for the *Ariel*'s assault expert, who was a completely different type of person from Franz. John was always open to ideas, though in truth Will had found little to contribute. Most of John's work was applied data theory, about which Will knew next to nothing. There wasn't much for him to do but follow instructions and pilot the odd decryption SAP John passed him. The SAPs were always inscrutable and filled with subtle cunning.

'What's a fascist?' asked Will.

John smiled wryly. 'It's an Old Earth term for an aggressive kind of nationalist. But the Earthers don't use the word properly. They mean someone who believes that one ethnic type is superior to another.'

'But we don't believe that,' said Will. 'Why do they call us that?'

Will had found watching the propaganda almost painful, so distorted was the news it put out. But once they'd positioned their spy satellites, there hadn't been much else for him to do. So he'd watched, and reported anything new he learned to John.

'It's an emotionally charged word with lots of historical connotations that they think fits because we practise genetic engineering,' John explained. 'As far as they're concerned, that makes us a separate ethnic type. And the fact that we keep doing it implies we think we're better than them.'

Will shook his head. It made him burn inside. How could he be hated so much by people he'd never met, over some aspect of himself that he never even chose?

'Why do they hate people with mods so much?' he said.

'Because they haven't got them,' said John with a smile.

'So what? What's to stop them from gene-tweaking their kids?'

'Lots of them can't afford to. Or they think it's wrong.'

That wasn't good enough for Will. 'But what right do they have to say what someone else should or shouldn't give their own children?'

John laughed. 'As far as they're concerned, someone else's choice limits their own kids' future. Someone with good mods is more likely to get a decent job than someone without.'

Will squirmed in his seat. Just like he could never hope to become a starship captain. 'But that's crazy,' he insisted. 'Mods exist. Everyone knows you can never put the technology genie back in its bottle. Sooner or later, everyone will have mods!'

'They disagree,' said John. 'Well, some of them disagree. And the rest of them just want to be sure that if someone's enjoying a biological advantage, it's them. Plus it helps to look self-righteous while you're murdering people. But I didn't come here to talk politics. There's a progress meeting happening upstairs in a few minutes and I thought you'd want to come along.'

Will nodded, not that he had much to contribute. 'Okay, I'll be there.' It had to be better than listening to Captain Huen Gupta.

Five minutes later, the crew convened in the *Ariel*'s upper chamber. Will surveyed the assembled faces as he pulled himself into the room. The stress of their work showed in their eyes – in Hugo's most of all. Gone was the talkative physicist so eager to expound on his pet subject. The constant risk of discovery, coupled with the academic frustrations of the last few days, was getting to him. He'd become sullen and withdrawn.

'All right,' said Ira. 'I've brought you together because we've been at this for six days now and I thought we should take stock.'

As always, the captain surveyed them with an easy if slightly detached confidence. His massive arms were folded across his chest.

'You've all been focused on your own tasks with only limited exposure to what the others have been doing, and pooling a little knowledge might help us all. I'll kick off because I don't have much to tell you. I've been monitoring our security situation. There's no sign that we've been noticed yet, so my guess is that we're safe here as long as we don't move around too much. Okay, that's it from me. John, want to go next?'

John smoothed the sleeve of his crumpled ship-suit as he spoke. 'Well, most of my time I've been working either with Hugo or Will. Our scans of the standard broadcast frequencies haven't turned up a whole hell of a lot, mostly the same old propaganda shit for the Following to lap up. The stuff with Hugo has been rather more technical, so I'll let him explain that to you.'

Hugo had been looking down at his hands and frowning while the others talked. Now he glanced up and surveyed the crew. He spoke slowly. 'As some of you already know, I've been trying to find out more about what the Earthers call the *suntap*.' He delivered the word with an ironic sneer. 'The name itself is evocative. The source of their apparently boundless energy is now clear at last. However, little else is.

'We have still found no information in their system that suggests how it functions. Had I but a few pointers, I don't doubt that I'd be able to replicate and surpass the Earthers' efforts with ease. However, there are no such pointers. I have even tried to interpolate a theory of the device's mechanism from the operating parameters of the starship components to which it is connected, though to no avail. Our examination of the engineers' working rules have revealed more than their technical files.'

Hugo shook his head in disgust. 'The only instructions the

engineers are given pertain to the unpacking and fitting of the device. They're forbidden from opening the unit. They are even banned from speculating on how it works while eating in their canteen.' His lip curled. 'In short, as far as the staff here are concerned, it is *magic*.'

John held up a finger. 'In my assessment, the reason we haven't found any data is that it's simply not here to find,' he said. 'The suntap doesn't come from Zuni.'

'Will,' said Ira, 'you've also been working with John. Anything to report?'

'No,' Will replied, wishing he had more to add. 'Other than a sick feeling from watching too much church TV.'

Rachel chuckled.

Ira glanced at her. 'How about you?'

She pushed floating hair away from her heart-shaped face. 'Well, while you've been listening, I've been watching. I've used the spy drones to carry out as close a survey of the whole facility as I can muster. The results have been interesting, if inconclusive.'

Will was surprised by how much he enjoyed listening to her again. He'd missed her, though it had only been a week since they'd last worked together. It was strange to feel that way about someone who hadn't been more than a few metres away from him the whole time, but with their shift differences and work patterns he'd hardly set eyes on her.

'The first thing I did was take a look at the g-ray banks on those new ships to see if there's anything different about them,' she said, 'and the answer is *no*. They're just a lot bigger. The technology appears to be the same as they've always used. Just as old. Just as clumsy. So then I took a look at their factory set-up – and that's where I found something. The antimatter plant, the factory asteroid and one of the habitat rings are all of Pioneer design.'

John smiled and nodded knowingly. 'I thought I recognised some of those power schematics.'

'That more than anything convinces me that the Earthers stole their new weapon technology rather than inventing it,' Rachel went on. 'I find it much easier to believe that the Pioneers found a way to tap a star's energy than that the Earthers did.'

Will couldn't help but agree.

'So that solves one of the mysteries about this place,' Rachel said. 'The Earthers built their fleet using equipment that was already here when they conquered it. That's why we haven't seen much traffic – they only had to bring in enough crew to man the place before they started churning out starships. Right now, though, I'm looking for ways we might stop that fleet before it leaves here. Haven't found one yet.' She gestured at Amy. 'Your turn?'

'I've been listening to ship gossip,' Amy said with glee. 'In other words, the executive channel tight-beam transmissions which John so kindly decrypted for me, and I've learned plenty. First, and most importantly, the majority of those ships don't have their suntaps yet. They might look finished, but they're not.' She glanced around at the others with triumph.

'Hah!' said Rachel. 'That's great!'

'Secondly,' said Amy, 'as we suspected, they don't have crews, either. We're definitely looking at a threat, but it's not nearly as immediate as it first appeared.'

Will exhaled and suddenly realized just how much tension he'd been carrying since they'd arrived. There was nothing like the possibility of impending extinction to put you permanently on edge.

'Thirdly, and I think most interestingly,' Amy added, 'is that the big boss who runs this place isn't here. He's someone called General Ulanu, and as far as they know he's on his way back here from Earth, where they gave him some kind of medal for the attack on Memburi.'

'Bastard,' muttered John.

'Undoubtedly,' said Amy. 'But the thing is, the guy he left in charge here is the one who did all the work, or thinks he did anyway. His name's Konrad Tang, and we caught some video footage of him talking to one of his aides.'

She tapped the tablet display. A picture of a furious man with a spherical head and a pair of outrageous eyebrows appeared.

'As you can see,' she said, 'Tang isn't happy.'

Will laughed. That was an understatement.

'Turns out that he not only planned the show at Memburi,' said Amy, 'but also oversaw the construction of this whole fleet. He's been away from his family here for two years building this stuff and he's mad keen to use it. But apparently he has to wait for Ulanu to give the word before he can go any further.'

'How come this Ulanu gets to call all the shots?' asked Rachel. 'What's his contribution?'

'Well, from the way they talk,' said Amy, 'it sounds to me like Ulanu is hardly ever here. He spends all his time at a place they call the "remote facility", which is where I suspect the suntaps are built. He's the man who makes it all possible, I guess.' She shrugged. 'As far as I can tell, he just ships the units in and gives the orders. But Tang is expecting some big changes when Ulanu gets back.'

'Any idea what kind of changes?' said Ira.

Amy shook her head. 'I think Tang's hoping it'll be news about the deliveries he needs. And an attack schedule.'

Ira frowned. 'And do they know when he's due to show?'

'He's late already,' said Amy. 'They expected him back days ago. I suspect that one of the reasons we got into the system so easily was because half their telescopes are pointed at Earth right now.'

Ira rubbed his chin. 'Hmmm. That puts us in an interesting situation.' He paused to examine the face on the tablet. 'Okay, Rachel, Amy, I need some estimates – worst case, from our perspective. Let's say this Ulanu turns up with two hundred full crews fresh from the Old World. He has to get them aboard, trained and ready to go. How long do we think that'd take?' He looked to Amy.

'If the crews are seasoned, a week,' she replied. 'If they're not, the better part of a month.'

'Let's work with a week,' said Ira. 'He also needs to fuel up those ships. Even if that little factory of theirs has full stores, it's not enough for the whole armada. How long till they're ready to go?'

Rachel tapped her chin. 'The quickest? About three weeks, I guess. Of course, he could always siphon off fuel from the troop ships he comes in with. That'd cut it to a fortnight.'

Ira nodded to himself. 'Okay. Finally, the good general has to install his suntaps. I think it's safe to assume he didn't take his top-secret tech with him to show off to the other sects on Earth, which means he has to go and get them and come back here. Any guesses?'

Amy grimaced. 'It's hard to say. If we assume this facility is at a neighbouring star, which seems likely, I think the closest one in the shell is at least three days away. A week if you're in one of those Earther buckets. So let's say a week there and a week back.'

'Then another two for installation,' Rachel added.

'So,' said Ira, 'assuming he does all this in parallel, the guy still needs a month to get ready, even if he's working flat out. Otherwise, it could be more than twice that. Then they have to cross their territory to our end of space.'

'Captain, where are you going with all this?' said Hugo. Will had noticed the scientist's doughy features slowly creasing with anxiety as the dialogue progressed.

'It's my guess that if we leave sooner than we planned, we could bring some battle cruisers back here before they get their act together,' Ira replied. 'One ship the size of the *Phoenix* could make mincemeat out of this lot if it caught them by surprise.'

'I could help with that,' said John. 'Give me a couple of days and I can halve their production speed and have them blaming each other for it.'

Hugo's cheeks reddened. 'Surely you're not thinking of leaving before this Ulanu turns up?'

Ira shook his head. 'Not if we can help it. We'll have a much better picture of what's going on once he gets back. But we can't wait for ever.' He surveyed the others. 'If we sit here for another week and he doesn't show, I think we can safely assume it's because he's bringing crews with him. We should head home and make our report.'

Hugo made puffing sounds. 'But Captain, Ulanu is the man who has the secret! If we don't wait for him, we might never get it.'

'I know that,' said Ira, 'but I think—'

Hugo cut him off. 'Don't you see?' he urged. 'Even if you return here in time and crushed the armada, we might not have another chance. And that would leave the Earthers with an intolerable technological edge. We simply can't take that risk.'

Ira sighed. 'I think we might have to.'

'Wrong!' Hugo exclaimed.

Will winced. That was no way to talk to the captain.

'What'd stop them from doing this all over again?' Hugo demanded. 'From causing another Memburi!'

The silence in the room that followed his outburst had a thick, charged quality. Will looked around at the others and spotted John and Rachel exchanging glances. Amy rested a very subtle hand on Ira's elbow.

Ira stared levelly at the scientist. 'We have to stack that up against the immediate risk to the home world,' he said slowly. 'I want that technology as much as you do, but I won't sacrifice my planet to get it. There'll be other chances.'

'But you'd be in breach of your mission orders!' said Hugo. 'I was told I'd have three weeks to study this thing, and I haven't even had one yet! What in Gal's name is the point of this mission if you don't give me the opportunity to do my work?'

Ira's face became stony. 'We're talking about something that hasn't happened yet, *Doctor* Vartian. And by the way, those are *my* orders. I'll interpret them as I see fit. Please remember that you are a guest aboard this ship. It is not your job to determine mission strategy.' He locked eyes with Hugo and didn't let his gaze waver.

Hugo went red in the face, turned and pushed himself quickly out of the meeting room.

Ira shook his head. 'One more week, everybody,' he growled. 'And John, why don't you start work on dropping their production.'

'Yes, sir.'

Ira rubbed his eyes with the heels of his hands. 'Okay, everybody, let's get back to work.'

Will couldn't help but smile a little as he slid into to his bunk. Despite the dire situation, it suddenly looked like they might be able to turn the nightmare of Zuni-Dehel around. Guiltily, though, Will realized there was more to his good mood than that. For the first time since coming aboard, he didn't feel like the outcast in the cabin. For a while, at least, Hugo had volunteered to fill that role. So far as Will was concerned, he was welcome to it.

5.3: IRA

Ira kept an eye on Hugo after the meeting. The man's attitude improved a little, but not enough. He stayed close to the boil and Ira didn't like the effect that had on the rest of the crew.

On reflection, he realised that focusing so much of his attention on Will during the flight out had probably been a mistake. He should have paid closer attention to the psych warning on Hugo's file instead, because the man was behaving exactly as it predicted. In short, he was confusing his own intellectual desires with the needs of the ship.

Ira suspected that Hugo's parents had probably been a little too generous with mods for curiosity. It happened a lot, particularly among Galatea's wealthier families. The more talent you forced into a human brain, the less likely that person was to wind up balanced. For all their sakes, he hoped the man's scientific thirst was slaked soon. Ira's alternative was to lay down some old-fashioned discipline – an option that seldom worked well with such a highly strung team. He hoped he wouldn't have to take that step.

Fortunately, he didn't have to wait long. Just two days later, Ulanu's ship arrived.

Every member of the *Ariel*'s crew listened in on the encrypted communications that followed. Through a comms window in his visor, Ira found himself looking at a lean man with skin like polished mahogany and eyes that gave new meaning to the word 'piercing'. He could have been a different species from the squat, sullen Tang in the window next to him.

'Admiral Tang,' said the brown-skinned ascetic.

'General Ulanu.' Tang nodded his respects with visible reluctance. Their mutual dislike was obvious.

'I have good news for you,' said Ulanu. Nothing in his face suggested he was pleased. 'We have received the order to attack at will.'

Tang's tightly held mouth curved up a little at one corner.

'I will be proceeding forthwith to the development facility and will bring you the remaining suntaps within a month,' said Ulanu.

'And the crews?' Tang asked hungrily.

'Already on their way from Earth.'

Tang's eyes twinkled. 'That's excellent. I'll start preparations immediately.'

'Don't rush it, Tang,' said Ulanu tersely. 'I'd rather we take our time and do it properly.'

Tang gave him a look of thinly concealed loathing. 'Of course.'

'One more thing,' said Ulanu. 'I'm sure you'll be excited to know that the Prophet has seen fit to attach one of his personal assistants to our operation. He will be accompanying me directly to the remote facility.'

Tang's private smile returned. 'Congratulations,' he said darkly. 'I'm delighted to learn that the Prophet has such interest in your work.'

'I'm sure,' Ulanu drawled. 'Good luck, Admiral. I shall see you again in a few weeks' time.' The general broke the link.

'He's running a diagnostic check on his engines,' said John. 'He'll be ready to leave in a few minutes.'

'Copy that,' said Ira.

He stared at the windows and thought hard. He hadn't expected Ulanu to leave so soon. John had barely started probing the new ship's security.

'Captain,' called Hugo from the lower bunks, 'we have to follow him!'

Ira shut his eyes. Just two days ago, Hugo had been exhorting him to stick to his orders. Now he was telling him to disobey them. Ira's mission plan said nothing about chasing ships away from the target star. He tried to ignore the scientist for a moment.

'John, any way you can stall that ship?' he said. 'Give it an engine failure or something?'

'Captain!' Hugo urged.

''Fraid not,' said John. 'Half a day and I'd have his ship running in circles, but he's using different codes from Tang's. It'll take me a while to break them. Tapping their shared traffic is the best I can do.'

Ira muttered curses.

'He's aligning for warp,' Amy warned.

'Match his heading to the stellar neighbourhood,' said Ira. 'I want to know where he's going.'

'Tried already,' she told him. 'Nothing there – he's hiding his destination.'

'Captain!' Now Hugo was actually shouting.

'Can it, Vartian,' Rachel growled.

Hugo didn't listen. 'He's going to get away!' he exclaimed.

Ira ground his teeth and tried to think. Ulanu was leaving without refuelling and forcing a course correction on himself – that meant his destination couldn't be far away. Ira had to weigh that against the risk of discovery if they moved without taking proper precautions.

The thing was, Ira wanted to go. This Ulanu character had sparked his curiosity, and if they were careful, they'd be able to use the general's warp bursts to hide their exit. That would be a tricky manoeuvre, though, and deadly dangerous if Ulanu decided to cut his engines for some reason.

Ira dearly hoped he wasn't sending himself on a wild goose chase. This little adventure could cost them valuable time.

'Captain! I really must insist—'

Ira interrupted his passenger in mid-outburst. 'All right, Hugo,' he said curtly. 'That's enough! Amy, I'm going to use his warp pulses to tail him out so I need a precision trace of his exhaust. Will, work with her. This tail has got to be *tight*.'

'I'm on it,' said Will.

'As for you, Hugo,' Ira growled, 'I don't want to hear another word out of you till I tell you otherwise. Do you understand?'

'Perfectly, Captain,' Hugo snapped. 'Only please hurry!'

Ira smouldered. Hugo's attitude would have to wait. He didn't have a second to waste.

'Rachel, give me rails.'

'Rails greasing.'

'Buckle up, everybody,' he said. 'We're heading out.'

The roar of the drive filled the tiny cabin.

As Ulanu's ship started to pulse out of the system, the *Ariel* was right behind it, slipping along like a shadow.

6: UPLOADING

6.1: WILL

Two days out from Zuni-Dehel, something strange happened. The first Will knew of it was from Amy. He was working with her on the tracking SAP they'd put together. She was scanning star maps while Will tweaked the SAP's parameters to cope with Ulanu's primitive but effective signature cloaking.

'It can't be,' she said suddenly.

Will looked up from his work. He was operating out of the *Ariel*'s astrogation subsystem, a virtual construct more abstract than most of Will's creations. It was like floating in open space, surrounded by slowly shifting stars.

He opened a window to Amy's bunk. 'What's the problem? Did we lose him?'

She looked straight up at the camera, her round face full of surprise. 'Far from it,' she said. 'Look at this.'

She passed a diagram into Will's metaphor that showed their flight path away from Zuni-Dehel. The predicted plane of the human galactic shell was shown as a thin pink sheet cutting across space. Their path curved gently outwards, away from the galactic core.

Will's brow furrowed. 'I don't understand. I thought it was impossible for a starship to come off the shell and still travel faster than light.'

'It is,' she said. 'And we're doing about a hundred lights, so we must still be on it.'

'But how?' said Will. The plot showed them practically flying straight out, with the center of the galaxy behind them.

Her eyes shone. 'I think we're on a Penfield Lobe.'

'A *what*?'

'It's the holy grail of interstellar travel – a kind of magic crossing place.'

Will didn't get it. 'A crossing to what?'

Amy laughed. 'Everywhere else.'

'I'm not sure I understand.'

'How much do you know about warp?' she asked.

'The basics. Enough to help Rachel fix the engines.'

'You're familiar with the First Law, I take it?'

'Sure,' said Will. 'A ship can only travel at superluminal velocities across a uniform curvon gradient.'

'That's right,' said Amy. 'We can only travel at a tangent to the galactic core because the curvon density behind a ship needs to be the same as that in front. Otherwise, you don't get a match between the space you're expanding and the space you're contracting. Your engine fouls. Thus we can go *around* the galaxy at speeds right up to the Shige-Mot barrier, but if we wanted to visit the core, it'd take us lifetimes. Then about seventy years ago, a man called Hiro Penfield-Weiss came up with a hypothetical special case of shell topology. The shell isn't smooth – we've always known that. It's bumpy!'

She waved her hands enthusiastically to show him and Will couldn't help but smile.

'*All* black holes radiate curvons,' she said. 'They can't radiate anything else, so their information debt to the universe is paid in spatial potential. The galactic core may be the biggest source of curvons in our neighbourhood, but there are plenty of others, and they all deform the shell. However, most black holes don't sit close enough to us to make a big difference. They just make it a pain in the ass to navigate from place to place. But if you position one just right, it makes a kind of pucker, a shape like a droplet that sticks out of the shell. And that's a Penfield Lobe!'

She grinned at him through the camera, her blonde pigtails bouncing. She was proud of her explanation, or her discovery, or both.

Will still didn't get it. 'But you said it was a kind of crossing place,' he reminded her. 'How does that work?'

'Good question!' said Amy enthusiastically. 'At a lobe, the curvon gradient is super-sharp because you're so close to an emitting source. It makes the shell wafer thin.' She held up two fingers close together to show him and peered between them. 'That makes it very easy to pass from one curvon density to another using conventional velocity – from one layer of the onion to another, if you like. So with a little bit of boost from your fusion torches in the right place, you can find yourself on a different shell altogether. You can access star systems that would take centuries to reach otherwise.'

Will's skin prickled as he started to understand. If Amy was right, this could be the doorway to whole new regions of the galaxy.

'No wonder the Earthers chose this place to build their fleet,' he said. Where better to conceal a laboratory than somewhere your enemies can't even see on their star maps?

'I have to tell the others,' said Amy.

With a little help from Will, she assembled a file of her evidence and threw it out into the *Ariel*'s public data space.

Rachel and John both reacted with enthusiasm and astonishment, just as Will had expected. Hugo and Ira's responses were somewhat different.

'How far does that put us from our nearest candidate star?' the captain wanted to know. 'This throws off all our estimates for Ulanu's range and timing. If he has an antimatter factory waiting for him somewhere out here, we could be screwed. We can't afford to chase him so far that we don't have the fuel to get back. Unless we intend to convince him to share his supply with us, that is.'

He had a point. Will had been so impressed by Amy's findings that he hadn't thought of that.

However, it was Hugo's response that surprised him the most. The scientist read Amy's file and then started giggling. From where Will lay on his bunk, he could see Hugo staring intently at the ceiling with his hands over his mouth, grinning to himself.

'Are you okay?' said Will.

Hugo turned abruptly to stare at him. 'Fine,' he said airily.

'It's pretty amazing isn't it?' Will remarked cautiously. 'This Penfield Lobe thing.'

'It's *too* amazing,' Hugo relied, with heavy emphasis. 'First the suntap and now this? That's two miracles in the same trip. Doesn't that strike you as a little unlikely?'

Now that Hugo mentioned it, it did. Will found himself vaguely unnerved.

'What are you getting at?' he said.

'We'll see,' Hugo replied coyly.

Will tried to draw him out, but Hugo refused to say another word on the matter. Will was left with the uncomfortable suspicion that there was another surprise waiting for them just around the corner.

As it was, he didn't have to wait long to find himself proved right – less than a day, in fact, when Amy identified their destination star.

'It can't be!' she blurted again. Only this time, she sounded far from pleased about it.

Will didn't wait for her to explain herself, just pulled up a view of her workspace. In front of him was a spread of windows. The largest showed a low-mass M-dwarf star with its spectrum laid out beneath it.

'Another miracle?' he asked.

'I... I don't know,' said Amy. She sounded troubled 'Take a look at that spectrum. See anything strange about it?'

Will wasn't used to analysing data from stars but he'd been bred to see patterns, and now that he looked something did jump out at him. Something impossible.

There were seven very strong absorption lines in the display. The distance between the second and third was twice the distance between the first and second. The distance between the third and fourth was three times that between the first and second. The gaps mapped out the first six prime numbers, in order.

'Primes,' he muttered.

'Is that what they are?' said Amy. She sounded afraid. 'All I saw was that the spacing looked far too regular to be natural. And that they didn't correspond to any metals I've ever heard of.'

'John?' she called across the cabin.

'Yep?'

'Have you been messing with my spectroscopy code?'

'No,' said John. 'Would you like me to?'

'Just check it over, would you, see if there are any bugs in my SAPs.'

'A problem?' asked Ira.

'I... yes.' Amy confessed. 'Take a look at this.' She dumped the problematic scan into the public space again for the rest of the crew to pore over.

Hugo took one look at it and burst into laughter. 'I knew it!'

'Knew what?' said Ira.

Hugo cackled for a while before condescending to answer. 'Don't you see it? I *knew* those Earthers were too stupid to come up with this technology on their own. They stole it!'

'We already know that,' said Rachel. 'From the Pioneers.'

'Not from the Pioneers,' said Hugo scornfully. 'From aliens!'

There was a cold silence in the cabin.

'Now you're not making sense, Hugo,' Ira said at last.

'Aren't I?' the scientist replied. 'Can you really not see it? Take another look at that spectrum. It's clearly artificial. Someone manufactured that star ahead of us, or changed it somehow. I wondered how the suntap could have appeared as a fully mature technology without spin-offs or consequences. Well, here's our spin-off, ladies and gentlemen. And here's the reason why the Earthers kept such tight security. They found aliens!'

6.2: IRA

The following day, The *Ariel* slid into the M-dwarf's gravity well behind General Ulanu's ship. Ulanu's destination was a close orbit around the only planet. Ira parked as close to it as he dared. Even with a vessel as hard to spot as the *Ariel*, he had to be careful. John and Amy started scanning immediately.

'I see six ships,' said Amy. 'Ulanu's, two large tethered vessels – one Earther, one Pioneer – and three Earther gunships of armada design. My guess is that they've got working suntaps.'

'Whoa, security's tight,' John remarked. 'About a thousand times better than it was at Zuni-Dehel. There's a micro-sentinel drone cloud around those ships. Our friend Ulanu doesn't want anyone coming close.'

The excitement was clear in their voices. Since Hugo's bold assertion, the mood in the ship had been fevered. Ira wasn't surprised. The discoveries they were making beggared belief.

Nevertheless, Ira found their predicament troubling. His hands hadn't stopped shaking since he'd realised the obnoxious physicist was probably right. He didn't know whether to be excited or terrified. Though he hated to be the anchor on the crew's mood, he felt he was the only person aboard holding on to objectivity about the mission. They still had a war to win. And no matter how remarkable the things they found were, they still had to get home.

He surveyed the system diagram. The Earthers' small fleet formed a tight cluster like a fist positioned just above the small grey world's equator. Ira wondered what they'd found down there.

'Will?' he said.

'Yes, sir.'

'You've spent some time in terraforming. Know much about planets?'

'More than I want to, sir,' Will replied.

'Then take a look at this one and tell me what you see.'

Will called up the displays. 'It's smooth!' the roboteer said suddenly. 'It looks like rock, but that surface isn't natural.'

'Of course it's not natural!' Hugo jeered.

The sullen scientist had vanished and the pompous enthusiast was back. Ira wasn't sure which side of Hugo he liked the least.

'At least we know the Earthers didn't find this place themselves,' said Rachel. 'That Pioneer ship clinches it. But what I don't understand is why they didn't tell us about all this before the war started.'

'Profit!' said John cheerfully. 'The one thing the Pioneers liked better than anything else. Bet you whatever you like they were going to poach technology and pass it off as their own.'

'John, any broadcast traffic?' asked Ira.

'Not a peep. Ulanu is keeping his comms on tight-beam and routing it through his sentinel cloud. This guy runs a completely different kind of show from Tang. It's going to be hard to crack.'

'Then you'd better get started on it, because I want them gutted,' Ira told him. 'Will, give him a hand.'

'Already on it,' said John.

Ira lay back in his couch and frowned at the display. Up until this point, he'd believed they were up against Earther technology. It had looked like they stood half a chance of out-thinking their enemies and developing a defence. Now all bets were off. How did you out-think an alien species that might be thousands of times older than your own?

If they still couldn't find a way to access the suntap schematic, Ira doubted they'd ever find a defence against it. It felt uncomfortably as if his chances of pulling off the mission were withering by the hour.

6.3: GUSTAV

Gustav's scientific team were waiting for him as he stepped out of the docking lift into the habitat ring of the observation ship. Something inside him relaxed as his eyes took in the sight of those scuffed plastic corridors again. More than any place in the galaxy these days, this ship felt like home.

'Welcome back, General, sir,' said Emil Dulan, his chief of research.

Emil's horsy face was sombre, his bearing formal. Good. That meant he'd received the advance broadcast Gustav had sent him from the edge of the system, warning of the disciple's presence.

'Thank you, Emil,' he said, hiding the sense of relief he felt on seeing his friend again. The disciple was right behind him.

'Team,' said Gustav, 'I'd like to introduce you to my new special assistant, granted to me by the Prophet himself: Disciple Jesus Rodriguez.'

He had to work to keep the distaste out of his voice. The flight hadn't improved after he and Rodriguez had their little chat. The disciple's presence aboard his ship rankled like a bad tooth. Gustav had made a couple of spectacularly unsuccessful attempts to build a bridge between them, but only managed to worsen their rapport rather than strengthen it.

Rodriguez nodded to the assembled scientists.

'Father,' said Gustav, 'I'd like you to meet my team: Emil Dulan, Kali Deseringer, Juliet Zhu, Pablo Kim, Margaret Banutu.'

The scientists nodded in turn. Rodriguez received looks of thinly veiled contempt from all of them – particularly the women, whose positions on the project were the most at threat from High Church involvement. The Prophet was famously misogynistic.

'Also, please meet Regis Chu,' Gustav added. 'Regis functioned as my assistant until your addition to the team.'

'Thank you, General,' said Rodriguez smoothly. 'It's a pleasure to meet you all. Please consider my presence here a measure of the Prophet's appreciation of your good work.' His voice oozed pious insincerity. 'If you don't mind, I'd like to take the opportunity to talk to you all one-on-one over the next few days, to find out what you do. I'm well aware that I have a lot to learn.'

Gustav watched his team's collective suspicion screw tighter. 'I've decided to relinquish Regis's time to you for the next few days, Father, to help bring you up to speed,' he said.

Rodriguez shot him a suspicious glance. "That was very generous of you, General." He turned his hard black eyes on Regis.

Regis smiled back blandly. Gustav was pleased. Apparently, Emil had briefed Regis well.

Gustav rubbed his hands together. 'Now, where should we start? I imagine you're keen to take a look around, Father? Perhaps you'd like to view the Relic with your own eyes.' He gestured invitingly down the corridor that led to the observation centre, as if he intended to walk that way himself.

Rodriguez nodded slowly, clearly surprised to find Gustav so cooperative all of a sudden. 'That would be my first objective, yes,' he said warily.

'Wonderful. Regis, please take good care of the disciple. I will be briefing my science staff in the ready room.'

Rodriguez's face hardened as he realised he'd been outmanoeuvred. Before the disciple could complain or change his mind, Gustav strode off in the opposite direction with his team following close behind. He felt a certain glee as he walked away. *Free*, for the first time in weeks, from the disciple's repellent smugness and psychotic schemes. The sense of relief was like a window thrown open in a stuffy room.

Though the ruse amused him, it was also a necessity. He needed to get his people away from Rodriguez as fast as possible, so he could explain the situation before one of them put their foot in it. After all, they had just weeks to persuade the Prophet's representative to see things from their perspective before the project was dropped. After that, Rodriguez would be free to try out his ideas for destroying the Relic.

Emil had a guard waiting at the door of the meeting room, just as Gustav had requested.

'Welcome back, sir,' the guard said with a grin.

'Good to see you, Assim,' said Gustav. 'I don't want to be disturbed, not by anyone or anything – particularly not by Disciple Rodriguez. If he tries to enter, call for Chu.'

'Yes, sir!'

Gustav ushered his staff into the meeting room and closed the door behind them.

'Sit down and listen,' he told them all. 'Save your questions for the end. I have a lot to tell you.'

6.4: WILL

Together, John and Will scrutinised Ulanu's security arrangements. It was becoming increasingly clear that to get at Ulanu's data they had no choice but to deal with the sentinel swarm that hung around the ships like a cloud of animate menace. Will manoeuvred their drone fleet and handled John's incomprehensible hacking templates. Meanwhile, John became progressively more agitated.

'Damn!' he exclaimed at last.

'What's the problem?' asked Will.

'That cloud is the problem. I just realised why I couldn't hack its swarming protocol –because it doesn't have one. The fucking thing is semi-random. It's some kind of chaotic, distributed set-up.' John pulled a sour face. He was not a man used to being thwarted. 'Not only are all the comms routed through it, but it scans the surrounding space for intruders, too,' he complained. 'Send a drone in there and you trigger an alarm. Try to intercept a sentinel and the same thing happens. Because they don't have any visitors, there's nothing to stop them from winding their security as tight as they like.'

'Can't you just send a tight-beam message through it to one of those ships' data ports and bypass the whole problem?' said Will.

'Not without knowing their encryption first. To find out what they're using, I have to intercept packets. And I can't get at the packets unless I know where the sentinels are going to be.'

Will stared into the ever-shifting swarm. 'If the sentinels' movements are random, how do they find each other?'

'It must be hard-wired,' said John bitterly. 'As far as I can tell, they read the positions of their neighbours and the ships they guard and then compute expected vectors. They probably just use some tweak of a standard chaotic function. The problem is, without knowing the exact formula, we don't stand a chance of replicating it.'

'Can I have a look at your workings?' said Will.

'Be my guest,' John replied distantly. His tone implied what he'd never say out loud: that he doubted Will would see something he couldn't. After all, Will was just a roboteer.

Will opened a window onto John's digital interpretation of the swarm. John had overlaid colour-coded velocity and acceleration vectors onto each sentinel, and they moved in slowly undulating unison like bright fish under water. Will stared at the image intently, determined to help. He'd not really had a chance to prove his worth since he stepped aboard the *Ariel*. Perhaps this was his opportunity. After all, this was just a pattern-analysis problem at the end of the day, and that's what he was good at.

Several minutes of staring and pondering yielded nothing, though. Will decided he wasn't close enough to the swarm. He needed to be in it. He dumped John's feed into a virtual room and stripped off the vectors to look at the raw motion. The swarm became a cloud of fireflies, the ships at their heart a cluster of burning embers. He walked around it, and through it, letting the ebb and flow sink into his mind.

'Will?' said John.

'Hang on, I'm thinking.'

The swarm had flavours of tides and flocking birds, but there was something else in the mix. He peered at the sentinels and watched them suddenly backtrack at speed in a surprising cascade.

He laughed, a crazy idea forming in his head. He pulled up a scalar velocity history of the sentinel that had caused the domino effect, and sure enough, there it was – a pink-noise curve, just as he'd suspected. Will would have seen the same graph if he'd plotted the behaviour of a piece of jazz. Whoever wrote this swarm code had taken their algorithm from a music package and beefed up the motion with extra dimensions. The solution looked strangely cheap and obvious now that he'd spotted it, but he had no doubt it was the right one. It fitted perfectly with the Earthers' *make do and mend* approach to coding.

Unfortunately, there was still no way for him to know the exact formula they were using. But that shouldn't stop him from improvising along with it for a little while. The idea amused him.

'What if we could make one of our drones move like a sentinel long enough for us to break the encryption?' he asked John excitedly. 'If it could fool its neighbours and intercept signals on their behalf – would that help?'

'Sure,' said John with a laugh. 'That'd solve all our problems. Assuming we could emulate their flight pattern down to the nearest metre for whole minutes without fucking up.'

'Okay,' said Will. 'I'll need a couple of hours.'

John glanced incredulously into his cabin camera. 'You think you can do it?'

'No harm in trying, is there?'

John raised an eyebrow. 'Not until we get our asses kicked, no.'

It took Will longer than he'd guessed. First, he had to trawl the *Ariel*'s entertainment archives for a decent jazz improvisation SAP. He beefed the code into shape, adding extra dimensions much as the Earther programmers must have done. Then he grabbed a handful of suitably complex songs from the music archive to act as base parameters. Finally, he needed a little magic: anticipation. He took that from a schoolyard tag program he'd written. Then he started knitting it all together so that instead of thinking like an ordinary machine, it guessed and played like a living thing.

This was Will's speciality. Common wisdom said that an SAP could only get so smart and still provide reliable behaviour. Galatean research had never been able to push artificial intelligence beyond the hypothetical Brache limit without creating minds that were dangerously erratic. Widen the aperture of consciousness and there was a corresponding drop in the frequency of rule creation. Narrow it and there was a limit to rule complexity and a tendency to obsess. Hence the need for a human handler – a guiding intelligence beyond the Brache limit that could handle ideas that were *strongly fuzzy*.

Will's fascination was with pushing that limit. After all, nature had done it with the human mind. Admittedly it had taken millions of years of evolution to achieve, but nevertheless, the presence of natural intelligence meant it was possible somehow. Will hadn't been able to break the limit yet, but he'd come close and this SAP was one of his finest.

John watched it with him as they dry ran the program. It matched the swarm's motion almost exactly.

John shook his head in disbelief. 'In Gal's name!' he said with a laugh. 'I wouldn't have believed it if I hadn't seen it.'

The others opened windows through their visors to see what Will had accomplished.

'Way to go, Will!' said Rachel with a grin.

Will swelled with pride.

'This is excellent work,' Hugo told him, sounding surprised. 'Really excellent.'

It was the first time the *Ariel*'s resident physicist had complemented Will on anything.

Ira rubbed his chin and nodded appreciatively. 'Clever,' he said. 'But you realise you're going to have to ride that drone in there the whole way, just in case. One mistake and those three gunships will fry us on the spot.'

'I know,' said Will.

John grinned broadly, his perfectly even white teeth flashing like a shark's smile. 'Let's go, then,' he said.

John selected the drone from their fleet with a physical profile most like that of a sentinel and slid it close to the swarm. Meanwhile, Will loaded the SAP into its hardware and jumped in after it.

The view from the drone was extraordinary. The sentinels ahead of him no longer looked like dull grey dots or even fireflies. Instead they were golden motes with silver tails of position-history snaking away in one direction and translucent cones of possible flight paths spreading in the other.

In a rush, Will saw the truth of what the sentinels were doing. They were dancing. With glee, he sidled up and joined their three-dimensional tango. The sentinels swerved around him, accepting him into the swing of motion as if he were one of their own. Will shared the spy-drone's delight.

'It's working!' John exclaimed. 'It's fucking working!'

Then, just as Will started to lose himself in the pattern, the sentinels started talking to him. Little snatches of data mentioned in passing like gossip on a ballroom floor. He dutifully delivered them to their intended destinations while John copied them back to the *Ariel*.

'This is great!' he exclaimed. 'Keep it up, Will. We're getting packets.'

Will danced between the stars. In the back of his mind, he could feel John's incursion into the Earthers' network and the chunks of data flowing the other way – architecture schematics, blueprints, passwords. In a few minutes, they'd have cracked the security altogether. The secrets of the strange, smooth world below would be theirs for the taking.

Excited chatter broke out in the cabin, back in the real world. Will could just about hear Hugo's urgent tones, but with his senses tuned to the dance, it was impossible to make out the words.

In fact, the next human word he heard properly was John's almost explosive yell.

'*Shit!*'

It came straight down the comms-line into Will's sensorium. Will flinched and narrowly avoided missing a cue to dart sideways as the swarm's flight-path cones flicked around in a spectacular wave.

'What is it?' he asked, as soon as the emergency was over.

'This fucking Ulanu,' John snarled. 'There's no soft copy of the swarm algorithm. He had the sentinels shipped in sealed with their behaviour blueprint intentionally missing so they couldn't be hacked. Now we know where Earth has been hiding all its decent scientists.'

No blueprint. Will's high spirits dropped. 'So what do I do?'

'Keep at it, if you can. We're going to try to piggyback the comms straight through you.'

Through *him*? 'For how long?' Will asked nervously.

'Till we've got what we need,' said John. 'Don't worry, I'll try to make it fast. Get ready for a full-scale data-trawl.'

Will braced himself. Suddenly the dance didn't feel quite so cheerful. He began to see the swaying golden spheres for what they really were: deadly moving triggers. This was a very dangerous kind of ball to dance at, he realised. Tread on just one foot and your dance partners were likely to kill you.

In the next second he experienced a dreadful shuddering sensation, like standing on a bridge over a mighty waterfall. A blur of words and images coursed through his head as the little drone he was piloting became the conduit for John's download. They were sucking information out of the Earther database as fast as the *Ariel* could read it.

Somewhere in the distance, Hugo shouted again. Ira said something stern and decisive.

'We've found a map of their soft core,' John explained, 'and we think we've located the access feed for the alien device. Hugo's going to try for a quick contact.'

'Can't we wait?' Will urged. 'I don't know how much longer I can keep this up with the trawl going on.'

'We may not get another chance,' said John. 'If there are hook mines anywhere in their data store, just reading them will raise the alarm. We have to be ready for a quick exit. Rachel's already gearing to go.'

Hugo's voice came over the line. 'Don't worry, Will,' he said. 'I'll be as fast as I can. This is simply an opportunity we can't afford to pass up.'

'Then get on with it!' Will snapped.

He swayed left and darted right. Some of the sentinels nosed closer to him, as if sniffing him over. He wondered if their tiny electronic minds had begun to suspect.

Then Hugo's new channel opened up inside him, like a door in his brain. Hugo fired through a simple electronic query – the database equivalent of *hello*.

There was a long pause.

Hello, came the reply.

Will shivered to himself. This was it. They were talking to aliens...

Hugo laughed uproariously. 'First contact!' he shouted. 'I've made first contact!'

More like third contact, Will thought. Both the Earthers and the Pioneers had got there first.

Hugo's next question was more complex and took the form of an invitation to self-identify. As soon as Hugo sent it, new data started passing back through the door. It was cleverly tagged to build itself into a complex data structure on arrival.

It assembled in Will's head in crystalline chunks. However, as it did so, Will realised it wasn't the reply Hugo had asked for. It was a set of instructions for building a machine. It was the suntap! Will was astonished. That had been easy. The alien hadn't needed much coaxing to hand over the secret of infinite power.

'I've got it! I've got it!' Hugo sang. 'I never expected it so soon! Hold on, I have another question.'

Will chanced a momentary flick to Hugo's soft-space to see what the man was planning. Hugo was using the alien's own self-assembly pattern like a skewer and stuffing a huge chunk of data onto it. As far as Will could tell, it was a potted history of the whole war and Galatea's role in it. Will realised then that Hugo had spent the last few days planning exactly this exchange. He'd anticipated this moment – or hoped for it, at least.

Will jumped back into the drone just in time to dive with the swarm. Even with his SAP in place, he couldn't risk letting go of the little robot for more than a vanishingly brief moment.

Hugo hurled his question through the data channel. Will felt it flash through him, into the dark, empty aperture that was the link to the alien. He waited on tenterhooks for the reply.

When it came, it was not what he expected. He'd imagined

Hugo might get a potted history of the alien object in return, or at worst another copy of the suntap. Instead, they received more self-assembling data-structures – dozens of them with nothing more than simple diagnostic routines inside. It was as if they were being scanned, or tested for something. Each structure unfolded, then sent a single response packet back into the alien maw.

With alarm, Will realised that the drone's own hardware had started to spontaneously unfold some of the alien messages. That could knock him out of the swarm. He reached out with his mind to shunt the structures up the comms-link to the *Ariel*'s own computers and felt a perceptual jolt.

It was like a flash of shared memory from another handler, but nothing he could comprehend. For an eye-blink, he saw things like giant icebergs in darkness, with surfaces that crawled and rotted. It was something that shouldn't have happened. Something he should not have seen.

Instinctively, Will drew back into the security of his home node. He reached for the fat-contact on his neck to disconnect but his arms were held tight. His physical body had been in the muscle-tank since they reached the alien system, on Ira's insistence.

The alien patterns Will had accidentally dragged with him started popping open in the stone-walled room of his private node. Inside Will's own head. He felt his senses tweak and flutter. Flashes of something vast and tortuously complicated revealed themselves.

'I'm not getting any data!' Hugo wailed. 'It's all going straight into Will's metaphor space!'

'Will!' John called urgently. 'What're you doing? What's going on?'

Will desperately reached out a virtual arm to shut down his link to the drone. Immediately, that part of his interface was snatched away from him, like a toy plucked from the hand of an unruly child. He tried to cry out a warning, but his voice died, too. Like a portcullis slamming down, all contact with his physical body was shut off. At the same time, the alien code kept forcing its way into his consciousness. It rifled his memories like a burglar. It probed every part of him. Will screamed to himself in perfect silence as the components of his identity shut down one by one.

7: INFILTRATION

7.1: IRA

Ira watched as alerts lit up right across his visor.

'What's happening, people?' he demanded.

'Will took my data stream!' Hugo shouted back. 'He diverted everything into his space and now he's gone offline. I can't contact him. How dare he – he's not qualified to conduct a dialogue of this importance!'

'I'm getting weird reports ship-wide,' said Rachel. 'None of my diagnostics appears to be working.'

'Something's happening,' said John in a strangled voice. 'I think the alien feed is hacking *us*.' He sounded astonished, as if he'd never expected to be vulnerable that way. 'I think they're hacking Will,' he added nervously. 'It's routing everything straight into him.'

'Shut the link down, John!' Rachel yelled. 'Shut it down *now*.'

'Do it!' said Ira.

'No!' wailed Hugo. 'Divert the feed to my console – I can solve this.'

Ira watched through his displays as John tried to sever the link to the spy-drone. The link cycled security modes nearly as fast as John could block them, but not quite fast enough.

'Got it!' said John triumphantly.

The link died. They were free. The data-corruption warnings in Ira's visor began to subside. He exhaled in relief.

John roared his triumph. 'Try to out-hack me would you? No chance, you alien sonofabitch!'

'John, can you reach Will?' asked Rachel.

But before John could answer, the warnings started to ramp again, even faster than before.

'I don't believe it!' John gasped. 'Where are they coming from?'

'We're receiving messages direct to our sensors,' said Amy. 'The telescopes are flooded with maser pulses.'

'Then stop it!' Ira barked.

'I can't,' said Amy. 'I'm locked out. It's coming in on top-level Fleet encryption.'

'H-how is that possible?' John stammered.

Ira had never heard him sound so worried. He cycled through the ship's external sensors. Almost all of them were blinded by the bombardment of data, but finally he found one that showed him what was happening. The *Ariel* had become the focus of a thousand flickering red beams. Almost every single sentinel in the swarm was firing messages directly at the *Ariel*. All the comms channels were jammed.

'What is this?' Ira demanded, shunting the image to John. 'Some kind of Earther defence?'

'It can't be,' said John, his tone nervous as his fingers flew across his keyboard. 'It's too sophisticated.'

The alternative was worse. Somehow, the alien had commandeered Ulanu's entire defence network to beam messages straight at them. To beam messages straight at *Will*.

'I can't lock it out,' John wailed. 'If it keeps pushing data at us this fast, the central processors are going to burn out!'

'Arming the manual reset,' said Ira.

He reached up to the top of his bunk and ripped open the panel that revealed the ship's primary comms-fuse. He'd never had to use it before. It was intended as a last-ditch defence against a viral soft assault. Which, he reasoned, was pretty much what they were facing now.

He flicked open the fuse handle. Alert icons popped up all over his visor.

'Captain, we'll lose power,' Rachel warned. 'Pull that and the whole ship will have to recalibrate.'

But Ira knew exactly what he was doing.

'Three, two, one...' he called, and yanked the fuse.

The lights went out. His visor died. Beyond the cabin walls, a thousand humming machines slowed to silence. They were lost in the total darkness of a cabin sunk below half a kilometre of solid machinery. For a moment, Ira felt the profound weight of his ship bearing down upon him.

Then red emergency lighting flared into life, drowning the cabin in bloody illumination. The air filled with the mournful clang of plasma-containment alarms. Fortunately, their sound was short-lived. One by one, the ship's systems leapt back from the brink.

As soon as Ira's visor flickered into life, he started checking the ship's systems.

'How are we doing, people?' he boomed. 'I want all our comms battened down. I want our external sensors offline till we work out what the hell happened. I want a full diagnostic on every system we have. And Amy, check on Will.'

But Amy was already there. She'd scrambled out of her bunk and propelled herself headfirst to the bottom of the cabin in darkness to check the life-sign readouts on Will's tank. Ira jumped down after her.

'How is he?' Rachel demanded.

'He's alive,' said Amy, 'but not conscious.'

Rachel groaned.

Amy's hands darted across the tank's emergency console. 'Ira, I don't like his vital signs – they're all over the place.' She looked up at him with that same sincere, motherly expression she'd had the day Doug died.

Ira roared in frustration and slammed his fist repeatedly against the cabin wall. Then he spun and jabbed a finger at Hugo. 'You and your fucking *alien*!'

Hugo recoiled.

Except it wasn't Hugo's fault, Ira knew. It was his. He'd made all the choices that brought them to this place: a crippled ship in enemy territory. *And one man down.*

'Captain, I—' Hugo started.

'Shut up!' Ira roared.

Hugo fell silent.

Ira rounded on John. 'What do you think is the likelihood the Earthers didn't notice that?'

John forced his lips into a miserable approximation of a wry smile. 'Slim,' he said, his capacity for wisecracks apparently exhausted.

'That's what I thought,' said Ira. 'Rachel, we need those engines up and running as fast as you can, just in case we still have a chance of getting out of here.'

'That could take hours,' she replied anxiously.

'Make it less!' he snapped. 'And Amy, I want sensors back online. But keep it to the minimum, and find some way of hot-coding them so we can turn them off if something like that happens again.'

Amy nodded.

'And keep Will stable,' he added. 'I *refuse* to have him die on this ship.' He turned away as her face melted into an expression of pained concern and glared at John again instead. 'I want our computers clean and stable,' he ordered. 'Get rid of whatever that alien bastard shot at us. Purge them all if you have to.'

'I don't know if I can,' John replied quietly. 'That thing went through every node in the ship. And if it buried itself in SAP code, it could be completely distributed by now. It'd look no different from ordinary memory trees. It might be years before we find it. And if Rachel needs robots, there's no way I can afford a full memory-wipe.'

'I'll need robots all right,' she put in.

'Great!' growled Ira and slammed the wall again, crumpling the padding right back to its metal frame. His ship was infected with alien software and there was nothing he could do about it. 'Just *great*.'

He rubbed his face with his hands. Floating like this, they were sitting ducks. The fact that they weren't already dead meant the Earthers hadn't found them yet. But as soon as their enemies regained control of their computers, they were bound to start looking. The *Ariel*'s time was fast running out.

'You!' Ira thrust his finger at Hugo again. 'Help John clean up.' He glanced around his small domain. 'I'll be in my bunk working with Rachel,' he said. He grabbed the handrail and yanked himself up to his couch.

7.2: GUSTAV

Gustav faced a room full of astonishment and black looks.

'You mean, if we don't agree to shut the project down, the Prophet might *kill* us?' said Margaret Banutu, her brow creased in appalled disbelief.

Having spent the last few months in the company of politicians, Gustav had forgotten that scientists could be equally annoying in their own way. How had these people lived so long and remained so naïve?

'There is an alternative,' he explained for the third time. 'Win Rodriguez round. That's all we have to do. He reports directly to Sanchez. A good word from him and the project could continue indefinitely.'

'That's *all*?' said Pablo Kim incredulously. 'How are we supposed to do that? He's High Church. A fanatic!'

Juliet Zhu held up her hands in dismay. 'I don't understand,' she said. 'Why is the Prophet so afraid of all this? Doesn't he see the good it could do?'

Gustav was readying himself to reply when Assim burst into the room.

'General, sir!'

Gustav rounded on him furiously. 'I told you I didn't want to be disturbed!'

Assim flushed. 'Yes, sir, but I thought you'd make an exception for this.'

'For what?' Gustav snapped.

'Someone's broken into the Relic feed, sir. And the whole defence network is down.'

Gustav felt the blood drain from his face. He slapped the compad on his belt – the compad he'd turned off to avoid calls from the disciple. It came alive now with wailing alarms. Gustav strode past Assim, then ran the rest of the way to the command centre. When he arrived, he found his men frantically at work on their consoles. The wall-screens were covered with alerts.

Rodriguez was already there, waiting. His turned to regard Gustav coldly. 'Is this what you call "tight security", General?'

Gustav ignored him and addressed the soldiers at the desks. 'Report.'

'We have no sentinel net and no Relic feed, sir,' the watch officer told him. 'Half our computers are down and in the process of emergency reboot.'

'How did it happen?' Gustav demanded.

The watch officer shook his head. 'It doesn't make sense, sir. Transaction records show a huge amount of data being shunted from the Relic feed to a non-existent network address.'

'Did you track that address?'

'Yes, sir. First entry we have for it was just twenty-one minutes ago, when it requested a high-speed diagnostic of all our systems. Then it started tapping the Relic.'

Gustav could barely breathe. It could only be the Gallies. His reassurances to Rodriguez sounded pitifully hollow now.

How? he asked himself. *How could they have possibly found this place?* And then it hit him: for this to have happened so soon after his own arrival, he must have led them here himself. They had followed his ship. A violent sensation of nausea swept through him.

'Where are they?' he gasped. 'Can you see them yet?'

'Where's who, sir?' said the watch officer nervously.

'The Gallies, of course!' Gustav shouted. His hands started trembling. He squeezed them into fists.

'N-no, sir,' said the officer. 'The sensor net is dead. It's still reconfiguring.'

'Find them,' said Gustav. 'They're out there somewhere. I want a full proximity sweep. We have to catch them before they leave the system. We're going to Code Red.'

'We're already at Code Red,' Rodriguez interjected with disdain. 'That was the first order I gave when I came in here.'

Gustav glared at him, but Rodriguez just glared back, eyes ablaze with righteous wrath. The man had no authority to issue that command. His decision, however, had been absolutely right.

'Signal the Oort drones,' said Gustav curtly. 'Put their sensors on maximum sensitivity. The Gallies must be close if they had a real-time feed running. And now they don't have a warp trail to hide in. We'll find them. I want those gunships to release every single suntap drone they're carrying,' he added, thinking fast. 'Spread them in a globular scan pattern, centred here. Kill anything that moves.'

7.3: IRA

Through the *Ariel*'s crippled camera array, Ira watched dismally as the space around his ship filled up with robotic weapons. This close to the star, they'd easily catch him before he left the system. Only the *Ariel*'s hull cladding was keeping it hidden now, and that wouldn't stand up to a thorough scan. The only hope they had left was if Rachel could fix the engines before Ulanu decided to fill the area with disrupter buoys. He was surprised it hadn't happened already.

Even as he pondered that oversight on his enemy's part, the reason for it became clear – a robotic messenger drone darted out of the Earther research ship and accelerated away in the direction of Zuni-Dehel.

Terrific. In a matter of days there'd be thousands of drones for Ira to hide from, not just a few dozen. The whole lobe would be teeming with munitions before he could get off it. The messenger flared to brilliance and then tore out of the system, its drive winking ever more slowly as it gathered warp.

'I need those engines now, Rachel,' said Ira, as calmly as he could.

She gasped her frustration. 'The diagnostics still aren't running properly! I can give you about fifty-per-cent power safely, no more.'

Ira watched as the inevitable disrupters started sliding out of ports in the gunships' sides in long, snaking lines. 'That'll have to do. We just ran out of time. Strap in, everybody.'

Ira had to move, and there was only one direction he could go: in-system. Closer to the star, his more efficient Galatean engines would have a distinct advantage over the Earther drones, even at half-power. It'd do him no favours when it came to escaping the system, but at least they wouldn't get frozen in place.

As soon as Rachel said the word, Ira hit the button and threw the ship into a mad sunward dive. The hammer-blows of the gravity drive slammed him into his couch.

As the *Ariel* fled, its limited sensors struggled to build a schematic of what was happening around him. But Ira didn't need to be told. He could *feel* those drones racing after him.

Ira pushed the drives as far as he could take them.

'Engines exceeding safety limits,' Rachel warned.

Fuck the safety limits. The only safety limit that made any difference now was the radius around the star beneath which the drones couldn't warp.

Gratifyingly, he saw the enemy munitions start to fall behind.

'Ha!' he shouted. 'Eat that!'

He waited till he was confident they were no longer within drone range and then cut his engines. There was no point in letting the Earthers know exactly how close to the star he could get. They were nice and close already. Against its glare, they'd be even harder to see.

'Rachel, collapse the drive stalks. I want us invisible.'

He turned on the fusion torches and pushed them gently further in.

'The enemy drones are reconfiguring,' said Amy. 'They're taking up a defensive spread.'

Ira scowled. He'd expected a response like that, but not so quickly. That damned Ulanu didn't miss a trick. His weapons were moving into orbital patterns aligned with the local shell, with the highest drone density in the direction of human space. If Ira tried to leave the system, he'd have a choice: fly straight into them or make a violent course alteration after he hit the heliopause that would make him a lot easier to intercept.

He tweaked his thrusters, putting the *Ariel* on a parabolic dive around the star that would at least have them coming out running. Unfortunately, it pointed him straight towards the uncharted space of the Penfield Lobe. The good news was that it looked as if they'd be safe now until they reached the other side of the star.

'Any chance of full engine power in the next couple of hours?' he asked Rachel.

'I don't know,' she replied tightly. 'I found part of the problem with the engines – the maintenance robots are all running active programs, but none of them are the ones I asked for. The damned things are wandering around in the mesohull like wild animals. I think Will is still interacting with them.'

Ira blinked. 'Still interacting? Didn't we sever his link to the ship?'

'No,' said Amy. 'I kept it open on purpose. The way his vital signs were looking, I was worried it might kill him. There's a tremendous amount of neural feedback going on in there, and it's increasing.'

Ira grimaced. 'Is there anything you can do?'

'There might be,' Amy replied. 'I've identified the focus of the activity, at least. Rachel, do you know much about micromachines?'

'Enough. Can I help?'

'Maybe. Take a look at this.'

There was a pause. Then Rachel spoke again. 'Oh my God!'

'What?' Ira demanded. 'Let me see it, whatever it is.'

Amy sent him a scan of Will's head. It showed a huge amount of cellular activity around his interface site. Ira had no clue what it meant, but he didn't like it.

'What's going on in there?' he asked.

'That's what I'm trying to work out,' she replied. 'I wanted to diagnose it properly before worrying anyone with speculation.'

Ira didn't like the sound of that. 'Why?'

'Because it has all the hallmarks of a violent viral infection. But it can't be that,' she added quickly.

'A virus,' said Ira flatly. More good news. Something infectious in a ship this size would kill them all.

'Don't worry,' Amy insisted. 'It can't be. There's no way he could have contracted anything. The alien data might have been dangerous, but it wasn't magic. You can't turn data into protein. You just can't.'

Ira winced. What was magic but technology you didn't understand yet?

'Amy,' he said, 'I want you to concentrate on Will till we get around the star. Rachel, help her if she needs it. Hugo, you'll have to take over Amy's scanners for a while and keep an eye on those drones.'

'But, Captain,' said Hugo, 'I've been looking at the suntap schematic—'

'It'll have to wait, Hugo,' Ira growled. 'I want you on the scanners.'

'But I'm not qualified!' said Hugo.

'Enough!' Ira shouted. 'I've put up with a lot from you, Vartian, but now it has to stop. You're drafted to full crew duty until we get the hell out of here. That means following orders and shutting the fuck up when I tell you to. It's that or coma. Do you understand me?'

'Y-yes, but I don't know how to—'

'You're a genius, aren't you?' Ira bellowed. 'So *learn*!'

For the next hour, he watched Ulanu's weapons slowly adjust their positions to prevent his escape. The only piece of good news he could glean from their strategy was that they'd lost sight of their quarry and were having to cover all their bases. That spread them thin, though not thin enough for comfort.

His observations were interrupted by a call from Amy at the bottom of the cabin.

'Ira,' she said softly.

He looked out of his bunk into her upturned face. She and Rachel had brought Will out of his tank, though his body was still covered in gel and stim-needles.

'Turns out I was wrong.' She sighed. 'It is a virus.'

Ira felt the pit of his stomach fall away.

'Somehow,' said Amy, 'and don't ask me how it's possible... but his micromachines have started assembling virions from the DNA in his own nerve cells, and they're attacking his immune system.'

'Will he live?' Ira asked hollowly.

Tears sprang to the corners of Amy's eyes. 'I have no idea,' she said.

'Yes,' said Rachel firmly. 'Because we're not going to let him die.'

Ira examined the edge of his bunk for a moment while he tried to think his way around this new addition to his woes. 'Is it infectious?' he asked at last.

Amy shook her head. 'We don't know. But if it's passed by contact, then Rachel and I have already got it.'

7.4: WILL

Will awoke with a snap, but his senses didn't come with him. He floated in darkness, silent and all-consuming. He had no awareness of his body, or of the internal spaces synthesised by his interface.

He tried to stay calm. Being disembodied didn't bother him – he'd done it to himself many times while calibrating his interface. What worried him was that someone – or some*thing* – had the power to strip his senses from him. He knew that if he spent too long in deprivation, he'd start to experience toxic feedback. The human awareness loop wasn't designed to take that kind of cognitive pressure.

As the isolation dragged on, Will's panic slowly mounted. It was impossible to gauge the passage of time trapped like this. It occurred to him that perhaps this wasn't the result of some alien force being applied to his brain. The alien might have departed already, leaving him like this permanently – trapped in the empty, senseless dark until his mind ripped itself to pieces. Terror gripped him. He knew his heart should be racing, but just like the rest of him, it was missing.

Then, abruptly, his senses started coming back online. They appeared one by one, like modules of a rebooting computer, smell first. Will gasped with relief. However, by the time he'd been given back his sight, he knew something was wrong. Though he was lying in his bunk aboard the *Ariel*, his experience of it had the flat, plastic quality of a recorded memory. His gratitude soured quickly into unease.

'Captain?' he said.

The hum of the soft, off-white walls was exactly as it should have been, as was the muted electronic cheeping of the crew consoles. However, there was no reply.

Will levered himself out of his bunk and looked around. The rest of the cabin was empty. No one home. The crew bunks were flat and bare, with visors and keyboards left unclipped from the walls, as if their occupants had floated out just moments ago.

Will drifted up to the meeting chamber and opened the hatch.

No one in there, either. The meeting tablet hung loose in the centre of the room.

Increasingly he had the sense that someone had created a perfect simulation of the *Ariel*, just to keep him isolated within it. If that were true, then pretty soon it'd become as claustrophobic as sensory deprivation.

'This is a pile of nano!' Will shouted at the walls. 'This isn't the ship. It's a fake!'

He slapped a bunk frame with his open hand, but it remained resolutely solid.

'Give me back my mind!' Will raged.

There was no reply.

Will shut his eyes and tried to introspect instead. He visualised his home node, but it refused to appear. His senses resolutely told him he was already there.

In desperation, Will started yanking open cabinets and hatches. If this was indeed his own mind, then surely there would be some symbol or cue he could use to reassert control over it. He needed something iconic to focus on – something imbued with the power of personal memory. He scrabbled madly through the cabin, shouting curses at his invisible captor all the while.

'Who are you, you bastard?' he demanded of the air. What's going on?'

The cabin walls hummed softly back at him. Will's movements became more and more frantic. Eventually, his search brought him to the privacy chamber. As the door slid back, Will found something which proved beyond any doubt that this version of the *Ariel* wasn't real.

It was a SAP pattern. The hairs on the back of Will's neck stood straight up.

The pattern floated in the middle of the little chamber like a huge piece of surrealist jewellery, a metre across. At its heart was a consciousness loop large enough to wear like a necklace, with fans of sense and action modules branching off the main throughput trunk on either side. Each module bore a sheaf of closely packed recall trees thick with memories like pearls held together with spider-silk links. Seen in this incongruously real setting, the program looked beautiful, and far more sinister than it had any right to be.

With a deep and crawling sense of unease, Will climbed slowly into the chamber beside it. He checked all around the SAP for any kind of clue as to its nature. The first thing he noticed was that it wasn't one of his.

He'd never lay a sense map out that way. It was weird. And the closer he looked, the weirder it appeared to be. It had the broad, many-fronded profile of a robot mind, and a highly sophisticated one at that, but the senses didn't correspond to any robot type he'd ever seen. Things that looked like taste and hearing analogues were all jumbled up. Some of the action trees ended in twisted little self-referential clusters like gnarled hands. It didn't take a great deal of smarts to realise that this thing wasn't the product of a human imagination.

'What am I supposed to do with this?' Will demanded of the walls.

Though he asked, he could already guess. He was supposed to run the thing – plug his own mind into it and see what happened. What else was there to do with an SAP?

He wondered what it would do to him. However, whatever its effect would be, the alien had already disassembled him once. It didn't need permission to mess with his head. At least if he played along, he might have a chance of finding out what was going on.

'All right,' he said nervously. 'I get the idea.'

He moved around the program. If he was going to run it, he'd have to fit adapter blocks onto its consciousness aperture. There was no way he'd be able to read those weird senses directly.

The components of his adapter toolkit appeared suddenly in the space above his head.

Will lurched back. His heart pounded, and this time he could definitely feel it. At least what he was supposed to do with the SAP was no longer in any doubt, he thought, as his pulse returned to normal. Whoever was in charge here, they definitely wanted him to run it.

'I'll need more than that,' he said carefully. 'I'll need a sense-analogue library for a start.'

All at once, the little chamber filled with a motionless blizzard of manifested software chunks. Will flinched less this time.

'Thanks,' he muttered.

If the alien was prepared to give him access to tools like these, perhaps there was a chance he could use the code to break its hold over him. Unlikely, though, given that the thing was probably monitoring his awareness loop, and therefore privy to every thought that ran through his head. Still, it was something to bear in mind.

Cautiously, Will set to work. He mentally instructed two adapters to join and watched them fly across the room to snap together. Apparently not all of his roboteer talents had been stripped from him. The alien was still letting him access those that served its purpose.

The adapters weren't hard to build, and within what felt like about half an hour Will was ready to go. It was just a matter of instructing the SAP to run and then dropping his perception into the harness icon he'd prepared for himself.

Except that now he was about to start, Will found he was afraid. He glanced around at the walls one last time.

'This is what you want me to do, isn't it?' he asked, but the walls steadfastly refused to reply.

Well, what else was he supposed to do? He couldn't stay trapped in this plastic cabin for ever.

Screwing up his courage, Will told the SAP to run. Flickers of light coursed through its memory pearls. Obviously the program was receiving sensory input from somewhere, though where, Will couldn't say. He fixed the harness icon in his mind and pushed his perception into it.

Will stood outside his breeding bower on the Plain of Second Chances. The mother sun was overhead in the sky, as it would be for the next four fathers. In the distance, beyond the whispering yesblade, he could see the empty, crumbling bowers of his long-dead uncles.

Will looked down at himself and saw something yellow with a dozen stick-thin limbs. He shivered, and all his body segments shuddered in sequence. It was the most peculiar sensation, even for a roboteer who'd inhabited countless artificial forms.

'Will,' said a clear female voice off to one side.

It sounded disturbingly like Rachel, despite the fact that he knew the words were spoken in the whistling Tongue of History. He turned to face the speaker, his limbs moving beneath him in a curiously fluid and perfectly intuitive way.

The speaker was a mottled blue thing, like a caterpillar raised up on spiny legs with four narrow arms hanging down in front. She was a Fertile of foreign lineage. With strange and joyful certainty, Will knew that her legs would break off after he impregnated her. She'd attach herself to a rock to produce larvae, and he would feed her till she died, as was right and proper. He felt the emotion powerfully, though it was not his own. His fear came back redoubled.

'What is this?' he asked the female. 'What's going on?' He waved his front two limb-pairs to illustrate.

'Listen to me, Will, if you want to avoid the destruction of your species,' the female said.

For a moment, Will could think of nothing to say. He peered at her through four different eyes. *Destruction of my species?* His human instinct was to frown, but this body couldn't do that. Instead, he secreted the Odour of Perplexity.

'What are you talking about?'

Those were very high stakes to open a conversation with – the kind that made you immediately suspicious.

'Your species has been granted access to a technology you refer to as the suntap. This gift was initially granted with the purpose of destroying you.'

Will didn't want to accept that. Nevertheless, he had a grim, sinking feeling in his abdomen. He'd wondered why the alien planet had so willingly handed out the secret of unlimited power. It had almost seemed in a hurry to tell them.

'I don't believe you,' he said. He paused. 'How?'

'Continued use of the suntap creates a clearly identifiable signature in the heart of a star. It is then straightforward for my kind to target those stars and manipulate them, just as the lure star that brought you here was manipulated. The resultant shock waves will kill all life near those targets.'

'Targeting *stars*?' Will repeated stupidly.

'It should not be difficult for you to believe,' said the alien. 'Examination of the suntap schematic will show you that we have the power to instantaneously sample and affect a stellar context at a distance. The lure star is sufficient proof of our power to tune stellar radiation to our needs. Do you suppose that, given access to suntap technology, humanity will prove restrained enough to never use it? Four human-occupied stars have already begun to show tapping signatures: the ones you call Zuni-Dehel and Memburi, along with two others your species use for fuelling.'

Will began to believe, and to be afraid. Four whole star systems that these aliens could snuff out at will. The moment the Earthers used a suntap in the home system, most of the human race would be at risk. Anger welled inside him.

'But why? We've never hurt you. Why would you do this to us?'

'To keep the galaxy safe,' the female said. 'We police the gate. All species that pass through it are given the gift. Safe species are permitted to use it. Dangerous ones are destroyed.'

Will's immediate instinct was to claim that humanity wasn't dangerous. But with war raging across every inhabited star system, that was hardly plausible.

'What're you saying?' he demanded. 'That you're going to kill us all just because we threaten you? You haven't given us a chance to prove ourselves. Until now, no one even knew you existed.'

The alien shuddered in a way that showed amusement. 'You do not threaten us. We judge you based on your threat to the galactic environment. In our experience, there are only two types of species: those who will eventually transcend, and those who self-destruct. Transcenders tend to increase the number of planetary biospheres where intelligent species may arise. Destructors decrease them. Transcenders are characterised by their capacity to constructively self-edit. You are our first evidence that humanity is capable of self-editing. We consider you and your Galatean culture promising. Until your arrival, your species appeared to fall clearly into the Destructor category.'

'That's revolting,' Will exclaimed. 'You mean you judged us on the basis of the Earther crusade?'

The crusade was without doubt the strongest and most populous thrust of human culture in their age, but it felt so unfair. His alien body secreted a muddle of powerful smells – flavours of guilt and anger, all red and black.

'Who the hell do you think you are?' he said. 'On what authority do you make this judgement?'

'On no authority,' the alien replied. 'Does a human gardener judge the moral value of each weed before he plucks it from the soil?'

'But we're not weeds,' said Will. 'You can't reduce the whole of human history to some shitty metaphor. We're thinking beings.'

'Then consider this,' said the female. 'Humans came to this place. Humans asked for power. We gave it to them. Humanity has not yet bothered to ask what the consequences of this request would be. Even without our intervention, sooner or later, humanity is certain to gain power beyond its maturity to handle. That has already come close to happening several times in the past. Eventually, your race will have to either change to compensate for its increased potential, or destroy itself. In dying, it would almost certainly destroy the potential spawning places for other races, just as it has already denuded the biosphere of its home world.

'All we are doing is improving the efficiency of this natural process to favour life. We optimise the galactic ecology for the creation of new biospheres. Thus, even if we are wrong about humanity, on balance we will still have added to the diversity of life in the universe.'

'But how do you know?' Will urged. He clicked his spindly legs together and cursed the limited range of expression the unfamiliar body afforded him. 'How can you divide all intelligent life into these categories so blithely?'

'Because we have seen thousands of them,' said the alien. 'Our policy is not based on speculation. It is the product of a billion years' worth of collected data.'

Will reeled. 'Who are you?' he demanded, a little more nervously now. 'God?'

The female shuddered with mirth again. 'We are the Transcended, of course. We are what every intelligent species becomes if it reaches the next stage. If humanity passes the test, it will join us.'

Will wasn't sure he liked the sound of that, either. Was that all the future held for them – extermination or amalgamation into some galactic super-mind?

'You can't make us,' he said.

'Of course not,' the female replied wryly. 'Self-destruction is always an option, and free to all.'

Will reared his sinuous body as upright as it would go. 'I won't let you get away with this! I'll tell people about the suntap. Even if you try to kill us, you won't get all of us.'

The female produced the olfactory equivalent of a smile. 'That was our intention in telling you. The one decision we make for each species is whether to tell it that it is being tested. We do this only when we judge that a species' fate hangs in the balance, when a small amount of information may encourage it to change its nature. Please believe me when I tell you that I would prefer to see humanity survive rather than die.'

'So you can absorb it into your culture!' Will sneered.

The female exuded the Odour of Polite Disagreement. 'Transcendence is something a species chooses for itself. It is never forced. Please also consider our contribution to your species before judging us as enemies. As well as the secret of unlimited power, we are giving humanity access to the galaxy through the network of gates we have created.'

Will froze. 'You *made* the Penfield Lobe?'

'Of course,' she replied. 'And hundreds of others like it.'

Will chattered his mouthparts in awe. What chance for independence did humanity have living in the shadow of a power that could make black holes at will? The galaxy no longer felt like such a large and open place as it had before.

'Had we meant you ill, we would never have chosen to speak with you this way,' the alien said. 'You are being given the chance to determine the fate of your species. We are aware of your conflict with the culture called Truism and we are prepared to help you resolve it. However, first you will have to provide further proof of your capacity for transcendence. The information we have placed in your mind is a test of sorts. If you pass that test, then you and your race will deserve to reap the rewards.'

'*My* mind?' blurted Will.

'Yes. You have been chosen to represent your species.'

Will balked at the idea. 'I can't do that,' he cried. 'I'm just a roboteer!'

'That is exactly why we have chosen you,' the alien replied. 'Because you represent the pinnacle of your species' ability to adapt.'

'No way!' Will roared. 'You can't put the destiny of the whole human race on my shoulders. I won't let you!'

He tried to back out of the simulation, but nothing happened. He scuttled in a circle desperately, looking for an escape route. He grabbed at the flimsy walls of the bower and started yanking furiously at them.

'You must rest,' said the female. 'Further alterations of your mind-body pattern are required.'

'No!' Will yelled, but there was nothing he could do. Piece by piece, the alien took him apart again.

8: CAT AND MOUSE

8.1: GUSTAV

Gustav stared fixedly into the display, willing the Gallies to appear. His instruments still couldn't see where the enemy ship had gone. It had appeared suddenly and fled into the sun's inaccessible region far too fast for their drones to follow. Now it was lost again, but not for long.

Gustav had set his drones out in an optimal pursuit configuration and had them madly scanning the region around the dwarf star for any suspicious signals. Fortunately, there were only a few places his enemy could be, and he already had them covered. If the Gallies wanted to get home, they'd have to go through him first.

Gustav felt nauseous with anticipation as he watched the search unfold. It didn't help that Rodriguez had stuck by his side the whole time. Since the emergency started, the disciple's mouth had been glued tight shut in a pucker of sanctimonious condemnation. As if this event somehow entirely justified the insane plan to try to destroy the Relic. Gustav dearly wanted to order the disciple out of the command room, but knew better. He intended to win this fight, and he wanted Rodriguez to see it first hand. As the minutes of searching dragged on, Rodriguez ventured a dry remark.

'*Still* not found them, General? Perhaps this is how you intend to introduce the Following to the Relic – by giving our secrets away to the enemy.'

Gustav shot him an impatient glare. 'They won't leave here alive,' he growled, then chastised himself – why was he bothering to justify his actions?

'Really?' said Rodriguez. 'A suspicious man might imagine you'd invited them in on purpose. There is much about you that is reminiscent of the Galateans, General. A lack of faith. An indiscriminate lust for knowledge.'

Gustav fought back the snide ripostes that sprang to mind.

'The moment you attacked Memburi, you must have known the Gallies would become curious,' the disciple went on.

And of course, Gustav had. He just hadn't expected it so soon. Nothing in Tang's report on the Battle of Memburi suggested that the enemy had made a successful soft assault, just glowing reports of perfectly executed manoeuvres. Gustav wished he hadn't let the admiral talk him into using the assault on Memburi as a test for their weapon. If they'd done as he'd originally planned and kept the suntap for the attack on Galatea, none of this would have happened.

Abruptly, an idea came to him. If the suntap had got them into this bind, maybe it could get them out.

'Do those drones have their suntaps online?' he asked the watch officer.

'Not yet, sir – they chased in with warp. But they can be ready in a matter of minutes.'

Gustav smiled. 'Have them fire in a scanning pattern across the range of the Gallies' possible location.' That way the bastards were bound to sustain some damage, if only a little. It might even render them visible. 'Tune the telescopes to look for any associated scattering that results,' he added. His eyes narrowed as he stared into the screen once more. 'Let's see how the gene-bending scum like it when we turn up the heat a little.'

8.2: IRA

There were long, gruelling hours of waiting while the *Ariel* dived around the sun. Inevitably, the ship heated up. It was used to receiving a lot of hard radiation, but nothing this intense. The star might have been relatively small and dark, but it was still a star.

From his bunk Ira could hear the ship expanding all round them, causing deep, miserable groans that echoed through the mesohull. The buffers zipped and crackled under the barrage of solar radiation. Yet, beneath the whole racket, Ira could still make out the gruesome sound of Will's ragged breathing.

'More drones closing in on us,' Hugo reported glumly.

Ira examined the enemy's spread pattern again. The one source of satisfaction he could find was that the Earthers had underestimated the efficiency of his engines. He'd be able to use warp earlier than they expected.

Unfortunately, it wouldn't do him much good. He'd be instantly visible, and dangerously slow this deep in-system. If he headed in any kind of useful direction, the drones would still intercept him long before he reached clear space. The trick was surely to get his ship out on an exit vector the enemy wouldn't predict, then to fly far enough away that a course change wouldn't buy him immediate trouble. He set a search SAP looking for flaws in the Earther containment pattern. Programming it was a clumsy process without a roboteer around to help out.

Thinking about that brought his mind back to Amy and her progress with Will. She was still toiling with him at the bottom of the cabin, looking for some kind of cure for his condition.

He leaned out of his bunk. 'Hey, Amy,' he asked softly. 'How's our handler doing?'

She leaned back and sighed. Her face wore hard lines. Ira knew that problems like this brought her maternal side out in full force, and it hurt her to not be able to help.

'It's too early to say,' she said. 'I'm trying to flood his body with antivirals, but it's not working. The damned infection changes as soon as I get a protein profile for it. There's no way I can keep his immune system intact without taking out his micromachines. And with the tools I have here, I can't do that without causing severe damage to his interface at the same time. I'm looking for other solutions.'

'How about just waking him up?' said Ira. 'Could we do that?

Amy shook her head. 'I don't think so. His interface is still locked in a feedback pattern. It's like full memory recall, only worse. I have no idea what's happening in there. Or even if he'll be quite the same Will when he wakes up.'

Ira winced. 'Is it really that bad? Could this thing actually change his personality?'

'We have no way of knowing. Think what the alien software did to this ship. For all we know, the same sort of chaos is happening inside his head.'

Ira didn't like the thought of a hacked person in his cabin. You could turn a computer off and reboot it. You couldn't do that with a member of your crew. The thought distressed him enough that he decided to change the subject.

'How about you?' he asked.

Amy tried for a brave smile. 'Well, I tested Rachel and myself for the virus, and although we both came out positive for exposure, the infection doesn't appear to be making any headway. It's just not that virulent without the help it's getting from Will's micromachines. Which supports the theory that we're dealing with something of technological origin rather than a true disease, I guess. But I've given Rachel and myself antiviral boosters just to be on the safe side.'

Ira nodded. 'And what about you, Rachel?' he said, glancing across at her bunk. 'Any news about the ship?'

'What?' Rachel sounded fraught and distant.

'Have you made any progress?'

'Some,' she replied morosely. 'I have a full set of robots back under manual control, but no SAPs to run them. The core systems look stable enough, though. We've got full engine power, but we should run another suite of tests before we use them again.'

'Run them,' said Ira.

'Hey, Captain,' John interjected. 'Remember that the longer we wait, the bigger the problem we'll have. If the Earthers alert Zuni-Dehel before we get away, we could have a whole fleet after us. We'll be the most hunted people in the galaxy.'

Ira breathed deeply. 'I know. But right now, we have pursuit drones closing on us from every direction, an alien virus on board and no SAP control. We can worry about being infamous later.'

The moment after the words left Ira's mouth, an awful snapping sound filled the cabin, like the crack of a mighty whip.

He glanced around. 'What the *hell* was that?'

'Secondary buffer damage!' said Rachel. 'We were hit with a g-ray. Hard!'

'Have they found us?' he demanded.

'Don't think so. Contact was very quick. Damage pattern is linear. Went straight across us.'

Suddenly, Ira guessed what was happening. Ulanu had taken to firing blind with his suntap weapons.

Crack! The sound came again.

'Secondary buffers at eighty-six per cent," said Rachel.

'Hugo,' said Ira, 'how long to warp altitude if we go straight up?'

Hugo grunted and cursed as he handled the unfamiliar interface. 'Er... about a minute. But we'd be completely visible the moment we fired the torches. I don't recommend it – there are an awful lot of drones out there.'

Crack!

'Secondary buffers at sixty-nine per cent. That one kept target for longer,' Rachel warned.

Which meant the drones were narrowing their search space. They must have got a signal bounce off the *Ariel*'s hull.

'Strap in, everybody,' Ira called. 'We're heading out.'

He examined the results of his flaw-finding program. There was a narrow aperture that the Earthers hadn't adequately covered, and with good reason. It was the direction that led directly away from home – the only flight path that did them no good at all.

'Amy, get Will back into that tank,' he ordered. 'Rachel, help her.'

The two women jumped into action and then scrambled madly into their bunks.

The moment Rachel gave him the all clear, Ira hit the torches.

G-ray beams from the drones converged and fired. There was an awful moment during which the buffers snapped and boomed like lightning. Ira veered the ship desperately out of the onslaught only to have them track him again.

At last, they reached warp altitude and Ira turned full power to the gravity drive. The warp engines punched on, accelerating them out of the alien system.

'Fire countermeasures!' Ira barked.

'On it,' said John.

Defence drones ripped away from the ship behind them, annihilating some of the opposition, but not enough. The race was on again.

'Amy, how're we looking?' said Ira.

'It's touch and go,' she replied. 'A dead climb and there's not much in it.'

Ira thought fast. 'Rachel – I want you to over-tune our engine burst rate.'

It was a stupidly dangerous thing to do so soon after repairs, but he could think of nothing else.

'Captain . . . ?'

'Just do it!' he shouted. Over-tuning the engine would burn juice fast and might well blow them up, but in a few minutes, that probably wouldn't matter.

It took for ever for Rachel to make the adaptation without proper robot support. While she worked, Ira watched the drones close inexorably upon them. Thankfully, they'd disengaged those terrible suntap rays, but there were still antimatter warheads to worry about.

'Done!' Rachel gasped.

Ira kicked in the new program and the hum of the engines rose to an ear-splitting whine. The M-dwarf shrank rapidly behind them, but the tidal effect of the over-formed gravity shell produced a foul thudding sensation. Gravity jumped sickeningly, as if someone were repeatedly stomping on the brakes in a ground transport.

'Ira!' Amy yelled. 'You're pushing Will's life signs into the red!'

Ira roared his displeasure.

'Trying to compensate with muscular injections,' she told him.

Ira held his breath as they reached the system's FTL threshold. The whole crew cheered frantically as they reached clean space, but they weren't out of the woods yet. They still had to make it impossible for anyone to follow.

'Prepare for immediate warp-scatter manoeuvres,' said Ira. 'Amy, I need a flight pattern.'

'I can't give you one!' she wailed. 'Not if you want me to keep Will alive.'

'Then forget it. Fleet standard will do. Hold on tight, everybody.'

He began the series of gut-wrenching course corrections required to disperse their warp trail. It was the only thing that would grant them any certainty of survival.

It was impossible to see who was after you in an FTL chase, but it was almost as difficult to do the chasing. Hang around long enough to see the radiation from your target and it meant he was already getting away. You could track him but never catch up as long as he changed course often enough. Unfortunately, that meant a fleeing ship had to make a violent change of direction at least once every five minutes to avoid being nailed. Let a pursuit drone get too close and he'd close on you from sheer spatial distortion.

Gravity swatted Ira sideways against the wall of his bunk, knocking the wind from his lungs. He gasped in surprise and reluctantly reduced the extra burn he was putting into the drives. If that turn had knocked the wind out of him, he hated to think what it had done to Will.

Fifteen minutes of body-busting course alterations later, they were outside the drones' flight range and still alive. The probability of pursuit had dropped to negligible levels.

'We're clear,' Ira breathed.

Clapping and nervous laughter broke out in the cabin.

'Okay,' he said, 'Amy, set a course for home whenever you can make it.'

Ira wasn't kidding himself that the danger was over. Ulanu would have drones ready to intercept him on all the most likely flight vectors. It was normally impossible to catch up with someone in deep space, but with the bottleneck of the Penfield Lobe to pass through, there were no guarantees.

Rachel spoke up. 'Captain, if the heat is off, we have some serious buffer damage to attend to. And without robot support, it's going to be hard to fix.'

'Get on it. Hugo, you help her.'

Ira readied himself to quash Hugo's inevitable complaint, but apparently the scientist had learned something from the last few hours. All Ira heard in reply was a slightly sullen, 'Yes, sir.'

With the crew at work, he set about trying to train a SAP to predict Ulanu's likely ambush points. The work was cumbersome, and Ira began to realise how stupid it would have been to leave

Will on St Andrews – even a vulnerable roboteer was better than no roboteer at all.

So engrossed was he in the tricky programming that he jumped when an alarm sounded from the flight-management subsystem. He glanced across at their vector and saw that it had changed dramatically without his intervention. Furthermore, they were losing speed fast.

His skin prickled. What was this – more alien trickery?

'Amy, what the hell's happening?' he said.

Amy's answer was a string of obscenities. 'We're not compensating for shell curvature,' she explained furiously.

'Why not?' said Ira. 'Didn't you give me an algorithm for that when we hit the lobe?'

'Yes, of course! I don't know why it's not—' Then she let out a wail of despair.

'What?' Ira demanded.

'We swapped shells,' she said miserably. 'It must have been your warp-scatter manoeuvres. With the curvon gradient being so steep up here, all those bursts of conventional acceleration jumped us to a different level.'

'Can we compensate?' He glanced across at her. Her brow was a mess of worried lines.

'Hold on.' She tapped furiously at her keyboard and then reached up to seize her pigtails in anxious hands. 'We're on a closed shell!'

'What does that mean?'

'It means we're deeper into the lobe. We're not orbiting the galactic core any more – we're essentially in orbit around the black hole. If we keep going this way, we'll head straight back to the place where the enemy is waiting for us.'

Ira stifled a moan of frustration. He wondered if Ulanu was bothering to expend energy trying to follow them.

'So we change course,' he said.

'That won't help,' said Amy. 'We have to return to the thinnest part of this shell just to get off it, otherwise we'll keep going in circles for ever.'

Ira took a deep breath. If straight back into the jaws of their enemy was where they had to go, then so be it.

'Set a course for that crossover point,' he ordered. 'We'll take whatever Ulanu thinks he can throw at us.'

He pointed his ship back towards trouble.

8.3: GUSTAV

'Sir!' said the soldier sitting at the astrogation desk. 'We've analysed the Gallies' exit vector – they're trapped in the lobe.' He smiled smugly. 'Shall I send ships after them?'

'No,' Gustav said, shaking his head reluctantly. It was a hard order to give after the humiliations of the last few hours, particularly after the remarks he'd had to endure from Rodriguez when the Gallies slipped through his fingers.

'Why not?' the disciple drawled. 'Afraid we'll actually catch them?'

Gustav rounded on him. 'I'm not chasing them because there's *no point*. The Gallies will be expecting it. And furthermore because it would be a waste of our resources.'

Rodriguez's nostrils flared. 'You call keeping the Prophet's secrets a waste?'

'What do you actually know about warp battles, Father?' Gustav snapped. 'Chasing people with FTL is like running around in fog. You can't see a damned thing. You can only catch the person you're chasing if they happen to brush past you.' He pointed a furious finger at one of the wall displays. 'Do you know what that means?'

Rodriguez set his jaw. 'If you think to belittle me by asking—'

'It's a map of their exhaust-radiation profile. They over-burned their engines to get out of here. We know they can't have fuelled since before Zuni, which means that for a ship that size, they have to be running low. What's more, their captain just made a stupid mistake that wasted even more of his antimatter and plenty of time. He's given us the opportunity to put every antimatter factory for light-years around on high alert. By the time he gets off the lobe, he'll be desperate. He'll either die in space, or he'll come to us.'

Gustav turned back to the desk. 'Comms officer,' he snapped.

'Sir!'

'Instruct Captain Wahid of the *Gaza* to head for Zuni immediately with new orders for Admiral Tang. He is to alert every fuelling star within sixty lights to look out for unscheduled stops, regardless of their apparent security clearance. He is to tell them that . . .' Gustav struggled for a suitable excuse. He certainly couldn't afford to tell the truth. 'That we have found a Gallie thief-ship involved in a Galatean plot to kill the Prophet. The ship has stolen information critical to the Prophet's security and may attempt to pass through their system with false clearance information. Tang is instructed to use the operational subset of the Zuni fleet to mark every potential Galatean fuelling star within the same region. The *Gaza* will act as flagship with Wahid in command. Tang is to remain at Zuni to fit the stockpiled suntaps to the remaining ships.'

The last thing Gustav wanted was to give Tang an excuse to play with his fleet. Better to keep him pinned down at Zuni with something to do.

'Sir,' said the comms officer, and strode out of the room towards the secure channel booth.

Tang would hate ships being taken away from his precious assault force, but he'd have to cope. The Gallies simply could not be allowed to return home. Whatever they'd done to the Relic, it had killed the Earthers' feed in such a way that Gustav's team was at a loss as to how to retrieve it. The alien world had fallen silent for the first time in two years. Gustav's gut tightened again at the thought.

Analysis of his ship's slowly rebooting computers had shown Gustav evidence of a message being passed to the intruders that was petabytes in size. With ten minutes' access, his enemies had achieved something with the Relic that his team had never come close to. That gave the advantage firmly back to the Galateans – an intolerable situation. Who knew what super-weapons they'd been given? He felt sick with envy. And with that feeling came a change of heart.

'Astrogation!' he barked.

'Sir!'

'Contact the *Saladin*. Tell them to lay in a slow pursuit course after the intruder. They don't have to catch the Gallies, just follow them.'

Finding where someone had been in warp after the fact was a lot easier than trying to keep up. Remote telescope drones could detect warp flashes for days after a ship had left. And warp always left a radiation trail of some sort, even with stealth technology.

'Make sure they don't get away,' he added. Better safe than sorry.

Surprisingly, Rodriguez didn't bother taking a swipe at him for issuing that order. Gustav glanced around to see what the disciple had to say for himself, but to his surprise the man had gone. Gustav frowned. *What prompted that?* he wondered. Nevertheless, he was grateful for the peace the disciple's departure brought. He returned his eyes to the board.

It was only a matter of time now. Then the Gallie ship would be in his grasp, and with luck, so would the secrets of the Relic.

8.4: WILL

Like a body dropped in cold water, Will came awake. He found himself back in the muscle-tank, where he'd been before the whole alien incursion started. Desperate with relief, he commanded the tank to drain its gel and free him. Dragging his limbs out of the confinement of the box was wonderful, though his body ached as if it had been soundly beaten. But he was back, and that was what counted.

He emerged to the sound of shouting. Ira was swearing at the top of his lungs.

'It's no good,' said Rachel. 'The buffers just can't be fixed out here. Unless we can get to a safe repair site, we're all going to die of radiation poisoning before we make it home. We can't even effect decent temporary repairs without proper working SAPs. But that's not the worst of it.'

'Dear God!' said Ira. 'What else is there?'

'We're also low on fuel.'

'She's right,' said Amy. 'Our detour around the shell has put Li-Delamir just out of our range.'

'Shit!' roared Ira. 'Shit! Shit! Shit!'

'As far as I can tell,' she added. 'the only system close enough for us to fuel at is Zuni-Dehel.'

'That's great,' John interjected. 'We just walk right into our enemies' hands. Hands up who likes torture.'

'Enough, John,' Ira barked. 'If I want your wit, I'll ask for it.'

Will listened with mounting alarm. What could have happened while he was unconscious? How long had he been out of the loop? And where in hell were they now?

He consulted the ship. Apparently, they were some distance out from Ulanu's secret system and stalled in space. Amazingly, just hours had passed since their brush with the alien data feed. He also learned that Amy's estimate was right – there was nowhere safe to refuel that was close enough to reach. In other words, they were trapped, dead and they'd lost Galatea the war. No wonder Ira was tense.

He smiled bitterly to himself. Here was one problem that the brilliant Transcended had failed to anticipate: that he'd be dead before he got the chance to take their stupid test.

But as he thought of the Transcended, something odd happened in his head. A memory surfaced in his mind like a chess piece being deposited on a board. There *was* somewhere they could go. Somewhere they *should* go, in fact. Somewhere very important.

'I know a place,' he croaked. His throat was raw, for some reason. It hurt to speak.

All the heads in the cabin whipped around to face him. Their astonishment was clear.

'Will?' said Amy incredulously.

'You're back!' Rachel broke into a smile of relief.

Ira just looked worried. 'What did you say?' he asked quietly.

'I have a vector,' said Will. 'I know a place where we can fix the buffers. Maybe even get fuel.'

Ira's eyes narrowed. 'Where?'

Will passed the coordinates from his interface straight to Ira's visor. He watched as the captain's eyes scanned the information.

'This star isn't on our shell,' said Ira flatly. 'This is uncharted territory.'

Will nodded. 'I know.'

Hugo spoke up. 'Then how do you—'

Ira motioned him to silence. His face was grave. 'Are you positive about this?' His eyes bored into Will's.

'Yes, sir,' Will croaked. 'The aliens, they . . . spoke to me.'

Will watched Hugo's eyes go round like dinner plates as a pained, jealous look entered them. It occurred to Will then that his experience was going to take no small amount of explanation.

'And you trust them,' said Ira sceptically.

Will nodded. 'I . . . I think so. I mean, I see no reason for them to send us into the middle of nowhere when we're just as likely to die here.'

'How about to take over our brains?' John remarked dryly.

Will grimaced. 'I don't think . . .' Then he ran out of words. After all, wasn't that exactly what had happened to him? 'I believe they could have done that here if they'd wanted to,' he said. 'That's not what they're about.'

'Do we have much choice?' said Rachel. 'It's this or Zuni.'

Ira rubbed his eyes with thumb and forefinger. When he looked up again, his face was full of grim resolve. 'I expect a full report,' he said, eyeing Will wearily.

'Yes, sir.'

The captain turned to his first officer. 'Amy, take a look at this course and set us up.'

'Will do.'

'Then take a look at our roboteer,' he added. 'If he's well enough, Rachel could use a hand.'

'I'm fine, sir,' said Will.

Ira regarded him uncertainly. 'The ship's doctor will be the judge of that. In the meantime, I want you to start that report.'

Will nodded. 'Okay, sir.'

As he turned back to his bunk, he couldn't help but notice the uneasy way the crew looked at him. He didn't blame them. In their place, he'd be doing the same thing.

9: UNCHARTED TERRITORY

9.1: WILL

Amy finished checking Will over and stepped back from his bunk.

'I don't get it,' she said, scanning the information in her visor. 'You appear to be fine. The level of virus in your blood is way down, though I don't see any evidence of antibodies at work. It's like the infection just gave up.'

She didn't sound particularly pleased about it, and Will could understand that. It was one more mystery of the alien assault. And no one was more unsettled about that than he was.

'How do you *feel*?' said Amy, peering at him.

'Fine,' he replied. 'Physically, at least. A bit bruised, and my throat is raw, but otherwise normal.'

'And mentally?'

Will was sure she meant the question kindly, but he didn't like the way it sounded.

'Just nervous,' he replied, a little curtly. 'An alien took over my brain. As far as I know, it's still in there. How do you think I feel?'

Amy winced. 'Sorry.'

'Hey, Will,' said Ira. 'You finished that report?'

Will glanced inwards at his home node where he'd been hurriedly writing his transcript while Amy ran her tests. It was a clumsy piece of text, but he doubted Ira was much interested in fine writing at this point.

'Yes, sir,' he said. 'What would you like me to do with it?'

'Just put it in the public space. We'll all take a look.'

Will would have preferred the captain to read it himself first. Cut down into bullet-point form, his experience with the Transcended made for melodramatic reading. The end of humanity, galactic gardening, billion-year programmes – it was a lot to take in. Reluctantly, he reached into his home node and transferred the file to the *Ariel*'s public domain. Then he lay back on his bunk and waited for the inevitable questions.

John was the first to make his feelings known, which he did by bursting into laughter.

'Oh my *God*!' he exclaimed. 'Will, are you serious? They actually said all this shit?'

'I'm afraid so,' said Will tersely.

'Well, hey, the nano really hit the fan-o this time! Looks like the whole future of the human race just landed in our lap. Gotta love that sense of destiny.'

It didn't sound like he believed it for a minute.

'Cut it out!' Rachel told him sharply.

Hugo, meanwhile, was making quiet plosive noises as he read. Will could see the man was mesmerised by the text. Then, abruptly, he turned and fixed Will with an urgent if slightly wounded stare.

'This must have been a very unique experience,' he said woodenly.

'It was frightening for the most part,' Will replied.

'Did the Transcended say anything about how they manipulate stars?'

Will shook his head. 'No.'

'Did they mention anything about particle resonance? Or collapsed-matter states?'

Will shifted uncomfortably. 'It wasn't really a technical discussion.'

'Why not?' Hugo demanded suddenly. 'You talked to them – you could have made it one. You could have asked them anything!'

'I was too busy finding out about the end of mankind,' Will retorted. He wasn't in the mood for one of Hugo's rants right now.

'If I'd been given the chance—' said Hugo, his voice trembling.

Ira interrupted. 'Will,' he said.

Hugo fell silent.

'Yes, sir,' said Will.

'You're convinced of the sincerity of this… alien.'

Will took a deep breath. 'I know it's a lot to swallow, sir, but I don't think they've got any reason to lie.'

'Oh, come on!' John said with a laugh.

'Quiet!' Ira snapped. 'Go on, Will'

Will searched for the words. 'I mean, they've proved they have the power. They made the suntap and the star back there. Who's to say they can't do the rest of it?'

'Did they say anything about how long we have to pass this test?' asked Ira.

'Not that I recall, sir.'

Ira grunted. 'Well, it doesn't matter a great deal anyway. There's nothing we can do till we've found fuel.'

'Captain,' said Rachel, 'if you don't need Will, I could use his help trying to set up a temporary buffer configuration.'

'Fine,' said Ira.

'I'm on it,' said Will, with more than a little relief. Work brought an excuse to escape from the cabin. He gratefully slid his consciousness into the relative sanctuary of the *Ariel*'s metaphor space.

Rachel's avatar met him in the Cold War Era situation room Will had made for the buffer maintenance node. The big display board showed buffer panels instead of continents. Three of them were shining bright red and several more were yellow, which meant they were already taking rads. They'd all need days in the scrubbing tanks if they ever got home.

'I guess we could take some of the intact secondaries and rig them over the damage to the primary sphere,' he suggested. 'It won't work for ever, but it might get us to the next system.'

'Will, forget all that for a minute,' said Rachel. 'Are you all right?'

Will glanced at her avatar. Her eyes were full of urgent appeal. He looked away again, into the glaring board. He'd prefer not to talk about it. But of all the people on the ship, Rachel was the only one whose company he wanted right now, and she deserved an answer.

'Will?' she asked again.

'I'm fine,' he said with a sigh. 'I'm sharing my brain with aliens, but other than that I'm fine, really. The hardest part of it is how everyone's looking at me. But I can't say I blame them.'

'Ignore them,' she said quickly. 'Really. John always laughs at anything that scares him, and Hugo's a genetically overcooked dork.' She shook her head. 'I can't imagine what it must have been like, having your senses stripped away like that.'

Will shrugged. 'I could deal with that. What worried me was being singled out from the whole human race for a job I can't do. I'm no saviour, Rachel. I'm just a roboteer.'

'Bullshit,' she replied. 'You were *never* just a roboteer. There's not many people who could have gone through what you faced and come out sane.'

Will doubted that, though her compliment warmed him. He was sure Hugo would have been thrilled by the experience. He'd have come out with a lifetime supply of scientific discoveries, though he might have neglected to listen to the warnings.

'You're not alone, you know,' said Rachel. 'I want to help if I can.'

Will smiled. 'Thanks.'

'Do you think . . .' She stopped.

'What?'

'Do you think they've left you alone now? Your mind, I mean?'

This was the one question Will had no desire to face. He didn't want to get his hopes up. He buried his virtual head in his hands.

'I don't know,' he mumbled. 'I don't know if I'll ever know again.'

The thought nearly made him laugh. It was so vast and frightening that he couldn't take it seriously. He'd assumed the aliens had finished with him when he woke up back in the tank. Then the location of the uncharted star had appeared in his head. Now he felt certain they hadn't.

'Jeez!' she said. 'What a mind-fuck.' She giggled nervously, as if realising just how apropos her words were.

'There's nothing you or I can do about it,' Will told her bluntly. 'Right now we wouldn't have anywhere to go if it wasn't for the Transcended, so why look a gift horse in the mouth while there are buffers to repair?'

She smiled at him with something like admiration. 'Okay.'

She appeared to think he was being stoic, when he was just desperate for the sanctuary of denial.

'I wish I was in there with you,' she blurted suddenly. 'In your virtual space, I mean. Or anywhere other than this damned cabin.'

A pang of desire struck at the centre of Will's chest. He stared dumbly at her blind avatar. For a moment, neither of them spoke.

'Sorry,' she said at last. 'Buffers.'

Will turned gratefully away towards the desk. His eyes skittered distractedly across it, looking for the icons that represented his buffer maintenance SAPs. It took him a minute to realised they weren't there.

'Where'd my robots go?' he asked.

'Oh, I had to take them offline,' she said. 'They started malfunctioning during the alien soft assault and I haven't been able to fix them yet.'

'Why don't I take a look?' he said.

Rachel unlocked the SAP programs and Will tried them on, one at a time. He could detect no difference in them.

'They feel perfectly fine to me.'

Rachel frowned. 'How come?' She ran through her diagnostics. 'Amazing. I checked them not half an hour before you woke and their awareness cycles were all over the place.'

Will ached inside as he recognised an expression of fading trust on her face.

'Well, there's nothing we can do about that,' he told her stiffly. 'They're working now, and that's what matters.'

Without waiting for her to comment further, he hurled himself into the mind of a buffer-jack and started work.

Will worked on repairs for the next two days as the *Ariel* pushed deeper into unknown space. Amy checked his body for infections from time to time and reported him miraculously cured. The others regarded him warily. They all had plenty of questions about his experiences, particularly Hugo. Unfortunately, Will didn't have any more answers. He found that the tank-time Ira had made him endure on the trip out was fast becoming a habit of his own. It was a refuge from the crew's attention.

Though he hid from them, Will hated the gulf that appeared to have opened afresh between him and his shipmates. Far from proving himself a part of the team, he felt as if he'd become a liability. In his spare time he ran diagnostic programs on himself in the vain hope of ferreting out more alien memories. He reasoned that if he could determine the origin of the foreign thoughts, he could purge them somehow and pronounce himself cured. But his programs revealed nothing. According to his memory logs, he'd known about the star ahead of them since childhood.

Then, as their fuel supplies dipped miserably into the red, their destination presented itself. It was a K-class star, a little elderly but still on its main sequence. Will found it ironic that, in simple physical terms, although they were just a few light-years from Zuni, the location couldn't have felt more remote.

Ira dropped warp outside the system and craned his head out of his bunk to speak with Will.

'Will,' he said sternly. 'I need to know. Should we be coming in on stealth?'

Will shook his head. 'I don't think there's any need.' He wished he knew why. It was hard to advise your captain with only a hunch to go on. 'I'd come in slow, though,' he added randomly.

Ira nodded. 'Slow it is.'

They cruised gently into the system. They'd barely gone further than the Oort cloud before Amy spoke up in a tense voice.

'Ira, I'm getting readings. Massive ones. And they're definitely artificial, not planetesimals.'

'Any signs of an intercept course?' said Ira.

'No. They appear to be in stable orbits – maybe habitats of some kind.'

'Keep your eyes open,' said the captain. 'John, I want you ready with torpedoes and countermeasures, just in case.'

Will had an urge to tell them that defences wouldn't be necessary, but chose not to open his mouth. He had nothing to base his opinions on other than a guess with suspicious origins.

They decelerated in-system and took up an orbit around the star. Ira cut the gravity drive so they could have a proper look around.

'Give me close-ups of those ships,' he said.

'Scanning now,' Amy reported.

Immersed in the *Ariel*'s astrogation node, Will was treated to the best possible view. It took his breath away.

They were surrounded by ruins. Lying all around them in vast profusion were the remains of a civilisation. They were gothic and immense – vast, dark, twisting shapes covered with rows of curving spikes. It was as if titanic brambles had grown wild in space. The *Ariel*, a full kilometre on a side, could have passed easily through one of the holes punctured in their weirdly textured hulls.

Greater than the sense of scale was the mood of the place. It had about it a tremendous sense of melancholy, as if tragedy had been wrought there on a scale too great for human comprehension. Will felt like a child trespassing through a giants' graveyard. And yet, beneath the weight of awe and despair, Will found himself touched by a sense of rightness as keen as a child's excitement.

Yes, said a voice inside him. *This where you are supposed to be.*

'Amy, give me a system profile,' Ira said into the hushed cabin.

Amy cleared her throat and spoke almost in a whisper. 'Four gas giants. Two solid planets, one V-rated, one M. One debris ring. Four hundred and seventeen alien habitats currently detected and counting.'

'Will,' said Ira, 'were these the people who made Ulanu's planet?'

Will was about to tell them he didn't know. But then, with a revolted shudder, he realised he did. He'd found another new memory. It was like discovering a pulsing lump of something foreign under the skin of his mind.

'No,' he said. Admitting the alien knowledge felt like a guilty confession. 'These were the last people to find it,' he explained. 'They were given suntap technology and then wiped out.'

'For being destructive?' asked Rachel.

'Yes,' said Will, surprising himself. It was like making up lies and discovering he had utter confidence in them. 'They controlled dozens of star systems and denuded every one. Left to their own devices, they would have swept through the galaxy. They would have reached Earth.'

The fact alarmed him even as he said it. 'If they'd lived, the human race would never have evolved,' he added in a hushed voice.

'Evolved?' said Amy. 'How old are these things?'

'About ten million years,' said Will awkwardly.

There were gasps from the others.

'To the Transcended, the Earther crusade looks no different from these Fecund,' he told them.

'The Fecund,' Ira echoed. 'Is that the name of these people?'

'I think so.' Like the rest of his explanation, the name had just popped into his head.

'What else do you know about this place?' asked Hugo suspiciously.

'Nothing!' Will replied quickly. Then, less defensively, 'I... I don't know.'

John chuckled to himself on his bunk.

'Ira,' said Amy, 'I've just completed a thermal scan and I can't find a single live energy signature in the whole system. There are plenty of blast sites that might have been caused by containment failure, but there's no actual antimatter.'

Of course there wasn't, Will realised with sudden chilling certainty. There was never going to be. This place had run out of antimatter while humans were still living in the trees. The pit of his stomach fell away. It appeared he'd brought them here to die.

Why? he asked himself. Why had the Transcended let him think they might find fuel here when it couldn't possibly be true? Why had they been brought here at all, if not for that? Simply to be made to understand humanity's fate, and then stand by while it was extinguished?

Will started to consider the things he'd been told in a different light. What if it was all lies, the test and everything? He couldn't be sure he knew what the thing in his head wanted, he realised, or what it intended to do with them.

'Unfortunate,' Ira rumbled. 'Well, people, I'm sure you're aware of the position that leaves us in. If we can't find juice here, we'd better hope that M-type planet is comfy, because there's no going home now. We just wasted what fuel we had left getting here.'

Will cringed at the bitterness in Ira's tone.

John burst into sudden hoots of laughter.

'What's so funny, John?' Rachel demanded.

'This ride!' he replied. 'The aliens fucked us over. Now *there's* a surprise! This has got to be the shittiest mission in the history of spaceflight. We should get a prize or something.'

'Quiet!' Ira snapped. 'I haven't finished.'

John's laughter dulled to suppressed sniggers.

'Amy,' Ira growled, 'check the whole system again. Make sure there's nothing we can use. Make triple sure. Rachel, look for buffer materials. Just because we can't find juice is no reason not to make repairs. There should be plenty of ship parts around here to cannibalise. Assuming they're not too old, and assuming we can tell what the fuck we're looking at. John, find what passes for a computer in this place, if there's anything left after all this time, and trawl it. That could save us a lot of search time. And Hugo, keep your eyes open for weapons. Since we're here, we might as well find out what these aliens could do. If we ever get home, it might win us the war. I want you all to report back to me the moment you find anything,' the captain told them. 'Do you understand me?'

There was a chorus of ayes. Ira fell silent.

Will waited for half an anxious, miserable minute before he opened his mouth. 'Sir, what should I do?'

'I don't know, Will,' Ira replied wearily. He sounded more disappointed than angry. 'Help Rachel. And if any way out of this fucking mess pops into your head, let me know.'

9.2: IRA

While the crew prepped for a robotic survey of the ruins, Ira stared out at the grim panorama of tumbling wreckage, his mind churning. He'd read about what happened on stranded starships. Admittedly the conditions had never been quite this extreme, but a single common factor stood out among all those that survived: morale. If there was one good thing about their situation, it was that Ira suddenly had time on his hands, which meant a chance to address the interpersonal issues he'd let slide since they'd hit Zuni.

'John,' he said, propelling himself out of his bunk, 'meeting room, right now.'

A smirking John slid into the chamber behind him. Ira sealed the hatch.

'What's up, Captain?'

'You,' said Ira. 'With respect, John, your cracks are showing.'

John's face stiffened.

'Ever since we got hacked you've been ratcheting up the laughs. You're not sounding balanced any more.'

John shrugged. 'Should I? They hacked my ship. What do you expect?' He shot Ira a meaningful glance.

They both knew what John's psych report said – *high-functioning sociopath with a strong loyalty complex offsetting severe interpersonal limitations. Level-three obsessive behaviour around security and control themes that is beneficial when suitably motivated.* Ira knew because he'd been briefed. John knew because he'd hacked the senior-officers' database years ago. There was an understanding between them that nobody kept secrets from John for long.

'I need you to put a lid on it,' said Ira. 'I know you can do it.'

John was an excellent officer – a man who literally laughed in the face of death and functioned coolly under the most incredible pressure. The fact that those talents came with certain behavioural consequences was something both he and the Fleet had been happy to overlook. After all, it didn't make him that odd. About thirty per cent of Galateans had a personality disorder of some sort by pre-diaspora standards. John was simply a starker case than most.

'Of course,' said John. 'You can count on me. You know that – Galatea comes first. I'll find another way to manage it, no matter how fucked up this trip gets. But while we're in here...'

Ira waited for him to finish.

John's face twitched. He smoothed his hair. 'We have a *slight* security problem, wouldn't you say? That's what I *thought* you wanted to talk about.'

'Agreed,' said Ira. 'But I don't see a way to fix it right now.'

'That doesn't mean there isn't a way to limit it. It doesn't mean there aren't steps we can take.'

'What do you mean, exactly?'

'Having a hacked ship I can fix,' said John. 'Lying next to a hacked person—'

'I know this isn't easy,' said Ira.

'How am I supposed to clear out the soft core when his fucking head is plugged into it all the time? It's like trying to clear the rat shit out of a ship full of rats without killing the fucking rats.'

Ira sighed. 'Remember, John, he's still your crewmate. It's your job to protect him as well as everyone else.'

'Sure. But that fucking alien is using him for cover, which makes him a human shield,' said John. 'And the Galatean Fleet has a policy on human shields.'

Ira was about to reply, but a ping from Amy sounded first. He touched the comm. 'What is it?'

'The robots are away,' said Amy. 'I think you're going to want to see this.'

'We'll pick this up later,' he told John as he slid back through the hatch. 'And thank you for listening. I mean it.'

With reluctance, Ira swung back into his bunk and pushed his visor on. His sense of claustrophobia returned as his field of vision filled with the view from the lead robot. The vast thicket of alien tatters lay straight ahead and a sense of wrongness at stepping into this awful graveyard gripped him like a palpable force. There was no room in his heart for excitement or curiosity. While he rifled through the ruins of another civilisation's dead, the Earthers were mobilising to invade his home world and turn it into a copy of the lifeless disaster that lay before him.

'Gah!' Amy exclaimed. 'I can't find anything that looks like an actual ship in this mess! There's nothing with a proper exohull, or even brollies.'

'There,' said Will, and dropped a marker into the display field. 'That's one.'

Ira zoomed in for a better view. It looked like the bud of some exotic flower floating in space. Delicate ferns of lacy, branching material arced forwards from a rounded base to surround a rust-red bulb. He could see no feature that made it look remotely like a ship. Ira's concern that his roboteer was no longer completely human increased another notch.

As the robots neared the alien vessel – if that's what it was – the sheer scale of it became clear. It was over two hundred kilometres long. What had looked like delicate fronds from a distance were in fact huge arcing towers of metal large enough to contain entire human cities. The red core hung before them like a world. The whole thing was surrounded by a halo of sparkling dust.

'My God,' Amy muttered.

Ira was awed, too, despite himself. They were the first human beings ever to lay eyes on such a thing.

As they came closer still, Ira made out features that might have been sensors and ports clustered in cryptic patterns on the core's surface. There were impact craters, too – thousands of them – and great, gaping rents, whether from collisions or warfare, Ira couldn't tell.

'Hugo,' he muttered, 'why don't you take your drone squad off and explore the surface for weapons?'

'I'll go with him,' said Amy. 'I want to have a closer look at that cratering.'

Hugo and Amy guided a third of the robotic fleet off across the rusty landscape while Will guided the remainder towards the closest hole in the hull and through it into a huge, dark interior space with twisted cables looping across it. Their robots' searchlights illuminated countless bits of drifting stuff like dirty snow. It was so thick they could barely see the walls.

'Not much shielding,' John observed as he examined the hull behind them.

Will cycled through scan filters till a regular arrangement of tunnel openings appeared out of the grubby haze.

'Will, any idea of the layout of this ship?' Ira asked.

'No. Sorry, Captain.'

Ira could hear the frustration in the young man's voice. He must be tired of people asking him questions about the aliens that he couldn't answer. But under the circumstances, he was just going to have to deal with it.

'Fine,' said Ira. 'Then let's head towards where the habitat core would be in a human ship. Want to lead the way, Rachel?'

Rachel chose a tunnel near the centre of the far wall. 'Let's try that direction,' she suggested, pointing with a data marker.

Will took them gently forwards into a long, curving passageway with rippled sides like the gullet of some prehistoric fish. They stopped shortly after, when they found something resembling a scorpion with a peculiar fanned tail hanging dead and blocking the way in front of them. It had shiny brown body-segments and was missing several of its legs. Fibres trailed out where the limbs had snapped off. Instead of pincers, it had something like armoured hands.

'Is that... one of them?' Rachel asked in a hushed voice.

'No,' said Will. 'That's a robot.'

Ira heard no doubt in his voice.

As they pushed nearer, it became more obvious that the scorpion-thing was artificial. On closer examination, it looked quite primitive. A triangle of lidless cameras passed for eyes. Its body was clad in bald plastic plates and there was no sign of anything like tact-fur. Humans hadn't built anything that clunky since the Martian Renaissance. Strange, Ira thought. As they passed the ancient robot, the exhaust from their thrusters sent it spiralling gently towards the wall. More limbs snapped off as it brushed past. Time must have rendered the thing as brittle as glass. Soon they exited the tunnel into a place filled with crazy interlacing metal rings that passed for a mesohull. Beneath it were more tunnels.

Ira found himself fascinated by the similarities and differences between his own ship and this one. Clearly, there were certain features all starships needed, and these Ira could just about recognise. But in other places, the engineering was bewilderingly different.

Eventually, they found their way to a sealed module that Rachel thought might be a habitat. It was at least fifty metres wide and held in place by great pistons. Its surface was clad in something like Casimir-buffers, except instead of panels, the material was laid in curved sections like strips of muscle, and fed by power cables that coiled like springs. Once, the buffers had been covered with something shiny. Now it was coming off in flakes.

'This is it,' Rachel exclaimed. 'We need to get some of those strips back to the ship to experiment on.'

Will sent a couple of small waldobots down to see if they could prise some off.

Ira watched the proceedings quietly. He wasn't sure he liked cannibalising this ancient ship. It felt vaguely sacrilegious.

'Ira, I've had a look at the hull,' said Amy. 'It appears to confirm

Will's story – everything here is about ten million years old. It looks as if the ship was hit by some kind of massive solar-flare activity. It was literally scoured clean.' She sent him pictures of the pocked surface and spectrographic scans of the samples she'd taken.

'A *flare* did all this?' said Ira. 'It had to be a pretty big one.'

'I'd say so,' she replied. 'That star down there must have sloughed its skin like a snake. Probably took a billion years off its lifespan.'

'I'm going to follow these wiring bundles,' said John. His marker pointed to cables like the tentacles of a mighty squid curling away around the surface of the module. 'They might be data links. And if they are, they might lead to an access tube.'

'Great,' said Ira. He was glad to hear John making a constructive and unironic contribution. Apparently he'd taken their talk to heart.

He returned his attention to Will and Rachel's work. A long piece of buffer was slowly peeling away from the ceramic surface underneath like sticky spaghetti. It ripped, leaving one robot holding a trailing end.

'Damn!' said Will. 'Sorry.'

'It doesn't matter,' Rachel told him. 'We'll have to reshape it anyway. It's the raw materials that count.'

Ira watched the robots painstakingly gather material to bring back to the *Ariel* until John claimed his attention again.

'Captain, I think I've found a way in.'

Ira flicked over to the view from John's lead robot. It was of an airlock, if a fairly basic-looking one. The whole ship was a weird mixture of styles, he mused – some high-tech, some clumsy. Who knew, maybe human ships would look the same way to an alien.

With a little help from Will, John's robots forced the airlock open. Ira half-expected atmosphere to start screaming out, but nothing happened. The habitat must have long since been violated. They yanked back the door and peered inside. Their searchlights revealed nothing but a blizzard of floating crap. Will took the robots slowly in.

The module was huge by human standards. Instead of being divided into rooms, it was one great open space filled with ladders of something like silk that tore as they passed through it. And everywhere was the obscuring mass of dirty snow.

'What *is* all this stuff?' Ira muttered in annoyance.

'I think it's what it looks like,' said Amy. 'Water ice.'

'What did they do in here, *swim*?'

'Maybe,' she replied. 'It's entirely possible that this race was amphibious.'

Then they bumped up against their first corpse. Everyone aboard the *Ariel* jumped in unison.

'Nice,' said John smoothly. 'I love a good surprise.'

'Will,' said Ira, shaken, 'get some waldobots over here and let's take a proper look at this thing.'

Will stabilised the spinning body so that the rest of them could see it properly. It was a beaked, quadrupedal creature about the size of a large dog, with hands on the ends of each of its four limbs and leathery grey skin covered with short spines. Its eyes were on little turrets. The fingers were webbed and looked highly dextrous.

'Amazing,' said Amy excitedly. 'An actual alien. Will, give me a hand, would you? I want to take some samples.'

Ira and the others spread the remaining robots out. Over the next half-hour, they found dozens of frozen corpses, large and small. Though the aliens' body plan remained the same, they varied in size from monkey to hippopotamus.

Ira's greatest surprise came when they reached what must have once been the bottom of the habitat. A huge, blunt-faced Fecund with a beak like an industrial shovel was curled up there like a gigantic baby, glued in place by hundreds of strands of silky web. Tiny aliens nestled all around it.

'Hey, everybody,' John called. 'Check this out.'

He drew their attention to a square section of the ribbed grey wall of the module that was covered with what looked like archaic switchboard controls.

'When we followed those links in, I thought I'd find some sort of computer core,' John explained, 'but there's nothing here, just a load of cut-out switches and dials with some lame-ass circuitry behind them. That's no way to run a starship. What do you suppose they did, twiddle their way from place to place?'

'The soft control over this ship must have been run from somewhere else,' Rachel suggested.

'I agree,' said Ira.

'I've dated the first corpse we found,' Amy interjected. 'It died at the same time as the ship. The solar radiation fried it.'

'Radiation?' said Rachel. 'But what about all those buffers? It would have been protected, surely.'

'All I can say is they must have been turned off before the blast hit,' Amy replied.

'But that's crazy!' Rachel insisted. 'Who turns off the buffers in a live starship?'

'Maybe they didn't turn them off by choice,' said Ira. 'We've already seen what the Transcended did to our ship. If they had a hand in this, what was to stop them from powering the ships down through a soft assault?'

'I don't buy it,' said Rachel. 'If the Transcended had that much hands-on power in this place, why didn't they just shut off everyone's life support?'

'No idea,' replied Ira. 'But I think we've found enough to be going on with for the time being. Let's get these samples out of here and back to the *Ariel* for proper processing. That might give us some of the answers we're looking for.'

He chose not to mention the fact that studying this extraterrestrial morgue was also giving him the creeps.

They'd started gathering bodies to take back when suddenly Hugo shouted from the bottom bunk. 'Captain!'

It was the first they'd heard from him since they'd come inside. The discovery of aliens didn't appear to have interested him in the least.

'What is it?' said Ira.

'I've found what I think are suntap weapons like the ones the Earthers are using, but on a much larger scale. Amazingly, they're in excellent condition! With one or two spare parts from the *Ariel*, I think I could probably get them working.'

He sounded immensely pleased with himself. Ira was less impressed. Relatively speaking, the whole ship was in excellent condition, given how long it had been floating here.

'Extraordinary,' he said unenthusiastically.

His appetite for control of the suntap had been thoroughly

quashed by what he'd seen here already, but he knew he'd be a fool to pass up the opportunity to learn more about the technology. In the event that the Earthers managed to track them here, they'd need to mount some kind of defence. They couldn't flee, and their chances of perpetrating a successful soft assault against the Earthers were at an all-time low. And besides, anything that kept the scientist feeling positive and engaged had to be worth the investment.

'Captain, this is a unique opportunity,' Hugo urged. 'We have to try!'

'Will,' said Ira, 'if we use a suntap here, are we going to incur the wrath of these Transcended of yours? Having seen the consequences, I've no desire to face down one of their solar shock waves.'

'I'm not sure, Captain,' Will replied. 'I don't think so. I think it's more likely that we've been brought here to make use of this technology to win the war.'

Ira wasn't convinced. If that were true, the Transcended would have shown them where to find antimatter. He was just going to have to take a chance.

'All right, Hugo,' he said. 'Fix up a weapon.'

Why not? Ira thought. While they were here, they might as well get on with the research that Fleet sent them out here to do. Without it, they were never likely to stand up to Ulanu's armada. Even knowing that, Ira had the uneasy feeling that he'd just made a deal with the devil.

9.3: WILL

A week into their involuntary stay in the Fecund system, Ira called a crew meeting. Will dragged himself reluctantly after the others to the upper chamber. The prospect of discussing their plight did not appeal, particularly given the mood in the cabin recently. The leaden sense of impotence hanging over them grew heavier with every day they spent in this dead place.

'The repairs are going well,' said Rachel. 'Will has helped me build a polymer substrate on which we can lay the Fecund composites.

We're lucky – about seventy-five per cent of the material has retained its picopore matrix. It's not perfect, but it should see us home.'

She was trying to put a brave face on it. There was still no antimatter. Going home was a fantasy.

'John,' said Ira.

John gave them all a winning, action-hero grin. 'Well, I'm no closer to finding one of those bastards' computers than I was when we turned up,' he admitted. 'The truth is, their IT is crap for the most part. Their wiring is awful and their comms are out of the Dark Ages. If it weren't for the fact they've got robots and wireless ports running through the whole damn ship, I'd think they never built a single processor.'

Will happened to know that John hadn't been looking very hard. After they'd discovered the dead aliens on that first day, his curiosity appeared to have fallen off sharply. Now he spent most of his time scouring the *Ariel*'s systems for signs of the alien code that had hacked his precious defences. As far as Will knew, he'd found nothing.

'I can tell you what I *have* learned, though,' said John, 'which is that there are a whole bunch of habitat cores dotted through that ship instead of just one. They had more crew than they could have possibly used. They were mad for multiple redundancy. As far as I can tell, this ship was designed to have the shit kicked out of it and still keep fighting. Which is weird, because it's got no exohull to speak of. I'm going to look at the base of those fern-things next – there's a bunch of complicated tunnels under them that we haven't explored yet.'

Ira nodded. 'Good. Hugo?'

Hugo steepled his fingers in front of his mouth for a moment and scowled. For a man with the galaxy's biggest scientific toy-box to play with, he'd been surprisingly testy over the last few days.

'The first prototype suntap is ready for testing,' he muttered. He met no one's eyes.

Ira tried for enthusiasm. 'That's great. You want to tell us how it works? After all, that's what we came here to learn.'

Hugo glanced sceptically at him. It wasn't often he was asked to volunteer an explanation these days. It was clear to Will, and no doubt to Hugo, too, that Ira was trying to draw him out.

Hugo's interaction with the crew had taken only one form this last week: picking on Will. Every time the physicist faced another frustration in his work, the first thing he did was ask Will for the answer. Except it wasn't so much asking as demanding, as if it was Will's fault that Hugo didn't understand what he was looking at.

For a few seconds, Hugo said nothing. When no one else spoke, he began. 'The principle of the thing is simple enough,' he said. 'A beam of entangled high-energy electrons is fired into the sun and energy is teleported out through them.'

'What do you mean?' said Rachel. 'You can't draw energy from quantum teleportation.'

'Clearly you *can*,' Hugo snapped.

Will saw Ira shoot him a warning glance. Hugo continued more calmly.

'There is a chamber in the device in which a field is established. The field is a kind of microgravitic agitation pattern that uses a similar principle to warp, but far subtler. The other halves of the electron pairs are held within it and forced into a state under which… their entanglement cannot collapse.' He said the words in a rush, as if he really wasn't happy with the idea, then carried on quickly. 'Radiation pressure on the electrons in the star forces energy into the trap through the electron bridge, which is collected with ordinary photoreceptors. Simple enough, as I said.'

Rachel folded her arms and stared at him. 'I don't get it. How does this field operate?'

'How do you expect me to answer?' Hugo demanded suddenly. 'My research is incomplete and there is no explanation provided in the blueprint.'

Rachel wasn't impressed. 'Then reverse-engineer the components that create the field,' she suggested.

'I did!' Hugo shouted.

Will felt little sympathy for the man. He contemplated saying something.

Ira beat him to it. 'And?'

Hugo turned sullen again. 'There's nothing there.'

The captain eyed him. 'What do you mean, "there's nothing there"?'

Hugo exhaled hard. 'I mean there's no system to control the gravitic generators.'

'There must be,' Rachel insisted. 'You're just not looking in the right place.'

Hugo glared at her with furious, pain-filled eyes and bunched his fists.

'Enough!' said Ira. 'Hugo, move on. Do you have anything else to tell us?'

Hugo blinked and returned his gaze to the chamber floor. 'Yes. The device has limitations. The electron beam needs time to reach whatever sun it is aimed at, which means it is impractical for deep-space conflicts.'

Ira's beaked face broke into an unforced smile. 'Excellent! That's our answer. Force out-system engagement on the enemy.'

'Furthermore,' said Hugo, 'the gravitic field is highly sensitive both to warp and conventional acceleration due to the ripple effect.'

Ira pounded his fist into his hand. 'That's why those drones chasing us stopped firing the moment they engaged warp. It's another weakness we can exploit – make them keep moving and they'll never be able to bring their taps online. Well done, Hugo. If we ever get out of here, your work may have saved us the war.'

Ira turned to Amy, but Hugo spoke again.

'There is more.'

Ira glanced back to him, one eyebrow raised.

'I have found other weapons with the... hallmark of Transcended *gifts*, if they can be called that,' said Hugo. 'One appears to be a large-scale coherent-matter cannon. As far as I can tell, a similar trick to that employed in the suntap is used to keep superheated iron plasma in condensate form. It can then be accelerated to near-light speeds and fired like a laser. However, the damage to these devices is too extreme. Without another blueprint from the Transcended, we lack the means to make them operable.' He looked meaningfully at Will. 'Will you supply such a blueprint?'

Will bristled. 'I can't,' he said.

Hugo's nostrils flared. 'Can't, or won't?'

'Concentrate on the suntaps, Hugo,' Ira told him. 'That should be all we need. If we survive the war, we can always come back here.'

Hugo met this suggestion with a sour face but Ira had turned again to Amy.

'I have made one other discovery,' Hugo added quickly.

Ira regarded him levelly. 'Really.'

'The hull of the Fecund vessel is lined with Transcended-type projectors of some sort. The projectors are routed directly into the exohull, which is made of an iron-based alloy. I can determine no purpose or value for the alloy. It doesn't appear to have been designed for structural strength or even field conductivity. Can you tell me what it does, Will?' He fixed Will with another piercing stare.

'No,' Will replied coldly. 'No idea. Sorry.'

Hugo turned his attention back to the captain. 'Sir, if the roboteer won't tell us what we need to know, I recommend that we relocate to the outer solar system where the damage to the remains is no doubt a lot less.'

Will shook his head in disbelief.

'Let's avoid accusations,' said Ira. He sounded tired. 'We'll stay put for the time being. If we can't meet our other objectives, you'll have the rest of your life to explore. Now, Amy, what have you got to tell us?'

Amy had been watching this interaction with a pensive face. She struggled for brightness.

'I've been looking at some of the corpses we found,' she said enthusiastically. 'It's more fun than you'd think, and the aliens were surprisingly like us in many ways. Organs in slightly wacky places and nerves made out of some kind of biopolymer, but otherwise more normal than I'd have guessed: carbon-based, cells with nuclei and all that. The tissue damage is extreme, of course, but there's enough material to build a composite picture. Their DNA-analogue appears to hold six different kinds of amino acid, for instance, none of them the ones used by life on Earth. It's a biologist's goldmine.'

She glanced around at the others as if trying to conjure excitement, then deflated a little. 'On a more practical note, I've been looking at the other alien ruins,' she added, 'and I've found something surprising there, too. Not everyone died at once. It looks like some of these ships arrived later, and their crews starved instead of being roasted.'

'Great!' said John. 'At least we're not the only ones.'

Ira glared him into silence.

Amy gave a brittle smile and carried on. 'It looks as if something prevented them from leaving. My guess is that their ships stopped working. Given that the Transcended can apparently alter a star, maybe they can also place it in a state in which suntaps won't work. From what Hugo just said, it sounds like the Fecund were pretty dependent on borrowed technology. They would have been crippled without it.' She shrugged tightly. 'That's it. Not much to report, I'm afraid.'

'Well,' said Ira, 'the bad news, ladies and gentlemen, is that there's no antimatter here. Amy and I have scoured the system. What's more, we can't find evidence of any of the juice-production methods we recognise. We even checked out the sites that looked like containment-failure cases. There's not much left, as you'd expect, and the remains don't tell us anything. The damage could equally have been caused by some kind of weapons fire.

'But don't worry, people,' he added rousingly. 'This is far from the end of the road. We haven't even started investigating Hugo's idea of a suntap-powered juice-factory yet, on the grounds that we've not known what to look for. There might well still be something we can use lying around in all this junk.'

'Assuming they even used antimatter,' Hugo put in.

Ira ignored him. 'Will,' he said. 'You got anything? Had any more realisations about this place?'

All faces turned to Will. Will folded his arms.

'No,' he admitted. 'Another puzzle appeared in my private node, as I already told you, but this one's harder than the last one.'

The puzzle had appeared three days before. It was another SAP, hanging there in the middle of his mental space one day when he woke up – a cold reminder of the fact that his mind was still not his own.

'I can't get any of my adapters to fit it,' he explained, 'so the senses are still unreadable. I have this feeling that the answer to the puzzle is somewhere in the ruins.' He paused. 'I still think I'm supposed to go and look in person.'

The puzzle had arrived with a strong sense that it was connected in some way to the Fecund ships, or something in them. Will had sent robots out in every direction to see if the data from them would trigger another alien memory, but nothing happened. The SAP senses he explored through were all too flat, too remote. The answer to this puzzle was something he needed to *feel*.

Ira's face was grave. 'I told you, Will – no way.'

Will clenched his teeth. That was the answer he had expected. He'd asked Ira if he could leave the ship two days before, when he'd first realised how hard the puzzle was going to be. Ira wasn't enthusiastic then and he was no keener now. Will hadn't exactly received a wealth of trust from the crew since his experience.

'Okay, Captain,' he said calmly. He knew better than to ask why. The captain already sounded weary of the subject.

'Anything else?' said Ira.

Will shook his head. Everyone knew exactly what he'd been doing anyway. When he wasn't helping Rachel with repairs, Amy and John had been conducting tests on his brain. Funny how that hadn't turned up as a topic for discussion. He'd been unconscious in the tank while it happened, of course, but their activity logs were in the ship's database for everyone to see.

'Mr Monet, may I ask you why you think the answer is out there among the ruins?' Hugo asked with mock-levity.

Will gave him a hateful look. 'A hunch, that's all.'

'I see,' said Hugo. 'A hunch. Captain, why do we have to tolerate this? It's obvious that the roboteer knows more about this place than he's telling us. Ever since we arrived he's been drip-feeding us information, yet whenever we ask him anything direct, he pleads ignorance. Well, I've heard this excuse too many times. It's gone beyond the point of believability.'

The spring in Will's insides coiled tighter. It was out in the open at last: the accusation that he was lying. He stared hard at Hugo.

'What are you saying?' he demanded. 'That I'm being controlled by an alien?'

'Far from it,' Hugo replied sharply. 'You showed your colours the day you deliberately routed the alien feed through to your private console. You've been holding information back from us ever since.'

'Gentlemen, please,' said Ira, but Will was already too angry to stop.

'*I* routed the feed?' he said incredulously.

'I don't see how you can deny it,' said Hugo. 'Your command signature was on the routing order. Did you think I wouldn't notice?'

'How about the fact that the alien had already taken my signature by then, fuckhead?' Will snarled back.

'*Enough*,' snarled the captain.

'Don't make me laugh, Mr Monet,' Hugo sneered. 'What possible reason would an alien intelligence have for communicating with *you* when there were better qualified minds on board?'

'Perhaps because it considered me more advanced than you, Hugo,' Will retorted. 'How come you can't comprehend that? That someone much smarter than you considers me a higher form of life than you are?'

Hugo's pasty features distorted into an ugly mask. He pointed a quavering finger at Will's face. 'Listen to him!' he hissed to the others. 'Have you ever heard such hubris? He might as well have proclaimed his guilt outright! Captain, as the senior scientific advisor for this mission, I recommend that we place the roboteer in restraints pending disciplinary action of the most severe order.'

It was too much.

'I'm sorry, Captain,' said Will, 'but I can't listen to any more of this shit.'

Will somersaulted and pushed off towards the door hatch, but Hugo grabbed his ankle while the door was sliding open.

'Oh no you don't!' said the scientist, his voice heavy with self-righteous anger.

Will had to bend upwards to prise Hugo's fingers off his leg.

'Let go of me,' Will warned.

'That's it!' Ira roared.

Hugo scrabbled for a grip but Will pushed him away. Hugo managed to grab Will's wrist and started lashing out at him with his free hand. He hit Will on the ear.

'Tell us the truth!' he shouted.

Will wasn't going to float around being mauled by an asshole physicist. He drew back his arm to punch Hugo's bloated face.

The next thing he knew, his arm had been seized. He turned to see John's grinning face.

'Sorry, guys,' said John cheerily. 'No nerd-fights allowed.'

John dragged Will away from Hugo with practised ease and shoved him hard to the far side of the chamber. Will bounced off the padding and massaged his wrist. Then he turned again and aimed for the open door.

'Stay right where you are, Mr Monet!' Ira boomed. 'Amy, please take our *passenger* outside for a moment while he calms the fuck down.'

'Aye, Captain,' said Amy.

It was at that point Will noticed that the first officer had to remove a restraining hand from Rachel in order to move.

John, meanwhile, had effortlessly grabbed a startled Hugo by his shoulders. He flipped the scientist in the air and threw him through the hatch head first like a missile.

'Score!' he said gleefully.

Amy followed quickly. The hatch snicked shut behind her.

As soon it was sealed, Ira rounded on Will and gave him a g-ray glare. 'What the *hell* did you think you were doing leaving a crew meeting without being dismissed?'

'Sorry, Captain,' Will replied curtly. 'I'd just had enough, that's all.'

'What kind of excuse is that?' said Ira. 'Do you think the rest of us haven't? Do you honestly believe that anyone else here likes this situation any more than you do?'

Will looked away.

'Feeling sorry for yourself, Monet? Well, snap out of it! There's no room on this ship for self-pity. It's too fucking small. You are crew. Hugo is not. Crew means being a professional all the time, waking or sleeping. In case you hadn't noticed, everyone aboard this ship is difficult to get along with, yourself included. Our *job* is to suck it up and stay alive. If you don't like what's happened to you, then I expect you to do something about it instead of whining.'

'Then let me, sir!' Will shouted back. 'Let me look at the ruins, because it's the only clue I have. And let's face it – without more help, we're screwed.'

Ira stared at him icily for a moment and then blinked slowly. He clearly didn't like the fact that Will had talked back to him, but some part of him must have seen the sense in it, because he didn't explode.

'Okay,' the captain said. 'Fair point.'

John folded his arms and grimaced.

'But not alone,' said Ira. 'I need a volunteer.'

'I'll go,' Rachel said quickly.

Will looked at her. She gave him a proud smile and then returned her attention to the captain.

'Fine,' Ira rumbled. 'But you'll both finish those repairs before you go.'

'Of course,' Rachel told him, then looked earnestly back at Will.

Will exhaled. He felt exhausted and angry, but somewhere deep inside him, a new spark of hope had kindled.

'Okay,' he said. 'Let's do it.'

9.4: IRA

With the meeting over, Ira ushered the others out and called for Hugo. He drummed his fingers on the wall while he waited and tried to figure out where he'd gone wrong. Clearly the disastrous meeting had been his fault. He should have come down hard on both of them long before things got so out of hand. If only he wasn't so tired. A powerful sense of failure at ending up in this hideous mess had robbed him of his ability to rest. He hadn't slept properly since they'd arrived. Every time he shut his eyes, visions of Galatea burning came unbidden to his mind. He needed to get a grip on his crew, and fast.

Hugo floated in with a wounded but defiant look on his face. Ira shut the door behind him.

'Captain,' Hugo started, 'I'm well aware that you're displeased, but frankly, I'm not sure you understand—'

Ira cut him off with a slice of his hand. 'I get it,' he said quietly.

'You think Will's been holding out on us. You reckon he's got something to prove and that he can't be trusted. He's unbalanced because he's a roboteer and they're all like that. You're worried that the fate of the human race hangs in the balance because we're indulging a single ill-informed individual.'

If Hugo had noticed any irony in Ira's words, it didn't show on his face. It never ceased to amaze Ira how dim the incredibly brilliant could be.

'Not quite,' said Hugo awkwardly. He looked surprised that Ira was giving him room to speak. 'There are actually two options. Either Will routed the feed himself, or the aliens were purposefully looking for a pliant host. In either case, duplicity is at work and we should not accept the status quo. It's your duty, Captain—'

'Don't tell me what my duty is. I just want to make sure we understand each other. You think the answers we need are right in front of us, and we only need to get Will to talk – is that correct?'

Hugo nodded. 'Or at least, if we don't explore that option—'

'I disagree,' said Ira. 'I disagree because, as captain, it's my job to trust my crew unless there's a damned good reason not to. And so far, though I hate every part of it, Will's story holds up.'

'How can you say that?' Hugo started. 'His remarks—'

'Shut up,' said Ira. 'I've heard your opinion of his remarks. You don't need to repeat them. Here's how it's going to be. From this moment on, every concern that arises, every quibble, every disagreement you have with our actions, you bring them straight to me. In private. And then you do *nothing* unless I give you the green light. I don't care how righteous or conflicted you feel, or how disappointed you are about what I choose to do. You suck it up like the professional you claim to be and let me make the decisions. And if you don't do that, the consequences will be very simple. I will destroy you. If we ever make it out of here alive, I will see you up in front of a Fleet court for jeopardizing the war effort and you will spend the rest of your life in a terraforming camp digging holes in the sand and drinking your own recycled piss.'

Hugo's eyes grew wide enough to fill half his face.

'Do you understand me?' said Ira softly.

As Hugo opened his mouth to speak, another crease of anger flashed across his brow. 'Captain—'

Ira held up a warning finger. 'Careful,' he said. 'Yes or no.'

Tears welled in the corners of Hugo's eyes as he struggled not to argue his case. 'Yes,' he croaked at last.

'Great,' said Ira, before the man could start up again. 'I'm proud of you. I'm glad you're on board because I *need* you on this team. You're a terrific asset, Hugo – a brilliant man. And we stand a much better chance with you than without you. That's all.'

He opened the door and pointed the way for Hugo to leave. Hugo had started shaking, he noticed, whether from anger, fear or disappointment, Ira couldn't tell. He dearly hoped he'd done the right thing. Men like Hugo were notoriously brittle.

As the scientist slid past, arms clenched tightly to his chest, Ira saw John waiting at the hatch.

'A quick word?' he said brightly. The light smile on John's face belied the urgent look his eyes.

'Sure,' said Ira. 'Why not?' He tried to think of a time in his career when he'd had to mentor his crew so much just to hold things together. There wasn't one.

John closed the hatch and fixed him with a curious, lopsided smile. 'Sorry,' he said, 'but I had to grab the moment. We're overdue for our follow-up chat.'

Ira nodded. 'You're right.' In truth, he'd been avoiding it. John's tone in the last meeting hadn't impressed him. He'd been hoping that his security officer would unwind on his own.

'Not a problem,' said John. 'We've all been busy. This time I won't beat about the bush. Will Kuno-Monet is compromised.'

'I know that, John,' said Ira sadly. He rubbed his eyes.

'Which means he's a potential threat not only to this ship, but, if we get back to civilisation, to every single person he comes in contact with. If that *thing* inside him starts making viruses again—'

'I think it's a little early to be talking about threats, don't you?'

John made a little huffing sound. 'Sorry, Captain, I said *potential* threats, not *threats*. I'm not proposing specific action here. That's not my job. I'm just reminding you that Fleet regs have a recommended protocol for scenarios involving a compromised roboteer.'

Unfortunately, John was right. Ira had tried not to think about it since Will came out of his trance. If Ira judged Will to be a danger to his mission or his crew, Fleet procedure required that they either had to coma him or kill him.

'I think you'd better break out the handler's shock key, don't you, Captain?' said John. 'Just in case.'

The shock key was the software code Ira could use to shut Will down via a neural blast to his interface. It was intended for emergencies and supposed to be harmless, but one time in ten it caused brain damage. The entire procedure and the key that went with it were, in Ira's opinion, hideous anachronisms. They dated from the early days of roboteers when they'd been practically autistic. Ships had required safety features like the shock key to handle screaming tantrums, not to shut down functional adults like Will.

Ira's mouth pressed into a thin line. The moment Will became a member of his crew, he'd come under Ira's protection, and Ira wasn't going to give him up any time soon. He wondered if Will understood. In their haste to pull data from Ulanu's network, Ira had put Will in jeopardy, something he'd sworn to himself he'd never do. Letting Will leave the ship broke that oath a second time. It was only when it looked like that policy was doing more harm than good that Ira had been prepared to relent. He would have preferred to keep Will safely in his muscle-tank for the rest of the mission.

'Point taken,' he said. 'I'll bear it in mind.'

'Glad to hear it,' said John, 'because here's my professional assessment, just so you know where I'm coming from.' He held up a hand to mark off his points. 'One: we have an alien aboard, alignment and objectives unknown. Two: this alien has made threats. Three: this alien has already engaged in at least one aggressive act. Four: the alien has manifested a biohazard threat to human life. Five: this alien has gone *way* out of its way to intimidate us with its supposed firepower. Six: this alien has deliberately resisted our attempts to remove its influence from this ship in a way that frankly pisses me off. Now, I like Will's story about as much as everyone else, but it looks pretty clear to me that whatever this alien's goal is, it's not the same as ours. It's not about which theory we like best, Captain.

In war it's always about the set of things that *might* be true. You know that.'

'I hear you, John,' said Ira. 'You've made your case. I'll activate the key.'

John's shoulders slumped in relief. 'Thank you,' he said.

Ira smiled. In truth, he had no intention of touching the key. As soon as he activated it, it would be wired into the rest of the ship's network, making it trivially straightforward for John to co-opt if he ever became frustrated or scared enough to disobey orders. That John could break through the key's security protocols was something Ira didn't doubt for an instant. But it had been clear that unless John received some kind of reassurance, he wasn't going to relax. Ira was gambling that by the time that John figured out what he'd done, it wouldn't matter. Ira didn't abandon his own people – not for anyone. He dearly hoped his loyalty wouldn't have fatal consequences for them all.

10: HANDS ON

10.1: WILL

Will stared out at the immense tangles of cracked tubing as they weaved their way between the Fecund habitats. Through them, he could make out the alien starship that had been the focus of their investigations. He'd never seen anything so pretty look quite so menacing.

'You brought me here,' he muttered to the thing in his head. 'Now you can damn well explain what it is you wanted me to see.'

'What was that?' Rachel asked from the seat behind him.

'Nothing,' said Will. 'Talking to my demons, that's all.'

'They say anything?' she asked, not quite carelessly. Will wished there was some way he could put her fears to rest. But he'd probably have to start with his own.

'Not yet,' he said.

He strained around in his seat to try to give her a confident smile. It wasn't easy – the cramped shuttle didn't leave much room for maneouevre, and the seats were a tight fit even without the pressure suits they were wearing now.

The shuttle was designed for short trips outside the *Ariel*. It had four seats arranged in single file, and Will and Rachel were in the front two. It was meant to be used when all the starship's gravity devices were safely off, but even so, it needed to be extensively radiation shielded. Thus its interior was cramped, and the only view they had of the proceedings was fed to them from external cameras.

Will watched as they passed between the arcing fronds that curled around the starship's core and sidled up to the blank, rusty face of the hull beyond. They anchored the shuttle against the exohull and crawled along the access tube to the small airlock.

Will found himself floating there looking at Rachel as the air cycled out of the chamber. She gazed back at him, her mouth set in an expression of easy confidence, but her eyes said otherwise.

'Here goes nothing,' she quipped cheerily.

The outer door slid open and Will got his first look at the universe through his own eyes in over a month. And what a view it was. Around him on all sides lay the featureless brown horizon of the hull. In the direction that his brain immediately wanted to call *up*, there arced the silver-black branches of the frond structures, like a canopy of monster trees that glittered in the harsh starlight. Above them was a sky full of floating stuff, like clouds from some heavy-metal hell – gunmetal clouds with thorns.

Below his feet, where ground should have been, was the hole they'd be exploring – a huge black chasm large enough to drop a small apartment building through. It had looked big through robot eyes, but not this big.

'That's some view,' said Rachel breathlessly.

Their robot chauffeur slid up beneath them. Will had arranged for one of their escort machines to give them a lift into the ruin's interior. It was a standard free-space waldobot, a dozen metres long with a pair of fuzzy giant's hands on the end of powerful articulated arms.

Part of the reason for the scale-shock was that Will was used to looking through waldobot eyes and judging the hands to be the same size as his own. In reality, the robot could squash his head between its thumb and forefinger analogues without noticing.

Despite knowing that everything inside the ruined ship had been dead for aeons, Will was glad to have the waldobot along. He and Rachel clipped their suits to the maintenance rings on its back.

'You ready?' he asked.

She exhaled hard. 'As I'll ever be.'

The robot tilted ninety degrees so that it was pointing down into the hole and then turned on its searchlights. Bottomless, shadowy depths filled with twinkling snow revealed themselves. Will urged the robot on. They descended into the dark.

Without the sense of detachment afforded by robot senses, the ship's tunnels looked sinister. The whole place was a mess of long, snaking corridors and junctions that prevented the mind from imposing any kind of orientation. The dead, grey ribbing on the walls had an unpleasantly organic appearance.

After a while, Will realised that without the software map running in his sensorium, he wouldn't have a clue where they were or how to get back. They'd be lost for ever in this maze of plastic gullets.

'Any idea where we're going?' Rachel asked him eventually.

'I have a place I want to start,' said Will. 'While I was reviewing John's search attempts, I found somewhere that gave me a funny feeling. I took some robots there to check it out, but that was all I got – a feeling. I'm hoping that being there in person will make a difference.'

'This whole place gives me a funny feeling,' Rachel muttered back.

Will's starting point was at the blunt end of the bulb shape, near where the stems of the outer fronds attached. It was a long, twisting ride away, through several kilometres of surreal interior. Will noticed that the further into the structure they travelled, the thicker the ice around them became. It clung to the walls and stuck out in jagged clumps – more evidence for Amy's theory that the Fecund had been amphibious.

At last, they reached the place. It was a near-spherical space, barely large enough for their robot to enter, where eight of the tunnels met. About a quarter of the chamber was filled with ice and some of the tunnels were completely blocked off.

'This is it,' said Will.

He squinted around at the tunnel openings, willing them to have some significance for him, but nothing happened. This was just another grimy, frozen junction like all the others they'd passed.

Was his helmet blocking his sense of connection? If so, then the Transcended could forget the whole thing. Will wasn't going to take it off. There had to be some other way of making him more connected to the space. He had an idea.

'Hold on,' he told Rachel, and unclipped his suit hook.

'What're you doing?'

'I'm not sure, but don't worry – I promise I won't do anything stupid.'

'You'd better not,' she warned. 'If you go weird on me, I swear I'll pull rank on you.'

'Yes, Ma'am,' said Will with a grin.

He pushed up from the robot and glided towards what he thought of as the ceiling. When he reached it, he grabbed hold of the ice to secure himself. The moment he did so, all became clear. A new memory asserted itself and overlaid the room like a fairy enchantment.

'There!' he exclaimed, pointing towards an aperture wedged tight with dirty grey bergs. 'We go that way! No wonder I couldn't see it – it's blocked!' He pushed away, back towards the waldobot, and reclipped.

'Watch out,' he told Rachel. 'I'm going to dig.'

Will swapped his perspective into the waldobot's idling mind and started ripping the glittering chunks away from the opening with massive, eager hands. Soon there was a gap large enough for them to squeeze through.

It felt *right*. The answer to all their problems wasn't far away. It was just a shame they'd have to leave the robot behind.

'Come on!' Will urged. He pulled himself over the ice and clambered impatiently through.

'Slow down,' Rachel told him firmly. She grabbed his ankle as she caught up and drew him gently back. 'Here,' she said, and attached a cable from her suit to his. 'That's better.'

Some childish part of Will was annoyed by this limitation. He was about to tell her it was unnecessary, that it would get in the way of his progress, but then he locked eyes with her and saw the look on her face.

Don't push it, her eyes said. Will realised suddenly just how hard Rachel had worked to keep the mood on this little adventure light. She wanted to help him, but there was a limit to how crazy she was prepared to let him get.

'What's the rush, Will?' she asked levelly.

Will's excitement drained away. More than anything, he wanted her with him on this journey. She was the one person aboard the *Ariel* who still seemed to believe in him.

'Good point,' he said quietly.

They advanced more slowly after that, picking their way over the debris and clinging to the slick ribs of the tunnel wall where necessary. They reached another junction. It was just a fork this time, but Will still had to choose a route. He hung there, looking this way and that, the lights from his helmet illuminating the equally unappealing choices.

'So, which—' Rachel started.

Will cut her off. 'Shhh! Did you hear that?'

There had been a sound, or something like a sound. It might even have been a voice.

Rachel gave him a look. 'We're in an evacuated tunnel, Will. There's nothing to hear.'

'I know,' said Will. 'But I still heard something.'

And then it came again – not so much a sound as the implication of one. A beckoning, leading them to the right.

'This way,' said Will, pointing.

The tube led them to another habitat core, though this one was markedly different from the ones John had found. The cabling running into it was far thicker.

'So what happens now?' said Rachel. 'We go in?'

'Of course,' said Will. 'Let's see if we can get that airlock open.'

From his previous robotic forays, Will had plenty of experience with the manual controls on Fecund locks. Despite a dead mechanism encrusted with ice, the simple hatch opened after just a few minutes' work. Rachel's extraordinary strength came in useful. Will did little more than supervise. She kicked the inner hatch open and drew back to let him enter.

'Ladies first,' she said, gesturing at the open doorway.

Will pulled himself inside, his helmet lamp scanning the darkness.

'See any good corpses?' she asked. It was clear from her tone that the thought of brushing up against dead aliens in person didn't appeal to her a great deal. She lacked Amy's fascination with medical matters.

'Not yet,' said Will.

He yanked himself through the cluttered space, using the tattered silk ladders as handholds. More often than not they shredded to nothing when he grabbed them. As he neared the far wall of the habitat, he saw something that stopped him cold.

'Make that a yes,' he muttered.

Strapped into a row of couches were Fecund bodies, or parts of bodies. Their eyes and limbs had been surgically removed and fat bundles of cables sewn directly into the stumps and sockets. Will didn't need to be told what he was looking at. These were the Fecund equivalent of roboteers. Will stared into their mutilated, eyeless faces and felt faint.

What kind of lives must these poor creatures have had, forever disassociated from their own bodies? A fate like this made the glutinous embrace of the muscle-tank look downright benign by comparison. No wonder the senses for the new SAP puzzle he'd been given didn't feel like natural fits. They weren't. They were meant to mimic the experiences of the beings that lay before him. Will had wondered why there was no correlation between the internal senses like balance and the external ones like sight. It was no surprise when the subject's physical body was in one place and the things he would have observed were in another.

Furthermore, the sight mapping on the puzzle had appeared to include a touch analogue, something that struck him as a crazy and purposeless addition. Now the reason became clear: visually mapped waldo control. The alien roboteer would have received data about his remoted hands in the corners of his field of vision, like a heads-up display seen through a visor.

He wrapped his arms about himself and shivered.

'I found it,' he said.

'Found what?' Two seconds later, Rachel's hand landed on his shoulder as she took a look for herself. 'Good God,' she exclaimed. 'That's revolting.'

The more Will thought about his solution to the puzzle, the more right it felt.

'I'll need my tools,' he told Rachel.

He shut his eyes and focused on his sensorium link to the distant waldobot. It was tenuous, but still intact. Through it they had contact with the shuttle, and from there Will could reach the *Ariel*. He dragged the software he needed into his suit's processor.

'Why do you need tools, Will?' Rachel asked nervously. 'What's the significance of this thing?'

'This thing is the key,' he said. 'It's what the Transcended want me to see. The new puzzle makes sense now. It had all these sensory features that didn't add up, as if whatever mind it was designed for was in two places at once. Well, guess what: that's exactly what they meant. 'Hold on,' he told her. 'I'll open the puzzle, then we'll get out of here.'

'Will, no.' She dug her fingers into his shoulder and glared at him. 'You're going too fast again. Wait and do it back aboard the ship.'

Will shook his head. 'I'm supposed to be here,' he said.

'Says who?' she snapped back at him. 'In case you've forgotten, the last time you talked to aliens you were out for hours while your body filled up with virus. I have no medical supplies here, no way of getting to your skin. It could kill you.'

Will met her gaze. 'It won't kill me,' he said softly. 'That's not what they want.'

'Will, you don't know what they want.'

Will sighed. 'I do know that this could mean the difference between us getting home and being stuck out here for ever.'

'But why open it here?' she demanded. 'Will, it's not rational. I'm going to call Ira.'

'Don't,' said Will. 'Please.' He grabbed her hand as it reached up to touch the comm-badge on her breast-plate. 'This is what I'm supposed to do,' he assured her. 'I can feel it. I wish I could explain it to you but I can't even explain it to myself. Hugo said he hated the drip-feed of information. Imagine what it's like to get that inside your own head.

'Look, if the Transcended wanted us dead, they'd have killed us by now. If they wanted to control my actions, they wouldn't have done such a lame-ass job of guiding me. We're here because they want us to *learn*. It's the only answer that makes sense. That means we have to trust them. We follow the lesson plan or we sit here rotting till the air runs out. It's our choice.'

She gasped and glanced away. 'How am I supposed to find my way out of here if you go offline?'

'I won't, I promise.'

She shut her eyes for a few seconds. 'You'd better be right about this.'

Will smiled. 'I am, don't worry.'

He turned his attention back to his home node. Now that he knew what he was aiming for, the puzzle was a simple matter of compensating for the artificial sense map with some blockers and remappings of his own. His mistake before had been imagining that he'd be able to correlate the SAP with a single coherent experience model the way he did with his own robots. This was more like partial thought-sharing with another handler.

Will started the program and panned back to regard his work. It was clumsy. And the SAP was clearly pulling data from somewhere in the *Ariel* because it was running very slowly. That didn't matter, though. He wouldn't notice once he was in there.

'All right,' he said. 'I've cracked the puzzle. My guess was right – the SAP's a sense map of one of these poor bastards.' He waved a hand at the ancient handlers. 'Looks like the Transcended want us to know how they felt. I'm going to run it now. It might take a little while.'

'I'll monitor your life signs,' Rachel offered grudgingly. 'But if I see any weird data traffic, I'm breaking the link to *Ariel*, okay?'

Will nodded. He took a deep breath and dropped himself into the puzzle.

It was nothing like the first Transcended SAP he'd run. This one was part slide show, part memory log and part dialogue. Will watched through the eyes of a robot as the current in the delivery tube rushed it to the damage site. Water surged around the plastic limbs folded back against its body. Will recognised the slick ribbing on the walls as it flashed past. It was one of the tunnels he'd come in through – they were a kind of hydraulic delivery system for robots! Water had once pumped around this ship like blood.

Will directed the robot to the access port, where it pushed through the retainer membrane into a scene of chaos and debris.

Electricity arced across a steamy chamber filled with the ruins of huge machines.

How were they going to rebalance the chamber? Will thought in horror. *It would take hundreds of units.*

The Fecund engineering philosophy unfolded inside his head. Durability first. They could take as long as they needed to fix this charging bank because the ship had dozens like it. Also, Fecund robots were simple but robust. Even a great nestship like the one he served on only had a few varieties. Their culture had refined robustness to a kind of elegance. They would throw as many robots at the problem as it took.

Will looked down at the hands of the machine he wore. They were well made but hard and insensitive. Surely, even with an infinite supply of such robots, there would still be delicate, complex tasks they'd never be able to perform.

The memory stream derailed as if in response to his confusion and Will found himself behind the eyes of another robot, performing a different task. He felt his heart swell with a peculiar kind of pride, tainted with bitter-sweet empathy. He was helping tend the babies. With his massive brown claws, he grappled a huge rectangular tank and dragged it across a birthing factory decorated in soft crèche grey. The tank was full of jelly-like spawn, and his destination was the oven where the eggs would be gently, lovingly overheated. It would ensure the young produced were neuter females like him, born for lives of willing servitude.

On a ship like this, ninety per cent of the crew were neuter females. Most were deemed *disposable* and sent to work in the mesohull. The lucky ones like him would be altered for robot work. He envied the disposables their knowledge of their own bodies and their camaraderie of physical contact, though not their brief, painful lives.

Will recoiled from the knowledge the puzzle pressed upon him. That was why Fecund robots were so simple: because they sent living crew outside the habitat cores to die. They sent their own children to their deaths. What kind of parents would do such a thing to their own offspring?

The memory track derailed again and Will discovered that he was monitoring the environmental controls for the executive module. He was overcome by fear. Everything must be just right or he would be replaced for sure.

In the pools below his camera-view, huge clan-parents wallowed. They would never leave the water, and in their lifetime would produce thousands of children, more than enough to run a ship. Thousands. Will reeled. What kind of world could have spawned such a race?

The puzzle showed him. Another change of context and he was watching soothing pictures of the home world while surgeon sisters made further adaptations to his maimed body. He saw vast seaweed forests and monster tides. It was a world far richer in life than Earth but more capricious in nature. Between the streaks of thick cloud he made out a huge moon hanging overheard like the yellow eye of some angry god.

The Fecund had evolved hands for moving around kelp forests in powerful currents, Will realised, not for swinging through trees. As he watched, three adolescent Fecund playing in the roiling surf were swept away. Disposable children – a part of life. With a home like this, Will thought, it was amazing the Fecund had ever managed to get off it.

On the contrary, the puzzle appeared to say, and pulled him through a bewildering series of snippets from what he could only imagine was a Fecund historical documentary. He saw cities built on scaffolds, amazing systems of dams and locks, and Fecund clinging to giant kites. It was clear that once this race had learned to make tools and change their environment, its development had been explosive. He watched simple rockets being assembled in giant silos, and a journey to the giant yellow moon. How tempting a destination it must have been for a developing civilisation.

The view swapped again, back to the repair scene where it had started. The action was further advanced, and Will was now following a robot scrambling through the damaged ship to a weapons array where energy beams of unbelievable potency were being fired into space. Will's robot looked out into the void between the vessels and saw armadas of such numbers of nestships that Tang's force was laughable by comparison.

They bred like locusts, Will realised. With the natural pressure of their environment no longer acting upon them, the Fecund had practically erupted into space. They fought each other for room and resources on every habitable world they could find and thought little of the loss of life their conflicts incurred.

Will grudgingly found himself in agreement with the Transcended. These creatures had to go.

'No,' he thought he heard the puzzle tell him. 'It is more subtle than that. We do not judge on speed of spread, but on consequences.'

To finish, the puzzle showed him the chaos aboard the nestship as suddenly the war beams all winked out. Fields of shimmering lustre cast from the frond-like warp inducers faded and died. The sun below them turned an ugly, bloated orange.

The Fecund had only a minute or two to panic before the shock wave arrived. Will's robot stared hopelessly at the mutating sun as a tsunami of boiling death enveloped the sky.

In the numb darkness that followed, a single final image appeared of a metal-clad sphere clutched by pistons in the bowels of the ruined ship. Ten thousand cables trailed from it.

'This is a nest archive,' the puzzle told him.

The program ended.

Will was dumped unceremoniously back into the real world – into a body gasping for breath. His pulse raced.

'—ou alright?' Rachel was yelling. 'Talk to me!' She shook him fiercely.

'Yes!' Will wheezed. 'I'm fine.'

Rachel collapsed against him in relief, then looked up again and fixed him with a glare. 'What the hell happened in there?' she demanded. 'Your vitals went crazy, just like you said they wouldn't.'

Will held on to her with trembling hands and pulled himself together. 'I'm alive, aren't I?' he said, trying for whimsy. 'It was just a bit surprising, that's all.' He shot her a weak smile. 'Thank you. Sorry.'

His head spun as he struggled to pull meaning from the experience he'd just endured. The Transcended had wanted him to see the dead alien with his own eyes, and then put him in that alien's shoes. *Why?* Just so he could view the consequences of being judged self-destructive? Will didn't believe that.

There was also the lingering question of how the Transcended had managed to capture the last moments of the Fecund roboteer's life. Perhaps the entire program had been a fiction, a near-accurate biography created after the fact, for his benefit.

But on reflection, Will thought not. There had been something too earnest about the puzzle for that. He was left with the unsettling suspicion that the Transcended had come here after everyone was dead and somehow pulled memories from the corpses.

He froze as the full import of what he'd watched dawned on him. This system wasn't just a graveyard: it was a memorial. It had been tended, maintained. The Transcended had left it intact on purpose because of its proximity to the lure star. As a lesson for other species, yes, but also as a resource.

He looked up at Rachel. 'I know where to go!'

The route to the nest archive was as clear to him as the walk around his local canteen back home. That was why the Transcended had wanted him to solve the puzzle here: because there was more to see.

'Go?' said Rachel. 'I thought we'd just found the answer.'

'We found the answer to the puzzle,' he replied with a grin. 'This is the answer to our prayers.' He tucked up his legs to launch off, back towards the airlock. Before he could move, Rachel grabbed him again.

'Will,' she said. 'I like you. I want to help you. But I can't do that if I don't know what's going on. You still haven't explained what this is all about. And you're scaring me.'

Will took a deep breath and nodded. He needed to slow down again. 'It's good news,' he told her, as calmly as he could. 'The puzzle ended with a kind of prize – something we can use to get out of here, perhaps an answer to our antimatter problem. And we were supposed to solve the puzzle here because the prize is here, too.' He gestured towards the door. 'Come on, I'll explain on the way.'

They clambered back out to the robot and followed the tunnels down through the ship in the direction the puzzle had shown him.

Meanwhile, Will told Rachel everything he'd learned about the Fecund.

'They sound horrible,' Rachel said when he'd finished. 'A species that murdered their own children and trashed every star system they got hold of? I'm not surprised the Transcended destroyed them.'

'I don't think that's it, though,' said Will. 'The puzzle was trying to tell me that it wasn't a moral decision. It was deeper than that. It was something about the way they lived.'

Rachel snorted. 'Briefly, by the sound of it.'

The archive was exactly where Will expected it to be, near the base of the bulb, close to the power system that fed the warp-fronds. It was the most important point in the entire ship. Set in the centre of another spherical chamber, the archive resembled a ball of twine some fifteen metres across clutched in the talon of a mighty mechanical bird. Countless cables snaked out of it in all directions and disappeared into sockets in the curving wall. The talon was a bracing device, nothing more than a gravitational stabiliser. The ball was where the action was. It was the hub of the data network for the entire ship.

'Is this it?' said Rachel.

Will nodded. 'This is what John was looking for. The Fecund didn't use computers as much as we do. They didn't trust the robustness of software, but they did store data. And this is the database all their roboteers were plugged into. There should be tons of information in it we can use. Stuff that will show us how to get out of here. And how to beat the Earthers.'

It was exciting just looking at the thing.

'That's great, Will,' she said. 'Really great. Now let's tell John and get the hell out of here.

Will's heart sank a little. 'We can't. We need to route power through it and hook it up to a zero-latency diagnostics rig. That's not possible here. We'll have to take it back to the *Ariel*.'

Rachel's face fell. 'How? There's about ten klicks of ship in the way!'

Will shook his head. 'Not true.' He pointed. 'We've come almost to the other side of the ship. If we keep going that way, there are only three bulkheads between us and the exohull.'

'But it's still an exohull!' said Rachel. 'And this thing must weigh tons. How're you going to move it? How're you going to unplug it, even?' She gestured hopelessly at the mad tangle of wire.

'That's what robots are for,' said Will. 'We can cut a hole in the bulkheads and drag the thing straight out.'

Rachel shook her head. 'I don't know,' she said. 'This sounds like an awfully big job to me.'

He sighed. 'I know how it sounds, but I can't think of a better option. Give me an hour. Let's at least try.'

She deflated. 'One more hour, then.'

Will grinned at her.

'Do you mind if I tell Ira now?' she added.

'Go ahead,' he said. 'I'll start work on the cables.'

By the end of that first hour, his progress was even better than he'd hoped. His robots needed barely any guidance. With the slightest encouragement from him, they set about their task with almost manic enthusiasm. Burners and cutters attacked the peculiarly fragile exohull, which melted like butter under their tools. Meanwhile, the waldobot made short work of the other decrepit walls standing in their way.

Will had the strong impression that the nestship had been made ready for this surgery in advance. There were no visible flaws in the bulkheads they tore down, yet when the waldobot hammered at them they broke in clean, straight lines. Was this more evidence of the Transcended's involvement? It suggested that someone had planned for this moment long before he was even born. There was something unsettling about that.

Rachel surveyed his progress with gathering surprise. 'I should learn to stop doubting you, Will Kuno-Monet,' she said, astonished.

Will smiled at her, a little nervously. He wasn't sure exactly how much he had to do with their success. 'It's not really me,' he said. 'They just drop things into my head.'

She snorted. 'They drop puzzles, Will. You're the one who solves them.'

A mere four hours later, they were ready to snap the final pistons holding the sphere in place and sail it out into the void. The shuttle waited just outside with grapples extended.

Rachel regarded the scene with a gleeful grin on her face. 'We did it!' she exclaimed. '*You* did it. You're amazing, Will.' She hugged him and blew him a kiss from helmet to helmet.

Ira's call caught Will in mid-blush. 'Rachel, Will, cease your activity. Shut down all radiation signatures and wait for further instructions. The Earthers are here.'

10.2: IRA

The Earther gunship crept into the system like a visitor to a haunted house. That caution was understandable. Ira could imagine what must be going through the captain's head – the same things that had gone through his about a week ago. He held his breath as he watched the Earthers edge up to the exact part of the ring where the *Ariel* was parked. It wasn't a great surprise. Ira had put the ship in the middle of the thickest concentration of ruins – it was the obvious place to look, and in retrospect he could see that he'd courted this. Part of him preferred the thought of being found and killed to eking out a pitiful existence among the dead for the rest of his life.

That was why he'd been so reluctant to let Will go, he realised. And of course, true to form, the Earthers had shown up the very moment when two of his crew were out of his sight. Their timing was about right for the luck he'd been having lately.

The good news was that he'd anticipated the moment and prepared for it. From the moment Amy's deep-space scans had given him warning, it had taken less than a minute to shut down the *Ariel*'s radiation profile. Now they were just one more piece of floating junk. The conditions for an ambush were almost perfect.

The only problem was the plume of heated matter that Will's little adventure had produced over at the Fecund ship. In the dead cold of the system, it glared like a beacon. But it was small. Hopefully the Earthers would never get that close. The Sargasso region Ira had parked in was still hundreds of thousands of kilometres across. There was plenty of it to get lost in.

'Hugo,' said Ira, 'it's time to power up that new g-ray of yours.'

'I haven't finished testing it,' croaked Hugo. 'Just two more minutes and I can at least run an ad hoc calibration.'

Ira breathed deeply. 'Too late for that,' he said. 'Turn it on.'

'You realise that at this distance, it'll still take about ten minutes for the suntap to come online?'

'Then we'd better get started straight away, hadn't we?' Ira growled. 'John, help him. Give him targeting support. I want a clean shot at their habitat core.'

If he could manage it, Ira wanted the Earther ship intact. Their antimatter could save his mission, and the element of surprise was about the only advantage he was going to get. The gunship was bigger than the *Ariel* and a lot better armed.

He watched with his heart in his mouth as the Earthers fired off drones to explore. Their weapons and defences were all running hot, at full battle status. He wondered what emotion was uppermost in the Earther captain's mind right now. His guess was either awe or terror, with an outside chance of jubilation at the thought of the bonus he'd collect when he reported all this. Not that Ira intended to let the captain leave.

The minutes crawled by. Finally, Hugo spoke.

'Suntap online!' There was no small amount of pride in his voice.

'Fire at will,' said Ira.

'Not yet, Captain,' John said quickly. 'We haven't got a clean line of sight any more. There's too much crap in the way.'

Ira gritted his teeth. If they misjudged the shot at this distance, they could hit the gunship's juice-containment system, and that would be bad news for everybody.

'Shit!' said Amy. 'They've found Will.'

Ira glanced over at the tactical display she sent him and groaned as he saw drones zero in on Will's plume.

'Reading broadcasts on the Earthers' primary band,' said John. 'They're not using tight-beam. They can't be getting line-of-sight, either.'

'What kind of encryption?' said Ira.

'Nothing I can't break.'

'You'd better hurry,' he warned. 'It doesn't look like we've got much time.'

The drones closed in on Will and Rachel but didn't fire. The Earthers must have been curious. The gunship powered across the debris field towards them on its fusion torches and then nosed in close with a few light bursts from its thrusters.

'Broke their level one,' John announced. 'Now we can watch, at least.'

He sent Ira a video feed. It showed a view straight into the hot little hole Will had dug for himself. The *Ariel*'s shuttle floated nearby in plain sight.

'Galatean agents!' the Earthers boomed over the Truce Channel. 'You are hereby claimed as prisoners of war for the Kingdom of Man. Reveal yourselves immediately! Any attempt at violence will be met with force.'

There was nothing but silence from the hole. Ira felt a surge of pride. His crew weren't the surrendering kind.

When the silence started to drag, the Earthers tried a slightly softer approach.

'This site has been deemed a scientific resource of the Reconsiderist subsect. You are trespassing. However, surrender now and you will be not be harmed. The captain is prepared to offer full sanctuary terms in return for strategic information.'

Ira didn't doubt that the Earther captain had plenty of questions, like: *What the hell is this place?* for a start.

There was still no reply from the hole. The Earther drones started moving. Several of them docked like lampreys onto the shuttle. Another, bristling with weapons, nudged towards the hole. Behind them, the gunship inched closer.

'We have line-of-sight,' John said triumphantly.

'Hugo, fire!' Ira ordered.

There was a grunt of surprise from Hugo's bunk as the suntap snapped on. For a second, all the *Ariel*'s exterior sensors wobbled. A deafening squawk drowned out the comms bands. Then the beam was gone.

John was the first to get his console back in shape. 'Earther broadcast channel is dead,' he said. 'Their drone control appears to be down.'

'No signs of retaliation,' Amy reported. 'Scanning their ship for damage.'

It sounded like a direct hit but Ira wasn't taking any chances. 'Hugo, give them another shot.'

'I can't!' Hugo whined. 'The circuits are all burned out – the weapon used a lot more power than I thought it would.'

Great, thought Ira. *Now we're sitting ducks again.*

Aloud, he said, 'John, ready torpedoes.'

'Ira, I'm not sure we need to,' said Amy. 'Earther defences are in passive rundown. They're drifting and they have a hull-scorch like nothing I've ever seen. I think we got them.'

Ira blinked. Could they really be dead already, from just one shot?

'I've cracked their level two,' said John. 'Want to take a look?'

'Go ahead,' said Ira, but no pictures appeared in his visor.

'Huh!' John grunted. 'None of their internal cameras are responding. No, wait – here's one.'

A window popped up at last. The view it showed was startling. Charred bodies floated in a sea of black dust. Everything inside was ruined. Every single buffer on the ship must have burned out as if it wasn't there. Hugo made a strangled sound.

Ira immediately thought of Will and Rachel. They were outside. And they hadn't been far away from that monster beam.

'Rachel!' Ira shouted into his mike. 'Rachel, are you there?'

The reply was faint and crackly. 'Here, Captain.'

'Are you all right?'

'We're fine, Captain,' said Rachel.

'What happened to you?'

'Will and I retreated into the tunnel system,' she said. 'Will was watching through the waldobot when there was this flash and all the Earther drones went dead. Was that Hugo's work?'

'It was indeed,' said Ira jubilantly. He found himself breaking into a massive grin. 'Any damage?' he asked. 'What do your Geigers show?'

'We're fine, Captain. Will's got a headache from being in the waldobot's mind when the flash came, but he'll live.'

Ira laughed in relief. 'Thank Gal!'

'We should be back aboard the *Ariel* within the hour,' said Rachel.

'That's excellent. Really excellent.'

Ira turned off the channel and leaned out of his bunk. 'Hugo, that was great! Well done!'

But Hugo didn't reply. Ira checked his bunk camera and found the scientist white and shaking.

'Hugo, what's wrong?' he said.

'I don't think he's ever killed anyone before,' said John.

Ira blinked. He should have guessed. His heart sank. Hugo was almost certainly in shock. As if the man hadn't been fragile enough already.

'I'm sorry,' Ira told the scientist gently, 'but it was them or us and I'm glad it's them. You did good, Hugo, even if it feels awful. You saved all our lives. You might even have saved the home world.'

He addressed the rest of the crew. 'I want a full investigation of that ship, and I want a fuel-transfer conduit set up immediately. There could be others coming in any time. I don't intend to be here when they arrive.'

Ira found it hard to suppress a mounting sense of delight. They were free of this awful place at last.

10.3: WILL

Ira didn't look particularly impressed when Will returned to the ship with a hundred-ton piece of cargo but was clearly too preoccupied to complain.

'Great, you're back at last,' he said as they emerged from the docking pod. 'I need you both to work on the fuel transfer right away. John's lined everything up for you – you'll find the details in your data spaces.'

'Captain,' said Will, 'I'd like to talk to you about what we found.'

'Me, too,' said Ira. 'Once we have this situation under control. Getting us mobile comes first. There could be more Earthers out there.' He turned back to John and Amy. 'All right, have we come to any conclusions yet?'

Will fought down his frustration. Had he not made it clear what the nest archive was? It was the answer to the entire war. He glanced quickly at Rachel to share his displeasure. She gave him a knowing look. *He's the captain*, her eyes said.

She was right, of course. Will slid into his bunk and plugged in. John's work on the conduit was laid out before him but Will chose not to completely immerse. He kept his audio link to the cabin fully open. He wanted to hear what the captain was planning.

'John and I have been looking over the charts,' said Amy. 'With what we can siphon from the Earthers, we should be able to get through the lobe and out past Zuni. The bad news is that we still don't have enough to reach Li-Delamir. However, the good news is that John's identified a system occupied by the Earthers with a strong resistance movement that could help us.'

'Which one?' said Ira.

'New Angeles,' John replied. 'They're well organised and have access to juice-factories. I know because I used them back when I did that project with Counter-Propaganda. We could arrive by stealth, link up with them and be on our way in no time.'

There was a pause.

'Do you trust them?' said Ira. He sounded unconvinced. 'Remember, we've been burned by local resistance people before. I don't like tangling with them unless it's under orders.'

Then don't, Will thought. Hadn't Ira received Rachel's report when they were freeing the archive? They already had an answer, if they could take the time to work it out. He was convinced now that this was what the Transcended intended for them, and that their solution was almost certain to be a better one than anything humans could devise.

'What do the rest of you think?' Ira asked.

That was enough. Will unplugged and drifted out of his bunk to join the conversation.

'John has convinced me,' said Amy. 'These people sound pretty reliable.'

'Hugo?' said Ira.

Hugo hung near the top bunks with his arms folded, looking uncharacteristically pale. 'I don't know,' he said.

'Rachel?'

Rachel shrugged. 'I don't see that we've got much choice.'

Will winced. How could she not?

'But I'd like to hear what Will says first,' she said, glancing back at him. 'I think he's better placed than any of us to comment right now.'

Ira turned to face Will. The captain's eyes had a kind of hungry, impatient look to them, as if he was about to demand to know why Will wasn't still working on the refuelling. Well, fuck that.

'I think we should stay,' Will said before Ira could get a word in. 'The answer to our problems is somewhere in that archive. I think we should be looking for it, not dashing out of here as fast as we can.'

Ira's face darkened. 'For how long?'

'I don't know,' said Will. 'Till we have answers.'

'And if there are more Earther ships on the way?'

Will spoke as calmly as he could. 'We give them the same treatment we gave that last one.'

Ira shook his head. 'We can't. That blast blew the circuits. Hugo says it'll take two days to get the suntap running again and he'll need to borrow more kit from the *Ariel* to do it.'

Will hadn't known that. But then again, they didn't need suntaps to rig an ambush. He opened his mouth to reply but Ira talked over him.

'Not to mention the fact that there's still a battle fleet waiting to turn our home into slag just a few light-years away from here. And now they know about us. We've found what we came for, Will – a working suntap and defences against it. But if we don't get home soon, they won't help anyone. Furthermore, I have no intention of being captured at the next place we refuel, and that means we need to leave in time to conceal our radiation trail. Which means *now*.'

Will frowned. Why was the captain talking to him like an idiot? Did he think Will was clueless about all this? It just wasn't as simple as Ira was making out. Since the Transcended had involved themselves, it was a whole different ball game. They were talking about the future of the human race here.

And why had Ira even bothered to ask the others if his own mind was already made up? To give the impression of it being a group decision? What a joke.

Will tried to speak again, but Ira interrupted a second time.

'Do you even know why you want to stay?'

'To read the archive,' Will said stubbornly.

'You can do that on the way home,' Ira countered.

'No. It has to be done here.'

Ira raised an ironic eyebrow. '*Why*, Will?'

Will folded his arms. 'I don't know. They haven't said. But what does that matter? We're being given clues here!'

But the captain pressed harder. 'Clues to what, Will? So far, your alien buddies have taken us a long way up shit creek, and this is the first paddle we've found. Do you know what *compromised* means?'

Will found something about Ira's question chilling. 'Yes,' he admitted.

'I have to consider the possibility that you've been lied to, Will,' Ira told him. 'That you're being used. The truth is, we have no idea what we're dealing with.'

'Exactly!' Will insisted. 'And this could be our last opportunity to find out.'

Ira smiled humourlessly. 'Now you're sounding like Hugo.'

Hugo looked up in surprise and regarded Will suspiciously.

'I'm sorry,' Ira said, 'but we can't afford to pin our lives on your hunches. If the thing in your head wants to come clean and tell us why we should hang around, now's the time for it to do so.'

Will scowled and willed the Transcended to offer him something. As usual, nothing happened. How could he explain? He turned to Rachel. If the captain wouldn't listen to him, maybe he'd listen to her.

'What do you think?' he asked.

Rachel sighed and looked at him sadly. 'I'm sorry, Will, but I think Ira's right. The repairs are complete and we can't afford to stay right now. If we can get ourselves out of this scrape, there'll be nothing to stop us coming back here. Nothing you've told us about the Transcended suggests they've given us a deadline. Once home is safe, the pressure will be off.'

She glanced down, as if in shame. 'Think of it this way,' she offered. 'You got the archive. If you're right, it contains everything we need to beat off the new Earther fleet. What more can this place give us?'

The crew's eyes were on him. Will felt Amy's concern, Rachel's regret and John's urgent desire to leave, which was showing ever more obviously though his veneer of amusement. Will's chest felt tight. They still didn't trust him, or what he'd become.

'Look,' he said, 'I know that none of you likes this situation. Nobody hates it more than me. And I know we're dealing with a lot of unknowns. But if it wasn't for the Transcended, we'd be dead already. They're helping us for a reason. This is bigger than just us. This is about our species.'

'Exactly,' said Ira, 'and that's what concerns me. How much do the Transcended care about Galatea, Will? We'd all like to see humanity continue, but personally I'd prefer keep my home world, too. Have they made you any promises about that?'

Will winced. Of course they hadn't.

'That's what I thought. Look. Don't think I'm taking what you've discovered lightly – I'd be a fool to do that – but remember that we're also trying to stay alive. And we understand that it's frustrating for you. Someone's dropping facts into your head and leaving it up to you to explain them to the rest of us. That must be maddening. Let alone the fact that you're expected to take the weight of the entire human race on your shoulders without even understanding why.

'So if you honestly think Galatea would be better served by me leaving you here with a shuttle so you can carry on with your research alone, we'll do that. We have enough spare robots to make that possible. But the *Ariel* needs to get home *right now*, and you must ask yourself whether you're still the roboteer on this ship – or not.'

Will's mouth twisted in frustration. He could hardly save mankind hanging around in this system on his own. But if he went with them, he might still stand a chance. And more than anything else, he couldn't bear to see Rachel looking at him that way.

'Okay.' He squeezed the word out from the pit of his stomach.

'That's what I like to hear,' said Ira, gracing him with a smile as if it were some kind of reward. 'Amy, plot us a course out. Will, how about finishing that fuelling?'

Will nodded and turned away. He found himself intensely disappointed with the captain. With all of them, in fact. But could he blame them? They were still themselves. They weren't sharing their heads with the unknown.

And maybe Ira was right. What did he really know of the Transcended? Just because they'd led him down a few tunnels and shown him some memory fragments, what did that mean? If he were in the crew's shoes, he'd probably want to leave, too.

Will told himself that, all things considered, they were doing the right thing. But no matter how hard he tried to convince himself, he couldn't shake the feeling they were making a dangerous mistake.

11: SICKNESS

11.1: GUSTAV

Gustav stared intently at the progress monitors in the brown, padded docking pod as it crawled from the hub down to Tang's habitat ring. He couldn't wait to get aboard and check on the details of the search. It had been nearly two weeks. By now, messenger drones should have come in from gunships investigating some of the suspected fuelling stars.

Gustav tried to keep his contact with Konrad Tang to a minimum, but now he needed to know exactly what was going on. He didn't trust the admiral not to have augmented the orders to the gunships with a few of his own, designed to speed up the attack on Galatea.

Then there were the protectorate governments – another headache. If the Gallies were foolish enough to head for one of the Kingdom star systems, he'd have even less control over what happened. All three colonies within the Gallies' maximum predicted fuel-range were under the jurisdiction of other subsects. And all of them were hungry for chances to improve their own standing at the Prophet's court at the cost of the Reconsiderists.

Gustav had given strict instructions for the Gallies to be well treated when and wherever they were caught, and for him to be informed as quickly as possible. However, most protectorates had a habit of interpreting such orders in their own ways. He could only hope his security rating scared them enough to keep their noses out.

If it didn't, Gustav's career – and probably his life – was over. His one remaining chance of getting out of this mess was to be the man who saved the day. It was a role that everyone else was certain to try to take from him. But if he could stay on top of things, he'd at least get to keep his life. If he made it that far, he could work on extracting enough leverage from the debacle to convince the Prophet that the Relic was safe in Reconsiderist hands on a permanent basis.

Behind him, Rodriguez hummed a hymn. Gustav's shoulders tightened. It was unfortunate that things had to happen this way. Tang would get to meet the disciple, which was something he'd hoped to avoid.

Thankfully, Rodriguez had been less of a pest of late, probably because he wanted to keep his lily-white robes clean of the whole affair. Then, when the time came, it'd be easier for him to stand aside and let the Kingdom's wrath descend upon Gustav's head. Gustav just hoped the disciple held on to that strategy once Tang was involved.

The docking-pod door slid open. The blunt, bricklike figure of Admiral Tang was standing in the drab corridor on the other side. He waited with his hands clasped behind his back.

'General,' Tang growled, with a barely adequate nod of respect. The fact that a Military Intelligence officer had been given authority over an admiral on what was essentially a fleet project had always been a sore point for Tang, and showing deference was a constant struggle. 'Welcome back,' he said, sounding even less convincing than usual.

'Why, thank you, Admiral,' said Gustav. 'And may I introduce Disciple Rodriguez, my new assistant?'

Tang gave Rodriguez a perfunctory, stiff-bodied handshake and immediately returned his attention to Gustav.

'I wish to register my disapproval of this search you have instructed me to conduct.'

Gustav hadn't instructed Tang to be involved at all. He restrained himself from pointing that out. 'Disapproval noted,' he said. 'I trust it has not prevented you from carrying out my orders swiftly.'

Tang's face coloured. 'No. The ships have been sent out as per your request.'

'Good.'

'Though quite frankly I do not think employing them as a

messenger service is an efficient or fitting use for them. These are state-of-the-art suntap gunships. They carry weapons with an *aleph* security rating. Sending them into protectorate star systems presents an unwarranted risk for this project. Any number of enemy spy cells may take the opportunity to observe them.'

'I am well aware of the consequences, Admiral,' said Gustav. 'There is no need to remind me of them.'

'Furthermore,' said Tang, ignoring him, 'the message itself is somewhat hard to swallow. An attack on the Prophet?' He made a sour face. 'Coupled with your name on the orders, it will not take people long to guess that this has more to do with Memburi than Earth.'

Gustav had heard enough. 'If necessary, we shall embellish,' he said firmly. 'The Gallies have stolen some of our superior technology for their assassination attempt, thus the reason for our involvement. I'm sure the palace will support us. They have at least as much reason as we do to keep this discreet. And now, gentlemen, let us proceed.'

He strode towards the strategy room, forcing a pace a little too fast for Tang's shorter legs. The admiral matched his pace with difficulty, his face getting redder still.

'Then there is the issue of the fleet position,' he added.

Ah, the fleet, Tang's private joy – Gustav had ruined his tidy little rows of ships.

'You have spread us out and revealed our strength before the strike,' the admiral said bitterly. 'This will make it *considerably* harder to launch the big push against Galatea.'

That was the task Tang had been salivating over for years. It was to be his moment of fame – the victory that he expected to catapult him into the history books.

Gustav stopped and swivelled to face the shorter man. 'Admiral, imagine for a moment, purely hypothetically, that the Galateans find a way to interrupt the suntap. What would you do if your fleet arrived in their system and found that your weapons didn't work at all? There would be no bold victory. In all likelihood, your forces would be slaughtered. I prefer to work from a broad, exposed position than face that prospect. I suspect you do, too.'

'I strongly doubt they could develop a defence like that in such a short time,' Tang blustered.

'Why?' Gustav asked coldly.

Tang's security rating didn't permit him full knowledge of what transpired at the *remote facility*. Thus he had no way to gauge the severity of this emergency for himself. He had to take the scientific assertions Gustav gave him at face value, something he hated doing.

He regarded Gustav with a loathing he could not disguise.

'As General Ulanu's assistant, I can assure you that he is fully cognizant of the weaknesses in his position and is ready to accept them,' Rodriguez put in smoothly. 'I would suggest that all we can do is assist him as best we can. In any case, you can rest assured that the Prophet will receive a fair and accurate impression of your role in these proceedings from me personally.'

Tang fixed Rodriguez with a startled expression, as if noticing the disciple's existence for the first time. His eyes lit up. Gustav could tell the man had spotted a potential ally.

Gustav had predicted this, though he was surprised by how quickly it had happened. It was inevitable that once those two got together, it would be the most natural thing in the world for them to try to conspire against him.

Let them, he thought to himself. He was alert to the possibilities, to the extent that he'd started carrying his executive automatic around in the pocket of his ship-suit wherever he went.

'You're exactly right,' he told Rodriguez, injecting a little menace into his voice. 'We are in a state of alert. Thus, as the commanding officer on this project, obedience is all I expect from either of you under these circumstances. But I expect it unconditionally.'

He fixed each of them with a hard stare. Tang met the look with sullen suspicion, Rodriguez with a pious, scornful smirk.

'Now, let us proceed to the planning room,' Gustav announced.

He walked on ahead again, leaving the two of them trotting behind him. As he strode down the corridor, he could feel the spot on his back itching where he was sure the knife was going to go.

11.2: WILL

From the moment they left the Fecund system, Will felt uneasy. With every day that passed, the sensation worsened. By the time he was four days into the flight back to human space, it was intolerable. Foreboding churned his guts and made his teeth ache. Sleep became impossible.

As a consequence he was awake when, on the fourth night, Hugo appeared at the side of his bunk.

'Will,' he said. 'I've been going over my results and I'd like to talk to you about them.'

'Now?' said Will blearily.

'Preferably.'

Will was instantly suspicious. 'But it's the middle of the night.'

He glanced up towards the top of the cabin. Only Amy was on duty, her bunk flickering with visor-light. The others were asleep.

'Please,' said Hugo quietly. 'I don't expect any answers from you, but what I have to say may trigger some of your artificial memories, and that would help my work immeasurably.' He looked down, as if embarrassed by the admission.

Will had barely exchanged a word with Hugo since their disagreement in the meeting room. That Hugo was suddenly interested in talking to him now didn't exactly inspire his confidence. But Will couldn't just ignore the fact that the man had extended an olive branch of sorts. He'd clearly suffered since being responsible for the deaths of the Earther crew.

Perhaps Hugo had chosen the night because he was embarrassed to make peace in front of the others. He might not try again. And if Will could convince Hugo of his good intentions, perhaps he could help lobby the captain to turn the ship around.

'Okay,' he said uncertainly.

Hugo smiled. 'This way, then. We'll use the privacy chamber.'

Will didn't feel entirely comfortable as he descended the ladder to the room below. He quickly checked his home node to make sure his memory logs were running properly. If Hugo got weird again, Will wanted the captain to be able to see what had happened for himself.

Hugo reached the bottom of the ladder and sat on the floor, his back against the wall. Will did likewise. The floor beneath him hummed with the pull of the gravity drive.

'So, what do you want to talk about?' said Will.

Hugo hung his head, shut his eyes and spoke. 'I have been checking and rechecking my data, and I have come to an uncomfortable conclusion. The suntap schematic is *definitely* incomplete.'

He glanced up at Will with accusation in his eyes. Will began to wonder if he'd made a mistake in coming down here after all.

'My original assessment of the gravitic-generator control system was accurate,' said Hugo in a quavering voice. 'The software that completes it is not there. It is added in from outside at the time of operation.' He regarded Will expectantly.

Will wasn't sure what he was supposed to say. 'So where does it come from?' he ventured.

Hugo drew a long, heavy breath. 'I know what it looks like, but it can't be true.'

'Well?' said Will.

'The blueprint makes it look like it comes out of empty space. From natural curvon polarisation patterns. We didn't know that curvons could polarise. That's why it took me so long to figure out. I had to advance Galatean science in order to comprehend the supposed purpose of the devices.'

'What's wrong with that?' said Will.

Hugo shot him a look of tortured amusement. 'Because it would mean the galactic core is broadcasting software patches. Consider it for a moment,' he said dryly. 'A black hole thousands of times heavier than the sun. The single most significant object in the galaxy. And we are expected to believe that its total output is being tweaked for our benefit as if it's nothing more than a cheap house-mast. An impossible result by all accounts. It's as if we're being made fun of!' Anger flickered back into Hugo's features for a moment. 'I have a much better explanation, if you'd like to hear it,' he added.

'Go on,' said Will uncertainly.

'I believe that the aliens download the software into the device's processors at run time. In order for a culture to have access to the suntap, their computers must necessarily come into contact with the lure star first. In doing so, they're infected with an alien virus, just as we have been. That virus monitors their actions and responds accordingly. Given that we already know the computers of both societies which have the suntap have been compromised, it is relatively safe to assume that this is the general case. And given the relative difficulty of engineering such a virus compared to that of manipulating the galactic core, Occam's razor would appear to support my argument. Do you not agree?'

Will wasn't sure he did. 'I see where you're coming from,' he said slowly. 'But how can I help you?'

Hugo nervously tapped his fingers against his lips. 'If we assume the validity of such a viral strategy, then we must ask ourselves why the Transcended refuse to provide us with the software directly.' He looked straight at Will.

'I don't know,' said Will. 'To maintain control over its use, I suppose.'

'Exactly,' said Hugo darkly. 'And, by extrapolation, every system on the ship dependent upon it. So, simply put: any civilisation that comes into contact with the relic world is lured by the promise of unlimited power and leaves with their technology under the relic's control to at least some extent.'

Put that way, the aliens sounded more than a little menacing. Will wasn't sure he liked where this train of thought was taking them and still wasn't clear why Hugo needed him for this exercise.

'Another line of reasoning I've followed concerns the remarks you made during our meeting in the Fecund system,' said Hugo. 'Let us assume that what you said is true, and that you were not responsible for wresting control of the data feed from me during first contact.'

'Yes, let's,' Will muttered.

'The next logical question is why an alien should choose you as a target for contact instead of me.'

Will frowned. He tried to phrase his next words as tactfully as he could. 'As I said in my report, because I represented the kind of constructive self-editing they were looking for.'

'But *do* you?' said Hugo, his mouth cracking into a slightly unhinged smile. 'I am as much the product of genetic engineering as you are. Arguably more so. Your mods may be extensive, but they are cheap and unrefined compared to mine. I have a counter-hypothesis. You were chosen for contact because of your interface. Because, being like a machine, you were the easiest to manipulate. Their abuse of your memory processes since appears to bear this idea out.'

Will's face hardened. He hadn't come down here to be told he was some kind of puppet. One more remark like that and he was going to leave.

'And if they chose a living contact on the grounds of pliability,' Hugo continued, 'then we have to examine the so-called Transcendeds' intentions, and regard their story in a somewhat different light, I think. I have to consider the possibility that you are the unwitting and unwilling subject of a very dangerous kind of alien control.'

'Right, that's it,' said Will. He got to his feet and set one hand on the ladder.

'I blame myself, really,' Hugo said, with a sorrowful shake of his head. 'Had it not been for my eagerness to seek out knowledge, you wouldn't be in this unfortunate predicament.'

'Thanks for the sympathy,' Will snapped.

'That's why I'm sorry for what I have to do next.' Hugo took a tablet out of the pocket of his ship-suit and thumbed it into life.

Will's skin prickled. 'Do what?'

Hugo fiddled with the device and spoke breezily. 'Since I worked out what you've become, Will, I have been looking for a lever of some kind to make your reluctant parasite divulge some of its secrets. I didn't want to damage you, or any part of the ship. Such an act would be counter-productive. Then you provided me with the answer. Your precious nest archive.'

Will's hand curled tight around the rung.

'It is an extraordinary device,' Hugo remarked. 'Robust enough to last for eons without degradation. Yet now that it is plugged into our computer systems, its somewhat more delicate memory architecture is vulnerable once again. I doubt it would handle power surges well. Particularly if someone routed primary fusion output through the hold patches.'

Will stared the scientist down. At the same time, he fired a message to the ship's alarm system to warn the captain and isolate the archive.

Hugo's tablet bleeped at him. He smiled. 'I wouldn't do that, if I were you,' he said. 'I've already taken precautions to ensure we won't be disturbed.'

Hugo took a deep, ragged breath. Will noticed the man's hands were shaking.

'You will now answer my questions to my full satisfaction,' Hugo breathed. 'Firstly, where is the rest of the suntap code?'

Will felt sick inside. 'This is madness,' he said.

In the back of his head, he reached out to locate the block Hugo had put over the comms. He found not one block but dozens. Hugo had plastered every software system in the privacy chamber with rerouting patches several layers deep. It would take him hours to find a way through. In the meantime, his interface was effectively paralysed.

'I ask you once again,' said Hugo, his voice rising. '*Where is the rest of the suntap code?*'

'I don't know!' Will blurted.

'Wrong answer.' Hugo stabbed the tablet with his finger. 'Archive integrity at ninety per cent,' the tablet said cheerfully.

Will was horrified. One-tenth of their hopes for winning the war had just been fried into static. He started towards Hugo.

Hugo twitched a warning finger. 'No foolishness, please.'

Will realised what he had to do. If no other device in the room had a link to the rest of the ship, Hugo's tablet must. Will hurled an emergency command at it to warn the ship. It didn't respond. He dragged a data model of the device into his private node and started bombarding it with every kind of request he could think of. There had to be some way in.

'For the last time, Mr Monet,' said Hugo. 'Where is—' His finger raised above the screen.

Will threw himself at the scientist. He grabbed Hugo's wrist and pinned it back against the wall. Hugo was strong, but Will's nights in the muscle-tank had paid off.

'What are you going to do, Mr Monet?' Hugo spat through gritted teeth. 'Kill me?'

Will's soft assault on the tablet finally yielded fruit. The light in the privacy room went red. The radiation alarm sounded.

Hugo grunted in fury and wrested his arm free. He was about to press the panel a second time when a figure bounded down through the privacy hatch and grabbed his arms. It was Rachel. She swatted the tablet from Hugo's grasp and slammed him against the wall.

Ira was the next one through the hatch.

'What in fuck's name is going on in here?' he bellowed.

'Just a little negotiation, Captain,' said Hugo. He managed to sound self-righteous despite the presence of Rachel's elbow against his windpipe.

'Negotiation?' Will yelled. 'This asshole just tried to destroy the nest archive!'

Ira regarded Will coldly. In that moment, Will realised that the captain didn't really want the thing on board. He feared it.

'Rachel!' Ira snapped.

She released the scientist. Hugo adjusted his ship-suit like a ruffled bird.

'Examine the camera records, Captain,' he said smoothly. 'You will see that Mr Monet attacked me.'

'Because you were going to kill us!' Will shouted. He turned to the captain. 'He tried to make me tell him things I don't fucking know!'

'I discovered that Mr Monet has the secret of the suntap, Captain, and that he's not telling,' said Hugo.

Will turned back to the physicist and shouted in his face. 'You're *mad*! What's wrong with the answer in front of your fucking face? Is it so hard to believe the Transcended broadcast code? They can tune stars. They created the black hole that made this whole stupid lobe! What's the difference between that and the one in the middle of the fucking galaxy?'

Hugo's self-satisfied smile dimmed a little. He hadn't known the black hole was artificial.

Wild with rage, Will pressed his advantage. 'Why do you suppose they're so happy to give the blueprint away, you idiot? Because it's nothing without their help. Just like the human fucking race! Nothing!'

Will turned away, his cheeks tingling, and realised that Rachel and

Ira were both looking at him strangely. With a start, it occurred to him that the reason Hugo hadn't known about the black hole was because that detail hadn't made it into Will's report on his contact with the Transcended. There had been so much else to say and Will had so little time to prepare it. However, he now sounded more compromised than ever. Ira stared at Will. Rachel just looked sad. Will was speechless. He wasn't sure he could stand it.

'Listen to him,' Hugo hissed. 'He doesn't even sound human any more. You know what I think? I think there never were any Transcended. The whole story is a lie. There are just the sick, twisted remains of a greedy species who ruined their own star. They've been waiting millions of years for something like their own expendable children to come along so they can start the whole hideous cycle again. And Will's the closest thing they've found. That's why they chose him. And that's why they're *training* him, Captain. They want a whole army of roboteers. Of programmable people they can use to take over human space!'

Hugo glanced around at the unconvinced expressions before him. 'Don't look at me like that. You're fools if you can't see it. Fools!'

Will itched to put a fist through Hugo's face, but it suddenly looked like Ira might do it for him.

'I'm not afraid to suffer for the truth, Captain,' Hugo sneered. 'Our species is at risk, and *your* ship is carrying the disease that could kill it.'

From the spittle on his chin and the manic look in his eyes, it was clear that Hugo was losing it.

Ira stared at the scientist, his nostrils flaring. However, when he spoke, it was with a surprising calmness. In its own way, it held more menace than any roar could ever have achieved.

'I warned you, Doctor Vartian,' said Ira. 'You violated a direct order. You're finished.'

'I regret nothing, Captain,' Hugo spat. 'I answer to a higher calling. Do your worst.'

Ira reached out a huge hand and patted Hugo gently on the cheek. Hugo flinched away, and for a moment looked genuinely scared.

Ira then turned to Will. 'And you...' he said wearily. 'Got any more gems of information you'd like to share with us tonight?' His expression was unreadable.

Will shook his head.

'Okay then,' Ira said softly. 'I want to see your memory logs for this little adventure in my visor. Now I'm going back to sleep, and then tomorrow, Will, you and I need to have a private chat.' He gave Will a last, highly meaningful stare, and then climbed up the ladder.

Rachel stood there for a few moments longer, looking worriedly at Will. Will wished he could think of something to say.

'Rachel, administer a level-two sedative to Doctor Vartian. Then go to bed,' Ira said from above. 'That's an order.'

She gestured to Hugo to ascend the ladder, then started after him. 'See you tomorrow,' she said to Will as she climbed.

Will stood on his own for a long minute. Then he pulled himself up the ladder, swung back into his couch and swapped into his home node to fume. He paced back and forth, cursing at the top of his virtual lungs. He felt stupid. That little outburst of his hadn't exactly helped his cause. Perhaps if he didn't feel so damned edgy all the time, it wouldn't have happened.

He glared at the familiar stone walls of the metaphor space. They'd never looked so foreign to him. He knew that somewhere beyond them lurked the Transcended. Watching him, listening to him, twisting him.

Will shouted at the walls. 'Leave me alone! I thought you were supposed to be helping me, but you're making it worse, not better! I can't work on your damned archive feeling like this!'

He spun around to deliver another tirade to the opposite wall, but instead found an SAP hovering just in front of his face.

'Gah!' he exclaimed and jumped back, his heart hammering.

The SAP was a cumbersome, ugly thing, all twisted rings and straggling memory trees like damp weeds.

Will narrowed his eyes at it. 'Fine! This is your answer, is it? Another fucking puzzle. What am I, a lab rat? How's this for a deal. I solve it, you fuck off out of my head. Sound good?'

He didn't expect a response, and one didn't come.

'Well, fine then!' he said, with a grand sweep of his hand.

If the aliens wanted another trick from him before they talked, that's what they'd get. And then he was going to give them a piece of his mind.

Unsurprisingly, the SAP required him to make a butchered mess of his mental processes in order to synchronise with it, even more so than last time. But Will was used to that by now. He ignored his usual restraint. He hurled together whatever processor modules the program required, regardless of the reason why senses might be grouped that way, or the effect they'd have on him. He was too angry to care.

In less than an hour, he had a finished solution. It wasn't pretty, but then neither was the puzzle it was built on. Will activated it with a click of his fingers.

'Come on, then,' he growled at the program and threw himself in.

He found himself lying in a berth aboard a slow-moving starship carved from the body of an asteroid. Through the touch console, Will could feel the outlines of the wonderful new world hanging below them. There were a few cities there, their fins sticking up above the dunes in orderly rows. It was a big improvement over the old world. He could remember it, a place with countless kilometres of tunnels, honeycombed to death, the bottom layers filled with industrial waste.

He snuggled up against his wife. He couldn't see her, but through a combination of other senses, he knew what they both looked like. *Ugly*, said the human mind. *Wonderful*, said the puzzle.

They had simple vestigial eyes like a spider's on blunt faces with huge teeth for gnawing. Where ears should have been they had noses that doubled as whiskers, big feathery protrusions like the antennae of moths. There were retractable spade-like claws on their hands. They came from a world of hot, subterranean rivers and limestone forests.

His wife spoke. Once again, the Transcended used Rachel's voice.

'You are experiencing frustration.'

The theft of her smooth, alto tones filled Will with further rage.

'Damn right!' he said. 'And the first thing you can do about it is lay off that voice! If you think it's going to win me over, you're way wrong.'

'We use the voice of your intended mate to increase your comfort and attentiveness, not to attempt persuasion,' said the Transcended.

Will was caught off guard. 'Intended mate?' He'd never let himself think of Rachel in those terms.

'Do you deny that this is your desire?'

Will wanted to deny it, but what was the point of denying the truth to an entity that had access to the inside of your head? That was reaching new levels of denial.

'You did not call upon us to discuss the voice of your intended mate,' said the Transcended.

Will recovered his momentum. 'No. You know exactly why I called on you – because I'm fed up with you messing around inside my head!' He jerked back and forth in the lightless berth, wobbling his long, hairless body.

'You refer to the sensation of discomfort you have experienced since leaving the Fecund star system,' said the female beside him.

'Of course I'm talking about the fucking *sensation*. I want you to stop it!'

'We cannot. We are not the origin of the sensation. You are.'

That took Will by surprise.

'It is a natural anxiety springing from an accurate comprehension of your situation,' the alien explained. 'By leaving the Fecund system, you are risking the destruction of your species.'

'I didn't have a choice,' said Will.

'You do not fully believe this remark. This is one reason why your anxiety is so acute.'

Will gnashed his enormous teeth. 'You could have helped me,' he insisted. 'We need not have left.'

'You believe we should have aided you in convincing Captain Baron to remain in the Fecund star system.'

'Yes!'

'You are mistaken,' the Transcended said. 'This was your responsibility. You may consider it a part of the test.'

'The *test*,' Will said with scorn, 'feels like a pretty arbitrary way to decide the fate of a species.'

'Yes,' the alien agreed. 'However, it is still the best option available to us at this point. When you activated this program, we began taking steps to equip you with the tools you will need to compensate for your changed circumstances.'

Will wasn't sure he liked the sound of that. 'Tools? What kind of tools?'

'Their nature will become clear to you if you solve the required puzzle necessary to activate them.'

'Look,' he said, 'you don't understand. Can't this whole test thing just wait? Just give us a while to stop the Earthers first!'

'You cannot stop them,' said the female. 'Captain Baron is mistaken in his belief that the knowledge he has is adequate to prevent his world from being overrun.'

Will froze. 'How... You can't know that.'

'We examined the memory hierarchies of the group you call the Earthers in great detail. Without assistance, you will eventually be overwhelmed by sheer force of numbers.'

'Then blow up Zuni-Dehel!' Will raged. 'You can do that, can't you?'

'That option was available to us when you made contact with the lure, but this test was considered a better solution. You no longer have access to the lure. Furthermore, you no longer have access to the Fecund star system.'

Will was aghast. 'Why not?'

'At thirteen forty-three ship time today, your fuel supplies became too low to enable you to return.'

Will was speechless for a moment. Ira had kept that mighty quiet. Will's sense of betrayal deepened a little.

'Why didn't you tell me?' he said.

'We were waiting to see if your natural anxiety was sufficient to override your group instincts while return was still possible.'

Will craned his bulky, seal-like body against the soft upper layer of the berth. 'You did *what*?'

'That motivation was not sufficient,' the female said, ignoring his outburst. 'It is our judgement that you sacrificed your desire to the perceived need of your social group. This trait is visible in many constructive species, so we have not condemned you for it.'

'This is insane!' said Will. 'You want us to go back, but you leave it till *now* to tell me we don't have that option?'

'No, Will,' said the alien wryly. 'We do not want you to go back. We encourage you to. Were we to have attempted coercion, we would have succeeded. We are only interested in what you choose to do. We intervene only to give you access to facilities we have already decided to put at your disposal. Here are two questions for you to consider. First, would you return to the Fecund system now if you were the only one at risk – if it was a choice for you to make alone?'

'Of course,' he said.

'Secondly, what are you prepared to sacrifice to create such an opportunity?'

Will paused. He didn't have an easy answer for that one.

'We recommend you contemplate that,' the alien said finally.

Will felt his senses lurch. The SAP was starting to disengage. 'Wait!' he cried, but it was already too late.

The puzzle dumped him back into the *Ariel*'s main cabin. He felt as if he'd been dropped there from a great height. He gasped for breath and stared at the ceiling of his bunk.

He was glad Amy wasn't monitoring his vital signs right now. They wouldn't have shown him in the best of health. The puzzle had left him with an overpowering sensation of nausea. As he lay motionless on his bunk recovering, Will found himself filled with dread.

It was too late to go back. That meant they had no choice but to try John's plan on New Angeles. Sweat rolled off his brow. He tried to reach up to wipe his face and discovered to his horror that he was too weak to move. Now that he paid attention to it, it was clear his body had changed since he'd launched the puzzle. It was burning up. The alien virus was back.

He tried to speak but couldn't even muster a croak. He was forced to cry out through his interface instead.

'Help!'

Even that frail effort was too much for him. He struggled to stay awake, without success, and tumbled headlong into the abyss of unconsciousness.

11.3: IRA

After the fiasco in the privacy chamber, sleep for Ira became impossible. He climbed up into the meeting chamber, unlocked the gym-system from the wall and started bench-pressing weights. He had to channel the physical tension in his body into something other than crushing Hugo's skull like an egg.

Infuriating though the scientist was, Ira knew he only had himself to blame. Things should never have got this bad. The Ira of five years ago would have woken spontaneously the moment Hugo started talking to Will. Hell, even the Ira of six months ago. His instincts had never failed him so badly. He was definitely losing his touch.

Worse still, Ira had known he'd been taking a risk when he threatened Hugo. Applying traditional stick-and-carrot discipline to men as genetically overclocked as Hugo Vartian never panned out straight. There was always the chance they'd snap, and Hugo had definitely snapped. Ira notched the weight setting up again to five hundred kilos and started a fresh set of reps.

The comm sounded.

'What is it?' said Ira.

'It's me,' said John. 'Can you spare a moment?'

Ira folded the weights back into the wall and thumbed the door open.

John's head appeared at the hatch. 'Hi,' he said and climbed in, shutting the door behind him.

'What can I do for you?' said Ira, wiping the sweat from his face. He didn't feel much like talking.

'It's about you, Captain,' said John. 'With respect, your cracks are showing.'

Ira scowled at him.

John grinned and raised both hands in submission. 'A joke! Really. I heard everything that happened and I didn't come up here to piss you off more. I want to help. It's clear we have a problem.'

'That's a fucking understatement,' Ira growled. 'We're going to have to put our goddamn passenger into coma. Which will make a mess of what's left of our meds and leave us a hand down right as we go into the lion's den.'

'We don't have to,' said John. 'That's what I wanted to say. I have an idea: we could just put him off the ship instead.'

Ira frowned. 'I don't get it. Are you proposing we shove him out of an airlock?'

John shook his head. 'Of course not. I'm talking about giving him to the resistance on New Angeles to babysit. Look, he's done his job – we already know how to beat the suntap. Now he's dead weight and causing problems. Setting him down would give everyone a break.'

Ira winced. 'I don't like it,' he said bluntly. 'For starters, he's got a head full of military secrets.'

'Is that really an issue?' asked John. 'How long can the war possibly last now? The suntap has totally changed the game. There are a few months left in it, tops, we both know that. Either we get home in time, build our own suntaps and force a truce on Earth, or Galatea will be crushed. Nothing in Hugo's head makes a whit of difference any more. Plus there's the fact that using coma is a problem, as you mentioned. If anything else weird happens to Will, we'll be out of meds. Do you want that?'

Ira squirmed inside. John's idea made sense. He dearly wanted Hugo off the ship but dumping him with a bunch of rebels still felt like a cruel choice.

'I'm not sure he could hack it,' he said. 'He hasn't exactly proved himself robust.'

'True,' said John. 'But you need Will, you need a functional ship and you need to be able to make it home even if some other crazy shit busts off on this mission. You have to ask yourself if you're prepared to risk Galatea's survival to protect a single, unbalanced physicist.'

Put that way the answer seemed clear, even if Ira didn't like it that much. He exhaled. The moment he let himself indulge the idea, he could feel a weight lifting from his shoulders.

'How do you expect to do it?' he asked. 'Hugo's not an easy man to handle. We can't afford to jeopardize your mission.'

John laughed. 'Not a problem,' he said. 'I promise. If you could have met some of the people I've babysat behind enemy lines, you wouldn't worry. For starters, there's only one of him and he's not trying to kill me.'

'And what do we tell Hugo? How do we get him to buy in?'

'Simple.' John waved an airy hand. 'We tell him that you can't stand the sight of his face, which is true. We say that I've requested help for the trip down to New Angeles, and that this is his chance to redeem himself. He doesn't need to know he's staying put.'

Ira pulled a face. 'You think he'd buy that?'

'I think he'd buy that we're desperate, which is enough. Furthermore, I think he'd see a chance to advance his own agenda by getting off your ship, which makes everything else moot.'

Ira stared at the wall and thought. He still didn't like the plan but he couldn't argue with the efficiency of it. It had the kind of cold, tidy logic John excelled at. Plus there was the churning, irrational sense inside him that at some level, Hugo deserved it. Maybe seeing what the rest of the war looked like outside his ivory tower would be the slap of perspective he needed.

'You're confident he'll be safe?'

John cocked an amused eyebrow. 'You're saying he'd be safe on the *Ariel*? He'll definitely be *safer* down there, but let's face it, that's not hard. You have to fly home unnoticed across all of Earther space while being hunted by the entire fleet. He won't.'

Ira hesitated, knowing he'd already been convinced. Another ping on the comm broke his thoughts.

'What is it?' said Ira.

John's brow creased in anger at the interruption.

Amy's voice sounded over the speaker. 'It's Will,' she said with a heavy sigh. 'His micromachines are at it again. I've no idea how or why they started up again, but it's far worse than before. The virus has invaded most of his major organs.'

Back in the main cabin, Ira viewed Will's medical profile with a mixture of fury and concern. It didn't surprise him that the mystery illness should appear the moment they turned their backs on the Fecund system. Ira wasn't doing what the so-called Transcended wanted, so they were using the best bargaining chip they had: Will's life. If these aliens expected him to trust them, they weren't doing a great job of convincing him.

A part of Ira did regret leaving the ruins behind. Perhaps Will had been right that an answer lay back there. But Ira was the captain of a Galatean starship, and he didn't have the luxury of following a series of cryptic clues when there was a deadline for the survival of his people. And anyway, what kind of ally opened negotiations with a threat to destroy the human race? When he thought about it too much, Hugo's ideas started to make sense.

'Is there any way we can deactivate them?' he asked Amy. 'His micromachines, I mean.'

'Not without taking them out. Which we don't have the tech for.'

He scowled down at Will's empty bunk. 'So where does that leave us?'

Amy sighed. 'Our best option is to contain the virus by leaving him in the tank. With a constant supply of antivirals, we might be able to keep him stable till we get home.'

'Might?' said Ira.

'I'd give it about ten per cent.'

'Then that's not an option. Anything else?'

Amy frowned. 'Not that I can think of. I hate this, Ira. It makes me feel sick. Never in my entire medical career have I felt so helpless around a patient.'

Ira shook his head. Even if Will *was* thoroughly compromised, Ira wasn't going to give up on him so easily.

'What if we sent him down to New Angeles?'

Amy blinked at him in surprise. 'An away mission isn't a safe place for anybody, let alone someone as sick as Will is.'

'John says it's safe enough for him to take Hugo.'

Ira watched the expressions cycle on Amy's careworn face: confusion, disbelief, hope.

'It would make all the difference,' she said slowly. 'Medicine on New Angeles is quite advanced. Their methods and focus are quite different from ours, but if we brought some skull schematics with us, it should be relatively easy for them.'

'Will he last till we get there?' he said.

'He should,' said Amy, her enthusiasm visibly rekindling. 'I've mapped the disease's spread rate. We'd have days to spare.'

Ira pondered the idea. It clearly wasn't what the Transcended had in mind, but maybe that was a good thing. At the end of the day, Ira needed his roboteer, and he needed him well enough to work. And if the planet was safe enough for Hugo... He rubbed his jaw.

Amy put a hand on his arm. 'Ira, if you think this is possible, we don't have a choice. It would save his life. In fact, it's probably the only thing that could. And it would make all the difference to the mission. He doesn't need his micromachines for his interface to work. All they do is lay down the protein tracks that keep his nerve endings connected to the implant chips. His processors and transmitter would stay in. Eventually he'd experience some degradation in performance, of course, as his neurons reconnected, but he'd keep his functions till we get home. We'd have our roboteer back. We'd have Will.' Her eyes implored him.

'Hey, John,' Ira called.

John looked out from his bunk, his expression carefully neutral. 'Yes, sir?'

'My apologies, but you're going to have to take Will down to New Angeles with you as well.'

John was silent for a second, and then came back with a brittle smile. 'I don't recommend that, sir,' he said. 'Hugo's one thing, but there's no way I can make contact with the resistance and nursemaid Will at the same time.'

'Fine,' said Ira. 'I don't expect you to. I'll send Rachel with you.'

John blinked rapidly. 'I don't think that's going to work, either. The more of us there are, the more likely it is we'll hit trouble. It's that simple.'

Ira contained his annoyance. 'Look, I'm aware of the risk, but babysitting people on New Angeles is either easy or it's not. Which is it, John?'

John's mouth curved in discomfort before breaking into a sickly grin. It looked to Ira like he'd just worked out that he'd argued himself into a corner. The security expert sighed and chuckled. 'Okay. You win, Captain,' he said. 'Four of us it is. I can tell you now, though, it's not going to be easy.'

'Nothing about this mission has been easy,' Ira retorted. 'Why should it start now?'

11.4: WILL

Will was woken by a violent shaking sensation.

'Sorry about that, everybody,' said Rachel. 'Air pocket.'

He forced his eyes to focus – something that felt unusually hard to do – and discovered that he was strapped into one of the seats aboard the *Ariel*'s shuttle. Rachel's voice had come from behind him, and he could make out John in front, tapping madly on his keyboard.

'What is this?' he said blurrily. His mouth felt dry and furry. His limbs were weak to the point of being lifeless.

'Will!' Rachel exclaimed. 'You're awake!'

'Just. What the hell am I doing here?'

'Don't worry, Will,' she said. 'Everything's okay. We're taking you down to New Angeles.'

They'd arrived already? He must have been unconscious for almost a week. And apparently, in that time, the plans had changed again.

'Why?' he croaked. 'What's happening?'

There was an uncomfortable pause.

'We're going to talk to the resistance, Will,' Rachel replied. 'About taking your micromachines out.'

At first, Will couldn't believe what he'd heard. Why would they do such a thing? Then he worked it out. The micromachines must have been the cause of his condition. Something in him squeezed tight. It was a mistake. The micromachines had been changed by the Transcended. For all he knew, they were a crucial part of his link to them.

'You can't,' he said.

'They're killing you, Will,' Rachel said gently. 'They're making the virus again, and this time they're not stopping.'

'I don't care!' Though Will dearly wanted his mind back, he wasn't about to take risks with what might be humanity's last chance.

'Will—' said Rachel, but John cut her off.

'Everybody shut up!'

The cabin fell silent. Then, over the speakers came an automated female voice.

'Welcome home, Trader Arturi!' it said. 'I trust your trip has been a profitable one.'

'I hope so,' John replied cheerfully. 'I won't know that till I sell these damn things.'

'Do remember that you have to quote for imported merchandise on arrival, on the basis of expected price,' the voice told him.

'Don't worry,' John told the machine with murderous lightness. 'I'm filing it right now.'

'Thank you, Trader Arturi. Wishing you a pleasant landing.'

'Thank you, Customs,' said John. 'Arturi over and out.' He punched a key on his keyboard and craned himself around in the cramped chair to face Will. 'Welcome back to the land of the living,' he said with a dangerous smile. 'Given that you're conscious, I'll go through the rules one last time. Our job is to make contact with the resistance, fix you up, agree a price or barter for fuel and return to the rendezvous with a fuel-laden ship. That's all. Everyone does what I say, when I say it. And if you step out of line, I'll kill you. Is that clear?'

The fact that John delivered this remark so easily, and with such empty goodwill, made Will's blood freeze. He might have been joking, but Will didn't think so this time. Something in the way John's eyes shone left little room for humour.

Will nodded.

'I'm sorry about your micromachines, but this is an away mission and therefore under my jurisdiction,' said John. 'I've been given orders to see that you get medical attention, and that's what I'm going to do. If all goes well, we'll rendezvous with the *Ariel* two days hence.' He made an inquisitive face. 'Am I right in thinking this is your first trip behind enemy lines, Will?'

Will wondered why he was asking. Of course it was. He nodded again.

'Then you're in the same boat as Hugo.'

Will blinked in surprise. Hugo was on the mission, too?

'Rachel has taken Fleet survival training,' John explained, 'so if I'm not there, you take your cues from her. If you want to make yourself useful, you can plug in and check the pilot SAP. We'll be landing in just a few minutes.' He turned back to his console.

'You should know what the Transcended told me,' said Will.

'It's not relevant,' John said casually.

'They said there was no way we could beat the Earthers without their help.'

'And you believed them.' The assault expert sounded almost pitying.

'Yes, I believe them.'

'You know, Will, that's exactly what I would have told you if I'd been trying to take over your head. Now please be quiet before you convince me you have to die right now for the good of the mission.'

Will sat in his seat and gripped the armrest with strengthless fingers. Whatever the Transcended had been up to, it didn't appear to have made his situation any easier.

'What the hell am I supposed to do now?' he shouted into his private node. But this time, no puzzle appeared.

John brought the shuttle in at an unmanned industrial facility that didn't look like it had seen any activity since the Earthers arrived. It was just a bunch of windowless barrel-roofed buildings in the middle of nowhere, with sand piled up against one side and a dusty landing strip. It looked like dozens Will had seen on Galatea, if perhaps a little on the primitive side.

He felt an involuntary squeeze of homesickness as he viewed the scene through the shuttle's external cameras. The sky was a dusty lilac instead of blue and the rocks were redder, but otherwise, it was all painfully familiar.

'Hey, Will,' said John. 'Want to get some of those robots to pull us in?'

Will glared at the back of John's seat. He considered refusing, but what was the point? Whatever scheme he cooked up to extricate himself from this mess would still involve finding juice for the *Ariel* and the survival of his shipmates. He used the shuttle's data ports to jerk the facility's old-fashioned robots into life.

With the palsied slowness of long neglect, the machines pulled the shuttle into one of the hangars. It was a dismal place, all artificial lighting and dust-creep. They docked against a personnel tunnel and waited while what passed for an engineers' habitat was pumped full of breathable air. When it was done, Rachel and Hugo carried Will out of the hot, ticking shuttle. Will couldn't help noticing that Hugo refused to meet his eyes. What a happy family they'd become.

'What's the matter, Hugo?' he asked.

Hugo's mouth tightened.

'Hugo's under orders not to speak with you unless the mission requires it,' said John. 'We've already had a chat. You won't get much out of him. This way, ladies and gents,' he added, strolling ahead of them.

He led them into a featureless plastic corridor. Once again, Will had the strong sense that he could have been somewhere on Galatea. Except the Galateans never let their buildings become this shabby.

'What is this place?' Will asked.

'Exactly what it looks like,' John replied. 'An unused freight station. They used to bring in luxury goods through here. Since the war, there hasn't been much call for them.'

'Won't the Customs people notice?' said Will. 'This can't have been where we were okayed to land.'

John shot him an amused glance. 'What on Earth makes you think that a single living person on this planet has a fucking clue what we're doing right now? Customs has been *fixed* – or didn't you catch that?'

John took them to a staff changing room where they removed their environment suits and stored them in a great bank of empty lockers. Underneath, John wore a full set of Earther-style clothes in unobtrusive grey – high-waisted trousers of some cheap-looking material with fancy embroidery along the seams and a large, blousy shirt. Over his eyes went a data visor disguised as a pair of sunglasses. Strapped to his wrist was a small keyboard designed to resemble some kind of Earther fashion item.

The others had nothing but their ship-suits. The *Ariel* wasn't equipped for four-man away missions.

'What are we going to do about these?' asked Rachel, nervously fingering her sleeve.

'Don't worry,' said John. 'It's on my list. I'm not having you all wandering around in broad daylight wearing Gallie Fleet colours.'

They followed a windowless tunnel to an environment door. On the other side of it was a small rectangular transit car seated on a rail leading out into the desert.

John ushered them inside. 'Get in, folks, this is our ride.'

Once Will had been bundled aboard, John tapped the console on his arm and the car set off. The trip across the desert was achingly reminiscent of home – the same buttes, the same scree fields. Will found tears springing to the corners of his eyes.

He realised then that he'd long since given up any hope that he'd ever set foot on a planet again, let alone his own. It was a terrible kind of tease, he decided, being here. It reminded him so much of the place he wanted to be, yet, if anything, it was more dangerous than the starship they'd just left.

The others looked similarly entranced. They watched the passing landscape, drinking it in. Only John appeared indifferent to the view. He scorned the seats and leaned up against the plastic window, tapping idly at the keyboard on his wrist, a fixed smile curving the corners of his mouth.

Eventually, a rose-tinted tent city appeared in the distance, like some enormous Old World circus set out in the middle of nowhere.

'That's our destination,' John told them. 'The city of Goldwin.'

Will had played memories of tent cities, but this was the first time he'd seen one with his own eyes. It looked huge and fragile beyond belief. Graceful white masts supported a skin of translucent polymer. Will could make out pastel-coloured buildings inside, gleaming like giant crystals. It was something out of a fairy story and it demolished the illusion of being home. No one on Galatea built anything that tall or flimsy. It'd be smashed flat in the first dust storm that came along. Clearly, New Angeles didn't have real dust storms. It was just one of the many advantages of not pursuing a terraforming project.

As they approached, the illusion of fairy magic began to fade. Will made out splotches of pale grey sealant foam on the tent wall – recent repairs, and lots of them. He could see black scorch-marks on the buildings inside, too. His sense of foreboding returned.

The mood in the transit car grew steadily sourer as they got closer.

John stopped smiling and began scanning the terrain outside for signs of enemy attention. Fortunately, there were none.

Will held his breath as the car slid into a cluster of drab, boxy buildings stuck to the edge of the city. The lilac-tinted light disappeared behind them as they entered another gloomy hangar lit by isolated halogen lamps far overhead. Huge stacks of cargo loomed on either side of them like blank-faced houses. In the background, Will could make out the lumbering silhouettes of heavy-duty lifter trucks.

The transit car slid to a halt against an environment door. John strode up to meet it.

'Wait here,' he told them. He disappeared through the moment it opened.

Hugo and Rachel helped Will to the doorway. Minutes scraped nerve-wrackingly by. Will began to wonder if John had decided to undertake the mission alone and abandoned them, but seconds later he reappeared and ushered them forward.

'Okay, come on. And keep it quiet.'

John led them out into a huge enclosed space filled with dry, tasteless air and the hum of fans. Robot motors whined somewhere nearby. It was a long time since Will had been exposed to such a large space without walls or a spacesuit screening him from it. It made him feel dizzy and free. And afraid.

John led them down a narrow path between stacks of huge freight containers stored in perfectly straight rows. Will bit his lip every time they passed an intersection. At the end of the path was an open area where the light was brighter. They stopped just before it.

'The guards' post is just up ahead,' John whispered. 'It'll take a moment to distract them.' He tapped on his sleeve. 'When I give the word, follow me. Stay close. Don't stop or say anything.'

From somewhere beyond the containers, Will heard the laughter of young men. The sound was followed by some enthusiastic shouting in one of the many incomprehensible Earther languages. Will realised it was the first time in his life that he'd actually heard the people they were fighting first hand. They sounded normal.

'Now,' John hissed.

The assault expert strode out as if he owned the place. The rest of them struggled along barely two paces behind. Will stumbled between his two human crutches, willing his body to walk.

Ahead of them was a broad polycrete forecourt where several private transports were parked – the sort Will had often seen on imported interactives. Beyond was a rectangular opening leading onto a road lined with blank-faced buildings.

John walked straight past a glass-fronted guardhouse to their left. From the corner of his eye, Will glimpsed a group of soldiers clustered around the light from a monitor screen in the corner. The sight of them chilled him.

Hugo hesitated in front of the guard-house for a moment like an over-stimulated robot, but Rachel dragged him forward. A private transport rolled through the opening and stopped right in front of them.

'Get in,' John said quietly. 'And make it fast.'

He opened the back door for them. They bundled Will in while John stepped around to the front of the vehicle. He slid into the seat and tapped something on the dashboard. The side windows went dark.

Hugo was the last to get in. As his door closed, John grabbed the steering column and drove straight out into the bright street beyond. Rachel gasped in relief.

'Don't relax just yet,' he told her. Almost on cue, they turned the corner of a beige industrial building to find a squad of Earther soldiers in bright red and yellow uniforms standing there with bulky pacifier-rifles slung across their backs.

'Don't look at them,' John advised. 'Stay low in the seats.'

For Will, that wasn't a problem. He could barely sit up.

John pulled the transport to a halt just a few blocks further on. 'Stay here,' he said, and got out. He strode away through the doorway of a white-fronted warehouse.

'What's he doing?' asked Hugo.

'How should I know?' Rachel snapped.

A military vehicle striped like a hornet passed them on the other side of the road. Will's heart waited until it was past to resume beating.

John stepped back out of the warehouse with some bulky

plastic-wrapped parcels under his arm. He strolled nonchalantly up to the transport and opened the back door next to Rachel. He hurled the packages in as if the passengers weren't there.

'Get dressed,' he told them and slammed the door. Then he got back into the front seat and drove on.

Rachel ripped open the packages. Inside were dark-coloured Earther clothes. Rachel started helping Will out of his ship-suit. He reached up to stop her with a trembling hand.

'I can do it,' he said. He was feeling a great deal stronger now than when he'd woken up.

Nevertheless, it was awkward getting dressed in the back of the transport. Thankfully, the one John had borrowed for them was significantly bigger than the public taxi-bugs on Galatea.

There were high-waisted trousers with flared legs and dark shirts for Hugo and Will. The shirts had brightly coloured highlights and symbols on the front, arrayed like medals. Rachel's outfit had voluminous skirts, a zip-up corset and a long black tube that covered her shoulders and head, leaving only her face exposed. She scowled as she pulled the clothing on.

'Will, you'll have to help me with this stupid thing.' She turned sideways so that Will could yank up the corset zip at the back. It took all of his strength.

'Breathe in,' John advised, with some evident amusement. 'It'll help.'

'Fuck you,' she snarled at him. 'You did this on purpose.'

''Fraid not,' he replied. 'This is all the rage on the crusader catwalk this year.'

Rachel didn't look convinced. 'Couldn't you have found something a little more appropriate? How am I supposed to fight in this if the nan hits the fan?'

'You don't,' John said coolly. 'If it gets bad enough that we need to fight, we're already dead. While you're here, you play at being a good little Truist woman. Keep your eyes down and don't open your mouth.'

She glared at him. 'Fuck you, John. You could have dressed us as natives.'

John had a good laugh at that. 'Forgetting for a moment that we don't look anything like the natives,' he said, 'you really do *not* want to be one.' He glanced at her. 'You think I'm joking. I'm not. You'd better start playing meek if you want to live. You'll see.'

Will watched the city as they drove through it. It took him a while to get over the novelty of a city built on flat ground, and the strange sight of the lightly streaked plastic sky overhead.

The industrial district gave way slowly to residential areas and there were other sights to claim Will's attention. He saw hordes of soldiers and buildings that were garish to the point of disbelief. Almost every one of them featured baroque turrets or crystal facades or some other kind of adornment that drowned out the shapes of the structures themselves.

But the most striking decorations had been added recently. There were bullet-holes and scorch-marks on the mirror-bright plastic walls. Many of the turrets were punched in, as if struck by gigantic fists. Some of the houses had been burned to the ground so that only twisted remnants of their ornamentation remained. Will had the impression of a children's fantasy in which devils had been let loose.

John took a left turn up a boulevard. Will inhaled sharply as the view of the street ahead swung into view. It was crawling with Earther troops dressed in every imaginable combination of colours. They appeared to be having some kind of party. Most were clearly drunk, though it was the middle of the day.

Rachel gripped her seat. 'John, are you sure this is a good idea?'

John chuckled to himself. 'Do you want to drive?'

Through the crowds, Will saw a soldier dragging a woman around on a leash. He looked away and caught sight of another woman being bent over a café table while a soldier unfastened his trousers. His friends cheered him on. A little further down, a smiling man knelt on the pavement while soldiers took turns to kick him in the face.

Will felt sick. He was reminded of the propaganda broadcasts he'd watched. Was this what the Earthers referred to as *enjoying a free expression of faith*?

'I thought you should see this place,' said John breezily. 'Take in a little of the local colour and all that.'

'You asshole,' said Rachel, shaking her head at him.

John continued as if he hadn't heard her. 'They call this place Party Town. It's where the off-duty soldiers come.'

'I thought we weren't supposed to be taking risks with the fucking mission,' Rachel snapped.

'There's no risk,' John replied lightly. 'These guys are far too busy having fun to pay any attention to us. Look, we're through the thick of it.'

It was true. They had already driven through the worst of the melee and were cruising down a street that had practically been demolished. Broken glass and plastic littered the streets. What had once been windows and doors were now empty eye sockets in lifeless buildings. It looked as if the non-stop party had already visited and wrung all life from the neighbourhood as it passed through.

John put the car on automatic and leaned over the seat to talk to them. 'New Angeles used to be the self-styled Planet of Dreams,' he said.

Rachel sat back in her seat, folded her arms and stared out through the window. John didn't appear to care. He addressed himself to Will and Hugo instead.

'Back when Galatea was in the patent-farming business, New Angeles had a different way of paying for their colony runs. They specialised in entertainment – canned stories, interactives, that sort of thing. You know much about that bit of history, Hugo?'

Hugo shook his head mutely.

'It was fucked up,' said John with a grin. 'Colonies had to bend themselves out of shape just to make enough money to keep food coming in from the home system. That's when we started giving our kids mods and taking risks with the atmosphere. Nobody guessed how high the cost of spaceflight was going to climb. The fucking trader companies had a nice little captive market going there. Mars got rich. Everyone else took it in the neck.'

He laughed and shook his head. 'Except of course, over here it wasn't about mods and nanotech. Instead, their culture got kind of weird. Fantasy and reality blended together there for a while.'

That accounted for the weird architecture, at least, Will thought.

'The Angelenos messed with all kinds of stuff to find ways to pay the rent,' John explained. 'They had interactives, passives, robotic sex dolls, drugs, cosmetic surgery, pleasure implants, you name it.' He gestured expansively as if to show the scope of the Angelenos' enterprise. 'Needless to say, after the Truists took Mars, they made a bee-line for this place. It was a perfect propaganda victory for them. Decadent colonists with twisted tastes and no defences to speak of. They turned it into an R&R planet for the crusader armies. And the soldiers love it. They brought some of their Earther entertainments here to add to the fun. Hope riots and blood-baptisms. That sort of thing.'

John shrugged. 'Of course, life hasn't been so great for the Angelenos. Half their female population is involved in prostitution, and about a quarter of the males. That's what happens to the local girls, Rachel. Take a good look.' He fixed her with a particularly unpleasant smile. 'Oh, and anyone with detectable mods ends up either castrated or burned, mostly at parties.' He sounded almost amused.

Will shivered. Was this the kind of fate Galatea could look forward to if the Earthers won? If it were, then maybe extinction at the hands of the Transcended would be a blessing.

'It's no great surprise this planet's got such a rabid resistance movement,' said John. 'They hate the Earthers like no one else. And they have the added advantage that most of the soldiers they're fighting are drunk or stoned or both. But the funny thing' – John raised a conspiratorial finger – 'is that the troops have got particularly out of hand recently. Despite the fact that they came here to save the locals from their depraved habits, they appear to have adopted a lot of them along the way. You're deeply surprised at that, I'm sure. But anyway, the black market in twisted entertainment ends up supporting the resistance. The fucking Earthers are paying for it out of their own pockets. Isn't that great?'

'Terrific,' Rachel snarled.

John gave her a bitter look. 'Not my fault if you can't appreciate a nice bit of irony,' he said, and turned back to watch the road.

He drove them to an apartment building in nondescript magenta on a quiet street lined with ginkgo trees that had been left to die. He stopped the transport and turned around to face them again.

'We know,' snapped Rachel before he could open his mouth. 'Wait here.'

'You got it,' said John with a wink. He exited the transport, walked up to the front door and disappeared inside.

Will and the others sat and waited. Minutes blended together to make an hour. An armed patrol in red and yellow strolled past them. They stopped to interrogate a girl in a short skirt and impractical shoes hurrying from one building to another. Will watched as she broke down in tears in front of them. They let her go with no more than a squeeze of her ass. Still John did not emerge.

'Do you suppose he's dead?' Hugo said at last.

'Shut up, Hugo,' muttered Rachel.

Eventually, John appeared in the doorway and jogged back over to them. Rachel exhaled in relief at the sight of him.

'Do we go in now?' Hugo asked as John climbed in.

'Of course not,' John snapped. 'That's not how it works.'

He drove off with a lurch. Evidently, whatever happened inside hadn't put him in the best of moods.

'You want to talk about it?' said Rachel.

'Not particularly.'

They pulled into the parking lot of what looked to Will like some kind of office building clad in contoured gold panels. Some of the panels had been ripped off. Others were crazed with fracture patterns from bullet impacts.

'All right, everybody out,' said John. 'Same rules apply – move quickly and don't talk.'

There was no door, only black scarring around the frame. John led them across the ruined, barren lobby and up three flights of utilitarian stairs to a room without furniture or decoration. There was a dented, plastic door at the far end and security cameras in the ceiling corners. Rachel and Hugo leaned Will up against the cream-coloured polycrete wall.

'Now what?' said Rachel.

'Now we wait,' replied John in a patronising voice.

So they waited for another hour as the sun slid down the Angeleno sky and shone in through the thickest part of the tent. It filled the room with eerie rust-coloured light.

At long last, the door opened. A man appeared on the other side dressed in a blousy shirt and trousers of matching cerise pink. He was unnaturally tall, with an absurdly handsome face, a shock of shoulder-length golden hair and eyes so blue they looked painted. He reminded Will of a character from a children's interactive, except that his rugged features were distorted into a very real expression of disgust.

In one hand, he held a small, equally real gun.

'In,' he ordered, gesturing with the weapon.

Inside was another bare room, windowless this time, and lit from above by a single lamp. In the middle was a table with four chairs on one side and one on the other. Four large Angelenos stood in the corners with arms folded across their massive chests and guns in their belts. All were as good-looking as the first. They could have been brothers.

John had been right, Will realised. There was no way they could have passed themselves off as Angelenos. These people made the crew of the *Ariel* look like ugly dwarves.

Seated at the table facing them was the most striking occupant of all – a hard-eyed, middle-aged woman with short black hair. Her doll-like beauty was marred by a scar running from her temple to her jaw. Her face was set in a scowl of barely suppressed fury.

'Sit down,' she told them in a drawly Angeleno accent.

'Metta, good to see you again,' said John with an easy smile.

'Shut the fuck up, Yoric.'

Will glanced at John. Clearly this was some pseudonym he used. *Metta* probably wasn't a real name, either.

'Have you any conception of the trouble your people have caused us?' Metta added.

John raised an eyebrow. 'Trouble?'

'We're facing the worst clamp-down we've seen in this place since the invasion and it's all over one fucking ship. A *Gallie* ship. And I don't doubt for a second that it's yours. This trouble's got your stink all over it.'

John sat back and looked surprised. 'We didn't have any trouble getting in.'

'Don't give yourself any awards just yet, fly boy,' said Metta. 'We've been running interference with traffic control ever since the new orders came in. We've got half a dozen agents still trapped in the outer system and your being here isn't making it any easier to bring them home.'

'I'm sorry,' said John.

'Don't be. It's none of your damn business.'

John leaned forwards again. 'We can be out of your hair in a matter of days. All we need—'

Metta's eyes narrowed. 'I know what you need and there's not a chance.'

'Metta—'

She graced him with a sneer. 'Do you really not know what's going on? Every fuelling star between here and your front line is under watch. The Earthers have put triple guard around all our factories. Half my agents in juice-production are dead. The rest are scared shitless. There is *no* antimatter.'

Will was surprised to discover that he felt relieved. Now they'd have to change their plans. Perhaps they'd hijack another starship instead and he'd get to keep his micromachines.

'That's not all we need,' said John. He gestured at Will. 'Our roboteer requires medical attention. He's suffering implant rejection, and if he doesn't get help soon, he's going to die.'

'John—' Will started, but Rachel squeezed his arm hard.

Metta surveyed Will with cold, china-blue eyes. He had the uncomfortable sensation of being assessed like a robot about to be broken up for scrap.

'Forget the fuel for a minute,' said John. 'Will needs help and you owe us. Or have you forgotten about the hackpacks I brought you?'

Metta snorted at him. 'Calling in favours, Yoric? You must be desperate.'

'He's not just crew, Metta,' said John. 'He's important to the war effort. Really. You have no idea how much.'

'No, I really don't,' Metta replied. 'Can you tell me what the fucking point is in fixing up handler-boy here if you can't get him home?'

John smiled. 'Plenty. We have new intelligence we can share with you like you wouldn't believe. And most of it's in his head. Plus I can help you with the fuel problem. Maybe get your people back, too.'

'I doubt it.'

'Just give us a chance, Metta,' said John. 'I swear in Carmen's name you won't regret it.'

Metta stared at him oddly for several seconds. 'All right. Someone will have a look at him,' she said at last.

Will's heart sank.

Metta turned to the man standing at the door. 'Stone, get them a destination.'

Stone nodded and left the room. He came back a moment later with a piece of paper in his hand, which he passed to John.

Metta stood. 'Don't leave this place for another thirty minutes,' she ordered, 'then make your way to the destination. No funny stuff, Yoric. We'll be watching you.'

With that, she left, her musclemen in tow. The door clicked shut behind them.

Will took his chance. 'John, we don't have to go through with this. Look.' He grabbed the table and levered himself slowly upright. 'I'm getting better fast.'

John shook his head. 'Sorry, Will. I don't buy it.'

'Maybe he's right, John,' said Rachel. 'We came here to stop the effects of the virus. We didn't even expect him to wake up. Now he's walking around on his own.'

John laughed at her. 'Because the thing in his head knows what's going to happen to it.'

'The *thing in my head*, as you call it, is trying to help us,' Will said impatiently.

'Right,' John retorted. 'Despite the fact that it started acting up the moment we stopped doing what it wanted.'

Will shook his head. 'It started acting up because I activated another puzzle.'

John looked unimpressed. He planted an indolent finger in the middle of his own chest. 'You want me to disobey orders? I'll kill you before I do that.' He walked away from the table to stand in the corner and tap on his keyboard.

A long, uneasy silence followed. Hugo spoke up to fill it.

'If the resistance won't help us, maybe we should make some other arrangement.'

'Like what?' Rachel snapped.

John only smirked at them.

When their time limit was up, they left the way they'd come and drove through the city again. Night had fallen. Drunken soldiers staggered down the street in packs. Fragile-looking women with unlikely physiques lolled in doorways, beckoning to them.

Their next destination was another anonymous apartment building much like the first. This one was built on a rise, near one of the great tent-masts. The mast made a long black stripe against the mauve glow of reflected city light on the polymer far overhead.

John led them into the building and knocked twice on a door at the end of a corridor with stippled canary-yellow walls. They were let into a high-ceilinged space that was clearly someone's living room. There was thick orange carpet on the floor and family holopanels on the walls. The room, however, had been filled with humming medical equipment.

A thin Angeleno dressed in a white smock with an elegant patrician face stood waiting for them. He had an old-fashioned data visor over his eyes and a hypodermic gun in his hand. Behind him was something like the Angeleno equivalent of a muscle-tank.

Will took in the scene with a sudden lurch of fear. He slipped into his home node one last time. 'Help!' he yelled.

Still there was no answer, but Will recalled what the Transcended had said last time. They wanted to see how he reacted. How far he'd push his social instincts. Maybe that was the answer.

He turned to John. 'I won't do this,' he said firmly. 'It's a mistake.'

'Fine,' said John. He took a gun from his pocket and fired it at Will's chest.

Will staggered back, astonished. Rachel looked at John in stunned disbelief. Then her expression turned to one of loathing. She took a step towards him, but John turned the gun on her.

'Don't get your corset in a twist. It's a tranquilliser. I knew he'd make a fuss sooner or later.'

'Bastard!' Will breathed.

Rachel took him in her arms as he sank slowly to the floor.

'Don't let him . . .' he said, but before he could get the words out, the apartment faded from view like a puzzle dream.

12: A CHANGE OF PLANS

12.1: WILL

Will woke to the sight of a pale ceiling painted with pink whorls. He lay in a huge bed covered with sheets that had once been luxuriously silky. That was before someone hacked at them with a knife and someone else had tried to repair the damage. The room smelled of chemical perfume and was lit by pink morning light streaming in through a single untinted window. Will suspected it was what passed for suburban normal on New Angeles.

The garish orange and pink walls were dominated by dead, grey wall-screens. The panels were cracked and bent, so the owner had hung pieces of brightly coloured fabric over them in an attempt to hide the damage. In one corner, an improvised hand crank connected a plastic belt to what was left of a robotic wardrobe.

Will tilted his head and found Rachel asleep in a chair next to him, still wearing her corset and head-stocking. Framed like this, the prettiness of her face was oddly emphasised. He lay still and watched her for a minute or two, dwelling on the little details – the fullness of her lips, the clear skin of her cheek.

It was far nicer to think about Rachel than what might have been done to his head. His micromachines were gone. Did that mean his species' days were numbered? How long would it be before the human stars swelled up and burned them all to ash?

It came to Will that he'd like to spend as much of the time that remained as possible looking at Rachel's face.

She twisted sideways, frowned in sleepy discomfort and woke. She blinked at him in surprise. 'You're awake!' she blurted.

'I guess so,' said Will.

She tested his forehead with the back of her hand. 'Doctor Vamou said it'd be twelve hours before you woke,' she said. 'It can't have been more than six.' She checked the watch built into her sleeve. 'How do you feel?' she asked pensively.

'Fine,' he replied. 'Doomed, but fine.'

A small, uncomfortable smile played on her lips. 'Stay here a moment. I'll be back.'

She got up and hurried into the next room, clutching cumbersome skirts in both hands, then returned moments later with the thin Angeleno in tow.

'More surprises,' he drawled, his finely chiselled face twisted into an expression of displeasure. He applied a small medical scanner to the side of Will's neck. 'Huh! His body has flushed out the neuro-suppressant already.'

'Is that bad?' said Rachel.

Vamou straightened. 'I don't think so,' he said in a peeved voice. 'All his metabolic functions appear stable. Everything looks normal. Or as normal as this man can be, anyway. You people with your mods... You've messed with his brain chemistry so much, who's to say what's normal any more?'

'Is there anything we should do?' Rachel asked.

'There's nothing *to* do. He's well already. Tell him to get up – my wife would like her bed back.' He stalked out of the room.

Rachel broke into a grin. She leaned over and hugged Will hard. Will found himself smiling back.

She took his hand and sat on the seat, staring earnestly at him. 'I want to apologise,' she said.

'For what?' Will was surprised.

'I should have stuck up for you the moment you said you didn't want to go ahead with the operation. I had a lot of time to think while you were out cold, and I realise I've not exactly shown you a lot of trust these last few weeks.'

Will made a wry smile. 'How could you have?' He meant it, but even so, it was nice to hear her say. 'I'm not even sure I trusted myself,' he added.

Rachel shook her head. 'I could have done more. It was just so hard to believe in the Transcended after what they did to you. And when that stuff about the black hole came out, it cast a shadow over everything we thought we understood about them. We had no idea how much they were letting you say. Then you got sick. We all thought they'd decided to kill you. John still thinks that bringing you down here was the only thing that saved your life.'

The thought of John made Will suddenly sick with anger. The man had shot him, for crying out loud, as well as ignoring everything he or Rachel had to say. Will wondered if he'd ever really known him.

'And what do you think?' he asked tightly.

Rachel shrugged. 'I don't know. I've decided to assume less and listen more. How do you think the Transcended will take this? You losing your micromachines, I mean?'

'I don't know,' said Will. 'It's hard to believe this is what they wanted. I keep wondering if we just lost our last chance to save ourselves.'

Rachel's face became grave.

Hugo chose that moment to wander in from the next room. He looked down at Will with something like a smile of triumph curling the corner of his mouth – as if Will losing his machines had righted some injustice.

'Hello, Will,' he said.

'Hello,' Will replied coldly. He didn't particularly feel like talking to Hugo so he returned his attention to Rachel. 'Where's John?' he asked.

She exhaled. 'Out. Again. Trying to talk some sense into the resistance. Come on, let's get you up. I'll run some basic tests on your interface, make sure you haven't suffered any loss of function.'

Will dressed and followed Rachel through to the doctor's front room. He was surprised and pleased to discover that he could walk unaided. Hugo trailed after them.

Rachel sat down at a bulky computer console in one corner and passed Will a cable ending in an adhesive patch.

'This is for your interface,' she said.

He sat down beside her, and together they ran through a battery of diagnostic tests. Will discovered with some relief that his sensorium functions still all appeared to be intact.

Rachel collected the test results and blinked in surprise as she examined them.

'Well, if anything, your signal quality has gone up since we took the machines out,' she said. 'They must have been interfering with your contact synapses. How about the Transcended – are they still there?'

Will projected himself into his home node. 'Anybody home?' he called. 'No response. But that doesn't mean anything. It's not like they're all that predictable.'

Someone knocked on the door. Vamou darted out of a side room to open it and John slipped inside.

'You're back!' said Rachel, getting up to meet him.

Will stayed seated. He felt nothing for the man at this point other than icy dislike.

'Wow!' said Rachel, looking at John's face. 'You look terrible.'

It was true. John looked more haggard than Will had ever seen him.

'I was up all night,' said John, giving them a washed-out version of his trademark smile.

'So what did they say?'

John rubbed his eyes with his hands. 'They agreed to provide fuel at about five-thirty this morning.'

Will felt some of his anger sliding away. Despite his unpleasant way of working, John had at least found a way of continuing the mission. Maybe there was still a chance, if Will could just convince Ira to turn back instead of heading home.

'That's excellent news,' said Rachel.

'If we ever get out of this, the home world is going to owe New Angeles a *lot* of support,' said John. 'But somehow I think it'll be worth it. Don't cheer just yet, though – I still have to talk to their pilot. Apparently he wants a private negotiation, the greedy bastard. But he's the guy who'll be risking his life, so I'll have to go out again.'

'Again?' Rachel looked appalled.

'I'll be gone for the rest of the day and overnight again, I'm afraid,' said John.

She made a disgusted sound. 'This isn't a resistance movement. It's a fucking bureaucracy.'

John shrugged. 'They're afraid and they're angry. And it's their show. I just stopped by to tell you the arrangements. We're pretty sure we'll be able to buy this pilot guy – he's only holding out for a bit of personal profit. We'll meet up straight after the deal and go directly back to the shuttle. It's on the way to the freight depot from here, so it should save us a little time.' He handed Rachel a scrap of paper. 'This is where I'll be. Do you think you can find it?'

She glanced at it. 'Sure, if they give me access to the city maps.'

Hugo wandered over. 'I go with Will and Rachel?' he said, looking confused.

'That's right,' said John. 'I'll meet you there, and then everything will be set.'

'What's this other address?' Hugo asked, pointing to the paper.

'That's the location of a safe house. If anything goes wrong while I'm away, that's where you should go. If Will has a relapse, or if you think you're being followed, someone there can help.'

'Are you expecting complications?' said Hugo.

John shook his head. 'As far as I can tell, we're on the downhill stretch now. I only insisted they give you an address to up my bargaining position. But hey – better safe than sorry.' He looked past the others to where Will was still sitting, watching, by the console. 'So how's our roboteer?' he asked.

'Fine,' said Will curtly.

John stepped over to him. 'Hey, I want to say sorry. I was just doing what I thought was best. Really.' He looked genuinely uncomfortable. 'No hard feelings?'

John held out a hand for Will to shake.

Will looked at it. What else could he do? If he didn't trust John now, it was only going to make things worse. He sighed and stood to face the shorter man, then took John's hand and shook it.

'No hard feelings,' he muttered.

John looked down and fumbled in his pockets. 'Look, I know it's not much of a consolation after what I did, but I got you this.'

He took out a flat, flesh-coloured oval about the size of the palm of Will's hand. 'It's a patch for your interface. With it, you should be able to reach pretty much all of Goldwin's public network, both Earther and native. It has some of my hackpack code on it, with SAP interfaces, so you should be able to access their command structures. I had the resistance make it for you specially.' John tried for another smile. 'I figured that while we've got you down here, we might as well make proper use of your talents. It puts you in the driving seat, I guess.'

Will was touched. It was a gesture of trust he hadn't expected. John was basically appointing Will chief hacker in his absence.

'Take care of Hugo and Rachel, won't you?' said John, with something like real concern in his eyes.

Will nodded. Maybe he'd misjudged the man.

John exhaled. 'I should go.' He turned for the door.

'Wait,' said Rachel. She hugged him quickly. 'Good luck.'

He gave her a crooked smile and winked at Will. 'Thanks,' he said, and slipped out.

12.2: WILL

The following morning, Will drove them through Goldwin's gaudy streets to the rendezvous point. It was in a row of derelict-looking houses that had once clearly been the homes of New Angeles's wealthy. The pastel-coloured onion domes had sagged in, and the fairy-tale spires were scorched and broken. Playful jumbles of silver boxes had been scraped back to the bland polycrete underneath as if by gigantic claws.

The rendezvous house was a historical fantasy – a miniature recreation of a cluster of twentieth-century skyscrapers, complete with hundreds of tiny windows. It was set in a garden arranged in striped, semi-regular sections, like little Surplus Age agribusiness fields. A path resembling a freeway led to the front door. The place was in better shape than most of its neighbours, but the garden had been trampled flat and left to rot.

Will pulled the transport up in front of the house and checked along the street. It was surprisingly empty, given how close it was to a main traffic artery. The resistance had chosen the location well.

'This is it,' he told the others. 'And we're right on time. John should be out any minute.'

Once again, they sat and waited.

'I don't like this,' Rachel said after a while. 'John's usually pretty punctual.'

'True,' said Will. 'But we're not exactly running on his schedule. The resistance here appears to specialise in delays.'

Eventually, the door moved. Rachel spotted it first.

'Look!' she exclaimed.

John stumbled out of the house, looking even more haggard than before. His clothes hung off him. Two sleepless nights had clearly taken their toll. Then Will noticed that John was clutching a gun in his hand.

'Oh my God!' said Rachel. 'What's he doing with that thing?'

John blinked at the bright sunlight and then started slowly down the path. Will opened the front passenger door for him. John turned blearily to look at it, but in that moment there came a growl of gunfire.

John was ripped apart. Shreds of his flesh sprayed across the garden like red confetti. What was left of him sloughed forward onto the ground.

A voice blared from loudspeakers somewhere. 'This is the Protectorate Police! Surrender your weapons and step away from the vehicle!'

Will looked frantically up and down the street. As if from nowhere, red and yellow military vehicles like glittering, poisonous insects had appeared to block both ends.

'Shit!' Rachel gasped.

Will looked to her. She was the superior officer now. 'What do we do?' he said.

'What do you think we do?' yelled Hugo. His eyes were wild. 'We get out of the car, you oaf!' Hugo thrust open his door.

'Hugo, wait!' Rachel shouted, but it was too late.

Hugo stood and started waving to the police. 'I'm unarmed!' he warbled.

The words were barely out of his mouth before the police guns growled again. They ripped into the transport door and chewed a chunk of flesh from Hugo's side, spraying a cloud of red mist into the air.

Hugo screamed. He spun as he crumpled to the floor. Rachel leapt across the transport's back seat and reached out an arm to grab him. She managed to yank him back inside just before the guns sounded again.

The polycrete road surface exploded in a cloud of grey dust as combat flechs raked the place where Hugo had lain. The door rippled and sagged under the impact of ultra-high-speed steel. Rachel and Hugo collapsed across the back seat together in a bloody heap. Will hurled himself sideways as flechs transformed the windscreen into plastic snow.

'Drive!' Rachel yelled.

Will rammed his mind into the transport's tiny control node. He could see the street from above now, blocked at either end by the flashing squares of police vehicles. As he watched, the police began to dash towards them from both ends, personal assault cannons cradled in their arms.

'Stay down!' Will warned and kicked the transport into motion.

He reversed violently, straight into the police lines. The men barely had time to aim before they were forced to scatter for their lives. Then Will hurled the transport forwards as flechs pounded the vehicle from all directions with a deafening roar. Half of Will's sensors winked out, but he could still see through the traffic-control cameras situated on the canopy overhead.

He accelerated towards the other police line and then swerved at the last moment, into one of the gardens to the right. He smashed through the hedge, showering the transport with vegetable shrapnel. It bounced madly as it ploughed over the landscaped ground, its ruined door flapping uselessly like a broken wing. Police flechs scoured them from behind.

Will drove straight through an untended pond of brackish water and over a cluttered lawn beyond it towards a high fence. He smashed through it and raced across a second garden while the wail of sirens mounted behind him.

In seconds, Will was out into open street. He threw the transport sideways into the traffic and sped away, weaving between the trucks and personal pods as fast as the engine would permit. He knew where they had to go: the safe house. The problem was how to get there. Will doubted the place would be much use to them surrounded by Protectorate Police.

He glanced between the seats at where Rachel was frantically trying to staunch the flow of Hugo's blood. They were both drenched in it. Will was astonished that so much could come out of just one person. Hugo was gasping like a landed fish while Rachel ripped strips of her skirt to make bandages.

'How's he doing?' said Will.

'He was lucky,' said Rachel. 'That was a standard-issue Earther cannon, as far as I could tell – no toxins or nerve agents so it's just tissue damage.'

'How long has he got?' said Will.

She looked up at him worriedly. 'I don't know. An hour, perhaps.'

Will could see no police behind them, but that didn't mean a thing. Police only chased people in historical dramas. Modern law enforcement used surveillance and simply trapped you.

He jumped his mind back into the transport, and through it out to the traffic system. Sure enough, their progress was leaving a wake of alarms wide enough for the whole city to see. Flashing police units were converging on them from all directions.

Will turned to the hacking code John had left him. It was depressingly limited – much less than John had given him reason to hope for, just some worms and cracking tools along with a handful of basic SAPs. He'd have to make the best of it.

Leaving the transport to drive itself for a moment, Will jumped through the traffic-control software till he found a portal to the Protectorate Police network. He fired a generic crash virus through it. That wouldn't buy them much time, but it'd have to be enough. All across Will's display, the police markers went dark. He threw the transport into a tight turn up an alley behind a commercial thoroughfare, keeping his eyes peeled. Unless they changed vehicles before the police came back online, they were dead.

He spotted a bright-green troop carrier parked idly at the back door of a pleasure palace.

'Rachel, get ready to move him,' said Will. 'We're changing vehicles.'

Through the traffic software, Will dragged up a portal to the troop carrier. Just as he'd hoped, it was the property of a different subsect from the one running the police. The police were under the jurisdiction of the Sons of Mao, while the carrier belonged to the Ecowarriors. And the suspicious, factional Earther groups had put plenty of security between their respective domains.

Will slammed one of John's password levers into the Ecowarrior network and had the carrier's engines running before they screeched to a halt behind it.

'In there!' Will told her, pointing at the new vehicle.

Rachel glanced nervously at the back of the pleasure palace. The door was open and rhythmic music blasted out from inside. She scowled at him.

'Are you crazy?'

'It's the best I've got,' said Will.

He shut down the transport, severing its links to the traffic grid, and ran around to help Rachel carry the limp and slippery Hugo into the open back of the vehicle. Rachel, though, was doing fine on her own. She charged forward like some blood-soaked Amazon with the scientist joggling limply on her shoulders.

Will leapt into the back of the carrier and took Hugo from her.

'Wait!' she ordered and dashed back to the civilian transport to grab their flech-riddled bags from the trunk. She hurled them into the carrier and jumped in after them, her face full of thunder. 'If I have to fight for my life, there's no way I'm doing it in this fucking corset.'

Will permitted himself a grin before diving back into the carrier's node and driving them out onto the main street towards the safe house. He checked the traffic-system status. The police units were coming back online with alarming alacrity. A pair of hornet-striped police vehicles sped past them, sirens blaring.

It was only a matter of time before the authorities found the transport, Will knew. And once they did, it wouldn't take them long to make the connection to the troop carrier. Assuming, of course, that the soldiers who'd lost it didn't report it missing before then.

'We're going to have to swap cars again,' Will warned.

'No shit,' said Rachel. 'Once they find this thing gone, they'll come down on us like meteors.'

Will scoured the traffic system for something he could use, well aware that he had only minutes to complete their escape. By now, the Protectorate Police were bound to have their finest SAPs on the case. What he needed was a vehicle that was clean and hard to trace, preferably one on a different network. Unfortunately, portals were slamming shut all across the system like starship airlocks. One by one, the disparate subsect domains were raising their alert levels.

Will groaned in frustration as the carrier ground to a halt at an intersection to let a maintenance robot lumber across their path.

Then the solution hit him.

'That's it!' he exclaimed.

The robots ran on guide strips by the roadside, barely integrated with the transport network, and the traffic system treated them as pedestrians. It took him precious minutes to find his way into the city maintenance system from the increasingly isolated traffic control, but once he was in, it was easy. He arranged for the carrier to rendezvous with a couple of larger robots behind an unused warehouse.

Will held his breath as they turned into the deserted lot, hardly daring to hope that his ruse had gone unnoticed. He grunted with relief when he saw the two robots standing there alone. They looked like a couple of animated trash bins, with small sensor heads and large hairy waldos.

Rachel stared at them with unabashed concern. 'We're going in *those*?'

Will nodded. 'There should be enough cargo space in the back of each for a couple of people. It'll be a tight fit, but hopefully untraceable.'

'Okay,' she said. 'I'll bring Hugo. You haul the luggage.'

She carried Hugo over to the larger of the two machines and laid him carefully in its cargo hopper. Will dumped the bags in the back of the other machine and climbed inside.

'Wait,' said Rachel. She ran over to him, grabbed his cheeks and kissed him hard on the mouth. Will's face tingled. His heart pounded. He blinked dumbly at her.

'What was that for?' he mumbled.

'That's in case we die before we get there. You did great, Will. Really great. See you at the safe house.' With that, she ran back to her robot and climbed inside.

Will set the troop carrier on automatic and sent it back to the place they'd found it. Then he sealed the lid of the hopper above him so that the only light came from a crack around the rim. The inside stank of surface dust and chemical adhesives. It was hot and cramped, but bearable. With his head still spinning from the kiss, Will let the robot trundle out along the street.

12.3: WILL

The trip to the safe house was a nerve-wracking one. Will watched police vehicles dash past via the robot's inadequate electronic eyes. He could hear the sirens around him with appalling clarity, though. Just a thin plastic wall separated him from the street.

He began to wonder if the hoppers were watertight. If not, Hugo's blood might dribble out onto the pavement, leaving a trail for the Earthers to follow. Rachel would be found. He'd have caused her death.

He was immensely relieved when both robots shuddered to a halt outside the front door of the safe house. He scanned the street using the robot's simple senses and waited till there were no passers-by. Then he leapt out and threw back the lid of Rachel's hopper. The inside wasn't pretty. Hugo was still losing blood. Rachel looked up at him with exhausted eyes.

'Stay here,' he told her. 'I'll get help.'

She nodded. 'Be quick.'

Will strode up to the door of a house that appeared to be made of yellow lace, surrounded by a dense garden of small blue-green pine trees. He pressed the visitor stud. A few moments later, an Angeleno woman with plastic-perfect features and a yellow dress that clung to her like paint opened the door. She surveyed Will's blood-spattered clothing and dishevelled hair with alarm.

'We need help,' said Will. 'My friends are back there, in the robots. One of them has been shot.'

She stared at him for a moment, her face blank. A terrible fear gripped Will. Could he have made a mistake about the address?

'Isn't this the safe house?' he said stupidly.

What would he do now if it wasn't? Kill her? Tie her up in her own home? Will doubted he could bring himself to do either.

The woman's face slowly took on a frosty aspect. She looked out at the robots for a moment, and then up and down the street.

'Bring them around the side,' she said tersely. 'Behind the trees.'

Will grinned at her in relief. He took a breath to thank her but the door was already closing. He hurried back to the robots.

It took a little coaxing to persuade the robots to abandon their guide strips, but Will succeeded in leading them along the gravel path to the back of the property. He found the woman waiting for them there. A huge, muscular youth with no shirt and pectorals like slabs of mocksteak stood beside her with a handgun tucked into his belt. Will helped Rachel out and together they retrieved the unconscious Hugo.

'This way,' said the woman.

She led them inside and down a flight of stairs to a simply furnished room behind a false wall in the basement. Will and Rachel lowered Hugo onto a narrow bed made of wipe-clean plastic. The youth with the gun watched them from the doorway, poker-faced.

'You'll find medical supplies in there,' said the woman, pointing to a blue plastic crate in one corner. 'I'll get help.' With that, she walked out, shutting the door behind her.

Rachel started carefully peeling away Hugo's improvised dressing. 'Will, help me. I'll need tweezers, disinfectant, plasmix, spray-skin and dressings.'

'I'm on it,' said Will.

He dashed over to the crate and started rifling through the contents. He spent the next hour following Rachel's instructions and accessing Goldwin's public medical database. Luckily, the safe house was well equipped. Beyond the room with the wipe-clean furnishings lay a bathroom and a basic kitchen. They were able to do a fairly creditable job of dressing Hugo's injury. They picked the bits of steel from his side, then disinfected the wound and patched it up as best they could. Rachel gave him a shot of repair accelerators and followed it up with another of neurostimulant.

'Isn't that dangerous?' said Will.

She nodded. 'Yes, but it'll be a lot harder to get him out of the city if we have to carry him. We've got a few hours tops before they figure out what's going on and lock the whole planet down, so we need him walking if we're all going to make it out of here alive.'

When they were finished, Hugo lay on the bloody bed, breathing shallowly but regularly. Rachel and Will staggered off to the bathroom, taking turns to shower and change back into their crumpled ship-suits.

Will felt the adrenalin drain out of him as he washed. By the time he was putting his boots on, his hands were shaking so hard that he could barely fasten the adhesive straps.

While Rachel dried her hair, Will wandered around the small suite, examining the facilities in a state of addled shock. Everything they might need for basic living was provided, along with enough dried food in the kitchen to last them for months. However, there were no windows or obvious escape routes.

Will wondered how long they'd be stuck there, and how hot a trail they'd left. He patched into the house computer system and requested a portal to the Protectorate Police. To his surprise, there was no reply. The house's metaphor space remained as windowless as the basement itself. That was down to resistance security, no doubt – it was understandable that they wouldn't want any live links to the authorities. Will, however, didn't like to be thwarted.

He returned to the medical database he'd used to fix up Hugo. From there, perhaps he could find a way to a local hospital and through that out into the rest of the network. But those routes were blocked, too. Eventually he realised that the database he was looking at was a disconnected backup, not the real thing at all.

On a sudden instinct, he strode into the main room and tried the door they'd come in through. It was locked.

'Fuck!' he yelled.

He raised his hand to slam the thing and thought better of it. There was always the possibility that Earther soldiers were searching the basement on the other side.

'What now?' said Rachel.

'We're locked in,' he explained, 'and there are no lines to the outside.'

Rachel frowned. 'It's probably just resistance paranoia.'

'Probably,' said Will, unconvinced.

He thought back to the woman's face when he'd appeared at the door. On reflection, her expression had looked more like guarded panic than surprise.

'Don't you think it's a bit odd that she didn't ask us what happened?' said Will.

'From the look of Hugo she could probably guess,' said Rachel. 'Plus it'll be all across the pervasivenet by now.'

But then something horrible occurred to Will. What if the resistance had something to do with their predicament?

'And why did the police fire at us in the first place?' he asked. 'They shot John before he even saw them.'

Rachel looked at him nervously. 'He was armed,' she said.

'But Hugo wasn't. He even told them as much. It's as if they wanted us dead then and there, regardless of what we did.'

'Are you surprised?' said Rachel. 'These are Earthers, remember?'

Her face, however, betrayed a mounting sense of alarm that echoed his. There'd been no time for either of them to think about the police raid till now. On reflection, there was something very wrong about the way it had played out.

'I don't buy it,' Will replied. 'They'd want to interrogate us, surely. Find our ship. Find out what we know. If they just wanted us dead, why did they bother to announce themselves as police? It doesn't add up... Unless,' he added slowly, 'they weren't police.' He started to get a sour, unpleasant feeling deep in his belly. 'What if they were resistance? Or police in the pay of the resistance, like the ones John mentioned? John probably worked out something was going down – that's why he was armed. The negotiations must have failed at the last hurdle. Either that or they set us up from the start, because of the heat we were bringing down on them.'

The more Will thought about it, the more convincing that interpretation became.

'Shit!' he exclaimed. 'I've gone and killed us by coming here. I've killed the whole mission!' He clapped his forehead with his hands. They were trapped in a locked room, most likely with assassins on the way.

Rachel grabbed him by the shoulders and stared hard into his eyes. 'No, you haven't, Will! Neither of us saw this possibility. And where else were we supposed to go? If we'd headed back to the depot, we'd never have made it out of the city alive. We had no choice but to trust them, and they might still come through for us. We have no idea what's really going on out there, and if we jump to the wrong conclusion it could lose us our last chance.'

Will looked down at the floor, appalled with himself regardless.

Rachel grabbed his head in both hands. 'Look at me, Will.'

He glanced up at her.

She kissed him then, for the second time that day, and Will's world suspended for a while. Nothing existed except Rachel's lips.

She pulled back and examined him. 'That's for getting us here in one piece,' she said.

Then she kissed him again, more softly this time. Will found his arms around her. She pressed against him.

'And that's for helping me with Hugo,' she said breathlessly. 'And this is just because I want to.'

They kissed a third time. Will felt his loins stirring. His mind filled with sparks.

She pulled away at last and held his hands in hers. 'While I was stuck in that hopper, I realised I wanted to kiss you again,' she told him. 'I wanted you to know what I felt before it was too late for both of us.'

'You like me,' Will said stupidly, barely able to grasp his good fortune. Somehow, it made the prospect of their impending deaths less frightening.

She smiled lopsidedly at him. 'Yes, I like you. I like you because of the way you treat me. And the way you look at me. The way you sneak a glance at me every time I step out of my bunk. And the fact that you bothered to make an avatar of me.'

Will flushed. How long had she known?

'You make me feel beautiful, Will,' she said. 'I've never felt like much except a starship officer before. Around you, I feel like a woman.'

'You don't mind?' he said. 'That I made an avatar of you, I mean.'

She laughed. 'No. It's very flattering, actually.'

'When... I mean, how did you find out?' he asked, but then guessed before she answered and regretted asking.

'John,' she said, her smile falling away. The mood between them cooled by a few degrees. 'It's a small ship,' she added, 'and he can be quite a gossip.'

Wrong tense, Will thought, but chose not to correct her.

Rachel looked away, hurt showing on her face. She stared into the middle distance. 'That's one of the reasons why our relationship never worked out,' she said absently.

Will's mouth fell open. 'You and he were... together?'

'Ages ago. Back in Doug's time.' The lines of pain around her eyes took on extra depth. 'We don't talk about it much. Old wounds aren't exactly good for ship morale.'

'I can imagine,' said Will.

'I could never get close to him,' she said, hugging herself. 'Whenever it looked like he was really going to become intimate, he'd laugh it off. He couldn't bear to let himself be vulnerable to anyone, I guess. Eventually, I got bored of trying. And now he's dead.'

Tears welled up in her eyes and she buried her face in her hands and wept. Will had no idea what to do. He didn't try to speak, just awkwardly wrapped his arms around her again.

'He's dead, Will,' she wailed into her hands. 'The stupid, smug bastard's dead.'

Will held her close.

Their moment of intimacy was broken seconds later when the door flew open. Resistance heavies strode into the room pointing personal cannons very much like those the police had used. Behind came Metta, immaculate in a form-fitting teal business suit.

Her gaze scanned across Will and Rachel, who were still holding each other in the middle of the room. She *tsked* to herself.

'Well, well, our *allies*,' she said with an ironic sneer. 'I wonder if you realise how difficult you've made life for us. I think it's fairly clear that we can't trust you any more.'

Rachel blinked at her. '*You* can't trust *us*?' she said incredulously.

But Metta wasn't listening. 'Boys, take them outside,' she said, jerking a thumb towards the door.

The heavies pushed Will and Rachel out of the room with the barrels of their guns.

'What about Hugo?' said Will.

'Don't worry,' said Metta. 'He's coming with you.'

Another couple of resistance men stepped in behind them and picked up Hugo's limp body. They were taken up the stairs and out through the back door the way they'd come in. A delivery truck was waiting there. The plastic plating that comprised the floor had been removed to reveal a space where the spare fuel cells should have been.

'Get in and lie down,' ordered one of the heavies.

'Where are you taking us?' said Rachel.

'Away,' said the heavy. 'Now shut up and get in.'

He prodded her hard with the muzzle of his gun. Rachel spared him a withering look and stepped inside. Hugo was placed in the truck next to them and the flooring laid back over their faces. It was a tight fit. There was barely any room to move and the darkness was total. Will noticed with concern that the hiding place had been lined against net traffic. His electronic senses were dead.

'If we get out of this, I'm never going to complain about the *Ariel*'s cabin again,' said Rachel, in an effort to break the tension. Will dearly hoped they got the opportunity.

With a whine from the truck's motors that reverberated around their heads, the truck set off, back into the streets of New Angeles.

13: BETRAYAL

13.1: WILL

They hadn't been travelling in the truck long before Hugo started to stir. The drugs they'd given him were kicking in fast.

'Where am I?' he groaned.

'In a resistance truck,' Rachel told him simply. 'Stay quiet and keep calm.'

But to Will's dismay, Hugo's disorientation rapidly turned to panic as he discovered the immovable floor pressed up against his face.

'Let me out of here! Help!' he gasped.

'Hugo,' Rachel hissed, 'shut up or you'll get us all killed.'

'Why are we here?' Hugo demanded. 'What happened?'

Rachel started to fill him in, but as she talked, the truck slowed to a halt.

'What's going on?' said the delirious scientist.

'Shhh!' said Rachel.

Will held his breath as he heard voices. Someone spoke in an Angeleno drawl. Rapid dialog in an Earther dialect followed. Boots clumped back and forth just centimetres above their heads. It had to be some kind of vehicle check. The Earthers must be on full alert, Will realised. Then, to his immense relief, the sound of boots receded and the truck started off again.

At least now he knew the resistance didn't intend to hand them over to the authorities, though that didn't exactly lift his spirits. The police would no doubt want live prisoners to interrogate. Will still wasn't convinced the resistance were as concerned for their welfare. After all, he and Rachel knew the location of one of their safe houses, which left their organisation exposed.

Half an hour's tense driving later, the truck stopped again. This time, the lid came off their secret compartment. Will held his hands up to shield his eyes against the sudden glare.

A large figure stood over him – Will recognised him as one of the heavies from their first resistance meeting, the one Metta had called Stone.

'Get up,' Stone said. 'It's time to go.' He waved the barrel of a handgun towards the truck's open doors.

Will levered himself upright. Together, he and Rachel helped Hugo out. Will was surprised when he emerged from the back of the vehicle into the parking bay of the freight terminus where they'd entered the city. He wondered if his fears about the resistance had been unfounded. Why would they have brought their Galatean charges here if they didn't intend for them to live? However, Will noticed that the four resistance men were still pointing guns at them.

A woman ran up from the direction of the guardhouse. She was dressed in an outfit that was revealing even by Angeleno standards.

'It's done,' she said. 'Their comm-links are all off and the men are high as kites.'

'Good,' said Stone. He turned to regard his captives with an unpleasant half-smile. 'You're leaving. You being here is making things too hot for us, but Metta says no hard feelings. We've arranged to make your exit a little easier. The guards should be out of action for a while – hopefully long enough to give you a clear run back to your ship.'

Will began to feel embarrassed by his own mistrust.

'But just in case,' said Stone, 'take these.'

Stone's men passed Will and his shipmates each a wicked-looking flech-gun.

'They're empty,' Rachel observed dryly.

'That's so you don't mess with us before we go,' said Stone. 'We left ammunition for you over there in the yellow container.'

He pointed diagonally across the broad depot forecourt to one of the great metal boxes at the far corner. The door stood slightly ajar, like the darkened entrance to a steel cave. Will's sense of mistrust came back redoubled.

'You can go and get it after we leave, but not before,' said Stone. Then he gestured to his men, who started to climb back into the truck. 'Oh, and a message from Metta,' he said, pausing by the driver's cabin. 'Don't come back unless you bring your Fleet with you.'

He chuckled to himself as if this was some kind of joke, then climbed inside and pulled the door shut. The truck reversed hard and turned sharply back into the street.

Will watched their departure with more than a little unease. For a moment, the three of them stood there wordlessly, not sure they could trust their good fortune.

'Come on,' said Rachel. 'We'd better get a move on.'

She and Will hurried across the polycrete apron towards the sanctuary of the containers, dragging a limping Hugo along between them.

Something about this exit was ironic, Will thought. They'd arrived with one weakened crewman, and that was how they were leaving. He doubted Hugo would find the symmetry particularly amusing.

A quick glance at the guardroom revealed that the resistance had been true to their word. Every man in there was sprawled in a chair, apparently unconscious. Smiles of mindless bliss curved their drooling mouths.

They were only halfway across the open area when they heard a screech of tires that echoed off the high ceiling. Will looked back and saw two red and yellow vehicles pulling up at speed.

'Halt!' commanded a voice from a loudhailer. 'Protectorate Police!'

Will's insides froze solid. Here they were, conveniently holding dangerous weapons on open ground, just as John had been. It was too perfect to be a coincidence. The resistance had led them into a trap after all – one that laid the blame firmly at the authorities' door, just like the last. Genuine police they might be, but Will didn't doubt they were in league with Metta, and likely to be generous with their ammunition.

'Hurry!' said Rachel.

They ran full tilt towards the closest containers as guns roared into life. Will ducked behind cover as streams of flechs ripped past him, smashing dents in the metal walls. The whole building rang with the clamour of their impact.

Rachel sneaked a look out and darted back. 'There's no way we can get to that ammo from here,' she breathed.

Will had already guessed that. The yellow container was two aisles away, with a door that opened in the direction of the gunmen.

'Forget it,' said Will. 'We've only got their word there's anything in there, and this looks too much like a set-up to me. We're armed, which gives them an excuse for shooting to kill. I say let's ditch the guns and get out of here as fast as we can.'

Rachel nodded quickly. She and Will threw down their weapons. Hugo looked unwilling to give his up but Rachel pulled it from his hand with a scowl. Then they hurried down the narrow passage towards the airlocks while Hugo breathlessly chided them for their foolishness.

'Do you think they're going to stop shooting just because we don't have guns?' he spat. 'They won't. In case you've forgotten, I tried surrendering already.'

The sounds of shouting and warning shots dogged them all the way to the end of the facility. As the bank of boxy doorways that led to the transit cars finally came in sight, Will reached out to the depot computer and instructed it to open one. The computer sent its apologies. The site had been sealed on police orders. Will's heart lurched. Of course it had. The resistance had never meant for them to leave here alive.

'They're locked,' he told the others. 'I'll need time to get them open.'

Rachel nodded grimly. 'Stay here,' she said, pointing to an open box at the end of the line. 'I'll try to make some kind of diversion.'

She ran off, leaving Will clutching a pale-faced Hugo. Will helped the man to shelter.

'Keep a lookout,' said Will. 'Rouse me if anything happens.'

He shut his eyes and dived fully into the depot computer. It was a mess. Old-fashioned Angeleno software laid out in hierarchical blocks had been overlaid with linked Earther security modules marked in warning colours. It looked like a cubist tree that had been assaulted by fluorescent ivy.

Will applied himself to the tangle of modules at the root node where the police control keys would be. He dug into the hackpack John had supplied and pulled out a cracker SAP to find an override code. The SAP went straight to work, ploughing through combinations faster than Will's mind could follow. But Will could see almost immediately that it was getting nowhere. Either police security had improved a lot in the last few hours, or the resistance had set the place up to be impenetrable. They'd probably used John's own software to do it, Will realised in disgust.

He grunted with frustration and jammed himself into the mind of the struggling SAP. Being inside a code-breaker was never comfortable – there was no good mapping between Will's senses and their input. But Will had endured plenty of that recently at the hands of the Transcended, and he could feel his mind intuitively adapting to compensate for the scramble of perceptions.

It was as if he were revolving the parts of some fabulously complex four-dimensional lock, looking for a straight line through it in which to fit a key. Though it stretched his brain just to look at it, Will refused to be beaten by the thing. He seized the lock in a pair of virtual hands and stared at it hard, willing it to explain itself to him.

Miraculously, it did.

His perspective shifted, and suddenly, patterns of shapes that had been meaningless before made perfect sense to him. Will spun the lock and shoved the key straight through it.

'Will!' said Hugo, seizing his arm and dragging him back to reality.

Will opened his eyes just in time to see two police in blood-red armour running around the corner of the container where they were hiding. At the sound of Hugo's voice, the men spun, bringing their weapons to bear. But in the split-second before their fingers could squeeze the triggers, a figure darted out from the aisle opposite armed with a long steel bar. It was Rachel.

With a roar to curdle the blood, she took a vicious swipe at the first policeman's head. It cracked sideways and the spray of flechs from his gun chased harmlessly up the wall. As the second policeman swung his weapon around, Rachel had already begun to kick. Her leg scythed through the air, sending the man's weapon flying from his grasp. She followed up with the bar, driving it straight into the man's visor and knocking his head back with an ugly snap.

She let go of the bar and threw herself into a somersault, seizing one of the fallen guns as she rolled. Rachel sent a stream of high-velocity steel into the chest of another policeman just as he came around the corner. As he toppled, she grabbed the remaining cannon and threw it to Will, who endeavoured to catch it with both hands as it flew towards him.

'You boys all right?' she said breathlessly, sweeping hair away from her eyes.

Will nodded, still awed by the speed and power of her attack.

'How's that security coming on?' she asked.

'Just cracked it,' said Will.

'Good,' said Rachel as the sound of fresh gunfire ripped the air, 'because we're pretty much surrounded.'

She dashed into the container after them as another assault cannon roared. She took up a position just inside the door and motioned them both behind her.

'You'd better do something, Will,' she said. 'I can't hold them off for ever.'

'Hold on,' said Will.

He jumped into the security system and drove an override code into the root node of the tree. The ivy turned a peaceful green from the system's root to the tips of its cubist leaves. Will dragged up a manifest of the depot's robotic resources. Sure enough, there were six very large lifter trucks idling there with not much to do. Will smiled to himself. He knew all about lifter trucks. With a flick of one virtual hand, he put them all to work. Their task was simple – to park themselves exactly over certain moving targets, namely the police.

Huge electric motors moaned like saurian carnivores waking up as the trucks stirred to life. It took the police a few seconds to work out exactly what was happening. Then there was a deafening screech of metal on metal and the sounds of screaming. Short bursts of gunfire sprayed randomly all around the depot.

Will watched with satisfaction through the security cameras high above as the ten-ton lifter trucks trundled this way and that, cheerfully knocking down bodies. The police peppered them with flechs, but the machines were invulnerable.

'Hey, Will,' said Rachel. 'How about that airlock?'

'Right,' said Will.

He chose the doorway that led back to the little transit car they'd arrived in and started cycling the air. A new voice came over a loudhailer from the depot's entrance.

'This is Coordinator Chopra!' said a furious voice. 'What the *hell* are you people doing using live ammo? Hold your fire! Use stun weapons only! I will personally execute *anyone* responsible for the death of these spies!'

So the real police had arrived. Will didn't know if that was good news or bad, but he had no intention of waiting around to find out. He took advantage of the lull in the fighting to make his move.

'Now!' he said. He and Rachel ran headlong for the airlock with Hugo between them.

The lock slid open at their approach and shut behind them. Once inside the transit car, Will braced himself against the wall and shut his eyes again.

'Get us out of here, Will,' Rachel urged.

'Not yet,' said Will.

With the authorities so hot on their tail, their exit was going to be painfully obvious. The Earthers would probably reach the shuttle before they did. They needed camouflage. A furious sweep of his arm across the depot's metaphor space readied every single train in the place. Eleven outbound tracks exited the building. Will intended to make use of all of them.

All across the facility, engines whined. Environment doors swung open. As a parting shot, Will opened a portal to the police computer system and fired through the most exotic-looking crash program in John's arsenal. A few extra minutes might make all the difference.

'Hang on, everybody,' he said. 'We're leaving.'

He gave the command to the transit car and it sped across the desert, accelerating as fast as it could go. A dozen alarms went off across the building as trains pulled away from their bays half-loaded and started speeding out onto the surface.

Rachel whooped at the sight and laughed. Even Hugo cracked a smile. And in less than a minute, Goldwin was a fairy-tale bubble once again, rapidly receding into the distance. Rachel hugged Will tightly and kissed him. This time, he was ready for it and returned the gesture.

They slouched exhausted in the plastic seats as the little vehicle raced across the rocky expanse. For a while, all was right with the world. They'd escaped the city alive – something Will had seriously doubted was ever going to happen.

But their mood soon turned from exhilaration back to worry. They weren't off the planet yet. And if they did make it into space, who knew what they were supposed to do next? They were still out of fuel, and even if they managed to run down some Earther ship, they had no John to make a soft assault. The Earthers now knew they were in the system and would be on full alert.

Will had to hope that somewhere between the nest archive and the Transcended in his head there was some trick that could save them. Assuming he still had a link to the Transcended, of course, now that his micromachines were gone.

After a long, uneasy silence, Rachel spoke up. 'Why do you suppose the resistance wanted us dead at Earther hands?'

'So they wouldn't be implicated,' said Will. 'Or that's my guess, at least. If they killed us themselves, the Earther forces would be all over them as soon as word got out.'

'But why did they want us dead in the first place?' Rachel pressed. 'Why go to all the bother of healing you and then killing us?'

'Maybe something bad happened during John's negotiations,' he suggested. 'Or maybe the Earthers got wind of their plan, and so they sacrificed us to save themselves.'

There was no way to know. They just had to be glad they'd got this far.

Will slowed the transit before they reached the hangar and queried the building through the car's information link. They couldn't be too careful, he reasoned. There was always the possibility that the police had worked out their destination and set up an ambush. However, nothing appeared to be out of place. There were no new vehicles present and the life-support systems were idling on minimum. None of the site security had been engaged, either.

'It all looks clear,' he told the others. 'I'm taking us in.'

'How long do you think we've got before the Earthers work out where we are?' asked Rachel.

Will shrugged. 'I can't say. With the authorities this edgy, our take-off is bound to draw some attention, no matter how good John's hacking was. I think we should get out as fast as we can.'

As soon as they reached the hangar, Rachel took up lead position with her borrowed assault cannon while Will and Hugo brought up the rear. Will checked the cameras and habitat settings in advance as they moved from room to room. Fortunately they were all empty, and they quickly retrieved their environment suits from the lockers. From there, it was a quick walk to the final airlock and their shuttle.

Will activated the pilot SAP and took them up in what he dearly hoped was a suitable approximation of a normal freighter's flight path. He kept an eye on air-traffic control as they went, expecting an alert at any minute. None came. The police system didn't respond to any of his queries. Apparently John's last crash program had been even more effective than Will dared hope. That was one blessing they could count, at least.

The flight out to the rendezvous point and the waiting that followed were horribly tense. Will spent the entire time checking and rechecking the scanners for signs of Earther pursuit. There was plenty of frenetic activity in New Angeles orbit and a few sorties into deeper space, but nothing that came near enough to consitute a threat.

Will could hardly believe their good fortune when the ship that finally descended upon them was the *Ariel*. It flashed in under stealth, swung up on its torches to meet them and cradled the shuttle to its massive belly.

As soon as the docking pod was extended, Will and the others made for the habitat module with all speed. Will tumbled through the opening door into the familiarly cramped cabin like a shipwreck survivor reaching dry land. He breathed in the familiar smell of recycled air with a grateful gasp.

Ira was waiting anxiously for them just inside the doorway, his face lined with worry. The last two days of sitting and waiting had taken a visible toll.

'Where's John?' he said.

For a moment, no one said anything. Then Rachel spoke.

'John's dead.'

Ira's face grew solemn. 'How?'

She set about explaining what had happened on the planet. Ira absorbed the news gravely, showing about as much emotion as a rock. When she'd finished her breathless account, he spoke again.

'Not good,' was all he said.

'Captain!' called Amy from her bunk. 'We have six Earther pursuit ships closing on us, fast.'

Will's heart sank. It appeared their escape hadn't been quite so complete after all.

Ira grimaced and looked at Rachel. 'Were you followed?'

Rachel shook her head vehemently. 'No, sir. There was no sign of enemy activity at any point before we docked. They might have tracked the shuttle from a distance, but there was no sign of a tracer scan.'

'All right, everybody,' said Ira, 'it's time to use up what little antimatter we have left. You three get to your stations. This is going to be rough.'

Rachel nodded and did as she was told.

Will yanked off the gloves from his suit. As the second one came free, a peculiar puff of smoke rose from the fitting.

Suddenly, Will discovered he couldn't breathe.

'Ca—'

That was all he managed to say before a black tide of nausea overwhelmed him. Then there was only darkness.

13.2: WILL

Will woke to a sense of profound discomfort. His skull felt horribly compressed, as if from the world's worst head cold, and his limbs were leaden and shot through with pins and needles. He opened gummy eyes and found himself sprawled out on a plastic floor, looking at several pairs of brightly coloured boots.

'Awake already?' said a voice. 'Sit him up.'

Two pairs of boots strode forward. Will was grabbed by the arms and hauled upright. For a moment, his vision narrowed again into nauseous darkness. He groaned. By the time his senses cleared, he'd been propped against a wall like a rag doll. He blinked hard and took his first focused look at his surroundings.

He was in a windowless room of lifeless beige. It could have been in any one of a thousand habitats across the human galactic shell. Four members of the Protectorate Police stood on either side of a plump man dressed in gold, red, yellow and black. His soft, round face and coffee-coloured skin were at odds with a pair of shrewd, pale-brown eyes. He looked inordinately pleased with himself.

'I wouldn't try to move if I were you,' the man said, bouncing on his toes.

That was the last thing on Will's mind. He was still reeling from being manhandled.

'You're recovering from a disabling immune response,' the man explained. 'I recommend remaining still and taking shallow, even breaths.'

Will attempted to voice his contempt but his throat was both constricted and raw. All that came out was a harsh wheeze.

'I expect you're wondering where you are,' the policeman said. 'The answer is the Protectorate Command Station in orbit around New Angeles.'

Will shut his eyes in misery.

'Ah!' the man said enthusiastically. 'Your associates are beginning to recover. Galatean physiology is a remarkable thing. Put them against the wall, men. They're not going anywhere in a hurry and I want to see their faces while I talk to them.'

Ira was dumped up against the wall beside Will.

'Let me introduce myself,' said the soft-faced man. 'My name is Civil Coordinator Enrique Chopra, and I'm the man who caught you. Who'd have thought it: a ship full of pure-bred geniuses captured by a peasant from the prote-farms. Where's your racial pride now, I wonder?' He chastised them with a wagging finger. 'You geniuses should have taken a closer look at your environment suits before you got back into your clever little shuttle. Once we received the tip-off that you were here, it was relatively easy to work out how you'd arrived. Just a process of simple deductive reasoning.'

It sounded as if he considered the reasoning anything but simple.

Chopra watched as Hugo, Amy and Rachel joined their crewmates in the line forming against the wall.

Will tested his limbs. He could move them a little if he tried hard. And it was getting easier to breathe, thank Gal.

'However,' said Chopra, 'I do have to congratulate you on the ingenuity of your security systems – Galatean software is indeed as good as I've been led to believe. Without the comms leeches I had attached to your shuttle's hull, we would never have been able to get into your habitat sphere to rescue you. However, you should feel fortunate that I took the steps I did,' he said with a grin. 'Without an antidote, the toxin you inhaled is quite fatal.'

He waved a hand. 'But here I am, talking about myself when I couldn't have done it without the help of our friend.' He surveyed the *Ariel*'s crew with a kind of hungry curiosity. 'So which of you do I have to thank for this moment? Which one of you is *Will*?'

Will's blood ran cold.

'No reply?' said Chopra with a cocked eyebrow. 'Well, I imagine it's still a little hard to talk, isn't it? Sergeant Wu, why don't you give them each another dose of clarifier.'

One of the police officers stepped forwards and started administering a hypodermic gun to each of the Galateans' necks in turn.

'Come now,' said Chopra. 'It must be one of you? Who sent us the tip-off with the rendezvous coordinates?'

Will was appalled. He didn't understand. Why would someone do such a thing and claim it in his name?

'Will, what's going on?' croaked Ira.

'I don't know,' Will gasped back.

'Ah!' said Chopra gleefully. 'So we have a face for our friend.' He fixed his gaze on Will.

'Fuck you,' said Will. 'I sent nothing.'

Chopra rolled his eyes in amusement. 'Well, we received a tip-off from someone.'

'Traitor!' Hugo hissed. 'He betrayed us, Captain. I knew he would.'

Will felt a fresh surge of hatred towards Hugo. Suddenly it all clicked together in his head – Hugo's bitterness, his cryptic smiles, his urgent desire to get out of the car the moment they were captured. He'd thought it was safe to sell them all out to save humanity from his imagined alien menace. But he'd reckoned without the resistance and their inside knowledge of the police. No wonder the poor bastards didn't feel they could trust the Galateans any more.

'You did it, didn't you, you stupid fuck?' Will grated. He tried to turn his unresponsive head to look Hugo in the face, without success. 'Why?' he demanded. 'Because you couldn't bully me into talking?'

'*Me?*' sneered Hugo. 'I never touched a keyboard the whole time we were there. You were the one with the data link on your neck.'

'Well, isn't this nice?' said Chopra with a gleaming-white smile. 'It's refreshing to see such a team spirit at work among the most highly evolved people in the galaxy.'

Will ignored him. 'Captain,' he said, 'you have to believe me. I sent nothing.'

Ira remained silent.

Chopra pointed at Will. 'Separate him from the others,' he told his men.

The guards picked Will up. He struggled feebly and, for a single horrible moment, got to gaze upon the faces of his shipmates, who were all staring at him. Their expressions revealed their opinions of him with awful clarity. Only Rachel's was free from doubt. Hugo's was red with hate.

In the next second they were gone and Will was being carried, helpless, along the gently curving corridor. They took him to an interrogation room and propped him up in a plastic chair on one side of a scratched and dented table. Chopra seated himself with some decorum in the chair on the other side.

'Leave us,' he told the guards, shooing them away with his hand.

'Sir—' started one of the guards.

'I said *go*.'

For a moment, Will glimpsed the hard man beneath Chopra's soft exterior. The last guard shut the door behind him.

Chopra arranged himself slowly, sitting at an angle to the table, his legs casually crossed, one elbow braced on the tabletop.

'It's okay now,' he said with a conspiratorial smile. 'You can drop your little subterfuge. No one believes you anyway, and nothing you say here will go further than these walls.'

'Fuck you,' Will growled.

Chopra sighed. 'Then you still claim you didn't send us the tip-off?'

Will glared at him.

'It will go easier for you if you confess,' said Chopra, ending his sentence on an expectant rise, but Will gave no reply.

Chopra looked genuinely confused. 'Why else was a note sent to us on a private channel identifying you as a willing defector?'

Will would have liked to know, too. Why had *he* been picked out to look like the traitor? Hugo's spite was the most obvious answer. However, the only reason Will could think of to explain why Hugo might betray them was if he believed the Transcended posed a greater threat to humanity than the Earthers. That certainly fitted the pattern of the man's behaviour, but it required him to have engaged in some very subtle spy work. Will tried to calculate when and how Hugo could have informed the authorities without the rest of the *Ariel*'s crew noticing.

Another possible culprit was the resistance. They'd provided him with the incriminating data link, and their animosity had been clear from the outset. But why would they have chosen to give his name in particular?

The last possibility was that Hugo was right, and Will *had* sent the message himself. Or rather the Transcended had, via Will. But he didn't believe they'd bother doing something as petty as that. They'd had plenty of chances to directly intervene in his actions before and taken none of them.

Whatever the answer, Will would certainly look like the guilty party to the others. And he'd further reduced his credibility with his crewmates by accusing one of his own people without thinking. Not that it mattered much now. The Kingdom of Man didn't have a great track record for human rights when it came to dealing with prisoners.

Chopra sighed, bored with the silence. 'I don't really know why you're here,' he said, 'but I can guess that it probably has nothing to do with assassinating the Prophet. Am I right?'

Will regarded him with confusion.

'I thought not,' said Chopra sitting back. The civil coordinator pondered for a moment, a hand over his mouth. Then he leaned forwards, steepling his fingers. 'I shall speak frankly,' he said. 'I represent the local authorities in this star system. Administering the police here requires a careful hand and a relatively ... *flexible* outlook. We Sons of Mao are far more easy-going than most sub-sects – and certainly more generous than the High Church.

'However,' he said ominously, 'we have received strict instructions not to interrogate any of you before representatives of a certain branch of Military Intelligence arrives. Their stated reason: that the information you hold could compromise the security of the Prophet.'

Chopra offered Will a wry half-smile. 'Needless to say, whatever the real reason, it might be to our mutual advantage if you voluntarily divulge what you know to us instead. You and your associates would then avoid the somewhat ... heavy-handed methods Military Intelligence employs. And being privy to such knowledge would increase my own standing, and that of the Sons of Mao, immeasurably. By speaking of your own free will, myself and my associates would be free of blame.' He turned his hands upwards, as if to prove them empty. 'I might even be able to put in a good word for you when they arrive. I am a strong believer in a civilised approach to law enforcement.'

Will remembered the scenes of ugly revelry he'd witnessed on the planet below. They hadn't looked particularly civilised to him.

Chopra waited for an answer, his impatience growing visibly. He tried one more time. 'I assure you,' he said, 'I am a much gentler man than those currently on their way to see you.'

Will considered telling Chopra everything. He had nothing to say that the man would enjoy hearing. He'd gain some small measure of satisfaction watching the policeman's face as he explained about their impending extinction and the church's lies to its own people.

Unfortunately, the truth was so inimical to his enemies that he doubted Chopra would believe it.

'No thanks,' he said. Even if his crewmates would never know it, he intended to remain true to his Fleet and his mission to the bitter end.

Chopra frowned and sat back. 'Perhaps I have misjudged you,' he said. 'I did wonder why you would send us a message giving us details so precious as the rendezvous coordinates for your ship, but lacking enough information to help bring you in alive. Perhaps you are a lunatic. You *want* to die, and that is why you refuse to speak now.'

Chopra got to his feet. 'I assure you, death at the hands of Military Intelligence is neither swift nor pretty. Tell the guard if you decide to talk.' He knocked on the door and was let out.

Will slouched in the chair, immobile. Chopra's ignorance of their mission had bought them a little time, but Ulanu and his people couldn't be far away. Will didn't doubt that, in contrast to Chopra, Ulanu would know exactly what questions to ask and have the means of extracting the answers.

How long would he be able to keep his mouth shut when they started torturing him? He shuddered.

13.3: IRA

Ira, Rachel, Amy and Hugo were thrown into a large bare room. As he began to recover the use of his body, Ira examined the walls and floor. There were no obvious means of escape. He noticed security cameras positioned in the room's upper corners. They were too high to reach and screened over with some kind of glass. Ira doubted there'd be much to gain from trying to damage them. Although at first glance the situation appeared hopeless, Ira was not the sort of man to give up.

Unfortunately, Hugo did not take their incarceration so stoically. Ira had forgotten what a pain in the ass the man could be.

The scientist propped himself up against the wall and shouted his rage at the top of his lungs. 'Stinking traitor! If I get my hands on him, I'm going to kill him! I tried to tell you. Ever since—'

Ira quickly interrupted him. 'Enough!' he barked. 'There's only one good reason I can think of for why we've been left together, and that's so the Earthers can listen to us. I don't want anyone discussing the mission. Is that clear?'

Hugo fell into sullen silence.

With some difficulty, Ira pushed himself upright. 'Let's use this opportunity properly,' he said. 'First, we take stock of our situation. One of our crew is dead. We've lost our ship. And someone has betrayed us, though we don't know for sure that the traitor is one of our crew.'

He looked at each of them intently and hoped they understood his meaning. The resistance could easily be responsible for their predicament, but even so, Ira didn't want to bring them up as a topic of conversation. The less the Earthers knew of their operation, the better.

'What are you talking about?' snapped Hugo. 'Of course it's Will.'

'Bullshit!' Rachel snarled.

'Oh, it's bullshit, is it?' the scientist retorted. 'He had the motive, and he had the means through that interface thing. He must have sold us out the first time he used it. No wonder the resistance turned on us.'

And there it was, out in the open: their connection to the resistance, exactly as Ira hadn't wanted.

'Hugo, I said *shut up*,' Ira growled. He wondered if he was a fool for even trying. Hugo wouldn't last long under proper interrogation anyway.

'Or what, Captain?' Hugo sneered. 'What are you going to do now? You don't have a ship to throw me out of any more. Or are you going to walk all the way over here and hit me? Care to give it a try?'

Ira glared at him and drew breath to speak, but Rachel beat him to it.

'You're an asshole, Hugo. Can't you see you're being manipulated? Blaming Will is exactly what they want you to do.'

'Bullshit!' he said, mimicking her voice back to her.

'Why did he take us to the safe house if he was trying to betray us, idiot?' said Rachel. 'In case you hadn't noticed, Will saved your life back there.'

'Only because the alternative was exposing himself,' said Hugo. 'He's been lying to us ever since he was compromised. We're not dealing with the same man we flew out with.'

'That's enough!' Ira roared. He drew the line at Hugo revealing their mission before they'd even made a stab at escaping. 'You'll shut up right now or I'll hit you so hard you'll wish you'd never been born.'

Summoning his strength, Ira clenched his fists and took a couple of unsteady steps towards Hugo. Hugo blinked in surprise at Ira's rapid recovery. He appeared to have forgotten that Ira's metabolism was designed to handle the worst rigours of spaceflight. A few Earther drugs weren't going to bother him for long.

'I don't want to hear another word from any of you,' said Ira. 'We'll stop bickering right now and start thinking up ways we can get out of here. But for God's sake, if you come up with one, don't say it out loud.'

At that point, two large Earthers tramped in and grabbed Ira's shoulders.

'What's this?' Ira said mockingly. 'Am I spoiling your little fact-finding effort?'

They steered him out of the room towards a separate cell. Ira chose his moment and tried to shrug them off, but resistance in his current condition was hopeless. The police barely heeded his efforts and threw him through the doorway. He sprawled across the floor as the door thudded shut behind him.

Now he didn't even have his crew with him. Ira gripped the floor and refused to despair. He needed to think about something else. Revenge sprang easily to mind – revenge on whoever had got him into this shitty situation. It wasn't rational and it didn't help, but right now it was the strongest, most productive emotion Ira could muster.

Who was it? He weighed the evidence. The suspects were Hugo, Rachel, Will and the resistance. Rachel he discounted immediately. Hugo had been shot for his troubles and appeared to have gained nothing. Unless his entire fragile persona was an act, it was unlikely to be him.

The resistance were strong candidates, but their motive wasn't clear. And from what Rachel had said, it sounded as if they'd exposed themselves quite badly through their actions.

However, believing in their guilt was preferable to the idea that he'd been sold out by Will. At the end of the day, Will was still one of his crew. Ira was responsible for him, and as determined as ever not to lose another roboteer.

Unfortunately, the evidence pointed straight at him – or to the alien in his head, at least. Perhaps it had done this in revenge for Ira's decision to remove Will's micromachines. Maybe it had decided that humanity wasn't worth saving after all, or was just pursuing its own unguessable agenda. Either way, Ira couldn't take Will's loyalty for granted any more. Though he hated the idea, if he ever escaped this place, he'd have to accept the fact that Will might need to die.

14: FACE TO FACE

14.1: GUSTAV

Gustav read the report from the New Angeles authorities while his starship was still decelerating into the system. It filled him with a kind of anxious excitement. The enemy was within his grasp at last. Not that he was out of the woods yet, of course – he still had a protectorate government to deal with, a project to save and a war to win.

As soon as he arrived, he made a bee-line for the habitat ring where the prisoners were being held. As always, Rodriguez came with him.

During the uncomfortable two weeks he'd spent with Tang, Gustav had experienced a reversal of attitude with respect to the intolerable disciple. He actually preferred to have him around. While Rodriguez remained in sight, he couldn't be off plotting. Gustav had found his new assistant huddled in furtive conversation with Tang once too often for comfort. It would also help if the revolting little man saw Gustav succeeding for a change.

At the habitat ring, Civil Coordinator Enrique Chopra was waiting for him. He met Gustav with a broad, gleaming grin and an outstretched hand the moment he stepped out of the elevator.

'Welcome, General!' said Chopra enthusiastically.

Gustav regarded the hand steadily until Chopra tucked it back out of sight. From the report Gustav had received, he knew Chopra was suspicious of the reasons for the *Ariel*'s capture, and the coordinator had done his level best to build himself into Gustav's operation. If he thought he could deal with Gustav as an equal in the negotiations that were bound to follow, it was better that he be disabused of that notion now.

Chopra's smile ground on with unyielding confidence. 'We have all heard the news of your commendation, General. My congratulations to you!'

'Thank you,' said Gustav curtly. 'May I introduce my assistant, Disciple Jesus Rodriguez.'

Rodriguez was only too willing to shake Chopra's hand. 'May I congratulate you on your capture, Civil Coordinator,' said the disciple. 'A brilliant piece of police work, if I may say so.'

Chopra beamed at him. 'You're too kind, Father.'

Gustav decided to wrest back control of the conversation before Rodriguez could enlist another ally in his machinations.

'I want to interview the prisoners,' he said.

Chopra arched an eyebrow. 'In person, General?'

'Why else do you suppose I'm here?' said Gustav. 'To watch recordings? Please take me to the man you identified as Will Kuno-Monet.'

'The mad one?' Chopra's professionally unreadable face betrayed a moment of intense curiosity. 'I would have thought you'd want to see the captain first, sir.'

Chopra was fishing. The report suggested he'd followed Gustav's orders to the letter. Supposedly, Chopra's men had neither interrogated the Galateans nor made any attempt to investigate the hard or soft contents of the impounded ship. Gustav was sure that was a lie, but they'd at least taken pains to conceal their efforts. He'd half-expected the policeman to announce his knowledge of the Relic and start bargaining for the price of his silence. Then again, the Sons of Mao could be relied upon for subtlety, if nothing else.

'You have stated that the captain's behaviour is stable,' said Gustav. 'Therefore, he can wait. I will see the *mad one*, as you call him.'

Chopra bowed. 'As you wish, General.' Chopra muttered some commands into the mike on his lapel and gave Gustav another winning smile. 'Please follow me.'

According to Chopra's report, Monet talked to himself. He made demands for help from an entity he called *the Transcended*. The moment he read that, Gustav's skin had prickled all over. That word, or something like it, had occurred eleven times in the garbled responses they'd received from the Relic.

Chopra had identified Monet as performing the role on the Galatean ship known as *roboteer*. This meant he was bred to think with the autistic clarity of a machine so that they could plug him into their robots like some kind of human strategy SAP. Gustav was revolted by the idea, but realised its potential all the same. If Monet was in effect part machine, was there some possibility that the Relic had influenced him, just as it had influenced their computers? Either way, it was clear that this Monet was involved in some way with the attack on their data feed from the Relic.

When Gustav learned of Monet's apparent betrayal of his crew, his suspicions were aroused still further. It suggested that something at odds with the Galatean agenda might be at work in his mind. If the man was as unstable as Chopra suggested, there was hope that they might be able to manipulate him to their advantage.

Chopra arrived at a door next to a panel of wall monitors. They showed a young man slumped in a chair from a variety of angles.

'I will talk to the man alone and in private,' said Gustav.

Rodriguez regarded him levelly. 'For what reason, General?' he asked coldly. Apparently he no longer felt the need to play at being an assistant, not even in front of the Leading members of other subsects. 'You don't want to give the impression that you're cutting deals with the prisoners that the Prophet would disapprove of, do you?' Rodriguez added.

'The Prophet will have to trust me,' Gustav replied with equal venom. 'I will go in alone.' He looked at Chopra. 'The man is appropriately secured?'

'Of course,' said Chopra cheerily. 'Motor-suppressants have just been applied. He can talk, and move a little, but not much else.'

'Good,' said Gustav. He tapped on the closest monitor, bringing up a command interface and used his security override to lock down surveillance in the cell. The images of Monet vanished.

'No recordings will be made of this discussion,' he said. 'If I find that there has been any attempt to subvert my authority, I will hold you in contempt of Kingdom security.'

Chopra nodded smoothly, not quite hiding his disappointment. 'Of course, General.'

'Open the door,' Gustav ordered.

Chopra keyed in the code and the door swung open. With some satisfaction, Gustav stepped through and shut it against Rodriguez's frowning face. Let the bastard wring whatever political advantage he could from this moment. Gustav wasn't going to miss his opportunity.

He turned to the prisoner. Monet was a tall man with a mop of floppy brown hair and some uneven beard growth. He sat slumped in his chair, dressed in regulation-green prisoner's overalls, looking for all the world like one of the drunks who used to pass through Civic Control back in Sophia.

Except for his eyes. The man's eyes stared fearlessly into Gustav's own. His expression might even have been called menacing. Gustav knew that the prisoner's slack posture was due to the motor-suppressants, but that wasn't how he looked. He looked like a supremely casual man considering murder.

Good, Gustav thought to himself. If he was lucid at the moment, he'd be that much easier to talk to.

'Good afternoon, Will,' he said. 'My name is General Ulanu.'

'I know who you are,' said Monet.

'Excellent,' said Gustav. 'Then you know why I have come to see you.'

Monet chuckled to himself. Gustav fought down a surge of impatience. If this little Gallie thought he could get away with playing mind games, he was a fool. Gustav had played with the best of them.

'I have come seeking knowledge,' he said simply. 'And I am prepared to ask nicely.' He sat down opposite the prisoner.

'How good of you,' Monet replied.

Gustav sighed and examined his fingers. 'Let me summarise your position. You and your crew are facing public execution. Your ship will shortly be broken up into pieces. Your robots will be dissected for analysis or forcibly reprogrammed. And your home world is due to be occupied in a matter of days.'

Monet looked remarkably unaffected by this list of misfortunes. An infuriating secret smile kept playing about his lips.

'If you know who I am,' said Gustav, 'then you also know that I am a powerful man. I can help you with one or all of these matters if you answer my questions. If you tell me what I want to know, you will find me surprisingly flexible.'

'Will you let me and my crewmates go?' asked Monet.

Gustav took a deep breath. Monet obviously considered himself a comedian. 'No,' he replied.

'Then you can't help me,' said Monet. 'You can't even help yourself.'

Gustav regarded him wearily and considered for a moment. A roboteer was supposedly a creature of logic and reason, so Gustav decided to take a calculated risk. He would give Monet as clear a picture of his priorities as he could afford.

'Perhaps I should explain a little about myself,' he said. 'I am, first and foremost, a scientist. I carry the rank of general because in the current political climate of the Kingdom, the military is the only source of research funding. For the last two years, I have worked full time studying the alien object we call *the Relic* – the object you attacked.'

At this, Monet's smile grew a notch wider. He snorted and shook his head.

'It is my desire,' said Gustav, raising his voice a little, 'to share what I have learned with *all* mankind. I believe that the human galaxy should be made aware of the existence of the Relic, and what we have learned from it. If you know the first thing about the Truist movement, you will also know that this is at odds with dogma. So you see, I am making myself vulnerable to you. I am making a confession to you that my enemies would be only too glad to hear. You may also consider it an assurance of the fact that this meeting is private. Nothing you say in this room will go any further.'

Monet laughed. 'That's what Chopra said.'

Gustav pursed his lips. 'Chopra is interested only in personal gain. I am interested in truth, nothing more, nothing less.'

'Really?' Monet leaned forwards and rested his arms on the table.

He moved surprisingly easily for a man supposedly doped to the eyeballs on disabling drugs. 'You might not like it.'

'Then you are prepared to talk?' said Gustav, excitement churning his insides.

'Ask your questions,' said Monet. 'I might answer.'

Gustav nearly betrayed his glee. Locked in this man's head might be secrets he hadn't even dreamed of.

'All right,' he said. 'How did you deactivate the feed from the Relic?' That had to be a good place to start. Since the arrival of the Galateans, the Relic had told them exactly nothing.

'We didn't,' said Monet. 'It stopped talking to you.'

Gustav peered at him. 'Why?'

'Because you were deemed no longer a useful part of the dialog with humanity,' the prisoner replied. 'I superseded you.'

Gustav bristled. The roboteer was almost as good at annoying him as Rodriguez.

'Superseded? In what way?'

'You spent your two years searching the Relic for weapons technology.'

He said it as an accusation. But what else could Gustav have done with so much pressure on him from the Kingdom to produce results? Did Monet imagine that would have been his choice if he'd been given free rein?

'In doing so, you convinced it that humanity is an unworthy species,' said Monet.

'Unworthy how?'

'Not useful for the galactic biosphere. Scheduled for extinction. The technology it gave you contains a deliberate flaw.'

Gustav recalled the long, anxious hours he'd spent poring over the incomprehensible blueprints and hid his alarm.

'Use it long enough and it marks the stars it draws energy from,' said Monet. 'The people who made your Relic can then detonate them at their leisure.'

A problem in the suntap, just as his instincts had warned him there might be. It was grave news for the Kingdom – if it was true.

'How do you know this?' said Gustav uneasily.

'I just listened,' Monet replied. 'Something you apparently failed to do.'

Gustav's shoulders cranked upwards. For two whole years, he'd done nothing but listen.

'Oh, and one other thing,' the prisoner said. 'It appears we Galateans have achieved one thing you Earthers have not. They call it *constructive self-editing*. It's the means by which a species is judged. If you can't do it, they wipe you out.'

Gustav's face hardened. Suddenly he could see where this was going. 'You mean genetic modification?'

Monet shrugged. 'That's part of it.'

The Galatean had blown it. He'd had Gustav worried there for a moment, but his story had just passed the point of believability. This wasn't the truth. It was a gene-racist's fantasy. Gustav was furious with himself for taking it so seriously.

'You mean to tell me that the survival of the human race is dependent on us all turning Galatean?' he said darkly.

Monet grinned. 'That's one way of putting it.'

Gustav stood. 'You disgust me,' he sneered. 'I gave you an opportunity to speak the truth.'

'And I told you that you might not like it,' Monet replied sunnily.

Gustav looked down his nose at the prisoner. 'You expect me to believe that an advanced alien race will kill us all if we don't adopt your people's revolting practices? That's a little convenient, don't you think?'

Monet examined his fingernails. 'Not really. We weren't thrilled about it.'

Gustav glared at him. 'To *self-edit*, as you put it, is to lose track of what it means to be human. No advanced race would condone it.'

'Are you so sure?' said Monet. 'Why not?'

Gustav contemplated ramming his fist into the Gallie's face. 'Because you people are building injustice into your very bodies! Look at yourself.' He gestured wildly at the prisoner's chest. 'Born to talk to machines,' he said with contempt. 'Selected for autism by your own parents, for God's sake. Are you going to sit there and tell me you're happy with that? Or are you so programmed by your own people that you can't see the freedoms they've stolen from you?'

Gustav saw Monet's smug mask slip for the first time. He'd struck a nerve. Good.

'You may be happy with your lot because it's all you've ever known,' he added, 'but I intend to fight for humanity. And if that means there'll be war and ignorance in the world, I think it's still worth it. It's better than changing ourselves into sterile machines.'

Monet shook his head. His expression had turned bitter. 'You don't get it, do you?' he said. 'I've no reason to lie to you. Listen, nothing lasts for ever. Put cavemen in charge of starships and sooner or later we're going to kill ourselves, with or without help. Either way, mankind's days are numbered.'

'Then let us be the ones who number them!' Gustav spat.

'Fine,' said Monet quietly. 'I don't care if you believe me or not. Unless you release us, it's irrelevant. You'll know I'm telling you the truth when whatever sun you're sitting near bloats up and fries you. It's just a shame you won't have long to regret your mistake.'

Gustav narrowed his eyes. This Earther might be mad but he wasn't stupid. He knew how to goad his adversaries. Gustav regretted his earlier honesty. Still, if the roboteer became a threat, they could always kill him. He turned to the door and pressed the stud.

'I'm finished,' he told Chopra bitterly.

The door swung back and Gustav stepped out into the corridor where Rodriguez and the coordinator stood with expressions of unconvincing innocence on their faces.

'Well, General?' said Chopra.

'Your assessment of the prisoner is accurate,' Gustav said coldly. 'His insanity is unfortunate. I will see the captain now.'

Gustav followed Chopra on down the corridor, leaving Monet's cell behind. The sick, uncertain feeling in his gut came with him.

14.2: JOHN

The captain's voice came over the bunkroom speakers.

'Fifteen minutes to Galatean defence perimeter. Weapons officers, report for duty in five.'

John put down the dull pornographic pamphlet he'd been staring at and exhaled slowly. At last! This had been the longest fortnight of his life. It was ironic that he'd spent none of it as himself.

When the Reconsiderist Subsect Starship *Fist of Vengeance* had finished planet leave at New Angeles, the Akbar Inglez who'd shuttled aboard was not the same one who'd left two days before. The real Akbar Inglez was dead. He'd died wearing John's face as he stumbled out of a resistance house clutching a gun. Now John had Akbar's face, his pass-codes and his scout mission to Galatea.

John had always prided himself on not feeling guilt. There was little room for that emotion in the life of a spy, but some of the *Ariel*'s crew had been close to him, and the cost of his actions had been hard to bear. He'd counted Ira as almost a friend. And he didn't like to think about Rachel.

When her face came swimming through his mind, as it did from time to time, he reminded himself that there had been no choice. The Angelenos would never have given him the antimatter. Not that he'd tried particularly hard to get it. From the beginning, he'd steered the negotiation towards a single place-swap with a crewman from an Earther ship. It was the only solution he could think of.

John knew what he had to do from the moment he looked at the star maps with Amy back in the Fecund system. He'd seen New Angeles sitting there just within their range and the plan had come to him fully formed.

The hardest part had been right at the start – convincing Ira that there was any hope of getting fuel there. Fortunately, the compromised roboteer had made that easy for him by kicking up such a fuss. Ira was too absorbed in getting the hell out of alien territory to think through the problems of obtaining antimatter in a star system at full alert.

It was fortunate that things worked out the way they had. Of the entire crew, only he and Hugo appeared to understand the potential threat the aliens posed. The bastards had cut through his finest defensive code as if it wasn't there, for crying out loud. He hated them for that. He'd decided then that the aliens represented an appalling threat to the human race – one he wasn't prepared to stand by and tolerate. Unfortunately, there had proved to be no way to purge the *Ariel* of the offending virus, which meant the ship couldn't be allowed to return home.

Sadly, John knew there was no way he could convince the rest of the crew of that. Had he spoken his mind, Ira would have ordered him not to act and thereby doomed them all. So he'd had been forced to arrange for the ship's destruction in secret.

Ira had made John's work infinitely harder by insisting he take the infected roboteer down to the planet. But in the end, John managed to turn even that problem to his advantage. Pointing the finger at Will ensured that even if his plan went off beam, he'd never be suspected. His method also had the added advantage of convincing the Earthers that the trail was cold. Assuming everything went as planned after his swap, the rest of the crew were already dead and the *Ariel* destroyed, along with its sinister alien cargo.

John knew that Ira would never allow himself to be captured. The moment those Earther ships appeared at the rendezvous, he would have either fled or self-destructed. And with the fuel as low as it was, there was nowhere for him to go.

Thus, tidily, the Earthers knew no more about the aliens than they had a month ago. In contrast, the Galateans would be receiving a full report couriered to them at full speed aboard one of the enemy's own scout ships. John was on his way home faster than he could ever have got there in *Ariel*, creeping around the perimeter of Kingdom space. He'd cut straight through the middle with priority fuelling stops all the way.

If there was one flaw to the entire plan, it had been the forced abandonment of Hugo. John had hoped to hand him over as part of his pay-off to the resistance. They would have gained valuable weapons expertise, while he'd have successfully planted someone with knowledge of the alien threat in a secure location. However, the resistance had shown little interest, so John had been forced to drop him. Still, in the grand scheme of things, Hugo's role was irrelevant and the universe was certain to be a slightly less annoying place without him.

In its own bitter way, this plan was the masterstroke of John's career. Unfortunately, there was no one he could tell. The Galatean Fleet would be unlikely to see his whole plan in a positive light.

They tended to take a dim view of officers abandoning a ship and colleagues, even under such compelling circumstances.

John sighed as he stood and shuffled over to the wash cubicle. He locked the door behind him and positioned himself in front of the sink. A foreign face stared back at him in the mirror. He missed his features. He hated his new squinty eyes, his broken nose and ludicrous moustache. He hated the man they belonged to. Akbar Inglez was boorish and ignorant. He had no wit, no real grasp of the weapons he ran and precious few social skills. Like most Earthers, he was little more than a peasant. But as Metta had pointed out to him, that made Akbar all the easier to pretend to be.

The gaps in his memory had raised a few raised eyebrows among his new shipmates, of course, but John had explained those away with tales of a drug binge gone horribly wrong. His gruff simulated embarrassment had been enough to make the revolting crew clap him on the back and laugh at his misfortune.

John pulled his overalls down to his waist, tucked a towel around them and held his left arm over the sink. Then, with exquisite care, he pulled out the bone and super-carbon-composite knife from the concealed biopolymer pocket in his flesh. It stung like mad. Red blood and ochre packing plasma dripped from his elbow into the sink. John gritted his teeth as he eased the weapon out.

There was a thudding at the door.

'Hey, Akbar, hurry up, you fat bastard. I need to go.'

That was Yuri, his bunkmate.

'In a minute,' John replied in Akbar's thick, deep voice.

The knife was out at last. It was a narrow, wicked-looking thing with a serrated edge that had been designed to sit alongside the bones of his arm unnoticed during an X-ray scan. John placed it in the sink, washed as quickly as he could and flushed the toilet.

He flexed his left hand. It still ached, but not so much that it wouldn't be useful in a fight. With calm efficiency, he pulled his overalls back up and carefully palmed the blade.

'Come on, Akbar,' said Yuri. 'Finish jerking off already.'

John slid the door open, keeping his right hand high at the edge of the door. 'I am done,' he announced.

'At last,' muttered Yuri. 'We're supposed to be on watch by now.'

Yuri barged past him. As he did, John let the blade slip around in his hand and dragged the edge neatly across Yuri's neck. Yuri's eyes bulged as he died. In case a slit throat wasn't enough, the knife's edge was coated with a nerve agent that had activated within minutes of John exposing it to the air.

John shut the cubicle door behind Yuri. He wiped the blade on his bunk-bag, palmed the weapon once more and stepped out into the narrow companionway, whistling one of Akbar's favourite tunes.

When he reached the weapons room, his team leader Gary Wu was waiting for him. The other two weapons operators were seated behind him, already strapped into their combat couches with bulky visors over their faces.

'Where the hell have you been?' Wu demanded.

John's knife flashed out and plunged into his heart. John side-stepped quickly, getting as little blood as he could on himself, and cut the throats of the other two men while they struggled with their straps.

John felt a certain satisfaction in these executions. He'd been listening to their light-hearted chat about genocide and the things they'd do to Gallie women for two whole weeks and had to laugh along with it. Now they were getting a first-hand taste of what genocide felt like.

With the ship's weapons staff dead, there were only two other stations on the small scout to worry about – engineering and command. Engineering first, he decided. Command was where he wanted to end up.

The engineering room had three staff, all strapped into their couches and frantically teleoperating robots that someone like Will could have run on his own and half-asleep.

The thought of Will brought with it another twinge of regret. The man had clearly been compromised, John reminded himself. Not really himself at the end. Only a romantic fool like Rachel could miss it. John gritted his teeth.

'Gunner Inglez! Can I help—' said the chief of engineering as John's poisoned blade slipped into his belly. The last, lucky engineer was halfway out of his seat before he died.

'Captain! Emer—' he managed to say into his throat-mike before John silenced him.

'What was that, Engineering?' came the reply from the captain.

John *tsked* to himself. That had torn it. He picked up the dead man's mike and spoke in a passable impression of the engineer's voice.

'Sorry, Captain, sir. False alarm. My mistake.'

He dropped the mike and stepped to the door. He'd have to move swiftly now. Even as he walked away, he could hear the captain's voice making fresh demands.

'Give me a full status report, Engineering. Engineering?'

John ran along the companionway as quickly as the narrow walls and juddering, uneven gravity from the engines would permit. He reached the door to the bridge and typed in the executive override code he'd hacked into the system on his third day aboard.

The ship's command crew looked up in surprise. The captain was there, surrounded by screens on his real leather couch. His three senior officers were positioned in front of him, walled in by the cumbersome crap the Earthers called 'technology'.

'Gunner Inglez,' said the captain. 'What in the Prophet's name is going on? Why aren't you at your post?'

By the time the captain had finished his question, he had an answer: John had dashed forward and stabbed the first officer in the chest. The three remaining men scrambled madly to get out of their couches. Two of them succeeded. The third died as he tried to rip open his last ankle strap. As he held a forearm up to protect himself, John did little more than rake the surface with the tip of his weapon, but it was enough. The Earther convulsed violently and slumped sideways over the couch, his ankle still trapped.

By that time, the real trouble had started. John ducked and rolled as the captain fired two whining rounds from his executive automatic.

'Iqbal!' the captain shouted to his remaining officer. 'Iqbal, over here! I'll cover you!'

John had to hand it to them – these top officers responded pretty fast. That didn't mean they got to live, though. John waited for Iqbal to make his move and dived the other way, against the captain's expectations.

'Doors, seal,' he ordered the computer.

The bridge's bulkhead doors started sliding shut.

'Doors, open!' the captain yelled, but the computer wasn't responding to him any more.

Just as John had hoped, the surprise of this held the captain's attention for the critical second it took for John to stand and bury his blade in the captain's neck. The captain slid forwards, letting the gun fall out of his hand.

John and Iqbal both made a desperate dash towards the weapon. Iqbal was closer, but John wasn't aiming for the gun. He was aiming for Iqbal's head. Even as the man grabbed the barrel, John's foot connected with his head, snapping it back and killing him instantly.

'Thank you,' said John calmly, plucking the gun from the dead man's hands.

He emptied a few rounds into Iqbal, just in case. Then he pushed the captain's corpse away from the command chair and sat in it. He surveyed the ship's performance stats and *tsked* to himself again. Not good. The very last thing the wily captain had done was to kick the ship into a fatal-overload condition.

John wrestled the antimatter feed profiles back to a semblance of normality. It wasn't easy. The simple Earther robots needed constant coaxing. With extreme care, he gently teased the ship out of warp – a task that usually required the attention of three men.

There was a gruesome bump as the gravity failed. Radiation alarms sounded across the bridge.

'Shit! Shit! Shit!' John shouted.

He pulled everything but the fusion cores offline as fast as he could. Unfortunately, the radiation alarms remained.

He quickly opened a tight-beam channel to Galatean defence. Then, with a wince, he ripped the message chip from the patch of false scalp on the back of his head and slapped it against the wireless port on the captain's chair. It contained a summary of his status and a highly compressed set of strategic recommendations. As soon as they received it, Fleet would hopefully come and rescue him.

Unfortunately, this far away from the primary defensive line, it'd be hours before his message arrived. Hopefully the bridge wouldn't flood with gamma rays before then.

He looked left, towards the captain's floating corpse. 'So,' he said, 'what shall we talk about?'

14.3: JOHN

As soon as the Fleet medics finished his anti-rad treatment, John was taken to see Admiral Bryant-Leys aboard *Evacuation Ark One*. The admiral strode across his huge office to meet John with arms open wide. His huge, rugged face was crinkled in delight.

'Lieutenant Forrester. John!' He took John's hand in both of his and shook it fiercely.

John winced. 'Careful, sir. The bones still ache a bit.'

'Of course,' said Bryant, his massive eyebrows shooting up. 'Sorry about that. Why don't you come over here and sit down. Take a load off.' The admiral put his arm gently around John's shoulders and gestured to the chairs by the viewing wall.

'Thank you, sir,' said John.

He hobbled over to the chair and sprawled gratefully into it. He'd made it home, and a few ugly days in a scrubbing tank was all it had cost him. He smiled to himself. No more vile ruins. No more horrible alien software creeping through his ship, keeping him up at night.

No more crewmates, his subconscious bitterly reminded him. His smile faded. Still, his guilt would fade in time. Guilt always did.

He looked to the admiral. Bryant was very obviously examining John's new face. John couldn't wait to get rid of Akbar's features. So far, all he'd been able to do was shave off the dreadful moustache.

'Extraordinary,' said Bryant. 'If I hadn't been told, I would never have known it was you.'

'Cosmetic surgery is one of the few areas where the Angelenos are ahead of us, sir,' said John, as airily as he could. He didn't want to talk about it. The doctors had expressed some doubt as to whether they could undo all the Angeleno cleverness. His face might never be quite the same again.

'I must say, sir, I'm very glad to see the arks in action,' he said, changing the subject. 'I was afraid my message wouldn't arrive in time.'

'We started priming them the day after you left,' said Bryant. 'When we spotted the Earthers making scouting runs, we began ferrying people from the surface. We were just waiting on some word from Ira before making the launch. You brought us that. On behalf of the Fleet, I want to thank you.'

John twisted uncomfortably in his chair. 'Just doing my duty, sir.'

'But it must have been the mission of a lifetime,' the admiral insisted. 'Alien worlds, shell distortions, fighting with the resistance.'

'You could say that, sir.'

Bryant read the pain on John's face. 'I'm sorry. That was insensitive of me.' He looked down. 'They were a fine crew.'

John nodded, keeping his expression carefully neutral.

'Captain Baron was a brilliant man, and a good friend,' said the admiral.

'Yes,' said John softly. 'Yes, he was.'

Bryant was quiet for a second and then looked up again. 'I apologise for raking over old coals, but I'm afraid I've brought you here to go through the whole thing with you again. Just to get the facts straight, you understand.'

'As you wish, sir.'

'I've read your report, of course,' Bryant added. 'It's the details I want to clarify.'

John nodded, suppressing both frustration and fear. What was there to clarify? He had brought back a full set of logs from the *Ariel*. What more did the admiral need?

'Where would you like me to start, sir?'

Bryant leaned back in his chair. 'At the beginning, please.'

So John talked. He said everything he could remember till he got to the alien software attack, which he chose not to dwell on too heavily. Even now, he hated how it had made him feel. It had scared him in a way he'd never experienced before. He hurried on to a description of the Fecund system, which held the admiral rapt. The next bit he glossed over was the betrayal on New Angeles, but this time, Bryant was not to be rushed.

'Let me get this straight,' said the admiral, leaning forward. 'You were set up by your roboteer, Will Kuno-Monet.'

'That's right, sir.'

'Extraordinary,' said Bryant with a shake of his head. 'He looked like such an excellent officer to me. A little wild, of course, but then our best ones always are – yourself included. He saved my life, you know.'

John nodded. 'Yes, sir. But I should say that it wasn't really Will who betrayed us – it was the thing inside his head. It took him over. Twisted his mind. At first, it appeared to be helping us. Then it led us to that alien graveyard. And when we insisted on leaving, it became dangerous. Consequently, it's my recommendation, sir, that once we win this war, all knowledge of the suntap be destroyed and the alien systems made off limits. These so-called Transcended can't be trusted. Their extinction strategy regarding the suntap illustrates that pretty clearly, I think.'

Bryant smiled at him kindly. 'Winning may be a little way off, Lieutenant. Right now, I think we'd settle for a draw. But back to New Angeles for a moment.'

John gritted his teeth.

'You say the resistance saved your life,' Bryant ventured.

John nodded. 'Yes, sir. We owe the Angelenos a debt of gratitude. When the Earther forces ambushed our rendezvous site and the shooting started, I was lucky enough to dive back into the house. The others died.'

'I don't understand,' said Bryant. 'So how do you know Will was responsible?'

'He was the only one with the means, sir,' said John, a little more curtly than he'd intended. 'I foolishly gave him an interface device to patch into the local network after his operation. It was a gesture of trust, but a badly chosen one. I hold myself responsible.' He looked down and tried for a suitably penitent expression.

Bryant leaned over and put a hand on his knee. 'Nonsense, Lieutenant. It's nothing I wouldn't have done in your shoes. Let's look on the bright side. You've brought us the plans for the suntap and our engineering labs are already working on it. Though we'll be careful to use it sparingly, given what you've told us. But, even more valuable than that: you've bought us a chance to escape. You're a hero, my boy.'

John winced. 'No, sir. Captain Baron was the hero. I was just lucky.'

Bryant regarded him with something verging on worship. 'Such selflessness does you credit. You should know, son, that if we survive what's coming, I've decided to personally see to it that you get a ship of your own.'

John managed a watery smile. 'Thank you, sir. Thank you.'

14.4: GUSTAV

Gustav sat in his cabin and pored over the notes from the interviews he'd conducted. The results were far from satisfactory. Like the two women, Captain Baron had refused to say anything. In contrast, the scientist, Hugo Bessler-Vartian, had rambled incessantly about an alien threat. The man was clearly obsessed with the roboteer to the point of mania.

Vartian had given his captors a list of demands: the isolation and careful study of Kuno-Monet, the cessation of all hostilities and the complete quarantining of both Galatea and the Relic system. When Gustav had refused to take the man's claims at face value, Vartian had become emotional, straining the limits of his motor-suppressants until Gustav had been forced to walk out on him. Gustav had his hands full just trying to make sense of it all.

There was a cough from the open door of the cabin.

'Come in,' said Gustav.

Emil Dulan, his head of research, stepped in. Emil looked excited. His long face was split apart with a wide-eyed grin.

'Sir, we've found something we think you'll want to see.'

'You've cracked the Galatean security at last?' Gustav guessed.

The *Ariel*'s computers had proven infuriatingly well defended. It was insane that they'd been able to get the crew out of the habitat pod yet were completely unable to access the ship's most basic records. It was as if the computer had a life of its own. They were learning more simply by cutting through the hull.

Emil shook his head. 'Better than that,' he said.

Gustav raised one eyebrow. 'Show me.'

Emil took him through the habitat ring to a study room lined with wall-sized screens that showed him a view through the eyes of their investigation robots. Hanging in front of them in one of the *Ariel*'s storage chambers was... *something*. It towered over them, covered in weirdly shaped sockets and dotted with unrecognisable characters. It looked thousands of years old. And the Galateans had connected it to their own data feeds.

Gustav didn't doubt for a moment that it was alien, and the hairs on the back of his neck stood up straight. This was the mother-lode. This was what he'd been waiting for. His people had scanned the blank face of the Relic hundreds of times and never found anything like this.

Which raised an important question: *where had the Galateans found it?*

'Forget the *Ariel*'s computers for a while,' Gustav said quietly. 'Forget the crew. Focus on this – and be very, very careful.'

15: LOSING POWER

15.1: GUSTAV

Gustav sat in his room, joyfully examining the latest update from the artefact. Life was looking up at last. It had exceeded his expectations. Not only did he have the Galateans, but they'd brought him this wonderful thing.

Despite some recent damage to its memory cores, they'd managed to work out part of the compression algorithm the alien object used. After ten days of feverish work, data was emerging at last, and there were intimations of secrets in it that would revolutionise the Kingdom. Weapons of unspeakable power. Starship designs like nothing he had ever seen. Star maps for great tracts of the galaxy that man had never visited.

There were mysteries, too, however, such as the fact that this device looked far less sophisticated than the Relic itself. The builders of the artefact appeared to have a relatively primitive approach to data storage, whereas the fiendishly subtle self-assembling structures that the planet had sent them were nowhere to be seen.

How could they both be products of the same culture? His best guess was that the artefact came from a far older site. Which suggested that perhaps the Galateans had managed to entice the Relic into giving up the location of the alien home world, and that they'd been there. If that was true, it couldn't be far away. For all they knew, it was just on the other side of the lobe.

'General,' said Rodriguez, stepping uninvited through the open door of his cabin.

'Learn to knock, Rodriguez,' Gustav told him.

He didn't bother looking up from his work. He had no time for the disciple now. As soon as they finished unravelling the alien archive, he'd have justification for his project beyond the Prophet's wildest dreams. Rodriguez would become an irrelevance.

'I have just received word from Admiral Tang,' said Rodriguez. 'I decided to bring it to you in person.'

Gustav suppressed the urge to shout and lowered the tablet he was reading from. After all, there was an outside chance that the message from Tang might actually be important.

He met Rodriguez's intensely shining eyes with a steady stare. 'Go on, then.'

The disciple looked more cheerful than he had any right to be. 'Admiral Tang says the fleet can wait no longer. One of the scout runs to the Galatean system has been lost. He is forced to assume that the enemy's swift and decisive response was intended to prevent our discovery of their defensive manoeuvres. He believes they have wind of our plans and has ordered a general recall of all vessels to attack immediately. He requests that you rendezvous with him at Memburi.'

Gustav's lip curled. 'Oh, he does, does he?'

That wasn't Tang's order to give, but Gustav decided not to jump to conclusions. It could be that Rodriguez had deliberately mangled the message in order to elicit some convenient response from him.

'Well,' Gustav continued calmly, 'then I shall tell Admiral Tang that he will have to wait. The value of our work here outweighs his desire for battle.'

Gustav had begun to wonder if attacking Galatea any time soon was a good idea. It would be far wiser to wring the truth out of the *Ariel*'s crew first. After that, they might test some of the inventions in the artefact. It had the potential to put their technology generations ahead of the Galateans'. That in turn would render taking possession of the colony world both swift and painless.

Rodriguez hadn't stopped smiling. 'That's where you're wrong, General,' he said. He drew a white and gold data card from the pocket of his ship-suit. 'I have here a dictate of emergency powers from the Prophet. It transfers control of the military component of this operation to Admiral Tang and jurisdiction over the Relic Project to me.'

Gustav stared at him. For an awful second, he felt as if his stomach had gone into free fall. Then he caught himself. Rodriguez's claim didn't make sense. How could the man have obtained such a thing? It had to be some kind of ruse.

'Oh, really,' he said, aiming for a tone of dry amusement. 'And how did you manage that?'

Rodriguez's smile became downright predatory. 'I requested special powers on the same day you sent word to Admiral Tang telling him to deploy his fleet to catch the *Ariel*.'

In other words, when Gustav looked the most foolish.

'I simply added a second destination to the messenger drone you sent,' the disciple continued. 'The Prophet received a full report, along with word of your decision to use a threat to his person as cover for your blunder. And now his response has arrived at last.'

The blood drained from Gustav's face. Now that he thought about it, Rodriguez's attitude had changed after that day. But Gustav had so much on his mind that he hadn't even thought to question it.

A cold sense of certainty settled on him. This was real. He stood up.

'You had no authority to do that,' he said hollowly.

'No,' replied Rodriguez. 'But thankfully the communications officer didn't appear to realise that. And now I do.' He pushed his shoulders back. 'Your commanding officer has issued you with an order. You and your staff will attend Admiral Tang at Memburi and assist him with the battle at Galatea.

'Don't worry, though,' the disciple added, raising a placating hand. 'As head of the Relic Project, I will take responsibility for the prisoners here as well as the new artefact. I have already made a request and a High Church research team is on its way here. They will handle interrogation while I focus on the alien problem.'

Despite a nauseating feeling of defeat, Gustav refused to give up. He had not survived the brutal days of the early church to have everything snatched away from him at the eleventh hour.

'I won't let you do this,' he said simply.

Rodriguez looked pleased. 'You have no power to prevent me.'

Gustav stared at the disciple and thought of the executive automatic still tucked in his pocket. Perhaps he should kill Rodriguez here and now.

'Then I'll make you regret it.'

'I'm glad you said that,' said Rodriguez. 'I had your cabin sensors activated just before I came in.' He gestured at the cameras in the corners of the room. 'This conversation and that threat are both now on record. And I warn you, any acts of aggression or attempted subversion of the hierarchy will be considered treason. You may, of course, lodge an appeal with your subsect leader if you so wish. If it succeeds, at that point you may have your object and your prisoners back. Assuming, of course, that there is anything left of them. In the meantime, they will serve my purposes.'

'What do you intend to do with them?' said Gustav.

'God's bidding, General, nothing more, nothing less.' Rodriguez let a little anger creep into his voice. 'A concept you appear incapable of comprehending. The Gallies will yield their secrets. Then those who can be made to serve the church will do so. The others will be silenced.'

'And the artefact?'

'Its teachings will be extracted to serve the church,' Rodriguez replied. 'Then it will be destroyed, along with the Relic world, as originally planned.'

Gustav's mouth twisted in bitter amusement. 'Does it not worry you that I was right?'

Rodriguez's brows shot up. 'About what?' he sneered. 'As far as I can see, you have done nothing but mismanage this project since the outset.'

'I said the Relic would prove able to defend itself,' said Gustav. 'It has. I said there would be more alien remains. There were. What do you intend to do, Father – wage war against the whole universe?'

'I will answer the call that God has given me,' Rodriguez snapped. His eyes lit up with zeal. 'With the knowledge in that artefact, I will make the High Church *free*,' he said, thrusting a finger at the images on Gustav's monitors. 'No longer shall we have to pander to the lesser churches and their vile machinations. We will be equipped to impose the Law of God directly. The discovery of other remains that concerns you so greatly will never be a problem, as future travel will be under the jurisdiction of the faithful.'

Gustav stared at him wide-eyed. Rodriguez was mad, he realised. He was talking about doing away with the subsects. He was talking about civil war. He wondered if Tang had the slightest comprehension of what his ally intended to do with the knowledge he'd gained.

'Well, good-bye, General,' Rodriguez said airily. 'I can't say it's been a pleasure. I have found your arrogant rationalism and contempt for faith equally revolting. I am quite relieved that I shall have to tolerate neither any longer.'

The disciple stepped to the door to leave and turned back at the last moment. 'Oh – I almost forgot to tell you. Given that you will no longer be enjoying the benefit of my assistance, I have taken the trouble to assign you two new assistants from the High Church to aid you in your somewhat reduced duties. Let me introduce Brothers Ulkin and Thaud.'

He gestured and two huge men dressed in High Church white entered the room. They were priests only in the loosest sense possible, being the sort of men used to arguing their beliefs with their fists.

Then Rodriguez was gone. Gustav stood wordless in the room, considering the brutish countenances before him. His mind raced. How could he win back control? Appealing to the Prophet would be hopeless. The old man had more power within his grasp now than ever before.

An unlikely notion popped into Gustav's head. He could arrange escape for the Galateans. If he changed sides, he was sure they'd tell him everything they knew. He grimaced, disgusted with himself. He was not desperate enough yet to throw in his lot with a bunch of capitalist mutants like Captain Baron. Better to play along until he could think of a better plan. He just hoped his prisoners would still be alive by the time he came up with one.

15.2: WILL

While his body lay curled on the floor of his cell, Will paced up and down in the seclusion of his home node. For the hundredth time, he debated with himself whether he should have told General Ulanu all that he had. He had no doubt that Ira would be furious with him. And in telling the truth as he saw it, he might have unwittingly given Ulanu a weapon to prise information out of the other crewmembers.

Why had he done it? Because he had found something that surprised him in the general – a kind of frankness, an urgent desire for knowledge almost as strong as Hugo's. But in Ulanu, it was tempered and controlled. He had looked genuinely honest, if rather unsettlingly cold and somewhat warped by his Earth-centric perspective.

Ulanu had kindled a small flame of hope in Will. A hope that perhaps this particular Earther might actually listen and be able to do something about their plight. The ones who'd come afterwards, the members of Ulanu's research team, had appeared blunt and ineffectual by comparison.

They certainly weren't what Will had expected to encounter at the Kingdom's hands. He'd experienced little more than a cuff across the face and a few days of carefully engineered starvation. Since then, he'd come to feel almost neglected. A week had gone by in which precisely nothing had happened. Even so, Will was determined to be careful. There was no way of telling when the knives would come out.

On the walls of his personal metaphor space, he'd mapped out his story in graphic detail to keep it straight. It included all the things he wanted the Earthers to know and those he'd rather they didn't, such as the location of the Fecund star system. It was becoming hard to manage, though. He was running out of space in his interface memory, and without connection to a proper computer there were no other virtual spaces he could reach. He was forced to rely on the resources of his own very human powers of recall.

Will heard a hiss as the door of his cell opened. He sat up and saw a stranger enter the room. The visitor was a soft, fat man dressed entirely in white with distant eyes and a small, V-shaped smile. The door closed behind him. The stranger appeared to be completely alone and unarmed but Will was not so naïve as to imagine he was unprotected.

'Ah, you are awake,' the man said. 'I'm so glad. Let me introduce myself. I am Father Gabriel Vargas. I am your new chief interrogator.'

A cold wind of unease passed through Will's body. 'What happened to General Ulanu?' he said.

Vargas made a vague gesture with his hand. 'He was called away. You and your friends have been passed to the jurisdiction of the High Church Inquisitory Branch. Things will be a little different from now on. But it's nothing to upset yourself about.'

He spoke in a mild, slightly condescending voice, as if to a child.

'You're very lucky,' said the priest. 'Disciple Rodriguez has decided that you're worth keeping.'

Will didn't like the sound of that. And who the hell was Disciple Rodriguez?

'What does that mean?' he demanded. 'What about my friends?'

'You'll see them eventually,' Vargas assured him.

His voice was no doubt intended to sound reassuring, but to Will it sounded so serene and oily as to be terrifying.

'Lots of exciting things will be happening,' said Vargas. 'First you'll tell us what you know, and then we'd like you to help us. Disciple Rodriguez has decided that you'll make an excellent leader for a subsect. A very minor one, of course.' He flourished fingers like well-fed maggots. 'But a fully fledged subsect nonetheless. We'll need people like you to help us bring Galateans into the fold after the occupation.'

Will couldn't believe what he was hearing. Was Vargas out of his mind?

'You're joking,' he said.

'Oh no!' said Vargas, gently inclining his head. 'I'm entirely in earnest, and leader of a subsect is a wonderful position. You'll live very well, and get to decide the common laws for your Following. Of course, most of them will be suggested by us, but I'm certain you'll agree with our recommendations. You're perfect, you see. The propaganda people are going to love you – a representative of one of Galatea's oppressed underclass who's seen the light.' Vargas's face glowed with sanctimonious delight as he imagined it.

'I'll never help you,' said Will.

Vargas carried on, apparently indifferent to the remark. 'You're going to love your new role. Except of course, we can't let you keep that interface thing of yours.' He waggled a finger at Will's neck. 'That's an abomination before God.'

'Don't you get it?' Will snapped. 'I'd rather die. Fuck you, and fuck your God.'

Vargas nodded knowingly to himself. 'Of course, a little re-education may be in order. We can't have you using such terrible language.'

The priest held up a hand and clicked his fingers. At the same instant, something small and sharp buried itself in Will's side. Will turned to find the origin of the projectile in time to see a small metal nozzle sliding back into the wall near the ceiling. As he stared at it, his vision began to blur. The room spun.

'Feeling a little tired, are we?' said Vargas, tilting his head as Will slumped sideways. 'Very good.'

15.3: WILL

Will awoke, lying on the floor of his cell. Groggy disorder clotted his thoughts. *Shot again*, he thought bitterly to himself. If there was one thing his experiences had made him deeply weary of, it was being knocked unconscious. Apparently everyone wanted a turn. His head ached abominably. He sat up slowly and called on his sensorium to dull the pain.

Nothing happened. His sensorium wasn't there.

Will emitted a garbled cry of fear and reached frantically for the back of his neck. He found a patch of artificial skin there, over a dent – a dent where his interface had been.

His grogginess immediately forgotten, Will leapt to his feet, his hands pressed desperately to the wound. He tried again and again to access his interface, but nothing happened. There were no extra senses. There was no personal node. His mind stubbornly refused to remove its focus from the tiny cell.

It was gone, the thing that had defined him since birth. With it had gone his access to all the mental spaces he'd created, as well as every mind he'd shared. He was no longer a roboteer. They might as well have cut off his arms.

Will cried out in anguish. He clutched madly at his neck and ran back and forth across the cell, unable to accept it. Then, slowly, the truth of his fate sank into him, like a cold, grey hand closing slowly around his heart.

He slid down the wall, staring at nothing. How could he tolerate this cell with no way to leave it? Never in his entire life had he been restricted to a real space this way. He would go mad! He was struck by a sudden, terrifying vision of the life that was left to him – a long, dark-walled tunnel, closed in on every side. Imprisonment, torture and death. He began to giggle. Tears rolled down his cheeks.

The door opened with a hiss and Father Vargas stepped daintily in. 'And how are we feeling today?' he asked sweetly.

Will screamed in fury and launched himself across the room at the man's face.

He didn't reach it. He'd barely taken a step before the pain stopped him. It was no ordinary pain, either. It had a terrible purity unlike anything Will had ever known – a brightness that burned away all other thought. It filled him and defined him. Will felt his mind come apart.

The next thing he knew, he was lying face down in the middle of the cell, his head spinning. The pain was gone, but the memory of it still rang in his head like an echo of rending metal. With a sudden start, Will drew breath. So powerful was the aftermath of that sensation that he couldn't bring himself to move. He lay there motionless, waiting for the sense of monstrous violation to fade.

From the corner of his eye, he saw Vargas step forward with a small plastic object in his hand.

'That's right,' the priest crooned. 'Lie down and relax.'

Vargas pressed his fat thumb to the object and Will's world split apart again, but this time from pleasure. It suffused every corner of him, drowning him in ecstasy. He gasped, speechless at the beauty of it. Drool spilled from the corner of his mouth. Then, all at once, the sensation faded. Its wake brought a feeling of terrible emptiness, a craving for the sensation's return that made him shake. Fresh tears rolled down Will's cheeks.

'While we were taking out your interface, we took the liberty of installing something else,' said Vargas. 'The implants already inside your brain made the process straightforward, and I felt sure you'd forgive us for it eventually. It's a thing the Angelenos invented. Some of them actually had it installed voluntarily.' He sighed. 'One of their many twisted sexual practices, I'm afraid. But don't worry, we intend to use it for far finer purposes – to help you discover your love for the church.'

Will tried to absorb the import of the priest's words, but it was too appalling for his mind to encompass.

'We will make the process as painless for you as possible, of course,' said Vargas. 'That little taste I gave you was just a warning of sorts. In self-defence, you understand. We will start you on a regimen of pleasure, I think, to teach you to value the stimulus. Then, as you grow to understand its importance, we will begin to give you simple tasks to perform in return for it. I feel sure we will be getting along famously in no time.'

He stepped back to the door. 'I'll let you rest for a while. You look like you need it.'

As the door slid shut, Vargas pressed the remote again and the pleasure returned. It was muted this time, but no less compelling. It washed Will's body in bright sunlight, bleaching the surfaces of his mind. He curled up on the floor, alone, mutilated and controlled, and couldn't help but enjoy it.

15.4: GUSTAV

After the most bitter journey of his life, Gustav arrived on the bridge of Tang's flagship, the *Sukarno*, at the insertion point outside the Galatean system. Gustav pulled himself in and, with a sensation of powerful loathing boiling inside him, delivered a zero-gee salute.

Tang floated at the centre of the busy, crowded room and regarded

Gustav with a grin that threatened to split his little round head apart.

'General, so glad you could make it,' he said. 'We didn't want to start without you.'

Gustav had flown to Memburi as slowly as his orders would permit, only to find that Tang had already left. More orders were waiting, instructing him to come to the Galatean front with all haste. Just two short weeks had passed since he'd left New Angeles.

He was unpleasantly surprised at the speed with which events had unfolded. They revealed quite clearly that Tang must have been planning the attack behind his back while he searched for the *Ariel*. Gustav had been forced to spend the next leg of his journey contemplating that fact.

Tang gestured to a couch situated just to the left of his own. 'I have reserved a place for you,' he said.

Gustav settled himself over the indicated seat. Its arms were blank. There were no controls on them.

'Why, thank you,' said Gustav frostily. 'And in what way would you like me to help you, now that you've brought me out here?'

'Oh, by doing what you've always done,' said Tang with gleeful emphasis. 'Support, advise. Offer a few words of wisdom on the suntap if it becomes necessary.'

In other words, nothing.

It was clear that Tang and Rodriguez had agreed this long before New Angeles. Rodriguez would get the Relic, and the *Ariel* if it was found, without Gustav there to comment or complain. In return, Tang got his battle and a humbled spectator to watch it.

'Certainly,' said Gustav. 'I have some new intelligence on its operation that my team was able to draw from the Galateans, if you'd like to hear it.'

Tang's smile hardened a little and he regarded Gustav warily. 'Go on, then. We don't have long – the scouts will be back in a matter of minutes with incursion clearance.'

'Well,' said Gustav, 'there's fresh reason to believe that the devices have a fatal flaw of the kind I originally suspected. If used heavily enough, they could induce a reaction in the target star, causing it to undergo a kind of small nova. If that happens, you'll lose the fleet and the objective. Thus, I recommend strongly against using them.'

Tang's face darkened into a murderous scowl. 'Is that right?' he snapped. 'Well, forgive me if I don't take your advice on this particular occasion, General. This fleet *relies* on weapons powered by suntap, as you well know, and I have no intention of sounding the general retreat at this point on the basis of your suspicions. So, if you have nothing more useful to say, I suggest that you keep your ideas to yourself for the duration of the battle.'

'Of course,' said Gustav acidly.

'Now, if you'll forgive me,' said Tang, 'I have an invasion to prepare for.' With that, the admiral pulled himself across the bridge to talk to his captains.

In fact, it was several hours before the scouts returned. Gustav had nothing to do but hang around and watch the activity. Tang flitted from one gaggle of officers to the next, discussing tactics and issuing orders like a squat, graceless hummingbird. The crews for his remaining ships were fresh in from Earth and needed plenty of guidance. They had hearts full of zeal and heads full of nothing. Gustav regretted ever delivering Tang his suntaps.

Eventually Tang returned to his couch, his self-righteous enthusiasm back at peak levels. He talked strategy at Gustav while he strapped himself in.

'The Gallies know we're coming, so we can expect a concerted defence. However, at Memburi I intentionally primed them to expect a single, rapid assault. This time, I'll be attacking in a series of four waves. It's my hope that the Galateans will be drawn into attacking the first wave and be surprised when the second arrives from a different vector.'

Gustav was no fleet strategist, but still he doubted the Galateans would fall for it. No matter how well Tang thought he'd primed the enemy, he'd be facing down a force of tactical geniuses. Making any assumption that bold about what they'd do had to be a bad idea.

In Gustav's limited experience, heavy-duty space battles always turned into a chess game. Thanks to warp, you had to anticipate where your opponent would mass his forces before you could see what he was trying to do. And the Galateans were excellent chess-players.

'To your places, please, gentlemen,' Tang called to his officers.

The wall-screens around the bridge flicked on, revealing an extraordinary view of the ranks of starships hanging there, bathed in the cold, white glow of the vessels' running lights.

'Ready the First Wave,' said Tang.

The tactical coordinators worked furiously at their consoles for several minutes. With a fleet this size, coordination was far from straightforward.

'First Wave ready, sir,' came the call.

Tang's voice swelled with pride. 'First Wave engage!'

Gustav looked across at the admiral's face and saw a man flushed with the anticipation of victory. Tang gazed into the wall-screen with something like rapture on his face. Gustav turned and watched the bank of sixty massive spiked spheres that constituted the First Wave power up. Lightning coursed crazily across their surfaces and became oval shells of light. The ovals stretched in unison and in a flash the ships were gone, flickering into the distance like fireworks. The bridge jolted from their combined gravity surge.

'Ready the Second Wave,' said Tang.

From the tense murmuring into head-mikes and the urgent tapping of control boards, Gustav guessed this would be the wave they went in with.

Tang looked barely able to survive the five minutes of waiting before his own illustrious charge into battle. He fidgeted and tapped and gripped his small hands together tightly. His eyes strayed back to the chronometer in the corner of the main display every few seconds.

'On my mark!' bellowed Tang. 'Second Wave, *engage*!'

Their field generators crackled. The screen was filled with jagged skeins of light and then the first hammer blow of the gravity drive struck home. Tang had decided to bring them in at full warp. Two-and-a-half gees of effective acceleration pressed Gustav into his couch.

The screen swapped to a diagrammatic display, showing their approach to the target system. The Second Wave would curve around the side of the star in line with the galactic shell and cross the outer defence sphere from above the plane of the ecliptic. No one talked during the long, gruelling minutes of flight.

'I hope it's not over before we get there,' Gustav remarked wryly.

Tang shot him a warning glance.

'Dropping warp in ten, nine, eight...' called the pilot.

'Comms officers at the ready,' said Tang.

The *Sukarno* arrived. At first, the screen showed nothing but stars and the glare of Galatea's butter-yellow sun dead ahead. Then, little by little, the display began to fill with multicoloured markers indicating ships and facilities.

Gustav winced. Unwilling to expose his flagship to too much danger, Tang had placed his Second Wave quite a distance from the star. It'd take them a long time to get their weapons up from here. Tang was counting on the Galateans being too busy to notice. Gustav hoped he knew what he was doing.

The murmurs of the communications officers quickly built to frenzied shouting. Apparently, things were going wrong already. Gustav bit his lip.

'Lieutenant Lee,' said Tang urgently. 'Give me an update. What's going on?'

'We don't understand it, sir,' said Lee. 'The Gallies appear to have built themselves some suntap stations.'

'What?' roared Tang.

Gustav's heart sank. How had they managed that, he wondered, when the *Ariel* was sitting back at New Angeles? Could there have been *two* spy ships? He shook his head in disbelief.

Tang glared at him. Gustav replied with a shrug. However the Galateans had managed it, it was out of his hands now.

'We count four installations,' said Lee. 'Big ones, positioned in the inner system. We think they're converted munitions factories. The First Wave ran pretty much straight into them. They were fired on before they could get their own taps online. We're getting damage reports in now.'

Lee was silent for a moment.

'Thirty ships destroyed, sir,' he announced in a quavering voice.

'Seventeen more are engaged in disrupter clouds and have sustained damage.'

Amazing. Out of sixty ships, only thirteen were still intact. If the news hadn't been so horrific, Gustav would have laughed.

'Incoming vessels,' one of the officers warned. 'Sir, we're under attack!'

No sooner were the words out of the man's mouth than eight huge Galatean cruisers flashed into existence around the Second Wave. They hit hard and fast with swarms of torpedoes and disrupters. In a matter of seconds, Tang's cumbersome fleet was paralysed, while the Galateans stayed way back and bombarded them with fresh munitions.

Tang screamed orders at his people as his ships vainly attempted to scatter until their main weapons could be used. Meanwhile the Galateans shot at them like the proverbial fish in a barrel. Gustav watched it all unfold with something between amusement and horror. What a way to die.

'No! No! No!' Tang roared. 'Broaden the spread! Use the drones! Draw their fire!'

'Suntaps online in ten, nine, eight . . .' shouted Lee.

'Now we'll show you!' Tang snarled.

But the Galateans had timed it well. Two seconds before the suntaps came online the enemy cruisers warped away, leaving antimatter mines in their wake.

'Mother of God!' Tang gasped, just before the blast wave hit.

The display screens blacked out, along with all the lights on the bridge. The starship shook. Tang yelled furious curses in his native dialect until the lights came back on.

'Status reports coming in,' warbled Lee.

Tang's Second Wave, battered and spread across tens of thousands of kilometers of space, had lost a dozen ships already, and there was now nothing within firing range to attack.

'Head in-system!' Tang shrieked, crashing his fist repeatedly against the arm of his couch. 'Make for those stations! We'll give those stinking Gallie *nenglak* filth some pain!'

The suntaps shut down and the *Sukarno* charged forwards again towards the Galatean home world and the beleaguered First Wave.

Their gravity engines shuddered and groaned under the pressure of forcing their way into the system's ion-cluttered depths.

'I want defensive drones in place the *instant* we drop warp,' ordered Tang.

'Dropping warp in six, five, four...'

The engines died and the *Sukarno* fired its defences.

Almost immediately, a bank of suntap-powered g-rays raked across the fleet, knocking out minor systems and evaporating half the unprotected drones in blasts of vicious radiation.

It looked like the Gallies hadn't had time to build large g-ray arrays since learning about the suntap, so they'd made up for it with numbers. Each converted factory was studded with hundreds of small laser installations firing in synchrony. The result was something like a gamma-ray cheese-grater, with Tang's fleet as the cheese.

Tang waved his arms and roared commands, his face red, spittle flying from his mouth. Gustav had no idea the man was capable of such animation.

'Focus your fire!' Tang screeched. 'No, you fool, further out, make them split their array!'

The Gallie battle cruisers returned in a blaze of light and fired swarms of torpedoes into the Kingdom ranks.

'Suntaps in five, four, three...' said Lee.

'Brace for impact!' warned Tang.

But this time, the Galatean cruisers warped out without dropping bombs. They were too close to their own installations to try that trick again. And now Tang had his precious suntaps at last.

'Annihilate them!' he spat.

Dozens of g-ray beams lanced out, focused on the closest station. It turned cherry-red and folded in on itself before exploding with a blast that rocked the bridge.

The attack came not a moment too soon – the Third Wave dropped out of warp just light-seconds away.

Tang cackled with mad delight. 'Prepare for attack! I want full disrupters!'

Sure enough, the Galateans appeared again to harry the Kingdom fleet before they could bring their suntaps online. The difference this time was that there were three times as many of them. They poured torrents of fire on the newly appeared vessels. Almost immediately, the Third Wave began to break apart under the onslaught.

But by now, Tang had established his bridge-head.

'Freeze those ships!' he ordered. 'I don't want a single one of them getting out of here alive.'

A massive swarm of fully charged disrupter drones swept up from the Kingdom fleet towards the Galateans, covered by a barrage of fire from Tang's lines. The Galateans were forced further and further back, and this time they were sustaining damage. Three of the huge cruisers crumpled and died under the momentous expenditure of solar power. A fourth exploded in a blast of radiation as Kingdom g-rays smashed open its antimatter trap. By the time the remaining Gallies warped away, Tang's standing fleet had increased to almost a hundred and fifty ships.

'Spread out,' Tang told his captains. 'Destroy those remaining stations and the inner system belongs to us!'

His ships crawled forward through the miasma of their own disrupter cloud, lancing the Gallie stations as they went. Despite their power, the improvised battle stations were no match for a sustained attack from Tang's fleet. One by one, they winked out. The tide had started to turn.

'The Galateans can't hide for ever,' Tang announced jubilantly. 'Otherwise we'll have their world surrounded before they can do anything about it.'

He was right. The Gallies flashed back into the fray, darting along the sluggish Kingdom lines just outside disrupter range to launch vast sprays of torpedoes. Tang's suntaps seared the space around them, but the Gallies were moving too fast for them to score many hits.

'Cowards!' yelled Tang. But he was laughing now, confident of his victory.

'Sir!' wailed Lee. 'The enemy munitions are doing something strange to our disrupter field.'

Tang's face fell once more. 'Show me.'

A bright field diagram overlaid the battle on the main screen. Somehow, the Galatean weapons were shepherding the disrupter drones together. The result was that, as the fleet's formation thinned, a cloud remained around each Kingdom ship but the space between them was rapidly becoming clear.

'Redirect the disrupters,' Tang ordered.

'We can't, sir!' said Lee. 'Not without reprogramming them. The Gallies have tricked their SAPs somehow.'

'Then pilot them by hand, for God's sake!'

All at once, the Galateans flashed back into their carefully prepared patches of clean vacuum and started firing with all weapons. Battle was truly joined.

'Admiral, sir!' called one of the comms officers. 'Communications down to ships eleven, nineteen, twenty-six—'

'Soft attack!' Tang yelled. 'Cycle the security codes!'

Fleet coordination evaporated under the onslaught and the battle dissolved into chaos, with ship fighting against ship. As Gustav watched, the flagship was separated from its escort and forced to take on the enemy ships one by one.

The Galateans fought like demons. They used every trick in the book, and plenty Gustav had never seen before. He had to hand it to them – they were impressive adversaries, even though their cunning was bought through butchering the natural order of humanity.

Then the Fourth Wave arrived. Tang issued a flurry of desperate commands.

'Cover them! Inform all ships on open channels!'

The order came too late, of course. The Galateans concentrated their fire on the vulnerable new ships, and a third of them were reduced to slag before their suntaps could engage. By now, though, it hardly mattered. Tang already had the advantage.

Gustav wondered what the sky looked like from the surface of Galatea tonight. Probably too dangerous to view with the naked eye, he reflected. Anyone with a brain in their head would be watching the display from a lead-lined bunker.

Slowly, Tang's hold on the star system became a vicelike grip. He ground down the Gallies through pure attrition, hurling dozens of ships and hundreds of lives at the enemy.

This was how Earth really won, Gustav knew. Never through technical superiority, rather with the most reliable force in the history of warfare: sheer weight of numbers.

In the end, the enemy simply ran out of tricks. Their star system was flooded with enemy vessels. Their home world was effectively surrounded. Each ship they had left was mobbed by a dozen Kingdom gunships.

After two gruelling hours of ship-to-ship fighting, Lee proudly relayed an incoming message to Tang.

'Sir! I have the Galatean admiral on the line! He says he wants to surrender.'

'About time!' Tang shouted.

His good humour had been battered flat somewhere in the madness of battle. Now he was just plain furious. More than half of his precious fleet had been destroyed by a handful of Galatean cruisers. It was by far the longest battle in the history of spaceflight, and without doubt the most expensive in the history of the human race.

'Instruct him to hand over his command codes and prepare to have his strategic facilities boarded,' Tang snapped, then slumped back into his couch and glowered.

'Congratulations, Admiral,' said Gustav smoothly.

Tang rounded on him. 'This was your fault!' he seethed. 'It was your delaying that caused this mess!'

Wrong, Gustav thought to himself. *It was your impatience.* But he didn't want to think about it any more. The whole process had left a sick taste in his mouth.

The final comic touch to the affair came half an hour later when the Kingdom's capture team processed the strategic information passed to them by the Galateans. Commander Lee had the unfortunate job of passing the news to Tang.

'Sir,' he said, in the tremulous voice that Gustav had learned preceded disaster.

Tang eyed him coldly. 'What?'

'We have secured the planet, sir, but only about half the population is there.'

Tang shut his eyes for a moment. 'Where are the rest of them?'

Lee cleared his throat. 'They've already been evacuated, sir. That includes the children, the elderly and everyone with expertise in maintaining the planet's terraforming systems.'

Gustav realised the import of that immediately. He shut his eyes and chuckled mirthlessly to himself.

'What's so funny?' Tang demanded.

Gustav gave him a pitying glance. Tang had clearly not done sufficient research on the planet he'd been so keen to conquer.

'Don't you see?' Gustav said. 'Without trained engineers, this planet's ecosphere will go into violent collapse in just a few years. You've captured nothing.'

Such extraordinary expense just to secure a dying world wasn't likely to impress many in the Holy Court. For the battle that was supposed to end the war and refill the Kingdom's coffers, it was a surprisingly poor result. Tang's face became a mask of pain.

'Evacuated to where?' he snapped.

'They don't know, sir,' said Lee. 'Apparently, their flight vectors were never disclosed to the rest of the Galatean Fleet.'

Tang pummelled the arms of his chair like a petulant child. 'Scan space! Organise searches!' he ordered through gritted teeth. 'They can't have gone far. We will find them, and then we will make the cowards *pay*!'

16: MURDER

16.1: WILL

Vargas came to Will's chamber every day. At first, he asked questions. How had Will communicated with the Relic? Where had his people found the artefact? Will refused to answer, despite the pain. Vargas quickly grew bored with his intransigence and concentrated on breaking Will's spirit instead.

His technique was simple but insidious. He gave Will orders. Obedience resulted in pleasure, disobedience in pain. Sometimes Vargas instructed Will to do things he'd do anyway, like sitting or breathing. Whenever possible, Will disobeyed. But then Vargas would create little challenges, like instructing Will not to harm or humiliate himself in certain specific, degrading ways.

Inevitably, Will's body started to crave the bliss Vargas meted out, and to fear the suffering. The sensations were so total that it was impossible not to. An awful voice gathered strength inside him, telling him over and over that it would be easier to simply submit rather than live like this. It echoed in his head at night, asking him if he honestly expected to see the light of day till he accepted his fate. It reminded him that his actions were irrelevant now anyway – that it was only a matter of time before the end of history. He might as well spare himself the torment.

Nevertheless, Will discovered that he had it within him to resist. The turning point came one day when Will was lying on the floor of his cell. Vargas was jolting him repeatedly and ordering him to get up. As Will gasped like a beached fish, he realised something important. Vargas could inflict limitless quantities of pain upon him, but he couldn't actually *make* Will change.

Will suddenly had a vision of his *self* as something totally separate from the world. It was a remote, indestructible thing like a hard black sphere, distanced from the flashing, glaring lights of sensation that impinged upon his physical person. The sphere could only be damaged if Will allowed it.

The only thing that still linked that sphere to the outside world was the insidious voice. In order to defeat the voice – and Vargas – Will had to protect the sphere. He had to maintain the separation between his mind and his senses.

From that day onwards, Will took to behaving as if the priest wasn't there. He pretended he couldn't hear the man's threats or enticements. He told himself he was in his private node, deaf to the world. After a while, it became easy to do – enjoyable, even. The fantasy of a private node helped a lot. Will found himself constructing a version of his old metaphor space out of pure imagination and residing there day after day, even when the priest didn't visit. It was a preferable reality to the soft grey walls of his prison.

Vargas didn't react well to Will's new strategy. With each passing day that Will refused to bend to his will, Vargas became more impatient. He changed tactics and embarked upon a programme of systematic humiliation.

Soldiers were brought in to brutalise Will. He was subjected to every kind of physical torment Vargas could devise and made to enjoy it. Will only retreated further into his mind, like a man sinking happily into a pool of viscous quicksand.

Had Will been inclined to focus on the world, he might have enjoyed watching the priest's persona of pious calm crumble into wrath. However, he was far away. Until the day Vargas changed his tack again.

He stepped into the cell one morning carrying his white priest's hat in one hand.

'Wake up, Monet,' he said curtly.

Will stared through him.

'Because your education has been coming along so slowly of late, I've decided to try a new method with you.'

Vargas clicked his fingers and the wall of the cell behind him sprang into life. It revealed three cells much like Will's own. Each one contained a familiar figure: Amy was sitting up against a wall, Rachel sleeping and Ira doing press-ups. It was the first evidence Will had been given since their capture that they were still alive.

The sight of their faces did what Vargas's voice could no longer do. It dragged Will towards awareness and tears sprang unbidden to his eyes.

'I have written down their names and placed them in this hat,' said Vargas. 'You will pick one of the names and that person will die. If you fail to pick a name, I will kill them all.'

Vargas held out the hat. 'Choose,' he snapped.

Slowly, the nature of the choice permeated Will's torture-softened brain. *This isn't good*, he thought to himself. It wasn't something he could ignore. He knew Vargas well enough by now to recognise that the man was in deadly earnest.

Will's eyes drifted up to the hat. He stared at it.

'Wait too long and your opportunity is lost,' said Vargas coldly. 'You have one minute.' The priest checked the watch on his sleeve.

Will held his breath as he tried to think. *He'll kill them all anyway*, he told himself. What difference would a few days make? But he couldn't bring himself to believe that while he was looking at his crewmates' faces. A lot could happen in a few days. Ira might find some way to get them out.

Death is better than living like this, the voice inside him said. But Will saw no evidence to suggest the others had been abused in the way he had. He'd be able to see it in their faces if they'd been treated like him.

'Thirty seconds,' said Vargas. 'Are you going to save two of your friends or not?'

Reluctantly, Will staggered to his feet. He looked inside the hat. The pieces of paper were folded over so that it was impossible to read them before he picked. In a way, he was glad of that. He knew that playing along could be a terrible mistake. Taking part in Vargas's games had never been a good idea before. However, this time the lives of two of his crewmates were on the line. Will could tell that Vargas didn't want him to choose. If he refused to play along, two useless deaths would be on his conscience.

Will screwed up his courage. 'Fuck you, Vargas,' he croaked.

He met the priest's gaze squarely and, without looking or flinching, drew out a slip.

The moment the paper was in his hand, an icy shadow passed across his heart. What if it was Rachel? It had been days since Will had thought or cared about anyone, but still he found himself praying it wouldn't be her.

He slowly opened the slip: *Amy McKlusky-Ritter*.

Will gasped in spontaneous relief and hated himself for it immediately. This was Amy, for God's sake – happy, loveable Amy. The person who'd stood up for him when he joined the crew. The person who'd hand-nursed him through the worst of the Transcended virus. And now she was going to die. How could he be relieved about that? Yet he was. Guilt clutched at his heart. Vargas had won anyway.

Vargas saw the expression on Will's face and smiled. 'Excellent,' he said. He plucked the slip from Will's limp fingers and read the name. 'Prisoner three to the execution room,' he said to the walls.

Will slumped back into the corner, curled his arms tightly around his legs and shut his eyes.

'Oh no you don't,' said Vargas cheerfully. 'You're going to watch this.'

Vargas gestured and two large guards stepped into the cell. One grabbed Will's hair and yanked his head up. Another applied a nerve-tickler to his face to force his eyelids open.

Will struggled but it was hopeless. The guards were far stronger than him.

'Fuck you! Fuck you all!' he screamed.

'Now enjoy,' Vargas said with glee.

The priest pressed the button and Will's body melted under a wash of pleasure. He had no choice but to writhe in delight has he watched four burly guards enter Amy's cell. She glanced up when they arrived, in hope at first. Then her face went stony with concern as they led her away. The cameras tracked her motion through the station's bland corridors.

'Is there any point is asking where you're taking me?' she asked her guards, but received no reply. 'I thought not.'

They led her to a huge, high-ceilinged room with wall-screens depicting the flags of every Earther subsect. In the centre of the floor was a kind of throne made from moulded black plastic with straps attached to its arms and base.

Amy hesitated at the threshold as she saw the chair. Her jail-worn features slid for a moment into an expression of fear and sorrow as she realised what was about to happen.

'Oh no,' she said quietly.

Then her face settled back into a mask of stoic calm. A gurgle escaped Will's lips as ecstasy and misery mingled repulsively in his mind and body.

The guards shoved Amy forward and bound her into the chair. She took the opportunity to spit in their faces. The guards glared at her but didn't bother to retaliate. They simply finished their work and walked away. The screen swapped to a frontal view of Amy on her throne, with the flags waving behind it.

'This will be used in our public-information bulletin tonight,' Vargas explained enthusiastically.

'Amy McKlusky-Ritter,' said a bold, masculine voice, 'the Holy Court of the High Church of Truism finds you guilty of the crimes of heresy, murder, espionage, withholding evidence and betrayal of the human race. The sentence is death by neural lash.'

'Go fuck yourselves,' Amy replied.

There were a few seconds of waiting, charged with dreadful anticipation, then Amy's face contorted in agony and surprise. Vargas increased Will's pleasure by another notch. He grunted in bliss as Amy spasmed.

Her face relaxed. She drew air raggedly and choked out a single sob before the lash came again. She arched in palsied torment. Vargas ramped Will's reaction every time her body jerked. Her screams echoed round the room. Meanwhile Will watched and endured. His body began to shiver uncontrollably.

At last, after thirty neural lashes, Amy slumped forwards in the chair, dead. Vargas gave Will one long, last surge of pleasure.

'Extraordinary,' the priest mused. 'Most people never live past twenty. But then I suppose she was a moddie.'

Will whimpered with incoherent loathing.

'You've had a busy day,' Vargas told him gently, patting him on the top of his sweating head. 'Why don't you relax a while? And then maybe tomorrow we can have a nice conversation about where that alien archive came from.'

The priest hummed to himself as he and his thugs sauntered out of the cell, leaving Will to collapse against the foam floor and shake.

In the hours that followed the execution, Will didn't move. He lay still as a corpse, his mind lurching between feelings of intolerable guilt and blinding hatred. Food was delivered through the slot in the wall but Will paid it no attention.

Eventually, artificial night came to his little world, but Will didn't sleep. He couldn't. He could only lie there, the memory of Amy's last moments still burned into his mind's eye along with the revolting knowledge of his own delight while she died.

Vargas had won and Will knew it. He couldn't take another day like this one. If they tried the same trick again with just two names in the hat, Will knew he'd break. He'd tell Vargas everything rather than squirm and moan like that while Rachel died. Which meant he only had hours left before it was all over.

As the last shreds of his precious freedom drifted restlessly, meaninglessly by, Will found himself hallucinating, as he often had in recent days. Disconnected fragments of his past came back to haunt him. He saw himself aboard the *Ariel*, talking to Amy. She was smiling at him, telling him about the Penfield Lobe. Then he was in the Fecund starship, crawling through the icy tunnels towards mysteries millions of years old. The hope he'd felt then seemed so ludicrous now. Will blinked and saw himself back in the security of his personal node, building a solution to an alien SAP puzzle – one that would save the human race...

That was enough. The memories were too hard to bear and Will forced them from his mind. It was better to forget than live in pain. But oddly, as the rest of the impressions faded, the SAP puzzle did not. It lingered hard and bright in his mind's eye, almost like the real thing.

Will scowled at it. It was more warped and convoluted by far than anything he'd solved on the *Ariel*, not so much a puzzle as a parody of one. It was the visual equivalent of those impossible problems one finds oneself trying to unravel in dreams. With a surge of self-disgust, Will tried to dispel the image again. He found he couldn't.

Gradually, he began to entertain the idea that the thing might actually be real. It was a strange notion, seductive and dreadful at the same time. He badly wanted the SAP to exist because that meant the Earthers had failed. Maybe Earther surgeons had botched the removal of his interface. Or perhaps new cells had grown across the fragments of it they'd left behind to install his nerve wires.

However, the more pragmatic side of him knew that in all likelihood the presence of the vision simply meant that madness was finally claiming him completely. His explanations for the program's presence were simply not plausible, no matter how charming they might be. They were the ramblings of a deluded, broken mind.

Then a new thought came to him, certain as stone. *The program is real.*

Will recognised the flavour of that idea immediately. It belonged to the Transcended.

Somehow, they were still with him.

He sat bolt upright. As he did so, the SAP took on solidity in his mind's eye. Will stared inwardly at it in awe. The program was literally thousands of times as dense as the other puzzles the Transcended had shown him.

He began to doubt his sanity all over again. A system this vast wouldn't be decipherable even given a lifetime of study. Why would the Transcended bother to present him with a puzzle he could never solve? He *had* to be imagining it. If his mind could produce a hallucination as crystalline as this one, convincing himself he'd heard the voice of his alien benefactors was a trivial act of madness by comparison. No doubt the illusion came complete with a suite of equally impossible senses that he was supposed to look through.

But when he glanced across the mad tangle of associations to the consciousness aperture, he stopped cold. The sense mapping was exactly human. In fact, it was cleaner than that. It was the mapping for a roboteer.

More disturbing still was the fact that the aperture was coursing with tiny, twinkling lights almost too small for the eye to see. The program was already running…

He glanced back across the massive structure in confusion. As he did so, his mind's eye came to rest upon a second shape hidden between the silken corrugations of the memory trees. It was a second program, small but deeply cryptic, keyed invisibly into the primary recall trunks – a program designed to tracelessly insert false memories.

Will scrabbled at the cell floor with both hands. This was no ordinary SAP program. He was looking at *himself*, complete with Transcended invader.

Will shook his head. How could it be him? He wasn't a program. No one had built his brain. Yet who was to say a human mind couldn't be represented as a SAP? He might be looking at a translation of sorts. In fact, he was hard pressed to imagine anything else it could be.

With understanding making his face and fingers tingle, Will considered the overall shape of the program again. It was certainly riotous enough to be a natural system. It was crammed with improbable connections that were nonetheless beautiful in their design. He zoomed in on the core consciousness loop. It was lined with peculiar Gordian kinks and staggered references to the memory structures. Pulses of bright activation coursed down its length in waves. Was this how evolution had passed the Brache limit?

He tried an experiment – a hefty piece of mental arithmetic. He thought up two random three-digit numbers and tried to multiply them together in his head. The kinks lit up like Christmas trees.

It *was* him. For the first time in weeks, Will laughed out loud. It was incredible, even if it was nothing more than an illusion. The Transcended had granted him a window into his own soul. He pulled his imagination back to admire the structure in its entirety.

Then he noticed the tools.

Arrayed around the mighty SAP in great marching banks were utility programs like the ones Will used to modify his robots' minds. Only these were utilities he'd never seen before. They were fiendishly complex, multipronged things – almost SAPs in their own right. And there were dozens of them.

Their shapes reminded Will of alien surgical devices from Old World science-fiction movies. With a gulp, he realised that was exactly what they were. They were tools for modifying the organic consciousness laid out before him.

Very nervously, Will instructed one of the alien programs to activate and present a profile for itself. Immediately, reams of foreign knowledge unfolded themselves into his head. The program was an unpicker-rethreader for distributed effector-control patterns, it told him. With it, he could remove the knowledge of how to operate his left thumb from his mind, or add the ability to move a sixth digit. Will took careful, shallow breaths and gingerly returned the device to its place in the array.

How could such devices be stored within him? He had no interface code to support them, no physical means of introspecting. There had to be terabytes of extra code here. Where was it all being kept?

He realised it had to be stored in the only place it could be: his brain. The alien virus must have distorted his neural pathways to include all this stuff, just like the false memories they'd given him. No wonder he'd spent days unconscious, with this going on in his head. Will remembered what the Transcended had told him in their last conversation. They'd told him they would provide him with tools to help him *compensate for his changed circumstances*. Well, these things would certainly do that, though not in any way he could have guessed. The prospect of performing surgery on his own consciousness cast the idea of constructive self-editing in an entirely new light.

The message of the tools was clear. The Transcended were giving him a choice. Rather than rotting here in this cell till the sun shed its skin or letting Vargas break him, Will could volunteer to alter himself.

That thought stunned him for a moment. He stared, amazed and appalled by the SAP before him. It hung there like a trussed animal surrounded by butcher's knives. His skin crawled.

The prospect of performing such intimate surgery upon himself made him nauseous, but the longer he thought about it, the less ludicrous it felt. Hadn't the Transcended already changed him? Wasn't that what Vargas was trying to do even now, in his own clumsy, brutal way? Why should Will be the only one not to get a crack at his own mind? He forced himself to consider his options.

The first thing that occurred to him was that he could carve out the Transcended program and save himself from doubts about their intentions for ever. It was tempting. Will had longed to have his mind back for weeks. But he couldn't do it. With the loss of the alien code, the option of further self-adaptation would disappear. He'd be back where he started.

The next solution that sprang to mind was volunteered by the all-too-familiar voice of defeat. He could give in to the Earthers at last, it suggested, and spare himself the pain of caring about it. Will set his jaw. He wasn't about to do that. He'd rather turn himself into a vegetable than submit to the foul priest. But that solution didn't satisfy him, either. It felt too much like abandoning hope.

He wracked his brains for a better answer. What he really wanted was some way to turn himself into a weapon – to get out of the cell and strike at his enemies before he died. He fantasised for a moment about the chaos he'd cause. And then, abruptly, he saw how he could do it.

Vargas expected Will to give in. His last words as he'd left the cell had suggested as much. So perhaps Will should give him what he wanted – or the appearance of it, at least.

He'd tried tricking the priest before, but Vargas had proved horribly good at finding degrading ways to determine whether Will's spirit was genuinely crushed or not. Will hadn't been able to fool him yet. The use of the alien tools might solve that problem.

Will could create a cut-down version of himself to act as a shell. That shell would be addicted to Vargas's remote, craven and utterly without hope. Will could even populate it with false but believable answers to Vargas's questions.

Meanwhile, the real Will would observe inside, insulated from the effects of the neural probe, waiting for the opportunity to act. Rather than wasting time, he could be working around the clock to free his shipmates and escape back to the Fecund system. Not even his shell would realise the truth until Will broke free to take full control of it.

He held his breath as hope surged through him. There would be a cost, of course. Will would have to watch himself become someone he despised. And Vargas might still order him to execute his shipmates as a gesture of faith. A situation like that would blow his cover before he had a chance to do anything.

Worse, perhaps, was the possibility that an opportunity to free his friends might never arise. He could spend the rest of his life as a puppet while his true identity chewed itself up silently in guilt and madness.

But what of the risks? The plan was better than any alternative he could think of. Assuming, of course, that the Transcended had in fact given him the tools to make it possible.

With new enthusiasm, Will scanned the pieces of alien software. He picked up each in turn, absorbing the knowledge of what it did. And as he learned, a way to solve his problem revealed itself.

Will couldn't copy his mind – there wasn't room for that – but he could bifurcate it. He could turn his real identity into an extra strand in his consciousness, like a buried personality. The real Will would become little more than a voice in his own head, while the shell would inherit all his exterior senses and functions. It sounded intensely claustrophobic, but it was still an answer.

With immense care, he took hold of the tools and started building. Creating a version of himself that was weak and pathetic disgusted him, but he stuck to it. He had to make it believable. A caricature would only raise his jailer's suspicions. It was several hours before he was done.

Will pulled back to regard his work. The shell itself was thinner and flatter than any SAP he'd written before and far more subtle. It reminded him of a glass mask, touched just enough with colour to disguise the true features of the face beneath.

Connected to it was a launcher program to handle the delicate transfer of power from one version of himself to the next without killing him in the process. As it ran, it would hand over his senses and memories one by one to the shell, leaving the real him as a buried stream of ideas. He would be reborn as a traitor.

Will drew deep, nervous breaths as he checked the code over. He examined each of the associative strands that would break him free from his mental prison when opportunity beckoned. Then he checked it all again. He dearly hoped he'd used the unfamiliar tools properly. There would be no turning back.

With gritted teeth, Will activated the launcher and threw himself in. At first, nothing happened. Then his senses started switching off. The internal ones like balance and body-position went first. Then taste, smell and touch all vanished. As they died in his mind, the memory structures associated with them went, too, so that Will couldn't even remember what it had been like to have them.

'To eat a good meal,' he said to himself experimentally, savouring the idea's new incomprehensibility.

Next went sight. The cell vanished, along with his recollection of how it had ever looked. Will had decided to keep hearing, with its rich weight of language, till last. Then that went, too.

The world shrank to nothing. There was only the idea of Will and his desire. It was not like a light or a place or a person, as Will no longer had the means to understand such things. It was simply a condition of thought. Then, with mechanical inevitability, the shell turned on.

16.2: WILL

The thought that was Will reflected upon itself and grew. Branches of implication were added and gathered texture, replacing what had been lost. Streams of input as varied and sophisticated as senses reappeared, looping back and gathering complexity with every iteration. Will remembered what it was to see.

He found himself floating in a vast galaxy of twinkling lights with a small black sphere hanging before him. An extraordinary sense of quiet rightness suffused him, as if he'd been seared clean in the fires of suffering and this was his reward.

It was not what'd he'd expected to see or feel, but he recognised the place immediately. It was his mind as he'd imagined it – his core self at the centre, with his senses arrayed around it. Except those twinkling lights were no senses he recognised. Each one was a complex ball of woven patterns that flickered with activity like the thoughts of a robot. They sang with life.

The sphere, too, was different. Looking at it, Will knew somehow that it did not represent his soul. It represented the Transcended.

'Congratulations,' said the sphere. 'You have passed the final test.'

Will looked around, bewildered. He was disembodied here, a piece of nothing.

'Is this my shell program?' he asked, with something that was not quite a voice.

'No,' said the sphere. 'This is your new mind. You are still welcome to activate the shell you constructed, but you may wish to consider other options first, which we chose not to disclose to you until now.'

Despite the detached, ethereal calm that suffused his mind, Will was immediately suspicious.

'What other options?'

'The use of your new internal systems. Those you see around you.'

Will glanced out at the vast, curving wall of software nodes. There was not enough room in his brain for all this, of that he was certain.

'I thought the mind tools were my new systems,' he said.

Somehow, the sphere managed to convey amusement. 'That was our intention. However, as you can see, our work has been further reaching than that.'

Will was baffled. 'How is this possible? My interface was lost.'

'It has been reconstructed and improved using the tools that were installed within your cellular structure,' said the Transcended.

Will wasn't sure he'd understood. 'In my *cells*?'

'After you activated the third puzzle, the tissues of your body were altered using the protein carriers you call viruses,' the sphere replied. 'Information was passed into your cells via the mechanisms in your implant. That information was then used to create running processor models similar to what you call SAPs.'

Will began to understand. His cells had become microscopic robots.

'Nanotech!' he exclaimed. He was alive with the technology that humanity had long since considered impossible.

'No,' said the sphere. 'The human conception of nanotechnology is stark and primitive. A better way to describe this would be *augmented life*. New protein machinery has been added to your cells' pre-existing mechanisms to enable them to operate as processors. A cell's behaviour and range of functions may thus be directly altered.'

Will was lost for words.

'All this,' he said at last. 'Why didn't you tell me before?'

'In part, because it was not ready,' the Transcended replied. 'And also because we wished to know that, given the choice, you would choose to retain those traits you refer to as "humanity". When presented with a suite of unlimited options, you chose to adapt, yet you did not give up hope. We were able to see that you understood a fundamental truth of constructive self-editing – that sometimes one must become something one fears or loathes in order for the greater self to survive.'

Will knew that had it not been for the strange, peaceful clarity of this place, he would feel injustice now.

'Do you mean you engineered my imprisonment just to push me into making this choice?' he said.

His supposed tip-off to the Angeleno police sprang to mind, followed by a memory of Amy's screaming face.

'Of course not,' said the Transcended. 'We have been required to adapt, too. It was necessary at times to augment your natural capabilities to ensure that you survived until your body was ready. For instance, your rate of physical recovery after being administered drugs was increased. Also, you were provided with extra insight to permit you to crack the depot security while still on New Angeles. However, it should be noted that for the most part, your survival was all your own work.'

Something melancholic settled on the sphere. 'We regret that our presentation of this solution comes after the death of your comrade. In part, your unwillingness to move since that ordeal was orchestrated by us, to enable us to finish our work rapidly before further loss of life was incurred.'

'What would you have done if I'd chosen to write a different kind of program?' Will asked. It appeared that an awful lot of work had been done just building up to this moment.

'You would have been allowed to run whatever you created,' the sphere said simply. 'The extermination program would have run its course unhindered.'

Will reflected on that. Apparently he'd narrowly avoided destroying the human race as well as himself.

'Do you now understand the difference between creative and destructive species?' the Transcended asked.

No, was the only answer Will could give.

There was no room for dishonesty in this place. Though he was pleased by how things had turned out, the Transcendeds' reasoning was still a mystery to him.

'Then look again,' said the sphere.

Will's reality twisted. For a few awful moments he was back in the body of a Fecund roboteer, manipulating the arms of poorly designed robots in return for a few jabs of artificial pleasure. It bore a chilling resemblance to his current predicament. Suddenly, he understood.

Both he and the Fecund roboteer had been adapted by their own kind to serve a technological end, but there was a difference in what had been done to them. The Fecund handler could never become more than the role it was born into. It was a slave. In contrast, Galatean roboteers, although shaped by machinery, were not defined by it. There was room in their lives to grow, and to find their own definition of self. Will had the potential to become more than he'd been designed to be.

He had it within him to become the starship captain he'd always dreamed of being if he worked hard enough. Assuming he ignored the pressures of his society, was prepared to compromise and never gave up hope. As long as the human race treasured that freedom, and the humanity that went with it, it would thrive. Resort to direct manipulation as Vargas had and it was doomed.

'We were never interested in forcing change upon you,' the Transcended told him. 'Nor were we interested in making it easy for you, either. We wanted only to see whether you were capable of meaningful adaptation if given the opportunity. You were. Thus, if you wish to save your people, your task is still the same. Return to the Fecund system. Take the archive with you and resume your work on it.'

Will felt a stirring of his former emotions – of rage and desire. The immense software vault rippled with the force of his feelings.

'Nothing would make me happier,' he said.

'During this process, we have come to understand humanity better,' said the sphere. 'We appreciate now that you are collective entities, but that your connections to others do not necessarily constitute weakness or lack of independence in your individual selves. We will understand if you wish to take your remaining crewmates with you.'

'I doubt they'd trust me now,' said Will, muted bitterness seeping back into him. 'They believe me to be a traitor.'

The sphere managed to look nonplussed. 'Then convince them otherwise.'

'How?' Will replied. 'I have no evidence.'

'Observe,' it told him. In the next second, Will was immersed in his own memory logs. They'd been lovingly stored, deep within his tissues.

The sphere showed him a much-slowed-down image of John stepping out of the house on New Angeles on that fateful day, gun in hand. Will watched John's eyes sweep across the car where he sat. No light of recognition appeared in his eyes. There was something off about his expression, too, and the set of his shoulders. It wasn't John.

Hugo hadn't betrayed them after all. Nor had the resistance, really. It had been the one man they'd all thought was dead. The realisation sent crackling discharges of disgust across the vast inner space of Will's consciousness. The powerful emotions this place held at bay were starting to reassert themselves.

'We will leave you now,' said the Transcended. 'You may continue with your original plan if you wish, or make use of these new capabilities in some way. You will find that every talent you had before has been restored, greatly multiplied. Your body contains records of every SAP template in the *Ariel*'s database, and many more that you may find useful. You will also discover that the remaining hardware implanted in your skull may be adapted to provide a communications channel. Through it, you should be able to reach external data systems. Good luck,' it added, and winked out of existence.

Will was left floating in the chasm of his own mind.

Damn right he was going to change his plan. He wasted no time about it. He scanned the vast array of programs stored in his mind till he found the SAPs inhabiting the cells that lived around his interface site. It felt supremely strange to share their thoughts. The cells had no eyes or ears, only a kind of sense-boundary studded with dozens of tiny mouths, each of which could taste with extraordinary specificity.

He located the invading fabric of the neural probe by the ion gradients that surrounded it. The impact of the clumsy surgery had left an immediately recognisable metallic taste in his head. It only took a few moments of Will's time to put the cells to work establishing new neural pathways and setting down microscopic circuits of protein filament that would convert the device into a transmitter.

He set other cells to work, repairing and improving his battered body. In the physical world, he smiled darkly to himself. By the time Vargas next came to visit, Will would be ready.

16.3: WILL

As morning rolled around, Will tested his new interface. But as he suspected, Vargas was taking no chances with his prize prisoner. The cell was shielded. No wireless comms could get in or out.

Will was almost glad. It would be a shame to leave without saying goodbye to Vargas first.

A few hours later, the door slid back and the priest stepped smugly in. Will felt a butterfly flutter of impending revenge in his stomach and got slowly to his feet. He stood, arms folded, and observed his torturer with a twitching smile.

At the sight of Will upright, Vargas's smirk dropped a little. 'My, you're looking well today,' he said sweetly. 'Had a little change of heart about cooperating, did we?'

Will couldn't help but laugh. It came out as a lunatic's giggle.

Vargas frowned and depressed the pain stud on his remote. Nothing happened, except that Will's grin widened dangerously.

'We'll have no more of that,' he purred.

Vargas stared at him blankly for a second before his wits kicked in. Then he turned and darted frantically for the door.

Will was faster. He leapt across the room, seized Vargas and slammed him against the floor. Vargas bounced.

'Help!' the priest shrieked, gesturing wildly to the cameras in the room's corners.

Hypodermic darts flashed down and buried themselves in Will's back. He barely noticed. His augmented cells dissolved the toxins in an instant.

'You are a very bad man,' said Will, his voice cracking, 'and so you must be punished.' With one hand, he seized Vargas's robe. With the other, he grabbed the priest's jaw, forcing Vargas to look at him. 'A very, very bad man,' Will added, tears stinging his eyes.

Vargas began to produce a muffled kind of keening. His fingers clawed helplessly at Will's chest. His eyes bulged.

Will realised then that he was crushing the man's jaw. He drew his hand away and looked at it. Vargas made a bleating sound somewhere between coughing and whimpering. The lower half of his face was a crumpled mess.

'Shut up!' yelled Will. 'Do you think I'm sorry?' He lashed out and slapped Vargas across the cheek. Vargas's head snapped sideways as his face erupted in a spray of blood. 'Do you?' he asked again. 'After what you did to me?'

He slapped Vargas's head back and forth, enjoying the simple childlike rhythm of the action for a while. Somewhere at the back of his mind, he was aware of the fact that his augmented arms had accidentally killed the man on his first swipe.

The appearance of armed guards in the open doorway broke his reverie. However, their presence meant the door was standing open. That gave Will access to the network nodes in the corridor. With John's full arsenal of code-cracking software at his instinctive disposal, Will ripped their security open like tissue paper. And being a prison block, this part of the habitat ring had weapons mounted beside the security cameras set high on the corridor walls. The guns turned as one. Before the guards could aim, their heads were peppered with high-velocity flechettes.

Will dropped Vargas's body then stepped over the guards and out into the hallway. He chastised himself. Three dead in five minutes. Funny to think he'd never killed before today. He mustn't let his experiences turn him into a monster.

He sauntered down the corridor while his mind explored the further reaches of the Earthers' computer system. He killed the alarms that had started to sound and locked down all the doors in the ring, trapping most of the Earthers safely into their rooms. That wouldn't account for everyone, of course, and many of the doors were fitted with manual override. However, it was going to greatly simplify Will's problem of getting to his friends.

He toyed with the idea of sucking all the oxygen out of the work and sleep spaces but decided it would be an uncivilised thing to do. He had no real grudge against most of the station's inhabitants. He contented himself with listening over the network to their cries of mounting panic as they realised they'd been trapped.

A quick examination of the prison block schematic revealed the locations of the cells where the rest of the *Ariel*'s crew were being held. He went in search of them, Rachel first.

Will reached her door unopposed and broke the code that held it shut as easily as flicking a switch. It slid back to reveal Rachel slouched against the wall. She looked thin and haggard, but intact. She got up and stared wildly at him has he stepped into the room. Her pale-blue eyes held more fear than relief.

'Hello,' he said. 'I'm here to rescue you.'

She clapped her hands to her cheeks and laughed once. She regarded him warily for a second or two, as if trying to decide whether he was a figment of her imagination. She made no move to approach him.

'Come on,' he told her. 'We don't have much time and we have to get the others out.'

He turned and stepped back into the corridor. It wasn't quite the reunion he'd been hoping for, but under the circumstances it would have to do. None of the *Ariel*'s crew was likely to be at their best today.

'How?' she said at last.

Will tried for a smile. 'The Transcended.'

She rushed forward and hugged him tight. Will hugged her back, wrapping his arms around her.

Three rooms away, a squad of four soldiers finally levered their reluctant door open and tumbled out into the corridor. Will turned the guns on them and fired. Rachel jerked away from his embrace as the clamour of shooting filled the air and looked about frantically. 'Where was that?'

Will stroked her cheek. He'd dreamed of doing that for weeks. 'Don't worry about it,' he told her softly. She wasn't that easily calmed. She didn't understand yet. He sighed. 'Come on, it's this way.'

Rachel hesitated a little when they reached the splattered bodies, but Will held out his hand to guide her past them.

'Did you . . .' she started.

Will nodded and pointed to the swivelling cannons high on the walls. She regarded their smoking muzzles in horror.

Will shrugged. 'I've no idea how you've been treated, but I don't have a ton of sympathy for these people any more.'

He turned and led the way. As they moved along the eerily quiet corridors, the only sound to be heard above the peaceful hum of the ventilator fans was occasional muffled thumping on the doors they passed.

Hugo's room was closest, and in another two minutes' walking they'd reached it. Will opened the door. Hugo sat inside, strapped into a torture chair like the one they'd used to kill Amy. His limbs were slack and his face appeared to have aged about ten years. He was wearing some kind of nappy. Will understood all too well the look of bottomless misery on the scientist's features. From the smell and the beard on Hugo's face, it looked as if the man had endured the chair for days.

As Will stepped in, a technician lurking inside the doorway sprang out armed with a scalpel. Will smacked him across the face with a negligent backhand blow as he walked past. The man crumpled and lay still, his limbs at unnatural angles.

Rachel watched Will's casual execution with mingled awe and alarm. Then she caught sight of Hugo.

'Oh my God,' she muttered.

Hugo regarded his saviours with a disbelief so blank that for a moment Will feared the man's mind had gone. Will could have cried. The sight of his former shipmate brought so low tore his heart and his dislike for the man evaporated, replaced with a kind of sorrowful kinship. Of all the crew, Hugo was most likely to understand what Will had been through.

It made sense that he and Hugo were the ones the High Church had chosen to victimise. Will had been selected for his political usefulness, Hugo because he possessed a head full of military secrets. Will was overpoweringly glad they hadn't found a use for Rachel.

'Don't worry,' Will said softly as he undid Hugo's straps. 'We'll get you out of here. No one's going to hurt you any more.'

As Will lifted Hugo out of his chair, the man stared at him with wide, liquid eyes.

'Why?' he whimpered.

Will wondered what Hugo meant. Was he asking why Will had betrayed them, or why he'd come back? Will decided on an answer as vague as it was true.

'Because you're my shipmate,' he said. He hefted the boneless scientist over his shoulder and turned to Rachel. 'Time to get Ira,' he said.

16.4: IRA

Ira was exercising when the first of the strange sounds reached his cell. He heard muted shouting and banging through the walls from somewhere nearby. The Earthers must be celebrating. Either that or a new prisoner had been brought in.

He stopped and listened anyway. He always did when there was a chance to gain new information – anything that might add to his meagre store of hope. Staying in shape in the cell was easy. Keeping up morale wasn't. Nevertheless, Ira had fiercely retained his belief in the possibility of escape throughout his incarceration. It mattered not to him that he was surrounded by Earthers, trapped inside a habitat ring closed in by empty space. There was always a way out.

It had been easier to believe that while they were still questioning him, of course. He'd had something to bargain with, then – a way of fishing information out of his captors. Then they'd stopped asking. They'd gone from being fiercely keen to learn his command codes to apparently indifferent overnight. No one had visited him or spoken to him in days. Had it not been for the arrival of rations through his food slot, he could have imagined he'd been forgotten altogether.

The sounds disappeared for a while and then returned, louder than before. They were a strange mixture, some violent noises, some plaintive. He heard something he could have sworn was gunfire, yet no alerts were sounding. Ira's hopes rose. Maybe a great accident had befallen the station, or his Fleet had come to rescue him. Or perhaps the sun was swelling up, he thought darkly, quashing his insurgent optimism before it caused him to lose focus.

He tested the door. It was still locked. Just in case, he positioned himself carefully to the side of it and readied for attack. He wasn't a moment too soon, for just then the door shot back. Ira sprang forward.

He managed to rein in his punch at the last instant. It wasn't an Earther guard he was looking at. It was Will Kuno-Monet. Will's green prison overalls were covered with blood, and there was a strange, serene smile on his face.

'Hello, Captain,' he said dreamily.

'You!' Ira exclaimed.

'We've come to get you out,' said Will.

Ira's mind raced. The boy didn't appear to be in his right mind, and the circumstances were not exactly the ones he'd expected in a rescue situation. Was this some kind of trap? Were the Earthers finally enacting some kind of ruse to make him relinquish the *Ariel*'s command codes?

'How the hell did you get in here?' he demanded.

'I killed the guards,' said Will.

He made it sound like *I made you some tea*.

Ira examined the roboteer's narrow frame. Something in this picture didn't add up.

'Ulanu told me what you said to him,' said Ira. 'You told him about the Transcended.'

Will nodded.

'That's one betrayal,' said Ira, his fist still poised and ready to strike. 'Who's to say you're not capable of another?' He cracked the bones in his neck. 'Tell me why I shouldn't kill you right now.'

Will sighed. Rachel appeared in the doorway, propping up a broken-looking Hugo.

'He's on the level, sir,' she said. 'The Transcended have given him some kind of power over the habitat computers.'

The sight of his engineer, alive and unharmed, was better than a blue sky to Ira. He hadn't dared to hope. But that wasn't a reason to let his guard down just yet.

'Did you forget that it was probably the Transcended who landed us in this mess?' he told her.

Will shook his head. 'That was John. I've been back over my memory logs and found the evidence. He never managed to negotiate the antimatter – all he negotiated was his own escape. The man we saw killed was someone else.'

Ira blinked in disbelief. John was certainly capable of such subterfuge, but Ira had worked with him for years. He was no traitor.

'I don't buy it,' said Ira. 'He wouldn't do it.'

'He might if he thought it was the only way to save the mission,' Rachel retorted.

Ira stared at her. 'You believe this?'

She nodded.

'Look,' said Will. He pointed to the wall-screen in Ira's cell. 'This is from my memory logs.'

Ira watched as a man with John's face stumbled out of a house on New Angeles in slow motion. As he did, the truth of Will's words settled into him like a boulder in his gut. It wasn't John.

He turned back to Rachel. 'Is this what you saw?' he demanded.

Rachel nodded hurriedly. 'Yes! Come on, sir. We can worry about it later. Right now the important thing is to get out of here alive.'

Ira nodded. Regardless of Will's intentions, this still represented the best chance he'd had to escape. He needed to take it.

'Okay,' he said. 'Let's go.'

Will pointed along the curving corridor. 'The exit to the prison block is this way.'

Ira grabbed his arm. 'Not so fast. What about Amy?'

Will's face drained of all expression. Ira saw something cold in the roboteer's eyes that made the hair on his arms stand straight up.

'Amy's dead,' he said.

Ira froze. She couldn't be. Not Amy.

'They executed her,' said Will, and walked on without looking back.

Ira felt faint for a moment as that old numbness crept over him again. But just like last time, Ira couldn't afford to mourn. He drew a lungful of air.

'Give me Hugo,' he told Rachel.

Hoisting the human burden across his shoulders, Ira set off after the roboteer. Doors opened before them and closed behind. It was both intoxicating and unsettling to have so much freedom after being trapped in a single room for so long. Ira savoured every sinister moment.

Then they reached a door which drew back to reveal a line of maintenance robots parked in front of them. They were squat, wheeled things with rudimentary tact-fur and pairs of telescopic arms. The lighter ones were armed with habitat carbines. The heavier machines carried two-metre-long bulkhead-repair plates.

'What's this?' said Ira.

'This is the end of the prison block,' Will explained. 'The funny thing is that it'll be more dangerous from here on. There are no guns in the walls and not half so many doors, so I've arranged for an escort. You can put Hugo down if you want – the machines will carry him.'

Hugo waved an arm. 'It's okay,' he warbled. 'I think I can walk.'

Will smiled at him. 'Nice to have you back, Doc.'

Ira glanced at both of them. Something in Will had *definitely* changed. He put Hugo down gently, keeping his eyes on the robots. It was very obvious this was Will's show, and he wasn't entirely comfortable with that situation.

'And where is this escort taking us?' he said.

'To retrieve the archive,' Will replied. 'It's in one of the holds on the inner level. The Earthers have turned it into a research lab.'

Ira didn't suppose there was much he could say about that. Apparently Transcended technology was getting him out of jail. Given that, it would be churlish to deny the Transcended an objective or two.

'Lead on, then,' he said, with a sweep of his hand.

They walked for what felt like miles, ascending ramp after ramp as the gravity progressively decreased. Ira found the station's empty passageways disturbing. Every now and then they passed a door on which someone was furiously banging, or through which muffled shouting or wailing could be heard. Other than that, there was no evidence of human life.

Just how had Will managed this? Whenever Will first shut the doors, there must have been some people in the corridors. Where had they all gone?

'Hey, Will, where is everybody?' he asked. His voice echoed off the metal walls.

'Around,' said Will. 'I'm taking us on a route that avoids trouble. And I've managed to convince some of the Earthers to leave the halls on our behalf – they think there's an air-management crisis. They're not all convinced, though. The High Church put a lot of extra security around the archive. The automated systems are under my control, but I haven't been able to convince the squads posted there to leave. They've entrenched their position, so we have no choice but to go through them.'

That didn't sound good.

'How many men are we talking?' Ira asked.

'About forty.'

Ira shot him a look. 'And how are we supposed to manage that?'

'With robots,' Will replied mildly.

Ira glanced quickly at Rachel, but she didn't look remotely fazed by the answer. Maybe there was something wrong with her, too.

However, when they rounded the top of the last ramp, Ira saw what Will meant. The high-ceilinged upper level was crowded with autonomous machines of all descriptions, everything from heavy lifters to cleaner bugs.

'Are you sure you can run all these things at once?' said Ira.

Will chuckled. 'No problem.'

Ira and his crew bounced with feather-light steps through the huge, echoing hangar hallway. Will stopped them outside a pair of sealed doors three stories tall.

'I'd stay back if I were you,' he said. 'You won't be needed for this.'

Ira was about to comment, but Rachel took his arm.

'Leave him,' she said softly. 'He knows what he's doing.'

Ira reluctantly allowed himself to be screened behind the robotic shield Will arranged for them. He watched as the roboteer took his place in front of the doors with his army of machines positioned about him. He gestured with his hands and the massive doors rolled back.

Almost immediately, there was a barrage of gunfire from the other side. Flechettes sprayed off Will's barrier of bulkhead plating. Protected by his retinue of robots, he stepped forward. Will's army powered into the room beyond. Lifters wrenched up the barricades the Earthers had created to defend themselves as if they were made of matchsticks. Maintenance robots tore guns from the hands of soldiers while cleaners darted about their legs, tripping them and spraying them with adhesive foam. Erratic gunfire and cries of panic echoed through the chamber. Will walked through it all serenely, tilting his head from time to time as if listening to some inaudible tune.

Will jerked once as a stray flech ripped into his shoulder, but walked on as if he felt nothing at all. Ira stared at him in disbelief. If Will had so much power over these machines, why had he bothered to enter the room and expose himself to danger? He could have fought the battle from anywhere.

Will turned slightly. Ira caught a glimpse of his face and understood. A soft, insane smile curved the roboteer's lips. Will wanted this. He wanted his enemies to see his face as he smashed them. Ira grimaced. The old Will didn't have this kind of appetite for vengeance. What had the Earthers done to him, for crying out loud?

Within another few seconds, the fight was over. The Earther positions had been demolished and the soldiers were either unconscious or helpless. The air was heavy with the sound of their plaintive cries.

Apparently many of them had broken limbs, perhaps deliberately caused.

Amazingly, the entire operation had been conducted without Will's force firing a shot. Though as the robots pulled back, it was clear that a soldier or two had been mangled beneath the lifters' wheels.

'You can come out now,' Will called to his friends. 'It's safe.'

Ira wasn't exactly pleased at being treated like a delicate civilian, but he was too astonished by Will's achievement to care. He stepped up to examine their prize. In the middle of the storage chamber was a bank of screens and sensors. A small cluster of white-robed technicians huddled behind it. Behind them was the immense scaffold in which the archive sat.

'Your services are no longer required,' Will told the technicians. 'You may go.'

The technicians fled in a series of frantic, graceless leaps, their terror outweighing their attention to the meagre gravity. Will's robots set about dismantling the scaffold and moving the archive into the cargo airlock at the back.

'We've done what can be done here,' he said. Blood oozed sluggishly from his shoulder, but Will was apparently indifferent to it. 'The robots will take the archive outside and shuttle-bugs will carry it to whatever ship we decide to take.'

Ira fixed him with a look. 'I can't imagine there's any question about that. We take the *Ariel*.'

An expression disturbingly akin to pity crossed Will's features. 'We can't,' he said.

Ira's body tensed for a confrontation. 'And why the hell not?'

Will stepped over to the technicians' monitors and pointed to one of the screens. It flared into life.

'Look,' he said.

Ira looked. What he saw appalled him. The *Ariel* was in pieces. Great swathes of its exohull cladding had been removed, exposing the workings underneath. Whole field inducers had been stripped away.

Ira's chest tightened in pain. His ship! That vessel had been his pride and his home. It had been his *life*. He felt the loss of this mere machine savagely, in a way he hadn't been able to with the news of

Amy's death. Maybe because it was safer to grieve after a piece of metal than his best friend. For a moment, he felt his entire emotional landscape tilt. Tears clouded his vision.

'I've been looking over what the Earthers have got,' said Will, but Ira barely heard him. His eyes were glued to the dreadful sight of his dead ship. 'What do you think of this one?' said Will.

The image on the screen changed. Ira reeled back. He took a deep breath and tried to focus on the new vessel. It was a battle cruiser, a vast, unwieldy monster a couple of dozen kilometres from end to end. Ira could see at a glance that it was a graceless, brutal thing. A piece of shit. Nothing like his *Ariel*.

'Too big,' he said emptily.

That he should have come to this – Amy lost, no ship and his mission in tatters. If he ever laid eyes on John, he'd rip the bastard apart with his bare hands. You didn't kill your own shipmates to save yourself. Regardless of what the scheming bastard believed about the mission, he should have known that.

Will touched his shoulder. Ira looked up suddenly.

'Did you hear me?' said Will.

Ira shook his head. 'Sorry, what were you saying?'

'I said it doesn't matter how big it is. You just have to be able to pilot it. Rachel and I will do the rest.'

Ira looked back at the ugly cruiser.

'Captain,' said Will. 'We have to make up our minds fast. Word's already out to the rest of the system that something's going on here. They haven't acted so far because they don't want to fire on their own space station, but they'll get over that soon enough.'

'Okay,' said Ira, screwing shut his eyes. 'I can fly it.'

With leaden steps, he followed Will out of the storage bay and along the great, echoing tunnel to a bank of docking-pod locks. Ira forced himself back into the moment. There would come a time for avenging the *Ariel*, and Amy. First they had to get away from New Angeles.

'I'll need your help plotting a course for Galatea,' he told Rachel. 'I have no idea what the warp profile is like on that thing.'

Will turned to face him. 'Sir. Ira. That's not where we're going. I'm taking her back to the Fecund system.'

Ira stared at him. Did Will really imagine he'd changed so much that he could ignore his commanding officer?

'Sorry, Will,' he said slowly, 'but we have to get back to Galatea while there's still a Fleet there to report to.'

That look of pity appeared on Will's face again. 'There's no point,' he said.

Ira found his heart hammering. 'No point? What do you mean, *no point*?'

'The invasion fleet has already left,' said Will. 'Galatea will have been attacked by now. What's done is done.'

Ira's chest tightened again. In other words he'd failed to fulfil his mission, and his home world was under the thumb of a horde of genocidal madmen.

'I don't care!' he shouted, surprising even himself. 'We can rendezvous with the evacuation arks – I know the rallying coordinates.'

Will shook his head. 'Sorry, sir, but we've got to go back.'

'Have you thought for a moment about what you're suggesting?' Ira yelled. 'That fucking hulk you picked out doesn't have stealth!' He jerked a finger back towards the room with the monitors. 'You'd be leading the rest of the Earther fleet straight to a lifetime supply of alien fucking technology! I'm giving you a direct order, Mr Monet. We're going home.'

Will looked sadly at the floor. 'Stay here, if you prefer,' he said.

'*What* did you say?' boomed Ira.

'I said stay if you want,' Will repeated quietly. 'You gave me that option. Or take another ship. All of you.' His eyes flicked to Rachel and Hugo. 'I'll give you SAPs that will make it easy. But I have to go back, and I hope you'll come with me.'

'I'll come,' Rachel said softly.

Ira stared dumbly at her.

Will turned to Hugo. 'How about you, Doc?'

Hugo's lips pursed. He nodded vaguely.

Will smiled at him. 'No more worries about the alien menace?'

Hugo's mouth trembled into a bitter smile. 'I have worries,' he replied. 'This change in you means nothing – you still have nothing but their word to go on, and everything I said may yet be true. But since we arrived here, I have had certain...' His eyes drifted for a moment. He looked like he was about to cry. 'Experiences . . .' he finished raggedly. 'Given the choice between Truists and aliens, I choose aliens. I would like to see the church . . . crushed.' The corner of his mouth twitched upwards. 'Yes, crushed.'

Ira shook his head in disbelief. 'This is fucking *crazy*! You're heading to a dead system with no fuel in it. We'll be right back where we started!'

Will shook his head. 'We won't need fuel.'

The door to the docking pod opened. Will stepped inside, followed by Rachel and Hugo.

'You're violating a direct order,' Ira shouted.

Will nodded. 'Are you coming?'

They were going to keep him away from his people. Away from reporting. Away from John.

Ira crunched his hands into fists and stormed in beside them. 'I hope you realise that this little power trip of yours is entirely temporary,' he told Will, and stabbed the close stud on the door.

17: BACK IN THE SADDLE

17.1: WILL

As the docking-pod door opened, Ira thrust himself out into the cruiser's orbital corridor. Will was just behind him.

'Which way to the bridge?' said Ira.

Will asked the ship. Pieces of himself were already infiltrating every part of its primitive network.

'That way,' he said, pointing right.

Ira grabbed the handrail and dragged himself off at great speed. Will followed. Whispering SAPs informed him that the other ships in the system were taking a lot of interest in the station and had started cycling their encryption. That meant they didn't have long to escape New Angeles orbit alive. Even so, Will found it impossible to feel hurried. The strange sense of numb serenity that had settled on him after he killed Vargas hadn't lifted.

The bridge, when they reached it, was like something out of a history interactive. Bulky acceleration couches with consoles on their arms faced a wall filled with monitors as if it was some kind of window.

Ira took the pilot's seat. Rachel looked around for something that was recognisably an engineering console. Will pointed it out to her.

'Hugo, do you think you can run astrogation?' said Ira.

Hugo nodded. 'I'll try.'

Will took the captain's seat. Ira scowled at him as he sat down. Will felt a moment's annoyance. What else was he supposed to do? It was the best place from which to monitor all the ship's functions.

And in the absence of a proper crew, that was exactly what he'd have to do.

'All right,' Ira growled. 'Let's get this shitty tub afloat.'

'Not yet,' said Will. 'There are some things I need to do first.'

He shut his eyes and stretched his mind out through the starship's comms-ports back to the space station. Since leaving the prison block, Will had been gathering robots together from all across the forty-kilometre-long structure. They'd brought with them anything and everything that Will could imagine might be useful in the Fecund system, from welding torches to medical supplies.

Now he directed them towards the loading trucks that ran to the ship's cargo bays. For the job that lay ahead of him, Will was going to need every pair of hands he could get. He packed machines designed for gravity environments into storage containers. The rest he moved into the ship's open portals, along with the shuttle-bugs that carried the archive.

'Captain,' said Hugo, 'I think we have a problem. The two ships that were posted in sentinel orbits are moving towards us. I'm receiving data packets from them which I believe are some kind of identification test.'

'Will, we need to move,' said Ira.

Will watched train after train of loaded cars trundle into the massive hull.

'One more minute,' he said.

'Message coming in on the public channel,' Hugo reported.

'Let's hear it,' said Ira.

A voice blared into life through the bridge speakers. 'KMS *Nanshan*, this is Captain Yuen of the *Third March*. We can see you loading. What's happening over there, *Nanshan*? Can you tell us why the station blacked out? We haven't heard anything for over an hour.'

Ira opened his mouth to speak but Will got there first.

'Good to hear you, Yuen,' he said, trying to sound relieved. 'This is Acting Captain …' He rapidly scanned the station's database for a real name. 'Kay Aquino. There's been an outbreak of a computer virus of some kind, sir. The people are safe for the most part, but comms are down and security's not responding. We think the outbreak came from the High Church research lab on Level A, so it could be of Galatean origin. We've also had some trouble with robots, sir, so we're moving as much vulnerable hardware out of the way as quickly as we can. We should be done in a matter of minutes.'

Will simultaneously instructed the station's computers to make it look as if he was telling the truth. He fired a couple of half-hearted infection attempts at the approaching ships from the habitat ring.

'They won't buy that for long,' Ira warned.

'They won't have to,' said Will. He quickly pulled aboard the last of the robots and retracted the loading rails. 'I'm done. We can go.'

'About time.' Ira's fingers flew across the board. He powered up the engines.

Almost immediately, Captain Yuen's voice returned. 'What are you doing, Aquino?'

'Moving a safe distance from the station, sir,' said Will. 'This is the only uninfected ship and we need to get clear.'

'You do not have permission. You are to hold your position until your status has been validated.'

Will grimaced. 'Can't do that, sir. The docking systems stopped responding when we disconnected. They won't let us back on.' He turned his mind to the *Nanshan*'s external sensor array just in time to see the *Third March* launch its disrupter swarm. It held them steady in an attack configuration.

'If you cannot dock automatically, make a manual tether,' Yuen ordered. 'Prophet knows you've got the machines to do it.'

Meanwhile, the other Kingdom ship had swung around the station and was closing on the *Nanshan* from the opposite side. Both vessels were smaller than the one Will had stolen but they were far from harmless.

'Sir, I think it's time to leave,' Will told Ira.

'I couldn't agree more,' said the captain. 'Hold on tight.'

He ignited the fusion torches and the *Nanshan* pulled away from the station at full conventional thrust – a pitiful three gravities. The Kingdom ships sped after them, matching course and speed. The *Third March*'s disrupters surged forwards and spread around the *Nanshan* like the talons of a mighty claw.

'This is out of order, Aquino!' barked the voice on the speakers. 'Power down your engines or we'll fire.'

Then let's beat them to it, Will thought to himself. He fired a volley of well-aimed g-rays into the disrupter swarm and launched the cruiser's defensive drones. On a ship this primitive, there wasn't enough processing power for him to do anything particularly clever with them.

'*Third March*, please ignore that last assault!' Will cried down the public channel. 'We were wrong about the virus, sir. We are infected. Repeat, we *are* infected. The weapons array is not under our control! In the name of the Prophet, please retract all weapons immediately! We will attempt to move the ship to a safe distance until the virus can be combated.'

'Negative, *Nanshan*,' said Captain Yuen. 'Power down engines and prepare to be boarded.'

Will shut the channel. 'Any chance of some evasives here?' he asked Ira.

'We're running them already!' Ira snapped.

Great. The cruiser was so cumbersome that Will hadn't noticed.

This problem was going to need a different solution. Will threw a handful of SAPs at the *Third March*'s security. The cruiser wasn't equipped with all the fancy tools the *Ariel* had enjoyed, but it did have the advantage of a full suite of Earther security codes in its command cores.

'Second ship just launched disrupters,' said Hugo.

It only took them seconds to close on the *Nanshan*. Will tried to fend them off with more g-ray fire, but keeping the enemy buoys from surrounding his ship wasn't easy. Running three weapons banks and several dozen tiny spacecraft simultaneously had his skills at full stretch, even with his new abilities.

'How long till warp?' he grunted as his mind flickered from problem to problem.

'We're trying!' Rachel replied. 'This engineering set-up was built for a crew of five. I don't have the software for it.'

While still struggling to outmanoeuvre the disrupter swarm with his drones, Will ducked into the vault of his new mind. He threw

Rachel every engineering program his body had access to. They started popping up all over her console.

'Hurry!' he urged.

It was no use. The disrupters closed and fired. Every time Will targeted one, another started up, increasing the distance before they could warp out.

Finally, one of Will's security SAPs came back. It had matched the attackers' encryption cycle. Will cackled and cracked the *Third March*'s main computer open like a walnut.

'Take that!' he yelled, firing an order for assault-system shutdown straight into their primary processors.

Half the disrupter swarm fell away. Before Will could repeat the trick, however, the second ship swapped cycles.

'Four more cruisers moving in from the outer system,' Hugo warned.

Will gritted his teeth. There had to be a better way to fight this battle. He reached back into the *Third March* and started pushing SAP code into the compromised computers. He didn't have time to make the new software particularly strong or sophisticated, but he only needed control of the enemy ship for a minute or two.

With ponderous deliberation, the *Third March* retrained its weapons on the second Kingdom vessel and started firing everything it had. Will smiled as he listened over the public channel to the shouts of panic and confusion that ensued. The rest of the disrupter swarm fell back, drawn into the conflict Will had created.

He turned his attention to the four new approaching ships. He tried a couple of long-range viral attacks but their encryption was already up and running. This problem was going to be a lot trickier.

'I've done it!' Rachel gasped. 'Ready for warp!'

Will quickly sucked his drones back through the exohull.

'Munitions retracted,' he told Ira.

'Firing engines in three, two, one...' called the captain. Then he hurled on the power.

The cruiser surged forwards but the four Earther vessels veered madly to match course. The sound of the *Nanshan*'s engines rose from a pounding to a whine as Ira took them up and out into the safety of interstellar space.

'Get ready for the nastiest warp-scatter manoeuvres you've ever experienced,' said Ira as they neared the system perimeter.

As soon as he was clear for FTL, Ira broke off warp and fired the thrusters at full tilt. The enormous ship dragged around on its axis. Ira warped again, stopped, applied thrust and warped, over and over. The effects of jerking and turning in such a big ship were far less aggressive than aboard the *Ariel* but no less sickening.

Fifteen minutes later, the *Nanshan*'s warp trail was a sprawling mess. It would take their pursuers hours to find them.

'We're clear,' said Ira.

Will passed him a course that would take them straight to the heart of the Fecund system and then flopped back into his couch.

They were free. New Angeles lay behind him. He could hardly believe it. The weeks of torture and isolation were finally, undisputedly over. Without quite knowing why, Will folded his knees up to meet his chest, buried his face in his hands and began to sob.

17.2: GUSTAV

Gustav stood with his hands clasped tightly behind his back and looked out from the balcony of his new office in the trench town of Perseverance. Golden light streamed down in dusty shafts through the curved glass canopy overhead, illuminating the tiny twisting paths and glittering fishponds in the park far below. Across from him were stacked layers of Galatean homes with their curious outdoor walls made from nothing but white sheets. They reminded him of washing days in the Sophia of his childhood.

Perseverance might have been still and beautiful, but it was also chilling in its emptiness. The town was virtually dead. There were no voices, no people visible below except the occasional Kingdom marine cradling an assault cannon. In the short weeks that he'd been there, he'd already learned to hate that quiet.

Apparently only half the population was missing, yet Gustav had never been anywhere that felt so desolate. There was nothing to hear but the distant rush of the air fans and his aide, Regis Chu, standing behind him, reciting the depressing details of the day's status report.

'Our troops have been all the way up the northern transit line to the settlement at Hope Canyon,' said Chu. 'The pattern appears to be the same – no children left, no environmental maintenance personnel. Only adults, and all of those appear to have volunteered to stay behind. I had Colonel Hassan sweep the town for hardware. Unfortunately we, er... lost four men to a chemical explosion of some kind and a fifth to a suspicious airlock failure.'

Gustav shook his head. 'Did Hassan retaliate?'

In his experience, marines always retaliated, usually before they knew who was responsible for attacking them.

'Yes, sir,' said Regis. 'Three locals were killed and one of our men was accidentally wounded in a friendly-fire incident. An atmosphere supply pipe was ruptured. I have a repair crew looking at it now.'

Gustav rubbed his eyes and groaned. Tang had known exactly what he was doing when he'd stuck Gustav with the job of Planetary Consolidator. It was spite in its most transparent form. Gustav was trapped on this denuded, hostile world for the weeks or months it would take for the new Protectorate Authority to arrive from Earth while the rest of the Kingdom celebrated. His task was not helped by the fact that the force of Kingdom marines he commanded appeared to be spectacularly inept.

'My God, Regis,' he said. 'I thought these troops were supposed to be our finest. I expected them to be clumsy, but they've exceeded even my wildest expectations.'

'There may be a reason for that, sir,' said Regis. 'Doctor Wei at our med-centre has been running blood tests and he's found that the soldiers coming in have some very unusual hormone levels. His current theory is that the Galateans have poisoned the local food supplies, maybe even the air, with some kind of agent for which they've already taken an antidote.'

That would explain why Gustav had been feeling so bitter and listless lately, at least.

'He recommends that the troops be restricted to landing rations until he can find out what's going on,' Regis added. 'He also says we should consider using environment masks.'

Terrific. Discipline was already strained. Cutting the soldiers off from the spoils of their victory wasn't going to go down well. Gustav straightened and sighed. It appeared that in the process of capturing Galatea, the crusade had turned its inhabitants into exactly the kind of people Gustav's own ancestors had been – terrorists and freedom fighters. There was irony in that, but also something to learn.

The Galateans weren't like the people of the other colonies. It was as if they *expected* to suffer. They actively courted it. Still, it would be different when the High Church Repentance Squads arrived. Then the natives' games would only make things worse for them.

Gustav's compad chimed. He drew it out and found Tang's personal insignia flashing there. Gustav was required immediately for a video conference with the admiral.

'The rest will have to wait,' Gustav told his aide. 'Restrict the troops to rations and give Wei whatever resources he needs.'

He strode over to the corner of the huge Galatean room where he'd set up a working console. He pressed the answer stud on the compad and sat down in front of the monitor. Tang's frowning face appeared on one side of the screen like an angry moon. To Gustav's immense surprise, Rodriguez appeared on the other, and he didn't look happy, either.

Gustav nodded to them. 'Admiral, Father,' he said coolly. 'What a nice surprise.'

'There's nothing nice about it, Ulanu,' Rodriguez snapped. 'The artefact has been stolen and a Buddha-class battle cruiser along with it.'

Gustav stared at the disciple in disbelief for a moment and then fought down a bray of laughter. Could it be that the mighty Rodriguez had failed to keep his hands on the Galateans? Of course he had! Gustav was only surprised that he'd managed to make such a mess of it so fast. He had come running here for help, no doubt.

Rodriguez read the light in Gustav's eyes. 'Are you *amused*, General?' he spat. 'Fifteen of my men were killed including my best interrogator. The Sons of Mao lost eight others. And my work on the Relic solution has been set back by months.'

'I'm very sorry for your loss, Father,' Gustav said unconvincingly.

'Disciple Rodriguez came as quickly as he could via high-speed scout,' Tang put in. Gustav didn't doubt it.

'Can I also assume that the Galatean prisoners escaped?' he asked sweetly.

Rodriguez turned scarlet. 'Of course they escaped! Who else do you suppose was responsible for all those deaths?'

You, Gustav thought. 'Father,' he said, 'may I ask, what vector did they leave on? Were they headed here?'

'No,' Rodriguez replied, 'though I'm sure you'd have liked the answer to be that convenient. They disappeared somewhere in the direction of Zuni-Dehel.'

'I see,' said Gustav, nodding sagely.

That was disturbing. Gustav thought that home would be the first place Captain Baron would head for. Failing that, he'd have bet on the rendezvous points for the Galatean evacuation arks.

'Well, Father, I'm grateful that you came all the way out here to tell us, but I'm not sure there's a great deal we can do about it,' said Gustav. 'The problem now lies within your jurisdiction, after all.'

Gustav glanced at Tang's face and saw some of the tension go out of it. It was clear that the admiral didn't want this problem. He might even be prepared to abandon his ally to avoid it.

'Wrong, General,' said Rodriguez. 'The High Church does not get involved in direct military action, and as the senior officer most recently responsible for those captives I consider it your responsibility to retrieve them.'

Now there was a surprise.

'Furthermore,' said the disciple, 'if your men had properly searched the prisoners for concealed weapons, this breakout would not have occurred. It is therefore your fault.'

So that was why he'd come in such a hurry – to hand off blame.

Gustav smiled back at him. 'Firstly, Father, those men were searched thoroughly. The nature of the scans and their results are all on record. Secondly, your grasp of the military hierarchy appears to be flawed. Responsibility for chasing spies cannot be retroactively apportioned to reassigned personnel, as you so colourfully imagine. From the moment the orders you passed me took effect, Admiral Tang became responsible for all military aspects of the Galatean problem. If you wish to second me, you must approach him, as it will be to his report sheet that my activities are appended. Thirdly, by coming here rather than following the Galateans directly, you have lost the opportunity of finding them. Neither I nor any other person alive has the ability to reliably follow a two-week-old warp trail.'

'I know that!' Rodriguez seethed. 'Chopra's men have given chase. I have come here to instruct you to depart to oversee the operation.'

Gustav shook his head. 'I cannot. Wherever they were going, they will in all likelihood have reached their destination by now. The best that we can do, in my opinion, is remain here and reinforce our defences. It seems certain that the Galateans will attempt to return home eventually and we must be ready for them when they do. Do you not agree, Admiral?' he said, glancing at Tang.

'Yes. Yes, of course,' said Tang, nodding vigorously.

Gustav smiled to himself. Tang's contempt for his old boss appeared to have been forgotten. Apparently, the moment the admiral's credibility was under threat, he was only too happy to hide behind whoever was closest.

'This is preposterous!' said Rodriguez. 'What if the Galateans are on their way to bomb the Earth in retaliation, just as the Drexlerians attempted?'

'Unlikely. But in such a case, we would bomb Galatea,' Gustav said smoothly. 'That is how deterrents work, Father.' He chose not to reveal the fact that Galatea was effectively doomed already. 'We have what they want most, and that is this planet,' he went on. 'With respect, we would be fools to take our eyes off it, as I'm sure Admiral Tang would agree.'

'Absolutely,' Tang said quickly. 'I'm sorry, Father, but our job is here. Those rebels are no longer our concern. That responsibility is yours, I'm afraid.'

Rodriguez tried to give his ex-ally a significant look. 'Admiral, I beg to differ,' he said. 'The suntap project and your fleet have been associated from the outset.'

'Not any more,' said Tang bluntly. 'The target planet has been taken. The crusade is over. We have no further interest in suntap production or its difficulties.'

Rodriguez's face went puce with fury. 'The Prophet will hear about this!' he hissed. 'You may like to think your hands are clean, but responsibility lies where he wills it!' He cut off the link.

Gustav turned calmly to the admiral. 'May I recommend that we mount extra defences with all haste, on the off-chance we're facing some kind of Galatean counter-attack?'

Tang nodded. 'For once we are in agreement, Ulanu. You will be responsible for the operation, of course. Please send me a summary of your intentions by close of fleet day.' With that, Tang signed out.

Gustav sat back and exhaled hard. Rodriguez had begun his inevitable fall from grace, which was wonderful. His threats of a 'freed' High Church already sounded hollow and laughable. However, the news that the crew of the *Ariel* were loose in the galaxy again with a repository of alien weapons technology was worrying in the extreme. Instinct told him that some kind of confrontation was inevitable. This time, he intended to be ready for it.

17.3: WILL

Will kept the cruiser on alert as they flew into the Fecund system. If one Earther gunship had been able to find the place, so could others. He transmitted a friendly welcome message under the Earther protocol and, to his immense relief, received no reply. Nothing moved out of the debris ring to attack them, either. The place appeared to be as dead as when they first found it.

Ira slowed the ship as they approached the drifting hulks. Everyone watched the monitor wall as their sinister, barbed forms loomed into view. They shone balefully by the light of the system's wounded sun. Will had forgotten what this place was like. There was something infinitely cold and sad about it, beyond the reach of words.

For a while, they just watched. Then Ira took the initiative.

'What now?' he said.

Will scanned the ruins. 'Hold on a minute.'

He found what he wanted floating a few AU away at the ring's far edge, where the Transcended files in his new mind said it would be.

'There,' he said.

He brought up a picture of a nestship to show the others. It was in far better shape than the first vessel they'd looked at. Its rust-red hull was smooth and unbroken. The immense fronds he now knew to be warp inducers were completely retracted, protected from collisions and radiation. Just as Hugo had predicted, the ruins at the outer rim had taken much less damage than those further in.

Ira regarded Will levelly for a long moment before changing course.

'Okay,' he said. 'And what do you intend to do with it?'

Rachel and Hugo turned around in their seats expectantly to hear his answer.

Will pursed his lips. The right time to explain his plans to the others had never really come up. He'd been kind of crazy while they were breaking out of New Angeles. For a couple of days after that, he hadn't been able to do anything without wanting to cry. He'd spent his time on the bridge working or alone, much to Rachel's apparent distress. It had taken him a while to find himself again. Now that he had, his doubts had come back, too.

He felt sure Ira could guess what he intended. In fact, he suspected they'd all guessed.

'I'm going to repair it,' he said.

Ira nodded knowingly to himself. 'Do I need to remind you that the Earthers will be here very soon? That we have about three days?'

'I know that,' said Will.

'Okay,' said Ira. 'So are you going to tell me how you intend to repair a ten-million-year-old starship ten times the size of this one by then?'

Will cleared his throat. 'With robots.' It sounded ludicrous even to his own ears.

Ira shut his eyes for a second. 'I see. And where are you going to find fuel for it?'

'We'll make it,' said Will. 'The ship has machines.'

'Of course it does.'

Will flushed with anger. He'd had it with being treated like a flake.

'This is what we're supposed to do,' he insisted. 'The alternative is death by star-burst. We'll make it work.'

Ira gazed at him impassively for a little while and then turned back to face his console. Without saying another word, he steered the ship towards the ruin Will had selected.

Will's anxiety grew as they got closer, but so did his excitement. It was much like the first ship they'd examined, only far less battered and, if anything, slightly larger.

It took a long time to find some way to park the *Nanshan*, but eventually Will spotted a fissure near the rounded stern of the alien ship. He sent out waldobots to anchor the cruiser in place and extended a loading rail towards the breach. Along the rail went score upon score of robots. They spread across the surface like ants, exploring the opening, and then poured inside.

Will started receiving images from the interior and directed them straight to the monitor wall for the others to see. To his initial dismay, the inky, icebound mess that appeared was much like the interior of the other nestship. He noted with relief, though, that there wasn't quite so much free-floating snow. Maybe the fluid-transport systems hadn't ruptured as badly on this vessel.

'This ship was designed to take an incredible pounding and still work,' Will reminded the others, as much for his own benefit as theirs. 'It has massive redundancy built into it. Plus the only damage it's sustained has been from space exposure. This one arrived after the star-burst – you can tell by the exohull's composition spectrum.' He glanced at them. 'And we don't have to fix up the whole thing, just the basics.'

Except, of course, it was also supposed to be manned by a massive number of crew. Will didn't simply need to repair it. He also needed to control it. Robots would have to take the place of the Fecund slave caste. And he was going to have to rig a whole new network of comms-nodes to talk to them. At the moment, he had about eight thousand autonomous units on board. He'd require ten times that number, maybe more.

The nestship had originally been equipped with a huge supply of disposable multi-purpose robots. They'd be worthless scrap by now, but there were automated factories on board to build the things. Getting those back up and running would have to be Will's first priority.

He stared into the monitors, contemplating his options, till he noticed that the others were staring at him. For a moment, he wondered why. Then he realised they were waiting for him to say something.

'Well?' Ira drawled. 'In case you forgot, this is your plan, Will. Does this ship fit your needs?'

Will nodded.

'Then we'd better get working, hadn't we?' said the captain. 'Hugo?'

The scientist blinked. His face was drained of emotion, as usual these days. He'd barely spoken since they'd freed him.

'I want you to see what you can do with the weapons and defence,' said Ira.

'I'll give you a team of robots to work with,' Will put in.

Hugo nodded.

'However,' Ira added, 'your first priority will be to rig up a few more of those suntap cannons like you did last time. That way we'll at least stand a chance when the Earthers turn up.'

Ira glanced at Will as if expecting a challenge, but Will wasn't about to debate the idea.

'Okay,' he said. 'Sounds like a good idea to me.'

Will would have to quintuple his workforce before he started on anything he'd need Hugo for anyway.

The scientist nodded again. 'It should be easier this time, now that I know what I'm doing.'

Ira turned his attention to Rachel. 'I want you to start looking at the engines,' he told her. 'That wreck may be older than the human race, but if we can run, we might last long enough to do something with it.'

Will winced. 'No,' he said. 'I need her help with the robot factories first. We have to make sure we can keep the ship in one piece before we try moving it.'

Ira cocked an eyebrow. 'My, that's reassuring. In that case, Rachel, go ahead, you're with him. And Will, if you don't mind' – the captain gave Will an exaggerated zero-gee bow – 'I'm going to work on a defensive strategy. Forgive me for being sceptical, but I suspect we're going to be attacked before you finish work.'

'Fine,' Will replied, trying not to let too much relief creep into his voice. Usurping Ira's authority was still deeply uncomfortable for him. It'd be easier for him to do what he needed to with the captain somewhere else.

Ira clapped his hands together. 'Right, everybody, let's get to work. Hugo, over here. Let's start with a review of the defences we already have.'

Ira led Hugo off to look at the *Nanshan*'s weapons desk.

Rachel floated up beside Will. 'Can we talk privately for a moment?' she said quietly.

Will nodded. She gestured for him to follow her out into the companionway.

'I want to clear the air before we start work,' she said once they were alone. 'I think we both know you've been avoiding me.' She winced and looked off to the left. 'I just wanted to say that if you feel what happened between us was a mistake, I can deal with that. You only have to say.'

Will shook his head. 'No, it's not that.'

Her face relaxed immediately, though a look of anxious curiosity remained. 'So what is it?' she said.

Will tried to find the words. 'I didn't really tell you about what it was like for me in that prison back at New Angeles.' He gritted his teeth. It was still impossibly difficult to talk about. 'Let's just say it was worse than that chair they found Hugo in. It was ...' Unwelcome tears sprang into his eyes again. He wanted to say something about what they'd done to him but the words steadfastly refused to come.

Rachel looked at his expression in horror. 'Oh, Will,' she said, and hugged him hard. 'I'm so sorry. If you want me to back off, just say the word. I mean it.'

'No, I don't,' he said. He stroked her hair and kissed it, very gently.

She smiled at him, her eyes full of earnest, desperate positivity. 'I have faith in you and what you're doing. What *we're* doing. The Transcended gave you the tools. Now it's just a matter of us working out how to use them properly.'

Will agreed, and was grateful for her tactful change of topic. But what had he really got? A head full of SAP interface and a body populated with half-sentient cells. Remarkable tools in their own right, but what use was robotic blood when you were repairing a starship?

And then he saw it. He'd always thought those transport tubes that ran through the ship were like arteries. Who was to say they should be pumping water just because that was what the Fecund had used them for? Maybe the vessel would be shielded enough for a dilute solution of his own augmented cells to flow through those pipes and survive. In a very eerie way, the ship would become an extension of him. He already knew from the puzzle dream he'd had right here in the Fecund system that the radiation levels in the outer hulls of nestships were lower than aboard Earth vessels. Otherwise the slave workers wouldn't have lasted a minute, even with the help of suits.

Will knew it was a stretch. It was one thing to replace a few microscopic wires and quite another to patch hundreds of kilometres of tunnel lining in a frozen, radioactive starship. But he had a funny feeling it would work. The answer felt *right*, as if the Transcended had laid the ship out before him like another puzzle. The solutions to his problems would be built into it if he was smart enough to find them.

He stared intently into Rachel's eyes. 'You've just given me a crazy idea.' He took her hand. 'Come on, we're going to the sick-bay.' He pulled her down the passage, explaining on the way. As he spoke, her eyes grew wider and wider. 'If I can get enough of the network repaired to start pumping fluid around, then the blood will be able to detect the smaller ruptures from temperature and pressure variations.'

'You're right,' she said when he was finished. 'That is a crazy idea.'

But she still followed him.

The *Nanshan*'s sick-bay was little more than a cubicle. They crowded inside and Rachel started looking through the cupboards.

Will flexed his arm. 'I want you to transfuse about a pint,' he said.

Meanwhile he started setting up the rest of his experiment. When they left the space station, the medical robots he'd taken had brought with them several tons of supplies. Those included forty-five litres of artificial plasma, which Will moved to a tank in a shielded area outside the habitat core. He'd use that as food. Then he descended into his new mind and told his blood what to do.

Rachel brought out a hypodermic gun and carefully decanted Will's blood. It took a little careful replumbing of the habitat core to pump the stuff out into the tank Will had prepared, but they managed it. Ten minutes later, Will was watching his cells diffuse into the tank through the eyes of the attendant robots.

'If we can create the conditions the cells need to multiply, the number we have to work with should increase exponentially till we run out of protein,' he told her.

Rachel smiled at him. 'Are you kidding? The one thing Fecund ships don't lack is protein.'

She was right. The ship was full of corpses. In fact, the whole star system was full of corpses. Protein galore. He broke into a grin.

18: TROUBLE ARRIVES

18.1: WILL

Ira was wrong. A full four days passed before trouble hit.

On the first day, Will and Rachel hurled themselves at the task of refitting one of the robot factories. It turned out to be a simple matter of extruding and replacing those components that time and harsh conditions had destroyed. There weren't that many. By the time they got it running, his other machines had carried out coarse-grain repairs on dozens of kilometres of fluid-transport conduits. Will saved hours by not checking for tiny fractures his cells could repair for him.

On day two, Will set his new robots to work repairing the second factory, a task for which they were perfectly designed. Meanwhile, he and Rachel synthesised twenty gallons of smart-blood solution. It took them hours to get the conditions right for cell multiplication, and even longer to make the cells do anything useful. It became clear that the smart cells in themselves were not enough. Will was going to have to create a dedicated communication system for them, too. In the end, he solved his problem by losing another sample of blood, this one carrying new orders.

By the end of the day, he had a transmitter in the tank that had become the hub of an extraordinary network of nerves. The fact that the same kind of nerves would have to run through many kilometres of tubing was a thought that disturbed him deeply. However, he had two factories working.

On day three, Will collected hundreds of Fecund bodies and

experimented with using his new blood to break down and utilise their tissues. The experiment was a success. His new cells, he learned, conveniently contained a suite of programs for exactly this kind of work.

Will also rigged heaters fed by the *Nanshan*'s fusion cores to melt the thousands of tons of ice already in the tunnels. By the end of the day, he had over a thousand litres of smart plasma and a hundred and eighty kilometres of transport tunnels repaired.

By the close of the fourth day, the ship was starting to look promising. And by that time, Will was no longer surprised at his own success. As each of his gambles paid off, it grew increasingly obvious that it wasn't a coincidence. As he'd suspected, the ship had been made ready for someone to resurrect a long time ago. Will could feel the hand of the Transcended in everything he did. They were present in every robot that fulfilled a repair task perfectly without his supervision, and every engineering problem that turned out to have a tidy, clever solution. At times, he felt like a dog being given treats in return for performing tricks. He also found himself wondering how many other solutions to species' problems lay floating out there in the dark.

When fate finally caught up with them, Will was deep in the bowels of the alien vessel with Rachel, overseeing the repair of some fluid heaters. Their discussion was interrupted by a call from Ira, still on self-imposed watch at the *Nanshan*'s sensor console.

'Will, Rachel – it's happened.'

Will stopped talking mid-sentence.

'The far-field scans just picked up the entry flashes from six ships,' Ira went on. 'That means they'll be here in minutes.' There was a strong note of *I told you so* in his voice.

Will and Rachel exchanged nervous glances. Will felt the pit drop out of his stomach. Despite their successes, they were nowhere near ready.

'They still have to find us,' Will ventured optimistically.

Ira laughed. 'That'll take them about thirty seconds. This crate isn't the *Ariel*. There's no way to lock down its infrared profile. If you want to live, I recommend getting to your battle-stations right now. I'm going to fire on them as soon as they're in range.'

'I hear you,' said Hugo. Hugo was out on the far reaches of the nestship's exohull, tinkering with the vessel's defences. 'I'm heading for the primary habitat core. The shield should be ready to activate, but I'll need Will's help.'

The shield had occupied all of Hugo's attention since Will had given him the archive files on it on their first day of repairs. If it worked the way Hugo hoped, it would buy them enough time to finish fixing the ship. If it didn't, they stood a good chance of vaporising all the nestship's outer defences at a single stroke.

'I warn you, though,' said Hugo, 'I haven't run any tests yet.'

'There's no time like the present,' Ira retorted.

'I'll see you there,' said Will.

He broadcast instructions to his robots to report to their action stations. He hadn't finished clearing tunnels but it was too late to worry about that now. It was time to put the ship's arteries to work.

'Ready?' said Rachel.

Will nodded.

Together they clipped their suits to the heavy-duty waldobot they'd been using for transport and sped off towards the nestship's core.

18.2: IRA

Ira strapped himself down in front of his improvised weapons array and cracked his knuckles. It was years since he'd run an assault position. He hoped he hadn't lost his touch.

On the screen before him were the marker icons for the six incoming ships. Four of them were clearly the light cruisers that had chased them from New Angeles. The other two looked unpleasantly like troop transporters.

Only Earth bothered to train zero-gee troops. Everyone else in the war had used robots. But then, only Earth had a steady supply of suicidal young men angry or vicious enough to sign up for such dangerous work. Earther space troops had a reputation for erratic, senseless violence that made their tactics very difficult to predict. Everything they touched turned into a bloodbath. On no account could Ira afford to let those ships get close. Unfortunately, all of them were heading directly for the *Nanshan*.

Ira shook his head. Just as he'd suspected, it hadn't taken the Earthers long to locate their target. They were being drawn to the *Nanshan* like flies to the dead.

Ira wished that Will had given in to his request to move the stolen ship to another part of the debris field. Will had refused on the grounds that they were still using it to power and coordinate the repairs. Thus, the two ships were still bound together by a hundred different kinds of struts and cables.

The good news was that, thanks to Hugo, Ira had three working suntap g-rays positioned in the debris field nearby. He'd powered and primed them the moment he saw the first flash. With luck, it was just a matter of waiting for the perfect shot.

After an initial surge of speed, the Earthers crept towards their target. Ira could understand their reticence. The enemy crews were certain to be experiencing awe and fear as they neared the ruins. Ira was counting on that to keep them distracted. Little by little, ships drifted into perfect positions. Ira waited with his heart in his mouth for a targeting lock. The computer chimed as his best-placed weapon zeroed in.

He fired. The suntap cannon channelled a torrent of radiation at the lead cruiser. It died instantly. A split-second later, the other ships were scattering into the cover of the ruins.

Ira cursed them as he struggled for another targeting lock. These guys were quick off the mark. He grazed a second ship before it could put a tumbling alien habitat between itself and his death ray.

He scowled into his monitor. That hadn't gone the way he'd hoped. He didn't dare fire again till he got a clean shot, otherwise the Earthers would be able to pinpoint his closest g-ray and take it out. Time to roll out the conventional defences.

He fired the *Nanshan*'s drones. With luck, a heavy enough assault would drive the Earthers into exposing themselves. However, the answering release of munitions that came from the Earther ships was startling. There were hundreds of them – far more than vessels that size would normally carry. With a grim, sinking feeling, Ira realised why the Earthers had taken an extra day to arrive. It wasn't that they couldn't follow his manoeuvres. They'd been preparing.

The enemy drones converged on his own. All of them mutually annihilated with alarming speed. Ira keyed in the new tactical program codes Will had given him as fast as he could. They slowed the attrition rate, but even so it was guaranteed to be a losing battle. He was barely going to touch the Earthers, let alone drive them out.

There had to be at least a dozen men commanding the enemy machines, and all of them more familiar with the equipment than he was. It didn't help that half of the fight was happening behind debris, where he could only see the action through slow relayed images. There was nothing to do but issue his fleet broad commands and hope.

His drones were rapidly overwhelmed. With a snort of disgust, Ira realised he had no choice but to pile on the power. He started firing again with his closest suntap-ray, taking every free shot he could. Two enemy ships received glancing hits and Ira had the satisfaction of watching their inducers flare and die.

This time, though, the Earthers retaliated and their sporadic shield of covering fire quickly became focused. Ira's best-placed suntap died in a flash of radiation. He roared his displeasure and slammed his fist on the arm of the couch.

The Earthers followed up their attack with another sudden burst of fire, this time aimed directly at the *Nanshan*. Ira scrambled madly to defend the ship as the buffers around him crackled under the onslaught. Clouds of countermeasures sprayed out from the *Nanshan*'s hull. But as his hands flew madly over the keyboard, three dark shapes slunk out across the debris field towards him.

Troop shuttles. They were headed for the *Nanshan* and using the floating wrecks as shields. Ira watched the little ships close on him with horrified fascination. They were flying insanely fast for such dangerous territory, but Earthers had always been good at risking lives. He tried desperately to block their advance using the *Nanshan*'s own underpowered g-rays but was hard pressed enough just keeping his buffers alive. The shuttles disappeared behind the curve of the nestship's hull, hugging close to protect their final approach.

Ira bellowed obscenities at them. There was no way he could get a lock on them now. They'd converge on his location in a matter of seconds, and in no time at all the nestship would be crawling with Earthers. There was only one thing to do: tell the others and hope they could pull some kind of alien rabbit out of the hat before it was too late.

He hit the intercom button but nothing happened. A warning message popped up across his monitors – *comms systems down*. The Earthers' tidy firing pattern had knocked out his primary and secondary antenna arrays.

'Fuck!' yelled Ira.

There was only one way to raise the alarm now. He'd have to chance it that the Earthers wouldn't use g-rays with their troop shuttles in the line of fire and go in person. He grabbed his suit, threw himself down the corridor and piled into the docking pod as fast as he could. He watched the action on the monitor screen as the pod sealed and proceeded with painful slowness up to the exohull. The shuttles were slithering over the side of the nestship's hull like vipers towards the *Nanshan*'s helpless bulk.

'Come on!' Ira boomed, bashing the docking pod wall with the flat of his hand. 'Can't you go any faster, you fucking machine?'

The pod reached space at last and trundled unhurriedly along the docking proboscis. Ira immediately hit his suit intercom and started broadcasting.

'*Ariel* crew, listen up. Earther arrival in the nestship interior is imminent. I repeat, *imminent*.'

The first shuttle swept into view around the curve of the hull below him. A tactical laser lanced out from its nose, severing the rail ahead of him, and Ira's pod ground to a juddering halt.

'It's just not my day,' he muttered as he slammed on his helmet and yanked the lever on the pod's emergency door release. He gripped the handle hard as air flooded out of the chamber. Then he held his breath and hurled himself into the half-kilometre gulf that still lay between him and the great rent in the nestship's side.

Ira turned lazily end over end as he soared across the void, struggling to stabilise himself with the suit's feeble thrusters. As he did so, he caught sight of a line of Earther soldiers in dogfight harnesses being spat out of the nearest shuttle's hull like peas from a child's mouth, and they were accelerating towards him.

Ira contemplated firing the small vacuum automatic clipped to the suit's leg, but the distance was too great. Truthfully, he wasn't equipped for zero-gee combat. They'd catch up with him in no time. He used what was left of the juice in his thrusters to propel him towards the jagged edge of the hole below.

Despite being wafer-thin in starship terms, the exohull was still several metres thick and not easy to grab hold of. There was a dreadful moment when Ira bounced at the lip of the rent and started to drift clear. He was almost out of reach before his hand lashed out to seize a nearby spar of tortured iron. He hung there, clinging to the ship with nothing but a single slippery hand. The laser sighting dots of Earther space-combat rifles wobbled briefly across his legs.

With a grunt of effort, Ira pulled his body back towards the wall of the ship. He half-flew, half-climbed hand over hand into the nestship and along the inner wall away from the hole. The chamber he found himself in was a huge, mottled polygonal space like a bubble in some titanic metallic foam. It looked very different in reality from its image on a monitor wall. The scale was humbling, and without robots' light-enhancement filters to illuminate the space it was oppressively gloomy.

Ira glanced around for ways to escape. There were openings to access tunnels on the other side of the chamber but they were dozens of metres away across open space. The rail that Will's machines had constructed ran across to them but following it would leave him totally exposed. So he pulled himself hand over hand along the strangely pocked and bubbled exohull interior towards the one piece of cover available – Hugo's project.

Dominating the chamber and anchored to its coreward wall was one of the things the physicist called a 'quagitator'. It was a huge particle gun of some kind with helical accelerator channels and a broad crown of glassy spikes. It looked like a squashed helter-skelter topped by a head of violently stiff hair. Hugo had surrounded it from end to end within a turret of scaffolding and diagnostic sensors. It squatted menacingly in the dark.

Ira leapt for the scaffolding and started pulling himself down towards the accelerator's base. In the next second, the Earthers arrived. The searchlights on their dogfight harnesses flicked on, filling the chamber with crazily swooping circles of light. Laser sights flickered against the struts ahead of Ira's hands. He grabbed the closest pole and headed inwards, ducking into the crevice between the quagitator's huge ceramic-clad coils. The machine was still warm from Hugo's tests and hummed beneath Ira's gloved hand.

Who knew how many rads he was taking just floating here? However, the good news was that no one in their right mind was going to shoot at him while he was close to such a machine. Starship equipment had a nasty habit of being full of antimatter or plasma or piped X-rays. Even the stupidest Earther knew that.

Ira unclipped his automatic and took pot shots at the Earthers as they zipped past He missed, and the soldiers started to clamber into the scaffolding above and below him. It was only a matter of time before they surrounded him.

'Fuck,' he muttered to himself. 'Still, at least I made it this far.'

'Sir, what's going on?' said Rachel's voice.

Ira blinked. He must have left his broadcast channel open when the pod died. Rachel and Will had been listening in ever since.

'Great,' he said. 'I'm stuck on a fucking quagitator. The one just inside the rent.' He instantly regretted his frankness. 'Don't worry about me,' he added. 'I'm fine. Get to the habitat core and start up the defences.'

'With all due respect, sir—' said Rachel.

'That's an order!' Ira shouted.

The last thing he needed was for the rest of his crew to blow their final chance to act because of him. He snapped the intercom off and started dragging himself down the quagitator's curving track. Who knew – maybe he'd make it to the bottom before they killed him.

18.3: WILL

Will and Rachel floated in the mesohull pathway that led to the habitat core and faced each other as they listened to Ira's last shouted command.

'Do you want to carry on while I go back for him?' said Will.

'No,' replied Rachel with a smile.

'All right then,' said Will.

He turned the waldobot around, and with it the small army of machines cluttering the passage in both directions. They started racing up towards the chamber where Ira was trapped. As Will rose, he reached his mind out across the slender communication lines he'd rigged through the nestship's labyrinthine mass and called for help.

'Any idea how to get him out of there?' said Rachel.

Will nodded. 'I'm going to take on the soldiers. You'll be covering his escape.'

More robots poured out of side-tunnels as they ascended, drawn by his call to battle. Will nudged a second waldobot up close.

'You ride that one,' he told Rachel. 'It's got manual controls. Take it to the foot of the accelerator. Grab him if you need to – I've set the hands so they won't crush him.'

'Right,' she said. 'What about you?'

'Don't worry about me,' Will replied.

Rachel gave him a look. 'That's what Ira said.'

Together they burst up through the opening into the outer chamber. Rachel's robot veered to the right. Will's headed straight up, surrounded by a shielding swarm of machines. He identified his targets through fifty pairs of artificial eyes and set about neutralising them with mechanical efficiency. At the same time, he launched a soft attack and started dismembering the Earthers' tactical network.

The soldiers' responses were the expected combination of random, disordered gunfire and incoherent orders. Will's robots seized the Earthers and immobilised them, stripping them of their weapons. But as he closed in on a knot of men taking shelter in the scaffolding, a rush of urgent commands came over the Earthers' main channel.

'Primary target acquired!' someone shouted.

'Commence Phase Two! Go! Go! Go!'

One of the Earthers shouldered a broad-mouthed cannon and took aim. There was a cough of icy vapour and a projectile of some kind ripped towards Will. He veered aside and drew up a shield of heavy-duty metal-movers. The device exploded against them. At the same time, Will's world burst open. A blinding, shrieking racket filled his head. It was an EM bomb.

Will instinctively clapped his hands to his helmet as the barrage of electromagnetic radiation scoured his skull. His less robust robots died immediately. They went limp and tumbled inertly off towards the walls. The few shielded for exohull work simply froze, their command stacks abruptly emptied.

In the moments of ringing shock that followed, the Earthers threw themselves at Will. He struggled weakly as they clustered around his body. Even in his addled state, he managed to thrust four of them aside through the sheer strength of his augmented limbs, but they jetted straight back into the fray.

Somewhere in the struggle, the soldiers clamped a kind of cage over Will's head. They seized his arms and trapped them by his sides with a suit-lock. Will squirmed and thrashed to no avail and his legs kicked harmlessly against vacuum.

Will cursed his own stupidity. He'd never suspected they'd use a weapon that damaged themselves along with him. But clearly this was a planned attack. They knew about him and his skills in advance and they wanted him alive. He groaned to himself as understanding dawned. Of course they knew about him. He'd left them all the evidence of his abilities they could ever need when he fled the station at New Angeles. He hadn't deleted the records of his escape. That meant the Earthers had video footage, data-transport records and over a dozen eyewitnesses.

Even so, the trap was still a cut above the normal Earther tactics. The soldiers had even come equipped for weightless combat. That was a rare thing in modern warfare, but simple analysis would have shown the archive had been stored in a weightless environment. Someone had paid attention to the details. Will suspected Enrique Chopra's hand in this affair.

The soldiers dragged Will to the inner wall of the chamber. As they pulled him along by the cage locked around his helmet, he noticed that the Earthers weren't remotely fazed by the comms blackout their weapon had created. They were signing to each other with their hands. That meant they had to be Spatials, Earth's crack zero-gee assault troops – the same butchers who carried out the

Ganymede Massacre in the first year of the war. No doubt Chopra had seduced them out of planet leave on New Angeles with promises of bonus pay.

Will made a tentative attempt to contact his surviving robots. He wasn't surprised when nothing happened. The cage was a signal blocker. It had probably been manufactured specially for him.

While the troops swapped gestures, Will's strength slowly began to return, and with it his determination to act. He could only think of one plan, and it was insane. He was surrounded by armed men and held in the grip of a solid steel band, but he didn't care. Will would rather die a dozen times than return to the hands of the High Church.

He shut his eyes and focused on his smart cells. His blood raced and his muscles tingled as he braced his arms against the suit-lock and strained. The metal band dug hard into his flesh. More significantly, it dug into the life-sustaining sleeves that surrounded them. Will pressed slowly but firmly – there was no point ripping his suit open unless he absolutely had to. He channelled his power, rearranging the body chemistry of his limbs. He let everything but the battle between him and the suit-lock's embrace melt away.

Nothing happened immediately, but eventually the lock gave sluggishly before snapping open. Will's arms flew up as they became free. Without pausing, he turned the motion into an attack, seizing the rifle of the closest soldier with one hand and grabbing the man's suit with the other.

Will hurled the soldier across the chamber, using the momentum it gave him to fly sideways. The soldiers' weapons whipped around to fire. They sprayed low-recoil suit-rippers into the space where Will had been a second before, their qualms about killing him apparently vanished. Will returned fire with deadly accuracy.

As the Earthers scattered for cover, Will reached up and tore the signal blocker from his head. Only three of his robots had survived the EM blast, but they were the biggest of his waldobots. They were all he needed.

He set permanent-kill programs into each of them before the Earthers got the chance to fire another EM weapon. Then he watched, smiling, as they ground, ripped and pounded the screaming soldiers into pulp. By the time his sideways vector brought him to the far wall of the chamber, the fight was over. He observed the fleshy remains with a certain crazy satisfaction and blinked himself back to sanity.

He looked around. Ira and Rachel were gone, and so were many of the Spatials. That wasn't good. Will asked the nestship network where they were, but there was no reply. All his local nodes for a dozen chambers in every direction had been fried when the bomb went off. Will had no idea where his friends were now or how to help them.

There was only one way he could find them now, and that was by getting his fluid transport system running at last. The mobile transmitters and sensors it carried would mean the Earthers could fire off as many EM bombs as they liked and Will would still be able to track his shipmates. He hailed the closest waldobot and set off as fast as he could for the habitat core, where Hugo no doubt waited.

18.4: IRA

While Will dealt with the Earthers, Ira and Rachel fled through the weirdly cellular interior of the nestship's mesohull. As they flew, Ira ranted.

'What the hell do you think you were doing, trying to rescue me?' he demanded. 'Didn't I give you a direct order? Does my authority count for nothing around here any—'

His tirade was interrupted by a hateful squeal as the waldobot they were clinging to twitched once and died. Then its headlamps went out.

'Rachel?' he said, but their intercoms were also dead.

Ira flicked through channels, trying them all. He looked up just in time to see Rachel's frantic gesturing. By the light of their feeble suit-guides, he saw that their waldobot was hurtling towards one of the chamber walls. He and Rachel leapt free of the machine just before it ploughed straight into the unyielding alien ceramic.

Rachel grabbed his suit and dragged him close enough for their helmets to touch.

'Was that what I think it was?' Her voice buzzed through his faceplate.

'It was an EM weapon,' Ira replied.

Rachel's expression darkened. 'Then Will's in trouble. We should go back.'

Ira sighed and nodded. 'Yeah.'

He had no intention of abandoning one of his crew. He just wished that circumstances hadn't conspired to make him look quite so hypocritical.

Rachel squeezed his arm and pointed back the way they'd come. 'Wait! Look!'

Through the doorway to the chamber behind them, Ira saw the beam of a searchlight illuminate the drifting ice particles. He scanned the space they were in – it was too large to manoeuvre in quickly, and they only had a dead waldobot for cover.

'This way,' he said, pointing deeper into the ship. Rachel nodded.

Ira led the way, flying desperately from doorway to doorway and squinting in an effort to make out the irregular shapes in the gloom. Two chambers on, he found a small space criss-crossed by plasma supply pipes and took cover behind a cluster of larger conduits near the corner. Rachel squeezed in alongside him. Seconds later, six Earthers poured into the room and fanned out, making complex hand gestures as they moved.

Rachel pressed her helmet to Ira's. 'We can take them,' she said. 'Six to two isn't bad.'

Ira grinned. He'd been thinking the same thing. The close space would give their lighter suits an advantage and the Earthers were bound to think twice about firing with so many pipes around. The odds were good. The enemy might be trained zero-gee warriors with thrusters, but he and Rachel were Galatean Fleet, bred for space.

'Okay,' he said. 'The three on the left are yours. The ones on the right are mine. We move on my mark.' Ira waited for the closest Earthers to drift near. 'Go!'

Ira exploded out into the room. The nearest Earther barely had time to react before Ira had wrenched the gun from his hands, turned it and fired point-blank into the man's harness controls. He brought his feet up and planted them hard against the Earther's chest. He launched himself at the next man, using the first as reaction mass and breaking his ribs at the same time.

Ira controlled his spin so that as the second man shouldered his rifle, Ira lashed out with the gun he'd taken, using the butt as a club. The plastic stock smashed the Earther's weapon sideways. Then, as he started to slide right, Ira fired once into the man's harness and a second time into the floating rifle, sending it spinning out of range. He finished off with a passing kick to the trooper's head.

By then, the third soldier had been given enough time to attack. He cannoned into Ira, sending them both crashing against the wall. Ira smiled evilly as they wrestled. The Earther had made a classic macho mistake. Direct physical assault was not the way to stop a Galatean starship captain. Ira yanked up his arms, freeing them from the soldier's grasp, and grabbed the man's right wrist. Then he forced the elbow back in a direction nature had never intended it to go. There weren't that many ways to really hurt someone in an armoured spacesuit, but aiming for the joints was always a good bet. While the Earther screamed in silence, Ira gave the other arm the same treatment. That was one trooper who wouldn't be firing guns at people for a while.

He looked up to see Rachel finishing off her set. Her style was very different from his – more like deadly combat pinball. She ricocheted around the room firing, spinning and kicking. The last man's head jerked sideways as Rachel's scissoring leg connected sharply with his helmet. She ended by tidily catching the gun Ira had left tumbling with one hand and arresting her drift by grabbing a plasma pipe with the other. She smiled breathlessly and shook the rifle. Ira pushed himself close so they could talk.

'Let's go and get Will,' said Rachel.

'Agreed.'

Ira unclipped the dogfight harness from the man with the broken arms and fastened it around his own suit. Rachel took another from one of her own victims. Better armed and better equipped, they headed back the way they'd come, rifles at the ready.

Ira slowed as they approached the outer chamber. He and Rachel nosed through the doorway, expecting to be surrounded and outgunned at any moment. However, a very different scene met them.

As Ira had expected, there were dozens of dead robots, but two giant waldobots were still alive. They hovered menacingly in the middle of a cloud of mashed Earther remains. There was no sign of Will.

Ira scanned the dark outer reaches of the chamber for movement. There was none. The roboteer must have survived the blast somehow and fled down a different tunnel. As he jetted over to touch helmets with Rachel, something overhead caught his eye. Crossing in front of the blanket of stars that filled the kite-shaped hole above them was the silhouette of a human figure, the first of dozens.

Searchlights stabbed down onto the chamber floor. Earther reinforcements had arrived.

'Oh, shit,' Ira muttered to himself.

He looked to Rachel. She nodded grimly.

Together, they started retreating again, firing as they went.

18.5: WILL

Will met Hugo outside the primary habitat core.

'What happened?' demanded Hugo. 'Where were you?'

Will had to broadcast direct from his implant to talk since the radio mike on his suit had been trashed along with everything else.

'Into the airlock first, then I'll explain.'

They clambered inside and Will told Hugo what had happened as the air cycled. Hugo's face became grave.

'So you see,' said Will, 'I need to get fluid transport up and running before we turn on the shields.'

For a moment, Hugo looked annoyed. His pet project had been shelved.

'There's little point in protecting a ship that's already full of Earthers,' Will pointed out, as patiently as he could.

Hugo nodded. 'I know. Let's get to work.'

They emerged into the recently cleaned habitat interior. Gone were the frozen bodies and the strange strands of alien webbing. The walls had been scraped back to the metal and re-clad with white impact foam. A flat plastic floor had replaced the clan-parents' wallowing pool, and the room now contained mounted combat couches and monitor banks pirated from the *Nanshan*. The empty space above was strung with elastic cords for easy zero-gee manoeuvring. The place smelled as clean and artificial as any ordinary vessel. But for the room's peculiar high ceiling and bulging walls, a visitor could be forgiven for thinking the place had always been occupied by humans.

Will started issuing orders to the nestship as he hurriedly shucked off his suit.

'Activate transport heater coils. Charge primary and secondary pump drivers. Initiate smart-blood infusion.'

All across the vast reaches of the nestship, machinery stirred into life. He pulled himself down to his new couch and strapped himself in.

'Hugo, I'll need you to watch over the safety metrics for me. This is going to be tricky.'

Hugo dragged himself into his couch and started tapping rapidly at his console.

'I'm ready.'

Will shut his eyes and concentrated on the ship. He could feel the smart-blood jetting into the vessel's massive arteries.

'Begin fluid transport,' he told the ship.

Immense mechanical valves began to pump like giant hearts. His new hybrid solution started circulating and, with it, the hundreds of robots and sensors it carried. Awful grinding sounds echoed as icebergs shifted and broke under the mounting pressure.

Hugo sucked air through his teeth. 'Gently does it,' he recommended. 'We nosed into the red just then.'

Will eased back on the pumps. The minutes ticked by but the situation didn't improve. The transport system was having none of the effects he'd hoped for. The sensors were moving far too slowly to do any good, so the patch where the EM bomb had gone off remained dead.

On a whim, Will searched his new mind for ways his smart-cells might help to break up the ice. Millions of tiny SAPs trawled their records and shouted back their answers. There were plenty. Apparently the smart-cells he'd been multiplying had already used such methods to adapt to the brutal conditions in his storage tanks. They had, in effect, become extremophiles, just like the single-celled organisms Galateans had been using for generations to build their ecology. They were perfectly equipped for the job. For a start, they could begin secreting a powerful antifreeze. Command sequences and molecular models floated to the front of Will's mind.

Will laughed aloud. Here was another piece of the Transcended puzzle – one he should have seen earlier. He passed the new orders to the smart-cells all over the ship. The results were practically instantaneous: the ice started melting, the pressure dropped and the model of the artery network that had been taking shape in Will's head suddenly surged with clarity and insistence.

It took Will a moment to realise why the effect was so pronounced. He'd never bothered to analyse the ice in the tubes. Now he could see that it was far from pure. There were plenty of organic compounds already in it and the cells were absorbing them at a voracious pace. By instructing them to melt the ice, he'd inadvertently doubled their food supply.

Will's model of the ship rapidly spread and grew, revealing things he hadn't even thought to look for – like the Fecund food stores. They contained as many tons of protein as he could ever need. Then there was an arsenal, where weapons were stored for the half-born to use in hand-to-hand fighting.

The dead patch in Will's map shrank to nothing and revealed that Rachel and Ira were in trouble. They were holding off a tide of Earther soldiers bearing inexorably down on the habitat core. Will woke his army of Fecund-designed robots. It was time to see what his new ship could do.

18.6: IRA

Ira threw away the empty rifle and brought up the spare he'd snatched on his way back through the plasma pipe room. At first, it looked like the frenzied, bloodthirsty attack from Will's two remaining waldobots was going to be decisive. But the new wave of troopers brought cutting lasers and more EM bombs. From the cover of the lower chamber, he and Rachel looked on as the robots were stunned and dismembered by dozens of swarming men.

Now the two of them were all that stood between the Earther hordes and the habitat core. Unsurprisingly, they'd steadily lost ground. For the last twenty minutes they'd been locked in a pattern of fire and retreat, taking as much tactical advantage of the narrow doorways between chambers as they could. But their ammunition wasn't going to last for ever. And with each step back that he and Rachel took, more side passages opened up for the invaders to explore. It was only a matter of time before they were cut off and surrounded.

Ira ducked as another volley of projectiles streamed past. In the unyielding silence and low light, the only way he could tell he'd been fired at was by the flash from the enemy's muzzles and the dull thudding as the ammunition hit the wall he was clutching. The shooting was fierce. The Earthers had entrenched again.

He glanced across to Rachel on the other side of the doorway. She nodded. On the count of three, they pushed hard away from their hiding places, firing between their feet as they flew towards the next chamber.

Ira roared at his enemy even though he knew they couldn't hear it. It helped him deal with the ever-present terror of having a ripper-round penetrate his suit. With a practised, synchronised movement, he and Rachel reached out to grab the edges of the entrance and swung themselves around into firing positions. This time, though, the Earthers were ready for them.

The moment Ira started reaching, the ceramic wall he was aiming for was peppered with tiny craters. He had no choice but to snatch his hand back and sail uninterrupted into the depths of the chamber beyond.

Rachel had made it to her shooting place and looked back at him in distress. The Earthers took advantage of her distraction and surged sideways into the newly secured room, firing as they came.

'Look out!' Ira yelled as he wrestled with his harness thrusters.

But she couldn't hear him. Rachel noticed just in time and rolled back from the doorway, losing her grip as she did so.

Ira groaned. Now they were separated and both exposed. Death wouldn't be long in coming. He fired and manoeuvred in a desperate attempt to regain the ground he'd lost.

He was so focused on the Earther soldiers darting back and forth on the other side of the deadly portal that he didn't notice the wall rippling at first. Only when the jets of ice started shooting out of it did it occur to him that something was happening.

The wall split abruptly to reveal a horribly organic-looking orifice. Through it tumbled things out of nightmare – giant scorpions, each twice the size of a man. They thrashed and flicked their way into the room in bursts of ice and leapt like fleas across the void towards the Earther forces. Ira had to thrust aside in a hurry to get out of their way.

At first, he could only gape at the emerging horde. Then he broke into a guffaw of understanding. Will was back.

The soldiers forgot Ira and Rachel in an instant and turned their fire onto the tsunami of furious machines. Another EM bomb flashed. The front wave of robots jerked and drifted lifelessly, but twice as many poured through to replace them. The results were inevitable. One by one the men were seized, either whole or in parts. They were dragged, kicking and thrashing, back through the aperture in the wall. Ira watched in wordless awe. The zeal with which the machines recycled Will's enemies was chilling.

Then, as swiftly as it had begun, the battle was over. Ira and Rachel hung wordless in the snow-filled room, watching the few remaining robots scuttle back to their orifice. The last one in line changed course and paused just in front of them. Ira's heart bobbed up to his mouth as he locked gazes with the many-eyed mechanical monster.

The scorpion gestured with a peculiarly delicate claw. *On my back*, it was saying. The motion was strangely human. Ira could almost imagine Will Kuno-Monet sitting behind its lidless eyes. He erupted into laughter again and grabbed on.

18.7: WILL

Will trembled as his new network gathered power. As the fluid moved faster and faster, it felt like parts of his mind he never knew existed were waking up. Of course, that wasn't far off what was actually happening. The smart-cells were rapidly laying nerve tracks along the tunnel walls and clustering together to form regularly spaced cognitive nodes. His mind was growing to fill the ship.

Will hadn't predicted this side effect of his idea. The sensation of empowerment was so strong it frightened him.

'Are you ready to activate the shield?' asked Hugo.

It took Will a moment to work out where the voice was coming from. Yes, of course, near his *human* body, down there in that tiny habitat core. Will opened his eyes and blinked hard.

'Yes,' he said.

Hugo smiled. It was the first time Will had seen any sign of happiness on the man's face since New Angeles.

'First, we need to power the associated suntaps,' said Hugo. 'I've marked them for you. They're in hull sections three, four, eleven, twelve, twenty-one...'

But Will had already guessed what to do. He could feel the quagitators waiting all over his inner skin and opened up the suntaps with a kiss of thought. They struggled a little at first, being so old and brittle, but Hugo had done his work well. Beams of electrons flashed out into the sun like the tongues of hummingbirds.

'Suntaps fired,' said Will.

Hugo stared at him. He had still been reading out his list when Will interrupted.

'Already? All of them?'

Will nodded.

'Right,' said Hugo. 'Well, at this distance, we'll still have a few minutes before they connect.'

'Nine minutes, fifty-two seconds and counting,' said Will.

'Right,' Hugo said again, sounding a little disturbed this time. 'That's... exactly right.' He paused. 'Listen, there's something I want to say.' The physicist stared into his monitor for a few seconds, then back at Will. 'I know I may have made a mistake I'll regret for the rest of my life, however long or short that might be, but I'm glad I chose to come with you. Otherwise I would have never seen all this. I would never have witnessed this moment.'

Will smiled. 'I'm glad, too,' he said, but Hugo held up a hand to silence him.

'Please, hear me out,' said Hugo.

Will grinned to himself. Amazing – Hugo still managed to be annoying even when he was trying to be nice.

'I want to say thank you . . .' Hugo paused, his face clouding with pain. 'For coming to get me. I didn't think—'

Will's smile fled. 'Forget it,' he said quickly. New Angeles was not an episode he wanted to revisit. 'Really.'

Hugo nodded. The two men sat in silence till power started to course back from the nearby star into the nestship's capacitor banks.

'It's time,' said Will.

All across the ship, Hugo's spiky accelerators began to fire. He watched the monitors avidly as beams of flickering violet light connected with the weird iron exohull. It became smooth and silvery as the metal rippled and began to run. The rupture near the stem sealed over as the weird substance sheathed the ship like a reflecting skin. The mystery of the peculiar alloy that had so distressed Hugo on their first visit was now explained.

Hugo cackled in delight. 'The whole ship is now covered in distributed matter, you see,' he announced excitedly. 'The space where the exohull sits is in a state of quantum agitation. Thus, the iron loses its particulate properties, just like the electrons in the suntap. It sits in superposition until you fire something at it, which temporarily collapses the wave. So whenever something hits the shield, it always interacts with a nucleus because the nucleons are everywhere! It's like being surrounded by a shell of solid quarks!'

Will nodded absently. He could already feel the theory of the thing in his head like a solid object, along with its cunningly contrived logical holes, courtesy of the Transcended.

'What shall we do about the Earthers outside?' he said. 'The *Nanshan* is still crawling with troops and we just effectively severed our tethers to it. All our supplies are aboard.'

'Yes, yes,' said Hugo eagerly, his eyes shining. 'We need some way to make the other ships back off.' He pressed his fingers against his lips. 'If only we had one of those bosers working, that'd solve the problem.'

'Bosers?' said Will.

'What I call the coherent-matter cannons. After *Bose–Einstein Condensate*. They're like the shield, only they fire distributed iron instead of holding it. The ship has eight of them, but I never had the time to look at them properly.'

'We could repair one,' Will suggested.

Hugo frowned. 'I doubt it. It was hard enough getting the shielding finished. It could take days.'

Will smiled. 'I don't think so. Show me which is in the best condition.'

Hugo regarded him nervously for a moment, then pointed out one of the weapons on his display. 'There.'

Will shut his eyes and extended his senses towards the boser mounting. The smart-cell nodes nearby started issuing instructions to the robots directly. They scurried across it, scanning and analysing. They reported what needed fixing and what would have to be replaced.

At the same moment, Will's factories started extruding and assembling the larger parts. Meanwhile, the microscopic components were constructed on-site by his smart-cells. The protein circuitry Will could make was far more efficient than the kind the Fecund had used.

Robots gathered the pieces and slotted them into place. In a matter of minutes, Will had the weapon repaired. He was barely involved with the process by the end. He watched in wonder with Hugo as the ship healed itself.

'We're back!' came Ira's booming voice from the airlock.

Rachel hurtled across the room and hugged Will hard. She kissed his head and face.

'Thanks for the rescue,' she told him.

Will blushed and shrugged.

'So, what's the status?' said Ira as he pulled himself down to his couch.

'Will is turning into a starship,' Hugo replied, clearly only half in jest. 'We're about to watch history in the making.'

'Really?' said Ira.

'I'm just finishing,' said Will. 'It'll be ready any second now.'

By the time Will had welded the final piece of the new weapon into place, he'd already charged the capacitors enough to fire it. Outside, the Earthers had started hurling antimatter warhead drones at the nestship while they lurked behind the Fecund remains.

Will aimed the new weapon at the closest ship.

'There's a lot of debris in the way,' he warned the others. 'Do you think it'll make a difference?'

'I have no idea,' Hugo replied. 'Only one way to find out.'

Will shrugged and fired. A beam of coherent matter, accelerated to ninety-nine per cent of the speed of light, stabbed out from the nestship, passed through the debris as if it were no denser than smoke and bored a clean hole straight through the Earther starship. As the beam moved, it cut like a wire through soft cheese.

Then the mighty capacitors drained abruptly and the beam died. The crew of the *Ariel* stared into their monitors in disbelief.

'Wow,' said Rachel.

There was a moment of chaos outside the nestship as the Earthers milled in panic. Then, as they watched, the enemy starships turned tail and fled at full warp, leaving dozens of men stranded in shuttles around the *Nanshan*.

Hugo waved his hands. 'See, I told you – Will's not strictly *Homo sapiens* any more. He's *Homo nestship*!'

Ira grunted in amusement. 'Let's finish fixing up this crate,' he said. 'It's payback time.'

19: JUSTICE

19.1: IRA

With a kind of feral glee, Ira piloted the recently christened *Ariel Two* into his home system. The warp hammer from the nestship's engines was incredibly fierce and his crew were pressed down into their crash couches, faces white and straining. Except Will, of course – he no longer appeared to be bothered by heavy gees. They drove straight into the inner system with the engines at full power. Ira dropped warp half an AU from the sun, just inside the orbit of the star system's innermost planet.

Will fired up the suntaps immediately and retracted the warp fronds. As soon as they were in, he started running the shield off the ship's prodigious antimatter reservoirs. It activated with just seconds to spare. Automated Earther defence drones had started chasing them as soon as their effective velocity had dropped to sub-light. They exploded against the liquid hull in bursts of harmless light.

The Earthers now had three and a half minutes to work out what the hell just happened and decide to act. After that, it'd be too late.

Hugo sent Ira a tactical scan. There were a hundred and forty-three enemy gunships in the system, all suntap-equipped and all in orbits beyond Galatea. They were fifteen minutes' flight away at Earther in-system warp speeds and none of them had yet activated their weapons.

Given the optical lag, that might have changed already, but Ira regarded the survey with satisfaction. It was a reassuring way for the confrontation to start. Even so, there were a couple of extremely good reasons for the *Ariel Two* crew to stay cautious. Firstly, the nestship was largely untested and still under repair, despite Will and Rachel working on it full time during the journey. Hugo had warned them all several times about the shield. According to his calculations, it was impermeable up to its threshold activation. After that, it might as well be made of cobwebs. Unfortunately, they didn't know exactly how high that threshold was. Ira hoped they never had cause to find out.

The second good reason was that General Ulanu's forces were perfectly placed to scour Galatea's surface. In the history of warfare, no one had ever resorted to a direct starship attack on a planet – but then again, no one had turned up in an alien battle cruiser before, either. The Earthers could be expected to get a little jumpy.

'We're receiving a broadcast on the open channel,' said Hugo.

Ira was impressed. 'That was quick. Let's see it.'

Admiral Tang's moody face appeared on the monitors. 'Galatean rebels, your planet has yielded to Kingdom control and your ship is surrounded. Prepare to stand down all systems and relinquish your command codes.'

Ira turned to his crew and grinned. 'Shucks. That takes all the fun out of it. I was looking forward to playing the alien invader for a while.' He looked back at Will. 'You want to talk to him?'

Will shook his head. 'You're the captain.'

Ira nodded. 'I was hoping you'd say that.' He flicked on his console camera. 'Good afternoon, Admiral Tang. Well guessed. This is Captain Ira Baron-Lecke, formerly of the Galatean Starship *Ariel*. If you don't mind, I'd like to speak directly to your superior officer to discuss terms for your surrender.'

It took a couple of minutes for the reply to arrive, and when it did, it wasn't a happy one. Tang had turned an unhealthy beet colour.

'I am the superior officer present,' snapped Tang. 'You will discuss terms for *your* surrender with *me*.'

'What happened to Ulanu?' Ira sent.

'General Ulanu is now under my command! I am not interested in chatting, Captain Baron. You have two minutes to relinquish your codes or I will commence firing.'

Ira leaned close to the camera and purred, 'Try if you like. And then get the hell away from my home world or I'm going to make you wish you'd never been born.'

By the time Tang's next riposte arrived, his eyes were bugging out of his face.

'Do I need to remind you, Captain, that you only have one ship, no matter how outlandish it is, and that I have a hundred and fifty?'

'It's not an issue that concerns me greatly,' said Ira.

'Then prepare to be destroyed!'

The connection went dead.

Ira leaned back in his couch and glanced over at Will. 'Ready to do your thing?'

Will nodded.

Ira chuckled and rubbed his hands.

19.2: GUSTAV

Gustav was on the bridge of the *Sukarno* along with Tang and a sullen Rodriguez, and watched Tang's dialogue with mounting horror. He'd expected the *Ariel* crew to come home and fight, but not like this. He'd imagined a stolen Earther ship equipped with a few choice pieces of alien technology plucked from wherever the artefact originated. He had not expected a fully functioning vessel hundreds of kilometres long built by an advanced civilisation.

As soon as Tang smacked the intercom's off button, Gustav turned to him.

'As the officer you put in charge of managing this confrontation, I must recommend that we proceed with extreme caution,' he said. 'We have absolutely no idea what that ship is capable of.'

Tang glared at him. 'What are you suggesting, Ulanu? That we flee because those freaks turn up in something we've not seen before?'

'Not necessarily, but I think a feint of some sort might be in order. The planet is already vulnerable. We could let them think they've won it for a bit. Meanwhile, we'd—'

Tang shouted over him. 'I did not come this far just so I could give up!'

Gustav realised then that the Galatean had done an excellent job of bruising Tang's fragile ego. Instead of learning his lesson from their last battle, he was desperate to keep what little he'd achieved.

'We've had nothing but tricks and lies from the Gallies since this war began, and I for one do not intend to be tricked again!' Tang shouted.

'I'm not suggesting a retreat,' said Gustav tersely. 'Just the calculated exposure of a limited force in order to draw out information about the enemy's capabilities. The tactical sacrifice of a few—'

'No!' Tang's eyes bulged at the thought of losing more ships. 'We will stand our ground and fight!'

Gustav fell silent. Clearly, saying any more would only make matters worse. Tang would only dig in his heels. Arrogant and foolhardy he might be, but Tang was not a bad commander. Better to let the man learn in his own way and hope they didn't lose too many people in the process.

Unfortunately, Rodriguez chose that moment to speak up.

'Listen to the general, Tang,' he said suddenly.

There was a tone in his voice Gustav had never heard before. It took him a moment to recognise it. It was doubt.

'I haven't been in the front line for years and even I know what he's saying makes sense,' the disciple added. 'I mean, look at the size of it.'

Gustav winced. He glanced at Rodriguez and was surprised to find an expression of strained puzzlement on the man's face. This, too, was quite a change. Since he'd joined the *Sukarno*, Rodriguez had offered little but threats and bitter remarks. This, however, was the first time he'd actually contradicted Tang to his face. Ironically, it was also the first time he'd sided with Gustav. Gustav wished he hadn't.

'Silence!' yelled Tang, jabbing a finger at Rodriguez's face. 'Your counsel was not sought, priest!'

Rodriguez narrowed his eyes. His moment of thoughtfulness was over. 'You're a fool if you think you can order me around,' he sneered. 'I represent the Prophet.'

Tang looked ready to pop. Gustav tried to save the situation the only way he could think of.

'Admiral, if this goes wrong, it could be a costly and embarrassing engagement. I know you don't want that. You asked me to take responsibility for the Galateans—'

'And now I'm taking it back!' Tang snapped. 'Commander Lee, inform all ships. Prepare for immediate convergence and attack with new suntap coverage pattern Tang Alpha One.'

'Yes, sir,' said Lee.

'Watch and learn,' Tang told Gustav coldly. 'Watch and learn.'

19.3: WILL

'How are the bosers looking?' Will asked Hugo.

The ship had plenty of g-rays he could fire, but he thought he'd start by making an impression.

'Good, I think,' said Hugo. 'I've ironed out most of the wrinkles.'

Hugo had been tinkering with the bosers during the flight, trying to moderate the extraordinary drain they put on the ship's power supply.

'I hope you're right,' said Will, 'because here they come.'

The Earther gunships advanced upon them under the thrust of their fusion torches. They approached in a series of carefully staggered waves with disrupters fully deployed and were careful not to get within targeting range until their suntaps had activated. Will waited patiently for them to fire the first shot.

When the attack came it was well coordinated, and from the whole first wave at once. Nine beams of intolerable power drove into the *Ariel Two*'s shield. They were quietly dissipated.

'That was your turn,' said Will. 'Now it's mine.'

He chose a ship from the front wave and fired a very brief burst of boser at it. The gunship split apart like an overripe fruit. Two seconds later, its antimatter containment failed and it exploded in a blast of blinding energy. The rest of the attack wave struggled to retain some kind of formation.

Will regarded his handiwork in disbelief. It was alarmingly easy, but then again, there were an awful lot of ships. He waited and watched to see if the Earthers had got the message, but seconds later, another – somewhat less coordinated – volley of g-ray fire hit the shield. Will selected a second ship and drilled a tidy hole straight through the heart of it. But the Earthers kept coming.

Will looked back at Ira. 'They don't appear to be getting the message. What shall I do?'

Ira shrugged. 'It's war, kid. Keep hitting them till they stop hitting you. They'll make it pretty clear when they've had enough.'

Will nodded and drove the nestship forward into the Earther lines, firing as he went. It was like fighting a crowd of tofu enemies with a carving knife. Each hit he scored took out a ship. However, he knew he wouldn't be able to keep it up indefinitely. Each volley used up a prodigious amount of iron from his reservoirs. He husbanded his resources carefully, keeping his blasts short.

As Will ground forward through their lines, warning icons started appearing in his sensorium. He was getting radiation leakage in the mesohull.

'Watch out!' said Hugo. 'It's happening. The shield is getting hot.'

Will realised that the Earthers had started concentrating their fire in earnest. The volleys hitting the *Ariel Two* were from seventy or eighty suntaps simultaneously, and they were tracking him with continuous beams. That wasn't good.

He piled power onto the nestship's matter-reaction jets to pull them out of the line of fire, but it was slow going. The *Ariel Two* might be blindingly fast under warp but it wasn't designed for conventional manoeuvres. As the shield grew steadily hotter, the smart-cell performance in the outer mesohull began to degrade.

Will cursed. The time for symbolic gestures was over. The moment had come to bring his own g-ray banks to bear. He farmed out targeting SAPs to the laser assemblies dotted across the hull and ordered them to fire. Forty-eight simultaneous lines of force lanced out from the nestship's hull and drove home against the Earther's buffers.

'Let's see how they like some of that,' he muttered.

19.4: GUSTAV

Gustav watched the monitor wall in wordless horror as four dozen of Tang's precious ships popped like soap bubbles. *Four dozen* ships from a single volley. Seen from the *Sukarno*'s safe distance, they appeared to bloom slowly into bright-white flowers of flame. In contrast, the alien vessel looked to have sustained exactly zero damage.

'Surrender,' Gustav told the admiral simply.

Tang just stared, open-mouthed.

'Surrender, damn you!' Gustav shouted. 'Can't you see? It's over, you fool!'

Gustav's outburst appeared to bring the stunned admiral to his senses. Tang blinked a few times and then turned to Commander Lee.

'Take us back to synchronous Galatean orbit. Full engines,' he said calmly.

The *Sukarno* broke formation and drove across the inner system at low warp. They left behind the battle where the alien starship hung surrounded by gunships, like a grizzly bear set upon by sparrows.

Gustav watched Tang with some concern. Why were they moving so far away from the fight? At this distance, optical lag would make it impossible to issue orders. What could the man be thinking?

As soon as they arrived, Tang gave Lee new instructions.

'Charge the suntap. Point the primary g-ray at the planet's surface. Target the city of Perseverance.'

Lee gawped at him. A gamma-ray laser fired straight at the city would vaporise it instantly.

'You heard me,' Tang said harshly.

Lee nodded and set to work at his console.

'Tang, don't be a fool!' Gustav urged. Tang didn't reply.

Lee cleared his throat. 'Suntap charging, sir,' he said. It was almost a whisper. 'Power delivery in eight minutes twenty seconds.'

'Fire when ready,' said Tang.

Gustav glanced at the monitor displaying the schematics of the battle. The Galateans didn't appear to have noticed the *Sukarno*'s withdrawal. They had their hands too full, even if they still didn't appear to be taking any damage.

'Tang!' he pleaded. 'Are you listening to me? Turn off the damned gun!' When that got no response, he tried another tack. 'Commander Lee, deactivate the suntap.'

'Ignore the general,' Tang said quickly. 'He is relieved of duty.'

Gustav glanced at Rodriguez in the hope of more support, but Rodriguez appeared to have changed again. He sat rapt, staring at the admiral as if in awe.

'Don't you realise what you're doing?' Gustav shouted. 'You're risking the Earth! What do you suppose the Galateans will do when they've finished demolishing your fleet?'

'They will submit,' said Tang. 'They have one world. We have twelve. They cannot win and I am tired of wasting time.'

The man had lost his mind if he thought the Galateans would just give up. He could be bringing about the deaths of billions. The truth was that Tang simply couldn't tolerate losing. He'd rather destroy everything they'd worked for.

Gustav looked back and forth between Tang and the monitor wall as the counter ticked down. He realised with terrible clarity that the moment had come to make an executive decision. He pulled the automatic out of his pocket, the same gun he'd carried with him every day since the trouble with the *Ariel* started. He pointed it at Tang's head.

'Turn off the suntap,' he said again.

'Lieutenant Gul, please arrest the general,' Tang said with a sigh. He didn't even look away from the monitor wall.

The lieutenant floated up from his couch by the door, reluctance plain on his face. He reached for his own weapon.

Gustav couldn't wait any longer. He shot Tang in the head. Tang flopped forwards as his brain sprayed across the cabin.

There was a moment of stunned silence on the bridge.

'I am now the senior officer aboard this ship,' Gustav announced. 'You will follow my orders. Commander Lee, deactivate the suntap immediately. Order the withdrawal of all ships.'

Lee stared at Gustav in blank panic and glanced for a moment at Rodriguez. Gustav swung around and trained the weapon on the disciple's face.

'Any man who obeys the general will answer to the Prophet,' said Rodriguez in a loud, almost jubilant voice. His arms remained folded across his chest. He regarded Gustav levelly, his eyes bright with zeal. 'So we see your true colours at last, General.'

'Yes!' Gustav shouted back. 'I will not stand by and watch

genocide!' He glanced quickly at Gul, who thankfully hadn't moved a muscle. 'Listen to me,' Gustav told the assembled officers. 'Rodriguez has no formal power here. You do not need to listen to him. Ask yourselves if you wish to be a party to this act. Use the g-ray deterrent against Galatea and you legitimise their taking *that ship* to Earth.'

'Turn off the ray and face the wrath of the High Church!' Rodriguez countered. His face broke into a beatific smile. 'I was confused when I first laid eyes on that monster,' he told the crew, his voice taking on the sing-song tones of a sermon. 'For a moment, my faith wavered. For our enemies, so thick in sin, to be handed so great a weapon horrified me. Had God abandoned us, I asked myself. I could not see what he intended. I even wondered for a moment if the general here might have been right all along! Then when Tang brought us to this spot, I understood. The Lord has merely raised the stakes again, my children! He wishes the Galateans dead and, in return, he will give us their ship! We must be fearless! We must act in his name regardless of the threat to ourselves! If that means we risk the Earth, then so be it.'

Rodriguez pointed a quavering finger at Gustav's chest. 'You cannot win,' he intoned, his sanity clearly at breaking point. 'Your career is already over. Put down your gun and submit before God!'

There was a coughing sound from Gustav's right. A red stain spread across Rodriguez's snow-white ship-suit. The disciple's eyes widened in surprise. He looked down at the wound and touched it with his outstretched finger.

'Oh,' he said, and promptly died.

Gustav turned to see Lieutenant Gul staring at the dead man, his gun hanging from his limp hand.

'I don't want to risk the Earth,' Gul said simply.

Gustav snapped into action. 'Commander Lee, follow my orders, please.'

Lee's hands flew to the control board. 'Suntap deactivated, sir. Retreat and surrender orders have already been sent to the fleet.'

Gustav exhaled and the tension went out of his body. He would have laughed if he hadn't felt so exhausted all of a sudden.

'Prepare to deliver our command codes to the Galatean captain with my compliments,' he said and slumped into his seat.

19.5: WILL

Will watched the Earther ships pull away with mingled elation and relief. Something about the battle had weighed heavy on his heart.

'Broadcast from General Ulanu,' said Hugo.

'Put it up,' Ira told him.

Ulanu's long, sober face appeared. 'Captain Baron, we surrender unconditionally. Furthermore, you should know that Admiral Tang, the man who ordered both the attack on your world and your ship, is dead. Please regard all Earther forces that remain as non-threatening. I have given the order for our troops to be removed from the surface of your planet, but that may take some time.'

Cheering erupted aboard the *Ariel Two*. The crew broke out of their couches and hugged each other. Rachel and Will embraced.

'You did it!' Rachel exclaimed. 'You beat them.'

Ira grabbed Will's shoulder. 'Thank you, Will,' he said. 'We owe this to you.'

Will shook his head. 'We owe it to the help we got.'

Ira cocked an eyebrow. 'I think your Transcended friends would disagree.'

Hugo shook Will's hand. 'Well done,' he said, a little shyly. 'Whatever happens next, at least we know we achieved this much.'

Will nodded and smiled.

Ira clapped his hands together. 'Okay, people, it's time to reply. The good general is waiting.'

Will took a deep breath and spoke. 'Tell him we accept on one condition.'

'And what's that?' said Ira.

'That General Ulanu comes to our ship. I want him with us for the job we're doing next.'

Rachel looked confused. 'What do you mean, Will? It's over, isn't it?'

Will sighed and shook his head. 'I'm afraid not. The Transcended charged me with convincing my species to change. I haven't even started yet.'

Ira peered at him. 'You want to go to Earth.'

Will nodded. 'You don't have to come with me. I can run the ship with SAPs. It'll be less efficient, of course—'

Rachel grabbed him by the waist. 'I wouldn't miss it for anything.'

Will looked to the others. Hugo grimaced, something of the old pain surfacing in his eyes.

'If they will suffer, I wish to see it,' the scientist admitted.

Ira considered for a second, then nodded once. 'Okay. Let's go and talk to the Prophet.'

19.6: GUSTAV

Gustav waited patiently as his docking pod crawled out to the aperture that had appeared in the side of the alien vessel. He watched the monstrosity looming in the monitor window with all the calmness he could muster. If it was his fate to lose, he was determined to do it with dignity.

The last few hours had been some of the hardest of his life. He'd asked himself a dozen times since he surrendered if he'd made the right choice. He'd given in to the genetic racists. Was anything worth that? His decision would affect not only the people of Earth, but in all likelihood their children and their children's children. Yet, even so, a struggling Earth had to be better than no Earth at all. Gustav refused to risk genocide, even if that made him a coward.

The price for his decision, it appeared, was to become a prisoner of war – a token in an unpleasant political game. Gustav was ready for that. He would turn this twist of fate to his advantage if he could and use it to bargain on behalf of his people. Maybe being so close to his enemies meant he could find new ways to fight his people's economic oppression.

The pod locked home. Its door slid back to reveal the interior of another pod just like it. Will Kuno-Monet floated there in a shipsuit, apparently unarmed.

Gustav was surprised to see one of his adversaries so exposed. He'd expected treachery or violence, but not this. That was why he still carried his executive automatic. It sat in the bottom of his pocket, waiting. It occurred to him that he might take the initiative and use it now. However, he was not so much of a fool as to initiate new violence on the Galateans' own ship. Not yet, anyway. He'd let the Galateans bring him to their habitat core first, before deciding whether to use it.

'Hello, General,' said the roboteer.

'Good afternoon, Mr Monet.'

Monet gestured at his own pod. 'Please, step aboard, there's quite a long way still to go.'

Gustav floated over the threshold and hovered next to the Galatean. As the door shut behind him, Gustav felt an episode of his life ending with it. He breathed deeply as the pod gently accelerated into the bowels of the alien ship.

'I've prepared one of the secondary habitat modules for your personal use,' said Monet. 'It's just next to the one where we're keeping the prisoners from the rescue of the *Nanshan*. You'd be surprised how many commandos your people left behind.'

Gustav's spirits dipped a little further. 'Am I to assume, then, that I too will be a prisoner here?' he said.

Monet shook his head. 'No. Far from it – I want your help.'

'I can't imagine what with,' said Gustav.

'To help arrange your planet's unconditional surrender.'

Gustav shut his eyes. Of course. He was a fool to have believed even for a moment that the Galateans would restrain themselves as he had done. He wondered how long it would be before a g-ray was pointed straight at Bogotá. He tried not to feel sick.

The pod ride ended at another airlock.

'Please, after you,' said Monet.

Gustav steeled himself and pushed through the doorway into a circular tunnel. It opened onto a near-spherical chamber that had been laid out as an extremely spacious and comfortable cabin. The standard Kingdom fleet bunk bed and wash cubicle bolted to the floor looked ridiculous surrounded by so much room. The Galateans had also set up a desk with a computer console for him. It was better than Gustav had expected. Nevertheless, it was still a prison cell.

Gustav smiled wryly. 'Far nicer than my current accommodations. I am very grateful for your attention and good treatment, Mr Monet, but I will have to disappoint you. I have no intention of betraying my world or my people.'

Monet fixed him with an oddly penetrating glance. 'I am seeking your help,' he said, 'and I'm prepared to ask nicely. If you're prepared to cooperate, you will find me to be surprisingly flexible.'

Gustav snorted in amusement, recognising his own words. 'Yes. An interesting reversal of fortunes since our last conversation, is it not?'

Will shrugged. 'Last time we met, you left me to be tortured while you came here to subdue my world. I will not do that to you.'

Gustav frowned. 'You misjudge me,' he said. 'I was not given a choice. I had no desire to leave you to the High Church, or to come here.'

'We all have choices, General,' said Will.

Gustav curled his lip. 'How quaint and naïve of you to say so.'

'Is it?' Monet replied darkly. 'Then I shall be quaint. I will explain to you what I intend to do and then give you a choice. You can either help me, or you can refuse. If you refuse, no harm will come to you. I will release you on Earth, unharmed.'

'You seek to threaten me by delivering me into the custody of the Prophet,' Gustav remarked dryly. 'No such luck, Mr Monet. My fate is already sealed. He will reach me wherever you set me down.'

Monet looked unimpressed. 'I have no desire to threaten you in any way. I'll land you wherever the hell you like when this is over. In the meantime, why don't you listen to what I have to say before assuming I'm playing some kind of mind game with you?'

Gustav spread his hands in a gesture of appeasement. It couldn't hurt to listen.

'Speak, then,' he said, arranging his features into an expression of polite attentiveness. 'Tell me what you have in mind.'

'I'm going to take this ship to Earth,' said Monet. 'I'm going to broadcast the truth of what we found to the entire planet. And then I'm going to demand they replace the Truist government with one that will cooperate with the Transcended. Ideally, I'd like you to lead it.'

Gustav laughed in his face. 'Be your puppet, in other words. Why, Mr Monet, I'm touched. But let me ask you – what in God's name gave you the impression that I'd be prepared to be Galatea's lapdog?'

'I'm not looking for a lapdog,' Monet replied coldly. 'And I chose you because you're the one Truist I've met who appears capable of seeing reason. You specifically said you believed the people of Earth should hear about the aliens. That's why I told you the truth that day in the cell.'

'The truth,' Gustav sneered. 'You told me that a race of ancient extraterrestrials had decided Galatea should win the war. I still find that rather hard to swallow.'

Monet folded his arms. 'Perhaps I didn't explain myself properly. The Transcended are not interested in our wars. What they want is an end to governance based on ignorance, and for our species to accept genetic modification and use it wisely.'

'The same thing,' said Gustav. 'You still expect me to believe that an advanced race condones genetic racism?'

'What's *racist* about modification?' Will snapped suddenly.

Gustav stared at the Galatean and then shook his head sadly. 'Can you really not see it? You who were bred to talk to machines? Humans should not be tinkered with like farm animals, Mr Monet. Because there will always be the designers and the designed. The owners and the slaves.'

'The Transcended have let us live *precisely* because it does not have to be that way,' Monet retorted. 'The requirement for our survival is for us to change without resorting to that.'

'Then what are we changing *for*?' Gustav demanded. 'If your Transcended are so interested in social justice, then we cannot be changing in the name of commerce or power. So what is it? What's wrong with simply having justice between *humans*?'

'Because it doesn't last!' said Monet, exasperated. 'Look at us.' He threw his arms wide. 'Why are we even fighting? We're destroying ourselves. Think what your precious humanity expends its energies on. Exactly those things you claim to despise: blind faith and callous exploitation. The same behaviours that have crippled us for our entire history. They're what ruined the Earth, for crying out loud! And did your people learn anything from that? No! The only force you could find that was strong enough to bind yourselves together was something even more brutal than what you had before.'

Gustav's hackles rose. That was a little too close to the truth for comfort.

'It doesn't have to be like that,' he said.

'Doesn't it?' said Monet. 'Thanks to technology, we live in a time when one ignorant man has the power to destroy millions with the flick of a switch. And unless human nature changes, there will always be powerful people who choose ignorance.'

'You're wrong,' said Gustav bitterly. 'It's poverty that creates fanatics, not human nature. And it's inequality that causes poverty. The genetic modification you're talking about *is* inequality. It binds inequality into our very cells.'

'Then how come Galatea hasn't destroyed itself in a blaze of injustice?' Monet demanded.

'Because it's *rich*!'

It was Monet's turn to laugh. Once again, Gustav considered killing him.

'Galatea's not rich!' he jeered.

'Isn't it?' Gustav snapped back. 'How else would you describe a world where everyone has more food and living space than they can possibly use? Where robots wait on you hand and foot!'

'I'd call it desperate. On the world where I grew up we *had* to cooperate because the alternative to pulling together was death for everyone.'

Gustav's almost spat his reply. 'You naïve little man! What do you suppose the Earth has been like since your ancestors left it to rot?'

'If it was so damned bad, why did your people build warships the moment you pulled yourselves together?' Will snarled, his hands shaking. 'Warships which you used to attack worlds that bore you no ill will.'

'To break the cycle of poverty! Or are you going to tell me that Galatean traders had no intention of exploiting our population?'

'Yes!' Will shouted, his face red with anger. 'What the fuck would we want the Earth for now? You left us in the fucking lurch back when you started murdering each other and we learned to do things for ourselves. There's *no one* on Galatea who's interested in exploiting the Earth. We're too busy trying to stay alive. Earth and Galatea are *not* the same. Your air never ran out because someone forgot to close a valve. You never saw a city crushed to death in a sandstorm. The Earth is still cosy enough for you to squabble over it. Your supposed suffering stems from the fact that you let people believe in *bullshit* without suffering the consequences. Well, guess what? Game's over.'

'Yes! The game *is* over, Mr Monet,' Gustav shouted back. 'So at least have the courtesy to admit the real reason why you're going to take over the Earth rather than blaming your actions on some aliens you have never spoken to!'

Will's eyebrows shot up. 'You doubt me? After all this, you still don't believe in the Transcended?'

'Would you, in my shoes?' said Gustav, disgusted. 'Where's the proof? I spent two years studying the Relic and I never heard a word of what you claim. For all I know, you stole this ship along with that artefact you found. You ransacked the Relic and now you're making up a convenient story to justify your revolting intentions.'

Monet stared at him long and hard. The silence stretched. Then the Galatean spoke again.

'Give me that gun in your pocket, General.'

Gustav tensed. 'Why?'

'I want to show you something.'

Gustav pressed his lips together. It didn't look like he had a great deal of choice. If Monet could scan him without his noticing, there were probably a dozen concealed weapons pointing at him right now. He slowly removed the weapon from his pocket and passed it reluctantly to the roboteer.

Monet took the gun. To Gustav's surprise, the Galatean pressed the barrel against the tip of his own thumb.

'Watch,' he said, and fired. His blood spattered across the immaculate decor.

To Gustav's astonishment, Monet's eyes never wavered. No pain registered on his face. The roboteer held his ruined hand out before him. The top of his thumb was nothing but a ragged mess of blood and bone.

'Look at it,' Monet ordered.

Gustav dragged his eyes away from the Galatean's fierce gaze and stared. New flesh was growing out of the ruined tissue at incredible speed. Gustav's skin crawled as he watched the new digit swell and quiver. This was not the work of Galatean modding. This was something else.

'They remade me, from the inside out,' said Monet, tossing the gun idly aside. '*Now* do you believe me? Or are you going to convince yourself that I stole the means to rebuild my body, too?'

In a moment of ugly comprehension, Gustav realised that the roboteer had been telling the truth, at least as he saw it. The aliens really were on his side. Monet's escape from the prison at New Angeles was suddenly a lot easier to understand.

But if Monet was to be trusted, that meant the suntap really was poisoned. And the Earth had been under threat from the moment he, Gustav Ulanu, had assembled the very first one. His mind cowered from the implications. Apparently his words to Rodriguez had been more pertinent than he'd realised. They were *already* at war with an advanced civilisation. They had been for years.

Gustav drew an uneven breath and met Monet's eyes once more.

'Temporarily, at least, you have convinced me,' he said, as evenly as he could muster.

His mind struggled to create a more mundane explanation for the thumb. There were plenty he could think of – psychotropic drugs sprayed on him as he'd entered the ship, holograms, a prosthesis. None of them had the ring of truth. Why would the Galateans bother to arrange so elaborate a ploy? And none of them had known he'd bring his automatic on board. He had to assume the Transcended were real.

It was therefore also highly likely that Monet believed everything he'd said about their intentions for mankind. Peace through genetic engineering still sounded like a lie to Gustav. So what did they really want? Clearly, they weren't bent on the destruction of the human race. With ships like this at their disposal, they could have achieved such a goal already. Nor did their intention appear to be to protect the human race, as the policy they were requiring looked certain to dissolve the definition of humanity altogether. They must want humanity alive for some other purpose.

'Do you completely trust these Transcended?' said Gustav.

'No,' Monet replied. 'But I trust them enough.'

'What is the purpose of all this modification?'

'To evolve and join them.'

The roboteer reddened slightly as he delivered this line. He didn't look that comfortable with the notion, either.

'Those species they consider likely to survive they help develop,' he added, sounding less confident than ever.

The skin prickled on the back of Gustav's neck. That sounded a lot like farming.

'I see. And did they tell you what kind of modifications we're supposed to get?'

'It doesn't work like that,' said Monet. 'They didn't intervene to tell us what to become.'

'Yet they chose to communicate with you specifically, I gather.'

Monet nodded. 'Yes.'

'Because you're a roboteer.'

'I suppose so.'

'So perhaps we should create a whole generation of roboteers?' Gustav suggested.

'Perhaps,' Monet replied stonily.

The irony in Gustav's voice appeared to have completely passed the roboteer by. A whole generation of autistic computer people for the aliens to tinker with. Gustav could think of nothing more likely to reduce mankind to the status of pliant machinery.

'Did it ever occur to you that there must have been species that developed without external help?' he said. 'That you may simply have been talking to the biggest bullies in the playground?'

Monet grimaced. 'Yes,' he snapped. 'Of course it did. But that doesn't mean it's true. For all we know, they could be the teachers, there to stop the fighting. But who they are is irrelevant. They hold the power. The role of humanity in this galaxy is about to change, and we all have to be ready for that. We have to stand together.'

Gustav nodded to himself. That much was evidently true. But to what end? In his experience, higher powers seldom had altruistic motives. It appeared likely that in their eagerness to win the war, Monet and his kind had delivered them into the hands of something vast and terrible.

Except that he, Gustav Ulanu, had started it. He was the one who'd gone seeking the secrets of the ancients. He was as much to blame as anyone. A tight knot of guilt formed in his stomach.

'Forgive me if I am not filled with enthusiasm for the new golden age,' he said, his voice less steady than he'd have liked.

'I don't care if you are or not,' said Monet. 'I just want you to help me bring the news to Earth.'

The Galatean was asking Gustav to inform his people that they'd failed. That despite all their efforts, they had overlords yet again. And this time they wouldn't be as easy to topple as a few colony worlds.

'The truth will be broadcast with or without your help,' Monet said firmly. 'The government *will* be changed. You have an opportunity to help make the society that follows it a reasonable one. The choice is yours.'

Gustav swallowed and shut his eyes. Nausea closed his throat. In all likelihood, Monet was asking him to usher in a new era of servitude. It went against everything he'd lived for.

'I cannot,' he croaked.

'Fine, then,' the roboteer snapped. 'I'm wasting my time.' He pushed himself up to the airlock. 'Sorry we can't see eye to eye, General. I'll speak to you later.'

The airlock slammed behind him with a thud.

Gustav floated motionless in the centre of the room and concentrated on his breathing. He covered his face with his hands. He, Gustav Ulanu, had opened Pandora's box. Perhaps it was fitting that he should be the one to tell the world what he'd done, though he knew it would break his heart to do it. The knot of guilt inside him swelled and festered.

Was it so wrong of him to have sought knowledge? Was it so wrong to believe that science and reason could save mankind? Even now, he found it hard to accept that ignorance would have been better. If curiosity wasn't worth the risk, then his entire life had been a cruel joke.

Something nudged his elbow. He looked down and saw the executive automatic slowly turning there. Gustav grabbed it, flicked off the safety and brought the gun slowly around to sit against his temple. He didn't believe in an afterlife, but still found himself thinking of the things he'd miss. His work, mostly – those wonderful days when it felt like he was unlocking the secrets of the universe. Before everything went sour. He began to squeeze the trigger.

'Please don't,' said a soft voice from behind him.

Gustav froze.

Monet drifted back into the room. 'It's not worth resorting to that.'

'Isn't it?' Gustav said hollowly. 'What exactly do I have to live for? I will not become a slave, and I would rather not see that fate befall my people.'

'No one is going to enslave you,' said Monet.

Gustav snorted in amusement. 'Wait and see, roboteer. Power always comes at a price.'

The Galatean sighed. 'Is it so hard for you to believe that the future might be good?'

'A good future is a free one,' Gustav replied. 'In a good future, there are no monsters looking over your shoulder.'

Monet was silent for a moment. When he spoke again, there was contempt in his voice as well as pity.

'We've never been free,' he said. 'And there have always been monsters. The only difference is that now we have to face them.' He shrugged. 'I thought you a rational man, General. Yet here you are, ready to end your life on the basis of a belief you can't let go of, just like the rest of your church.'

Gustav stiffened.

'Why don't you wait around and see what happens before assuming the worst?' said the roboteer. He turned and dragged himself back out of the room. The airlock closed a second time.

Gustav breathed deep. His finger tensed on the trigger again but this time he lacked the will to pull it. Will's words kept ringing in his head. If Gustav lived and died for an unsubstantiated belief, in the end how different was he from Rodriguez?

He let the gun slip out of his grasp and tumble slowly away from him. He'd made enough bad decisions. Perhaps he should gather some more data before he made another. Gustav buried his face in his hands once more and quietly began to weep.

20: ULTIMATUM

20.1: WILL

Ira brought the *Ariel Two* out of warp fourteen light-hours from Sol to survey their destination. They didn't dare come any closer. As soon as the Earthers got wind of their approach, things would become complicated.

The home star hung dead ahead of them, an innocent-looking point of light, little different from the billions of others that surrounded it. Yet the sight of it deepened the mood of impending finality that already suffused the *Ariel Two*'s improvised bridge.

Nobody spoke. The import of what they were about to do quashed conversation. Inhabited worlds were eggshell-delicate things. If they put one foot wrong in the home system, they'd either plunge humanity back into war or perpetrate the worst genocide the human race had ever seen. Even if their mission succeeded, their mark would shape human history for centuries to come.

Hugo tuned the communication array to sweep for broadcasts from Earth. To Will's surprise, what emerged from the cabin speakers was not military code but dance music. He shared a confused glance with Rachel before flicking his attention to the video feed. It showed people celebrating – millions of them, in rallies that spanned the globe. Apparently, as far as Earth was concerned, it had already won.

Will brought up another other channel to find footage of mass parties. Another showed speeches by jubilant subsect leaders. He flicked through the spectrum, finding the same pattern everywhere.

'...usher in a new era of peace and order...'

'...the Sons of Mao. Our only limit now is our imagination!'

'...give thanks, and remember those who sacrificed their lives saving human space from the twin sins of capitalism and genetic fascism...'

Will found it all rather chilling and ironic. The home world still had no idea that Galatea had been freed. But then, of course, how could they? The *Ariel Two* had only just arrived, travelling at nearly twice the warp of any Earther vessel. The celebrations, he realised, had probably been going on for days.

'I thought this might happen,' said Ira, watching the feed with a sour expression.

'Tang's report from the invasion fleet must have triggered this,' said Rachel. 'He basically let them think he finished us.'

'And why not?' said Ira bitterly. 'What was left? Saint Andrews, Destiny and Kurikov – three pitiful minor colonies who couldn't even put up a fight if they tried. And the High Church doesn't care that our Fleet got their evacuation arcs off in time. They're stealthed and travelling at sub-light. Where are they supposed to go?'

He killed the audio and turned to fix Will with a grim stare. 'Are you still sure you want to do this?' he said. 'This won't be the same as retaking Galatea. Even if we're lucky and they're celebrating so hard that they barely notice us, this is Sol we're talking about. We can expect more weapons, more panic and more hatred than you've ever seen. Twelve billion people are going to feel like you pissed all over their brand-new golden age before it even started. You need to be ready for that, because taking lives is not likely to be optional here. And even with a ship like this one, there's no guarantee we'll get out of here alive. We still have no idea what the *Ariel Two* can really do – or what its limits are.'

Will regarded the silent images of grinning faces and waving flags.

'We have to do this,' he said. 'Who else is there? Humanity needs to know, and it won't be easier later.'

Ira nodded. 'That's what I thought you'd say.' He turned back to his controls.

'Wait,' said Will.

Ira shot him a quizzical glance.

'I want Gustav here in the primary core with us.'

Ira's eyebrows rose. 'In here? While we face down the entire Kingdom? Are you in your right mind?'

'We need him,' said Will. 'Who else is going to help us manage a peaceful Earth if we succeed – the Prophet Sanchez? And if this ship is damaged, our last line of defence should be protecting one core, not two.'

Ira sighed. 'This is your show, Will. And you have a point, unfortunately.'

Will glanced over at Hugo to find the scientist looking at him with an oddly pained expression, his mouth pressed into a thin line. He looked away.

'If he tries to stop us, I will kill him,' said Hugo simply.

Ira snorted. 'Not if I get there first.'

Will wondered who'd actually be most at risk when they were all in the same room: them from Ulanu, or Ulanu from them.

He called the general's cabin. Ulanu looked up into the camera, his mahogany face as unreadable as wood.

'I'm sending you a docking pod,' said Will. 'I invite you to join us on the bridge. I recommend not bringing your gun.'

Ulanu's eyes narrowed. He stared at Will for a full twenty seconds before opening his mouth. 'I accept,' he said at last.

'Thank you,' said Will. 'See you shortly.' He killed the link and leaned back in his couch, hoping he hadn't made a dreadful mistake.

Ten minutes later, Ulanu drifted into the core, escorted by two maintenance robots Will had assigned, just in case.

He nodded to Ira. 'Captain.'

'General,' said Ira curtly.

'We're headed into the home system,' said Will, gesturing for Ulanu to take a seat on the couch he'd prepped. 'Do you have any recommendations for our approach?'

'Of course,' said Ulanu. 'By coming here, you risk the vast majority of the human race. How could I not want to advise you? First, the Kingdom will not take you seriously without a show of force. Without it, they will assume that any video footage of your actions at Galatea is doctored and that your arrival is a desperate ploy. I have tried to think of a way around this, but I cannot.

'Therefore you will have to make a point where they can see it. However, do it anywhere near Earth and you are likely to butcher millions. Do it too far away and it will take too long for the Kingdom to notice and respond. I therefore recommend the fleet shipyards at Ceres. The population there is tiny – a standard complement of fifty-five. However, the facility's value to the Kingdom is enormous. The defences are formidable, though not on the scale that this ship has already faced.'

'Why should we trust you?' said Hugo bluntly.

Gustav shot him a dry look. 'You don't have to. I was asked to give my opinion.'

Will brought a schematic of Ceres up in his sensorium, borrowing security details from the database core they had taken from the *Nanshan*. He saw a dozen ships – three heavy cruisers and nine gunships – along with extensive drone support from silos on the asteroid's surface. Before the *Ariel Two*, such a target would have been considered borderline suicidal. In the wake of Galatea, it looked like a couple of hours' work.

'What do you think?' he asked Ira.

Ira snorted. 'The Fleet have wanted to nail Ceres since the start of the war. It's never been an option. It's two-point-seven AU out, which means twenty-four minutes, give or take, for suntaps. That's a long wait. But the major fleets at Earth and Mars won't be able to respond in under thirty, which means we only have to take out local defences on our antimatter reserves.'

Will nodded. Gustav had chosen well. Ceres was big enough to get Earth's attention, but empty enough to not make them look like murderers. He wondered if they could trust Ulanu not to lead them into disaster. There was no way of telling how much the General's loyalties had shifted since their last conversation.

'You've been thinking about this,' he said, eyeing Ulanu's impassive face.

'How could I not? I have thought about little else since we left Galatea. The responsibility you wish to saddle me with is... unspeakable.' A brief tremor of emotion curled the general's lip. 'So let us understand each other. My cooperation hinges upon two conditions. Violate them and I will do my best to destroy you.

'The first is that I will not aid you in fighting my own people. I will not lift so much as a finger to help you kill Kingdom citizens, not even if my own life depends upon it. And I will not let you paint me as a traitor. Prior to our arrival at Earth, any statements of war you wish to make, you will make for yourselves. Is that clear?'

Will nodded. 'I would expect nothing less.'

'Secondly,' said Ulanu, raising a single, quivering finger, 'you brought me here to speak to the Prophet. That I will do. But we do it my way. Once you hand me control over communications, I expect no interference. None. Even if you do not understand my choices, you will respect them.'

'Works for me,' said Will. 'If we're going to trust you to handle Earth, we may as well start now.' He turned to Ira. 'Captain, I propose we lay in a course for Ceres.'

Ira regarded them both with a look of nervous uncertainty. 'Okay,' he said. 'Let's get this fucking war over and done with.' He brought the ship back up to warp and took them in-system as fast as the *Ariel Two* could fly.

It was not lost on Will as they dived crazily sunwards that this was his first ever visit to the home system. Before him lay the setting for every adventure story that had shaped his childhood and every great event that had informed his civilisation. Yet there would be no time for sightseeing. He was not here to enjoy history, only to make it. And possibly, if things went badly, to end it.

He, Hugo and Rachel all anxiously manned the sensors, watching for signs of attack while the pull of warp pummelled them into their couches. Gustav, meanwhile, lay on his couch, his eyes screwed tight shut as if to block out his own role in the affair.

The closer they came, the more the *Ariel Two*'s velocity dropped as Sol's radiation cluttered the enormous ship's warp field.

Ira broke the hush. 'Hitting sub-light speeds in ten, nine, eight...'

At sub-light, picking up a drone tail was inevitable even if they hadn't done so already. Since the Drexler colony's last desperate attempt to attack Earth two years ago, the home system had been littered with defensive munitions. There were millions of them, pumped out by automated factories. When *Ariel Two* slowed for orbit, they would catch up and smash themselves against the hull.

'Disrupter cloud, dead ahead,' Rachel warned. Will followed her marker and saw a billowing streamer of darkness stretched across the space before them, whole light-seconds on a side. That was the other issue with the home system: patrolling swarms of disrupters dumped smears of ionic crap at random intervals. While the chance of getting trapped in so vast a space was small, it still constituted a serious risk. Ira veered around the cloud, piling on the gees.

'I'm seeing our tail,' said Hugo. 'Fifty-nine drones and counting. Our lead is at seventeen seconds.'

'Another cloud,' said Rachel. 'Sending you the bearing.'

Ira veered again. Everyone in the cabin held their breath.

'Lead at nine seconds,' said Hugo. 'Drone tail up to three hundred and fourteen.'

Will's skin prickled with anticipation as they slowed towards Ceres. The approach seemed to last for ever. The drone tail slowly closed on them. He itched to act.

'Closing on Ceres in five, four, three...'

Ira dropped warp.

'Shields *now*!'

Will was already on it. The quagitators flared into life and wave upon wave of missiles erupted against the exohull in blasts of blinding incandescence. The drone barrage at Galatea had been nothing by comparison. Groans like some dying leviathan echoed through the ship as its entire structure flexed.

'Exohull stability at eighty per cent,' Rachel reported. 'Now sixty-five.'

'Firing suntaps,' said Hugo. 'Power in twenty-three minutes and forty seconds.'

The bombardment slowed and died in a final rumble of thunder. It took a full minute for the glare around them to fade. As it did so, the crew of the *Ariel Two* got their first proper look at Ceres.

Military engineering had transformed the asteroid into a dandelion head of orbital towers and construction frames. It was as if the tiny world had been taken over by enormous metal trees bearing huge surreal fruit. The fruit were starships. Will could see at least twenty under simultaneous construction.

'Holy shit,' said Rachel.

Galatea had nothing like this place. There'd have been no point – they didn't have the crews to man ships produced in such quantities. It put in perspective why the Earthers had been so hard to beat.

Ira sent the shipyard a hail on the truce channel. An astonished face appeared: a jowly military commander in a black dress jacket pulled over a canary yellow casual one-piece. Will could see decorations hanging in the cabin in the background – flags in the colours of all subsects.

'Unidentified ship!' the commander shouted. 'Who the hell are you and what in the Prophet's name is going on?' Outrage and panic were fighting for control of the man's face.

'This is the Galatean Starship *Ariel Two*,' said Ira smoothly. 'This facility has been selected for destruction to make a demonstration for your government. We are giving you advance warning to evacuate your staff and withdraw your defensive fleet before firing commences. We would like to minimize loss of life, so we implore you to take this recommendation seriously.'

The commander blinked at him in disbelief. 'Is this a joke? Galatea has already fallen. Everyone knows this. The war is over.'

'We liberated it,' said Ira. 'You have fifteen minutes to get your people out. Escape shuttles will not be targeted. That is all.' He killed the link and rubbed his eyes. 'Anyone want to take bets?' he said darkly.

Mere seconds later, the Ceres defensive fleet undocked and started to manoeuvre. At the same time, drones started pouring out of the surface of the asteroid in long streams.

'I guess they didn't need the fifteen minutes,' said Ira.

He backed the *Ariel Two* away. The drones kept coming and coming until there were so many it was ridiculous. There were thousands of them.

'Holy shit, again,' said Rachel.

'I told you the defences were formidable,' said Ulanu.

The *Ariel Two* wasn't moving nearly fast enough to avoid such a large drone swarm. Fresh impacts flared against the exohull.

'Will, thin that crowd, would you?' said Ira.

While the Fecund shield had done an excellent job at fending off g-rays, it clearly did less well against persistent physical bombardment on this scale. Will started picking off missiles with targeted g-ray bursts but found himself struggling almost immediately. With so many targets to keep track of, a lot of them were getting past him.

'Shield stability is back down to seventy per cent and falling,' said Rachel.

Suddenly, showing up unannounced in the home system was starting to look like a bad idea. Will needed more mental bandwidth for targeting. He pressed his thoughts deeper into the nestship's network, imploring his smart-cells to help him compensate. Something shifted inside his mind. His head swam for a moment, then abruptly the swarm of incoming missiles leapt into sharper focus, their flight vectors forming an easily comprehensible weave. Time slowed to a crawl.

'That's more like it,' he muttered.

He let the hidden patterns in the drone flight paths guide him. Two hundred simultaneous lances of hard light seared out from the *Ariel Two*, yielding two hundred direct hits. Will raked through the incoming munitions, toppling them like dominos. He realised with surprise that the drone wave was almost spent already. But the Ceres fleet had yet to act. He watched the starships position themselves to release another volley.

'Make your point,' said Gustav quietly. 'Quickly. The Ceres crew will never evacuate now. They would rather see you dead. Do it decisively and spare lives elsewhere.'

Will stared down at the factories below. Ira had been right. This *did* feel different from the battle for Galatea. This time he was the intruder – the one purposefully contemplating murder. Yet when he reached inside himself for a moral compass, all he found was a vision of Amy's screaming face. He just wanted the church finished and the war over. If this was the cost, so be it.

Will fired a tenth-of-a-second boser-blast into the heart of Ceres. The icy mantle of the asteroid erupted in a plume of steam. Shock waves rippled out across the dusty surface causing the orbital towers to sway and snap and the entire delicate structure began to come apart. Gouts of vapour jetted out from the tiny world along fissures miles on a side. They watched in silence as the Ceres facility crumbled in slow motion like a collapsing bridge.

From somewhere in the cabin where his human body sat, Will heard exhalations of surprise at the scale of the destruction. This, Will realised with horror, was a boser's true purpose, not skewering ships. A boser was a world-killer.

The shock of the moment gave way to chaos as the Ceres fleet started to pull desperately away from the *Ariel Two* and their mangled world. They launched a fresh wave of drones, but in a barely organized surge. Whatever they'd expected, it had not been the immediate obliteration of the site they were charged to protect.

Will reached out with his mind again and let the totality of the new assault sink into his extended consciousness. Then, with a twitch of mental muscle, he fired on them. Missiles died like firecrackers.

The Earther ships fell back, desperately throwing out gravity shields as they went. Gravity shields wouldn't do them much good, Will thought. He hadn't launched a single drone since he'd arrived.

'Will, Ira,' said Hugo, 'I'm seeing eight more battleships approaching. Big ones.'

'On what bearing?' said Ira.

'Out-system. They're coming from behind us. Origin unclear. Sending you coordinates.'

'My, how convenient,' Ira growled. 'An attack fleet appears whole minutes before we have suntaps online.'

Will opened his human eyes and saw the captain looking daggers at Ulanu.

'Did you anticipate such a rapid response, General? I thought we had about half an hour before the nearest fleet clued in.'

'I'm as surprised as you are,' said Ulanu, his tone flat. 'We appear to have been unlucky.' It was impossible to tell whether he meant it or not.

'Liar,' said Hugo. 'He set us up. I knew he would. I'm going to kill him.'

'Not while we've still got ships to fight, you're not,' said Ira. 'Leave that chair and I'll break your legs.'

Ira hailed the incoming fleet. 'This is Captain Ira Baron of the liberated world of Galatea. We are here to make a point, not engage in wholesale warfare. Power down your weapons and none of you will be harmed.'

They didn't have to wait long for a response. A man with a narrow, hawk-like face and dramatic eyebrows flashed up in a video window, his face a mask of fury. Will recognised him from the propaganda broadcasts he'd been forced to watch. The man was Admiral Kazak, the so-called 'Colony Crusher'.

'What point is that, Galatean terrorists? In case you hadn't noticed, the war is finished. You lost. The punishment for the murders we just watched you carry out is death. We have beaten you once. We will beat you again. Prepare to receive the wrath of the Kingdom of Man.'

Unlike the gunships at Galatea, these were old-fashioned warbirds – huge ships crammed with autonomous munitions of every kind. As soon as they came close enough to engage, they fired all of them in a full-frontal assault.

Will reeled at the scale of the violence and the lack of strategy behind it. The Earthers, he decided, must be *really* upset. He lurched back into his extended senses and the new swarm before him slowed as if dropped into treacle. He started picking off drones again with flickering beams like a pianist's fingertips dancing over their hulls. It pushed his concentration to the limit, but Will didn't care. What worried him more was that even while he was keeping the lengths of his shots minimal, their antimatter reserves were still dropping. Even if their shield stayed stable, they wouldn't be able to keep up this game for ever. Will checked the suntap countdown. Engagement was still nine minutes away – an eternity in battle time.

'More company,' said Hugo acidly.

Will pulled up the link to look. Another ten ships bore down on them behind the eight. And then behind them, another sixteen. It was as if there had been an entire fleet just waiting for them. The bottom fell out of Will's stomach. The *Ariel Two*, it appeared, had made them badly overconfident.

'How?' said Rachel. 'Where are they coming from?'

The new ships arrived in waves, throwing weapons at the *Ariel Two* with a complete disregard for the caution that normally came with space warfare. In the wake of Ceres, they must have realised that nothing short of a total onslaught would yield results. Will redoubled his efforts, but with attack now coming from so many sides at once, protecting the exohull was impossible. His mind was simply stretched too thin. The augmented concentration started to hurt.

'There's more,' said Hugo, his voice cracking now. 'Far scans indicate a hundred ships and counting.'

'Ulanu!' Ira shouted. 'Tell me what is going on, because even in my wildest dreams of fuck-up, I did not imagine this.'

'I don't know,' Ulanu snapped back. 'I gave you my best assessment.'

'Bullshit!' Ira roared. 'Lie to me one more time and I will snap every bone in your body.'

'And you'll get the same answer,' Ulanu said icily. 'Dispense with the threats, Captain. You are far less frightening than most of the people I've had to work with.'

'It's the celebration,' said Rachel suddenly. 'I just looked up the profiles on those ships – none of them is supposed to be here. The whole fleet must have been recalled to participate. They probably maxed out the docking capacity at Fleet HQ and parked the rest at Jupiter L-Four. Which means we flew straight past them.'

'Great!' said Ira. 'So we walked into a fucking parade.'

While the others talked, Will scrambled to vaporise the endless tide of munitions. His head ached. Breathing had started to become a struggle.

'Exohull stability now at twenty-five per cent,' said Hugo.

The limits of the *Ariel Two*'s capabilities, which had appeared so distant just days ago, now looked immediate and frightening.

'Fuck this,' said Ira. 'Sorry, Will, but we're getting out of here. Ending the war will have to wait.' He hit the reverse thrusters and started trying to back the ship out of the line of fire. 'We'll use what's left of Ceres to shield us till we have enough power to get out of here.'

Will could tell in an instant that Ira didn't have enough control over the ship to make that happen. They were surrounded already and the wrong moves would make the drone assault worse. It would take precision flying – non-human precision flying. Will plucked piloting control away from Ira's desk and did it himself. He routed power from backup systems, shutting down everything non-essential.

'My console is dead,' Ira shouted. 'Monet! What the fuck are you doing?'

'Will!' said Rachel. 'Your data load has gone crazy. Your vitals are spiking.'

Will knew she was right. He still needed more bandwidth – a lot more. He gripped his couch with white-knuckled hands, ordering his smart-cells and the entire ship to compensate. Blood pounded in his ears. His cheeks and fingers tingled as a barrage of weird neurochemical options thundered through his mind. He green-lit every one. Then, at last, his hold on the ship's systems started to swell and stretch. Entire tracts of his neural web throughout the ship appeared to blend directly into his subconscious. He had no idea how his body was doing it, but that was something he could figure out if they lived.

'We're sliding towards their disrupter cloud,' Hugo warned.

Will grabbed Hugo's sensor schematics and made them into extra eyes. He started patching all the remaining ship's systems straight into his interface. As he did so, he was distantly aware of the fact that the other people in the cabin were simply staring at him now. There was nothing left for them to do. He'd taken it all over. He'd explain later, he decided, if they made it.

Will moved as the starship, firing thirty-seven thrusters at once with microsecond-accurate bursts. Simultaneously, he bombarded the enemy with hundreds of g-rays, tiny facets of his personality managing each one. Other parts of him tracked individually every buoy and missile in the blizzard of weapons. He even started to feel the ebb and flow of the suffering quantum shield. He adjusted power to the quagitators, anticipating load before it arrived, balancing what capacity it had left. And one by one, he punched out each starship that swung in to join the fray.

The action became a blur. With a start, Will realised that the entire conflict could be seen as an abstract, higher-dimensional pattern. From that perspective, the untidiness of the attack appalled him. He used its asymmetries against it, nudging the ship this way and that to pit the drones of each craft against each other, just as he'd done back at Memburi. It felt so simple now that it barely deserved comment.

Just as Will's antimatter reserves slid dangerously into the red, the downpour of warheads dwindled and stopped. The remaining ships pulled back – all seventeen of them. Around the *Ariel Two* hung a dense soup of shrapnel and superheated ions.

Will stared at the last Earther vessels in surprise through a thousand lidless electronic eyes, waiting for them to do something. Part of him longed for the battle to restart. He hadn't got to finish tidying up their attack.

He threw a message out on the truce channel. 'Are you done?' he boomed. 'Is that all you've got?'

No reply came. It belatedly occurred to Will that they'd agreed to make Ira the face of their negotiations. Will didn't even know what image of himself his message had projected. Right now it was probably something a little odd. Never mind.

The Earther ships slid back out of targeting range and shifted to form a stationary globe formation with the *Ariel Two* at the centre. Will scowled at them. What were they up to?

'Monet,' said Ulanu, 'I recognize that pattern. The fleet is aligning for a suicide dive.'

With the exohull still radiating frantically, Will knew they wouldn't be able to take a coordinated blast of that magnitude. And amazingly, he still had ninety seconds before suntap engagement. They weren't seconds he could afford. He needed thrust now – and far more than the conventional engines could give him.

Without really thinking about it, Will routed power to the boser, using the super-accelerated iron as reaction mass, and hit all the reverse fusion-torches at the same time. The ship snapped backwards at a crazy angle, out of the field of red-hot debris. Will then threw them sideways, tumbling the huge ship end-over-end. Finally he piled on conventional power until he hit clear space and rammed them into warp. The ship arced around the back of the startled Earther formation and left them in the dust.

Enough messing about, Will thought to himself. It was time to take their point to the Prophet while they still could.

As Will raced towards Earth, antimatter depletion warnings

clanged in the cabin. Non-essential ship functions started shutting down. The quagitators died, leaving the hull a mass of liquefied iron alloy barely held in check by its magnetic brackets.

'Will, what are we doing?' shouted Ira. 'We need charge!'

Will dumped them out of warp a light-second from Earth and fired the suntaps. Any closer and he'd cause mayhem. He'd probably given Earth's partygoers a nasty sunburn as it was.

They now had six minutes of total vulnerability. The simplest conventional weapons could punch a hole in them. Will was gambling that with a two-hundred-and-forty-kilometer-long alien starship hanging over Bogotá, they wouldn't even try.

He opened his human eyes and found everyone staring at him, their eyes wild. And by the state of disarray in the habitat core, it was clear that some of his manoeuvres had shaken things loose.

'What?' he said.

Rachel glanced nervously at Will's hands. He looked down. They'd grown into the couch like bits of melted wax. In fact, all along his forearms, threads of organic matter trailed out, plugging him into every data port within reach. Weird bundles of semi-organic fibre had punched through the floor and hooked themselves up to his legs.

He tried to shrug, but apparently his spine was plugged in, too.

'Ah,' he said. 'Sorry, that looks weird, doesn't it? I needed bandwidth. Nothing to worry about. I think it's all retractable. Hopefully.'

He glanced across at Ulanu. The general peered at him with an expression both pained and astonished.

'General,' he said.

Ulanu kept staring.

'Gustav. You're up.'

'You still trust him after *all that*?' said Ira. 'Are you out of your fucking mind?'

'Yes,' said Will. 'He's what we've got.'

Ulanu ignored the captain and nodded gravely at Will, as if coming to some kind of final peace. He started typing commands into his comms console.

'Open a channel to the following secure address,' he said.

Will reached out to touch the Earth's pervasivenet and made the connection. The ringtone and wait-image they received on the bridge's monitor screens seemed incongruously mundane, given the circumstances.

Eventually, a worried-looking man with a lined face and dark skin appeared. Will could make out a grand white chamber in the background where men in brightly coloured robes were locked in fierce debate.

'Khan here,' the man snapped. 'This had better be good.' Then he caught sight of the face on the screen. 'Gus!' he exclaimed. 'Where are you?'

'I'm aboard the ship that just destroyed our fleet,' said Gustav.

Khan's jaw fell open. He was speechless for a second, then spun around to shout at the men behind him. 'Silence! Ulanu is aboard the intruder. We need order here.'

Several other faces crowded around the monitor as Khan returned his attention to the screen.

'What's going on, Gus?' said Khan. 'Are you a prisoner?'

'Listen carefully,' Ulanu told him. 'What I have to say may be hard for you to accept, so I've assembled an evidence package that I'm sending you on this line. Whatever you think of what I say, you have to hear me out.'

Khan nodded uncertainly.

Ulanu took a deep breath and spoke. 'This ship is an example of the technology available to an extraterrestrial civilisation called the Transcended. They have joined the war and *sided with the Galateans.* The Transcended have delivered us an ultimatum. Unless the Truist government is dismantled and mankind follows a programme they have laid out, they will take steps to extinguish the entire human race. I repeat: *the entire human race*. I am completely convinced of their sincerity.'

Ulanu paused. Every face Will could see on the screen was transfixed. Some of them bore expressions of horror, others of cynical disbelief, but none of them dared speak.

'It is the Galateans' intention to broadcast the truth about the relic and our involvement with it to the entire world,' said Ulanu. 'I will not be able to stop them. If we wish to prevent that, we must convince the Prophet to act instead. Oz, you must take the data I'm sending you directly to him. Then, when you've both looked at it, get back to me as soon as you can. Use this channel. Do you understand?'

'I think so,' said Khan uneasily.

'Good. I look forward to hearing from you.' With that, Ulanu cut the line and exhaled.

'What now?' said Will.

'Now we wait,' replied Ulanu.

The mood on the bridge of the *Ariel Two* was stiff with tension during the minutes that followed. The suntaps came online at last, but by that time Earth's defensive fleet had converged around them. Thankfully, though, they held their fire.

Will watched through the external sensors as the fleet surrounded the nestship like a closing fist, forming the same spherical configuration as they had at Ceres. Drones and disrupter buoys poured forth from the Earther vessels. Gravity shields took up positions and prepared to charge. This close to the planet, there was little they could achieve without causing wholesale apocalypse on the surface. Maybe the Earthers didn't care any more.

An hour passed. The shield cooled. Will sat sweating into his couch, his g-ray banks charged and ready, dreading the implications of another encounter. Then, at last, a call came in on Ulanu's code.

A split-screen image appeared on the monitors, showing two faces Will knew very well. On the left was the man they called the king, the Earth's nominal secular ruler. He had a round, softly handsome face, but weak, watery eyes.

The man on the right was the opposite – a frail and elderly figure with a wrinkled face and eyes like neutron stars. It was the Prophet, Pyotr Sanchez. Will stared at that face and felt a shiver of loathing. Suddenly it was abundantly clear how a weak old man had managed to hold almost every human world in his grasp. Willpower crackled out of him like inducer discharge.

The king regarded Ulanu with something between confusion and disbelief. The Prophet eyed him with raw hate.

'General Ulanu,' said the king.

'Your Majesty.'

'We have seen your evidence. It is startling, but as you know, the Kingdom does not bow to threats. You may tell these Transcended—'

Ulanu cut him off. 'As you will realise if you watched the entire package, your Majesty, the Transcended are interested in neither bargaining nor defiance. The simple presence of this ship in the Earth system is enough to give them access to our sun as a weapon. They will watch our behaviour and annihilate us if they see fit. You have already seen a small demonstration of their capabilities. Most of this was achieved by a *single human pilot* augmented with Transcended technology. I watched that process with my own eyes and I can assure you that we are utterly outmatched. Their ultimatum is not so much a threat as a statement of fact.'

The king's jaw worked from side to side. He was clearly not used to being talked to like this.

'I do not care how you choose to define it, Ulanu,' he said. 'You imagine that you can come here—'

'Quiet, Ramon.' The Prophet's voice was little more than a whisper but cleaved the air like a gunshot. The king reluctantly fell silent.

'I *have* watched your entire package, General,' said the Prophet with a disconcerting smile. 'It made for amusing viewing. Surely you realise it contains nothing that will sway the people of the Earth? Such an announcement as your Galatean friends propose would be immediately dismissed by the Following as propaganda. For all they know, the funny lights in the sky today were nothing more than fireworks. They are farmers and factory workers, Ulanu. They subsist on a diet of rice and faith. They have no interest in aliens. No understanding of starships.'

Sanchez chuckled to himself at the idea. 'You talk of statements of fact,' he said. 'Let me offer you one of my own.' He fixed Ulanu with a steely gaze.

Watching through his sensorium, Will felt the weight of those eyes upon him and shivered.

'The Earth will not change,' Sanchez purred. 'You cannot transform the belief system of twelve billion people in a day, or even a lifetime. You cannot stop them from fearing or hating. They will cling to what they know even if their planet stands upon the brink of destruction, as the last hundred years have shown us time and time again. So, if these Transcended intend to destroy mankind, let them try.'

He grinned broadly. 'If your Galatean friends wish to try to *save us* by imposing a government through force, let them try it. History has plenty of examples of where that leads. Or if your associates think to topple my church by destroying me and my palace, I *welcome* them. They will be doing my job for me.

'I am an old man, Ulanu. Holding the Kingdom together has been hard. Determining what to do with the church in the aftermath of war was already proving even harder. But killing me would create a martyr who would never die. It would crystallise my followers' faith and make my words live for ever. So you see, there is little for the Galateans' ludicrous behemoth to do, except perhaps fulfil the alien threat in advance and scour this world of life. Short of that, the only result they can obtain is to make us hate them.'

His smile vanished. 'And we already know how to do that. So leave, traitor. And take your laughable warhorse with you.'

Will found himself dismayed. There was an awful kind of truth behind the Prophet's words. The crusades had never been based on sound reasoning. Had they been fools to imagine that Earth would suddenly come to its senses just because they told it to?

Suddenly, Ulanu spoke. 'Are you finished, your Honesty?' he asked in clipped tones. 'Then permit me to reply. Your prediction regarding the truculence of the Following is enlightening, though it tells me more about your opinion of the people you rule than it does about them. However, it leads me to believe that you have failed to grasp the fundamental purpose of this visit.

'Let me present you with a simple choice. Option one is that you make a statement to the people of Earth yourself. You bring an end to hostilities immediately, renounce your claim on the colony worlds and withdraw your troops. You also announce the existence of extraterrestrial life, warn humanity of the threat from the Transcended and amend doctrine accordingly. In return for this, Galatea will sign a zero-exploitation contract with Earth. It will also agree to share the sum total of its robotics and genetic technologies with Earth for no cost.

'Option two is that you choose not to speak. In that case, the Galateans will destroy what is left of the Kingdom fleet. They will blockade aid from the colony worlds and put anti-aircraft sats into Earth orbit.'

Will's eyes widened in surprise. They'd discussed none of these measures against Earth with the general. He was making it all up himself.

'After that, we will broadcast the truth and leave for several years,' Ulanu continued. 'You may believe your church is solid enough to withstand such a test, your Honesty, but from my observation of it, it is already on the brink of self-destruction. Upon our return, I would not be surprised to find that the Earth has driven itself back into the Stone Age through purposeless squabbling. I doubt there would be much talk of Truism when we offer free food, aid and passage to the colonies for volunteers.'

The Prophet's expression didn't change one iota as Ulanu spoke. However, the king's eyebrows crept up into his hair.

'You have two hours to make up your mind,' Ulanu told Sanchez. 'Failure to communicate will be regarded as tacit selection of option two.' He stabbed the off key on his keyboard.

Will noticed that the man was shaking. He felt like congratulating the general but knew that nothing he could say would make Ulanu feel any better about what he was doing.

No one spoke for a while after that. Will felt the atmosphere in the *Ariel Two*'s bridge grow intolerably tense. The massive fleet of Earther ships held its position, while other munitions were ferried in from the outer planets.

If the Earthers did decide to fight, the *Ariel Two* would surely not survive another concerted attack in its current condition. His sensor SAPs counted over five thousand antimatter warheads out there. That was enough to crack open a small moon.

Time crawled tortuously by. Ulanu watched them silently like a ghost.

Will's hope turned to horror as the zero hour slid up to meet them.

'Guess that's it, then,' Ira said heavily. 'Will, you'd better get back to those g-ray banks. Let's try to not kill too many civilians as we leave.'

Will swallowed hard and turned his attention to the weapons

array. In the solitude of his mental vault, he watched the final seconds count down. He flexed a pair of virtual hands. The nestship tingled in readiness all around him.

Three seconds before the deadline, a call arrived.

'Hold your fire!' Ulanu shouted as he hit the button on his console.

On the screen, a single face appeared. It was the king. His cheeks were flushed. A bloody scratch marred his cheek. His hair was in disarray.

'Galatean Starship *Ariel Two*,' he said, slightly out of breath. 'This is King Ramon the First of Earth. The Prophet has been restrained. Please hold your fire and stand by.'

The message ended. Everyone aboard the *Ariel Two* sat in stunned silence. Will looked at Ulanu. Ulanu stared back at him with something between ironic amusement and tragedy showing in his eyes.

'Did we do it?' said Rachel. 'Is that it?'

Will had no idea.

Abruptly, a broadcast message filled the public channels, sending to the entire Earth system. It was the king again.

'People of Earth!' he said. The scratch had miraculously disappeared from his cheek and a cloak of gold and blue had been hastily pulled around his shoulders. His hair looked tidier.

'This is an emergency broadcast. In the last few minutes, the Prophet Sanchez has received a vision from the Lord. To reward us for our victory, the Lord has made shocking new information available to mankind. This information will result in an immediate and glorious change of religious priorities for the Kingdom. Having been taught a lesson, the fifteen colonies will be granted independence by celestial decree, and the Prophet is hereby retiring from office to pursue a new spiritual quest.'

Will didn't hear the rest because the bridge of the *Ariel Two* erupted in cheering. Rachel sprang out of her couch and grabbed him in her arms, at least so far as his nerve-tendrils would allow. He gingerly pried his arms free of the couch and hugged her back, his fingers trailing moist alien flesh.

'It's really over this time, isn't it?' she said.

'Yes,' Will replied. 'It's really over.'

21: CAREFULLY EVER AFTER

21.1: IRA

Ira was at the Fleet station when the last of the arks finally returned home. He waited in the transit lounge with a squad of military police behind him. He knew from *Evacuation Ark Three* security that John had boarded this shuttle, so he'd be here somewhere.

Ira scrutinised every face that came through the doorway. Then, near the back, a man appeared with the right height and the right walk.

Ira squinted at him. The face was similar to John's but not quite right, and the hair was dark rather than blond. But he'd been told to expect that – he'd read John's security report the moment he got home and learned all about John's change of face and his daring capture of the Earther scout ship.

He'd also read the lies. Strangely, it wasn't the ones about New Angeles that upset Ira most. It was the ones about the threat from Will and the Transcended.

The man sauntered out into the transit lounge along with the others until he noticed Ira's eyes boring into him. His footsteps slowed to a halt. A sheepish smile came to his face.

'Hey, Captain,' he said. 'Nice to see you.'

It was John all right. Ira would recognise that expression anywhere. He strode straight up to the man and threw his full strength behind a punch to his jaw. John flew backwards and landed hard against a bank of seats. He shook his head and gingerly fingered his face.

He blinked up at Ira from the floor. 'I guess I had that coming,' he said.

Ira had prepared a dozen things to say. Now he couldn't remember any of them.

'You lost me my ship and my best friend,' he stated simply. 'I should kill you for that.'

John's bruised face twisted into a broken, guilty smile. 'I tried to do what was best for the mission,' he said. 'And for Galatea.'

'Is that why you lied to the authorities the moment you arrived?' Ira asked.

John grimaced. 'I couldn't have told them the whole story. They'd never have understood.'

'No,' Ira growled. 'I don't suppose they would. If your little trick had paid off, we'd have lost Galatea. And you'd have left the human race to be fried.'

John's face contorted. 'You don't know that, Captain. The aliens can't be trusted! They *hacked* us, for crissakes! They hacked *Will*!'

To Ira's surprise, he saw that John was almost crying. Ira shook his head in contempt. That was John – paranoid to the last.

'Tell it to the court,' he said and gestured to the military police. 'You can take him away now, Sergeant.'

The police stepped forward and pulled John up off the floor.

'Ira, believe me,' John implored him. 'I'm sorry for what I did.'

'So am I.'

'I did it for Galatea!'

Ira looked the other way as they dragged him from the room. In truth, he was sure John believed in what he'd done. But how to end the mission had never been John's decision to make. It had been Ira's.

He squinted hard at nothing and tried not to think of Amy, his great arms folded across his chest.

The sergeant stepped up behind him. 'Are you coming to the debriefing, sir?'

'No,' said Ira. 'Nor the trial. I've already made my statement.'

'But, sir—'

'I've got too much to do on the new ship,' Ira explained. In truth, he didn't want to attend. And ever since the Fleet had started work on *Ariel Three*, his plate had been conveniently full of other things to think about. 'I'm hoping to be gone by the end of the month.'

The Fleet had been on a mad building spree since the end of the war. With traffic to and from Earth due to increase and new frontiers opened up, there was a lot of call for starships. The remains of Tang's fleet were being recycled into new vessels with all haste.

'But, sir,' said the sergeant. 'Inspector Voigt-Drue said told me he was expecting—'

Ira managed a smile. 'Didn't you see the news?' he said, cutting the policeman off again. 'A whole new galactic shell has been discovered and I intend to be the first person out there.'

With that, he slapped the sergeant on the shoulder and walked away. He'd done what he came here to do. He'd made his peace with Amy. Now it was time to look to the future. There was exploring to do.

21.2: GUSTAV

The fanfare of horns eventually died down and Gustav entered the throne room. For the last time, he began the long climb up the stepped pyramid that led to the Prophet's throne. A golden spotlight followed his solemn progress. A choir of voices too perfect to be natural sang his praises throughout his ascent.

Gustav loathed this kind of pomp even more now he was the star of it. However, his new social engineering team assured him it was necessary, at least in the short term. The people had been conditioned to it. Their expectations would have to be changed slowly. Gustav intended to make damn sure it happened.

Just like last time, the chamber was filled with courtiers from all the subsects of Earth, dressed in their awful gaudy outfits. Unlike last time, the expressions on their faces were ones of thinly disguised fear and uncertainty.

Their mood was well matched by Gustav's own. Who knew what the consequences of this sharp political turn would be? A return to the chaos of the past? That wasn't something they could afford any more.

No doubt some of the courtiers' concerns related to Gustav's suitability as a world leader. Gustav shared them. He wasn't looking forward to wielding so much authority. He hated politics. He didn't want to be trusted by the Galateans, either. He still disliked everything they stood for. But to his great chagrin, they apparently liked him.

From the moment Monet had suggested it back aboard the nest-ship, Gustav had struggled to avoid a high-profile role in the new government. Then Monet made his recommendation to Ramon and the king's team had latched on to the idea immediately. Gustav would make a perfect new Prophet, they said. He was symbolically ideal – the man who'd returned to Earth carrying the seeds of the new faith. He was also the only man on Earth who'd dealt with the Transcended in person, however unsuccessfully.

Ramon had been particularly pleased by the idea. Gustav suspected it suited the man just fine to be answering to a Prophet less politically capable than he was. It retained the status quo whilst increasing Ramon's share of power. That alone was reason enough for Gustav to be nervous about the appointment.

Unfortunately, he couldn't find the flaw in Will's logic. Would he prefer to see one of his peers in the role? He couldn't think of a single one of them he trusted, or would rely on to treat the Transcended threat rationally. Even Oz wouldn't be right for the job. He was too much of an appeaser. Non-natives were out, too. A Galatean would last about five minutes in power before he met with some kind of unfortunate accident. Which meant it had to be Gustav.

At the top step, Ramon was waiting for him, his face unreadably regal. Above that was the throne where the Prophet sat. Sanchez had been carefully drugged and groomed for this ceremony. It wouldn't do for the old man to end his reign with a loss of dignity.

The public story was that he was leaving power because God had shown him the flaw in his teachings. He was passing on the torch to someone chosen by God to reveal a new truth to mankind. It wasn't a story Sanchez liked, but then he hadn't played any part in making it up.

Gustav reached the top of the steps. In round, ponderous tones, the king began his proclamation to the crowd about the coming of a new spiritual leader, etc., etc. Gustav barely listened. Instead he knelt as expected, his face upturned to the Prophet's.

'The Earth will crumble under your hands,' Sanchez whispered to him bitterly. Those dark eyes of his were as full of fire as ever, despite him being doped to the brim with mood-controllers.

'Maybe,' Gustav whispered back. 'But at least this time we will build on knowledge, and not ignorance.'

Sanchez sneered at him. 'Fool! Ignorance is reliable. Knowledge is not.'

Gustav managed a smile. 'Ignorance is death,' he said. 'And you are the fool if you believe otherwise.'

Gustav was glad of the opportunity to tell the old man that. It had taken him days to reconcile his actions to himself, but in the end, he had done it. If he did not like the way the future looked, he realised, it was his responsibility to grab it with both hands and do his best to change it. It was all he'd ever done his entire life. Nothing had changed when he surrendered at Galatea except the tools at his disposal – and, arguably, the ones he had now were better.

Ramon's speech ended. The king reached down and helped Sanchez out of his seat. The neural stinger in Ramon's sleeve aimed at the Prophet's neck was not visible from the broadcast cameras in the walls.

With Ramon's insistent help, Sanchez knelt before Gustav as Gustav took his place on the throne. The throne room erupted into carefully orchestrated cheering. The unnatural choir let loose with a triumphant anthem. Truism was dead. Long live Transcendism.

Gustav looked out across his room full of courtiers and found himself smiling just a little. He already knew a few of the decrees he wanted to make. His first would be to allocate the bottom twenty floors of the Holy Palace for housing the poor, whose prote-farms still covered the countryside in every direction. His second would be to reintroduce education for girls.

He raised his hand in salute as the king helped the ex-Prophet Sanchez slowly descend the stairs before him.

21.3: WILL

Galatea had only ever boasted two real restaurants and one of them hadn't survived the brief Earther occupation. Will and Rachel sat in the one that remained. It nestled in the middle of a park in the trench town of New Beginning under a canopy of genetically engineered Joshua trees. Hundreds of tiny lanterns had been woven around the branches.

Will looked at Rachel across a table littered with the remains of dessert and held her hand. She looked back at him.

She had voluntarily put on a dress that evening, something Will had never seen her do in his memories, or Doug's. She'd even applied a little make-up. It wasn't her usual style, but then it was a very special occasion: their first real evening alone since returning home.

Of course, they'd had snatches of private time here and there, but they'd spent all of those in bed. This was their first actual date, despite the fact they'd been home for three weeks. The days since they arrived had been swallowed up in an endless round of parties, functions and celebrations. It was as if the whole planet wanted to meet the heroes, and most of them felt they had a right to.

As well as Honorary President of the Roboteer's League and Chairman of the new Department of Xenocultural Studies at Galatea University, Will had also been made Ambassador to the Transcended – a job he already had. The Galateans had given the role to him anyway, with a ceremony that lasted for several dull hours.

He and Rachel had talked so much all day that now they were finding it hard to muster conversation. It didn't help that life kept threatening to sweep them both on. Will had his new post, along with a public acknowledgement of his command of the *Ariel Two*. Rachel had received a promotion to captain.

'So what did Bryant say?' Rachel ventured.

'We're going back to the lure star to talk to the Relic,' Will replied. 'Even if the Transcended don't talk back, I'm going to send them a full memory log of my experiences. We figure that this way, they'll be better equipped to judge other species in the future.'

Will was still painfully aware that the technology that suffused both his ship and body was on loan. It was no surprise that he was on tenterhooks to find out what the enigmatic race had to say for itself next.

Nevertheless, he wished he wasn't leaving so soon. Rachel had been put in charge of the first Galatean starship to use the new alien technology. It was a very illustrious post, but it meant they'd be apart again for weeks.

'Did you manage to talk to Hugo about it?' she asked.

Will nodded. 'He's coming with me, as scientific advisor. Or as the "helpful sceptic", as he calls himself.'

Hugo had made it very clear he still believed the Transcended represented a potential threat, and now that Will had been given time to think about it, some of his points weren't so crazy. Gustav's remarks about the aliens had resonated, too. And even if one presumed they had the best motives, exactly what the Transcended expected humanity to do next was still completely unclear.

Nothing about the coming years looked easy. As Sanchez had pointed out, the Earth would not change overnight. They were standing at the brink of the greatest social upheaval in human history with no notion of the terms on which they were now expected to live.

Even so, Will was optimistic. He saw no real reason for the Transcended not to speak plainly. Surely such an advanced race had little to gain by subterfuge. When and if humanity needed guidance, they would be informed.

Nevertheless, the human race would have to tread very carefully from now on. It was time to grow up. Who knew what they'd encounter in the new galactic shell?

'Did he tell you when your new commission is supposed to start?' Rachel asked.

'Friday,' he said glumly.

'Good. That'll give me time to pack.'

Will blinked at her in surprise. 'What do you mean?'

She grinned at him. 'I've decided to come with you.'

'But... Don't you have a starship waiting for you up in orbit?'

She nodded. 'It'll be here when I get back. I'm not in a hurry.'

'But didn't Bryant say—'

Rachel laughed. 'Isn't this what the whole test thing was about? That human beings don't have to be rigidly defined by the systems they create? It's time to start living it, Will. The future's ours to define.'

She was right, of course. He leaned across the table to kiss her.

The music in the restaurant changed. The robotic band broke into a piece of slow jazz that he recognised immediately. Will pulled away from her lips to laugh.

'What?' she said, pouting. 'Do I kiss funny or something?'

Will shook his head. 'It's the music. This piece. I used it as inspiration for a program I wrote – the one that decrypted Ulanu's security. The one that got us into all that trouble in the first place.'

'This is what you were dancing to that day?' Rachel looked delighted.

'In a manner of speaking.'

Her eyes lit up. 'Then dance with me now.'

Will raised his hands. 'I don't know how.'

'You did it with robots, didn't you? How different can this be?' She took his hand and dragged him upright. 'Come on, Mr Ambassador. No excuses.'

Will laughed and let her pull him down to the dance floor. They stepped out together, and, clumsily at first, began to dance under a canopy of lights like little stars.

Turn the page for a preview of
the sequel to *Roboteer**

NEMESIS

* Not final text

0: PROLOGUE

0.1: TOM

The end of civilisation looked like two angry red points. Captain Tom Okano-Lark scowled at them as they sat there in the centre of his retinal display, unwelcome and persistent. From the warning tags clustered around them, he knew what they represented – a pair of small gunships racing toward him at about a tenth of the speed of light. Both vessels bristled with cheap tactical weapons showing fire-ready signatures.

It wasn't the response to his friendly hail that he'd hoped for. But then, after forty-six hours of surveying the Tiwanaku system, Tom hadn't held onto much hope. Since their arrival and the initial unpleasant surprise, his expectations for the outcome of the mission had darkened steadily, along with his mood.

The settlement on the planet in front of him shouldn't have existed. The fact that it did was going to make a lot of people very upset for one simple reason: it represented the end of thirty years of interstellar peace.

Wendy Kim, the *IPS Reynard*'s first officer, spoke up, breaking the silence.

'Four minutes to engagement radius, sir. Do you want to deploy gravity shields?'

Wendy ran the *Reynard*'s blunt sensor ops. Nobody had a more detailed or more disconcerting view of the approaching ships than she did. She lay prone on the crash-couch opposite Tom's on the other side of the Reynard's tiny central cabin. The other four crew members lay in the bunks stacked below them. None of them dared speak a word.

'Not yet,' said Tom. 'We have to play this *exactly* by the book. Otherwise they'll string us up the moment we get home.'

He hated risking his crew but the face-off had to be done right. That meant waiting and pretending the approach didn't look threatening until after a legally unambiguous dialog. The moment news of what they'd found got back to Mars, the finger-pointing would start. Shooting would follow.

Until Tiwanaku, unregistered squatter settlements - otherwise known as *Flag drops* - had always happened at well-established colonies. That way, the Flags could leech off the existing infrastructure and avoid the legal hassles that came with registering a new planet. IPSO law was remarkably forgiving when it came to protecting the inhabitants of an established world, no matter how they had got there. Frontier-jumping, on the other hand, was verboten. The fact that one of Earth's sects had now set up an independent world, without telling anyone, implied that they were finally ready to forgo the law altogether.

Tom hated how unfair that felt. He'd spent his career in the service of the Fleet, struggling to uphold the delicate balance of power between Earth and the Old Colonies. He'd spent far more of that time protecting Earthers than he had Colonials. Now Earth had gone and ruined it all. And for what? Money, as usual.

Had it been a simple scouting run, Tom would have turned back immediately and headed straight for New Panama, home to the Fleet's Far Frontier HQ. But the *Reynard* had come escorting families. A modified nestship ark, the *IPS Horton*, trailed behind them crammed with a thousand coma-stored colonists. And it had just dropped warp about 20 AU out. That meant his time for lying low had ended. Fecund nestships, even human-modified ones, did not arrive quietly. They left a gravity signature like a brick thrown at a pond.

'Sorry to put you all through this,' Tom told the others. 'Stay glued to your displays and wait for my word.' He knew his crew considered him a stubborn perfectionist. This time, though, they'd just have to put up with him. The stakes were simply too high.

As the ships raced toward them, he tried to get himself into a calm and diplomatic frame of mind. After all, who could blame the Flags for wanting to move here? Tiwanaku Four was a superb planet. It sat square in the habitable zone, swathed in salmon-coloured dunes, with a decent level of atmospheric nitrogen and fat, healthy ice-caps: a classic Mars Plus. It loomed in his display like a ripe peach. Not to mention the masses of Fecund artefacts drifting in the outer system, the signs of surface ruins on the planet itself, or the traces of non-terrestrial organic activity in the atmosphere.

Fecund ruins meant money. For decades now, mining the remains of that long-dead race for technological marvels had driven humanity's economy. Treated properly, Tiwanaku could become a thriving research centre and home for millions of Earth's struggling poor. But onto this gem of a world the Flags had dumped a clump of rickety habitat modules and a couple of thousand people, along with a cheap off-the-shelf industrial base that looked barely useable. Three orbital habitats hovered in geostationary orbit housing at least as many more settlers.

Given how much Earthers hated orbitals, that really said something. Whatever sect ran this place had clearly been shuttling people out here faster than they could put homes on the surface. And all this in the last nine months since the last survey pass, when the planet had been registered as 'colony pending'. The *Horton*'s passengers were going to be seriously peeved. Presuming they didn't all die first, of course.

'Their orbital suntap stations are targeting,' said Wendy. He could hear the strain in her voice. 'Even at this distance they might be able to nail us.'

Just the fact that they had suntap weapons here was insane. As far as Tom knew, nobody had been stupid enough to actually fire up a suntap weapon since the interstellar war. Keeping half a dozen suntap platforms and two orbital drone-stations for a tiny colony like this was like protecting a family-size hab-tent with a squad of titan mechs. The settlers had obviously expected trouble. They'd practically courted it.

Thank Gal they hadn't noticed the *Reynard*'s arrival until now, otherwise Tom knew he'd already have a disaster on his hands. Most of the time, he cursed the fact that scouts were little bigger than soft-combat ships. This time, it had probably saved his life.

'Sir,' said Faisal Koi, from the bunk beneath him. Faisal ran the fine sensors – the Reynard's most delicate and specialised scanning equipment. 'We've got audio from the incoming.'

'Let's hear it,' said Tom. Close enough to talk meant close enough to kill. He couldn't stall any longer.

'IPSO vessel, this is the captain of the war-shuttle *Sacred Truth*,' said the voice over the comm. 'You are in violation of our territory.'

The speaker sounded about fifteen. He had a heavy Earth accent, though Tom couldn't have guessed from which part. It didn't make much difference these days.

'You are instructed to leave this system,' said the Flag. 'Failure to comply will be interpreted as threatening action.' It sounded like he was reading from a prompt screen.

Tom flicked the comm. 'Whose territory is that, may I ask?'

'That not your business,' snapped the Flag.

'This is the *IPS Reynard*,' said Tom carefully. 'We are representatives of the Interstellar Pact Security Organization here in a peaceful escort capacity for the colony ark IPS Horton. We intend no violence. However, we are legally obliged to give you notice that your settlement is unregistered and therefore illegal. We also note that, A, you are occupying an unexplored alien ruin site in contravention of Social Safety Ordinances; B, that you are inhabiting a foreign biome without a license; and C, that you are using suntap technology at an unlisted star. All this will have to be reported. We strongly recommend that you power down your weapons and declare your funding body immediately. If you comply, you will not be held responsible for this settlement's existence.'

He didn't expect a reasonable answer but he had to try. Flags seldom understood the game they were caught up in. They were suckers a long way from home who believed they'd won a future among the stars. Meanwhile, the real bad guys made a fortune off them. A peaceful outcome would help everybody. Even so, Tom's finger hovered over the button for the gravity shields.

The reply came fast. The optical lag on comms had dropped to a matter of seconds.

'This an independent human settlement!' The Flag shouted. 'We don't recognise your IPSO and don't want your colony ark. If you don't charge engines in two minute, we open fire.'

Tom glanced at Wendy. Two days of stress had drawn lines on her usually serene oval face. Her dark eyebrows sat knitted together into a single, intense line.

'Can you believe this?' he said.

'I think they'll do it, sir. These Flags are set up for a fight. They've been waiting for this.'

'Send a warning to the *Horton*,' said Tom. 'Tell Sundeep to keep his engines warm and plot a course back to sanity.'

He flicked the channel back open. '*Sacred Truth*, please be reasonable. Consider the consequences of this course of action. We're not here to make trouble. If you make us leave at gunpoint, we'll have to come back here with a frigate and evacuate all of you.'

Not to mention that the breakdown of IPSO control would likely kick off a bloody scramble for control of the remaining Fecund stars and the alien riches they sheltered. They weren't supposed to acknowledge that fact in negotiations, even if everyone knew it.

'Your words mean nothing, Fleetie!' yelled the voice over the comm. It trembled with rage. The video stayed blank. 'We know you here to kill us but we defend our home to the last man. Go now and spare yourself a fight. No more talk. I mean it!'

Tom couldn't remember hearing a man sound so scared. Yet they were the ones pointing all the guns. He'd heard that Flags received a lot of political conditioning but someone had wound this guy up to breaking point.

'*Sacred Truth*, we acknowledge your request. As a sign of peaceful intentions, we will remove to a safe distance.'

'You will leave!' The Flag screamed.

'Okay, *Sacred Truth*, we're heading out. Please do not open fire. I am legally required to give you the opportunity to make a statement of claim before disciplinary action becomes unavoidable. If you want to keep any rights over the world you've settled...'

He let the sentence hang as he fired up the engines.

'Jawid, buffers to full strength. We're leaving. And quickly, please.'

'On it,' said his roboteer. 'Casimir buffers sizzling in five.'

'Brace for thrust, everyone.'

Throughout the four-kilometre sphere of the *Reynard*'s mesohull, robots raced to their action stations. Around the tiny central refuge of the ship's habitat core a dozen huge rad-shielding machines hummed into life, swaddling the cabin in a protective foam of pseudo-vacuum bubbles.

Their timing made all the difference. Two seconds after the *Reynard*'s shields saturated, a radiation wave slammed into the ship. Red warning icons splattered across Tom's display like blood spots. The buffers cracked like thunder just beyond the cabin walls. Warning clangs filled the air.

Tom blinked in confusion. 'Jawid, what was that?'

'Buffers at forty percent, sir! Compensating.'

'We've lost fine-sensor function,' said Faisal. 'Looks like g-rays. They fried the primary bank. Compensating with secondaries.'

Tom flicked the comm back on and set it to broadcast. 'Unregistered colony, I said *do not open fire*! We are prepping to depart.'

Silence filled the channel.

'I don't think it was them, sir,' said Wendy nervously. 'I'm picking up damage signs from their ships. That blast fried them worse than it did us.'

Tom selected one of the cameras that still worked and zoomed in for a closer look. Sure enough, both gunships had started drifting. One showed a rebooting engine. The other showed no activity at all.

His brow furrowed. 'Then who nuked us?'

'Scanning now,' said Wendy. 'Pinpointing the origin of the blast.'

She paused, her breath held. Tom glanced across and saw her frowning into her data.

'Sir, I think you should take a look at this.'

She posted a view to his display.

On the other side of the system, about ten AU from Tiwanaku's star, a cloud of *something* twinkled. Whatever it was, at that range it had to have fired its blast more than an hour earlier, and with prescient accuracy. Either that, or the wave had been broadcast – scouring the entire system.

'Those bursts look a lot like tiny warp flashes,' said Wendy. 'And I'm seeing visible growth in the cloud radius.'

In other words, it was headed their way. They could have company any minute.

Tom checked the *Horton*'s position. Compensating for light lag, it was still more than half an hour from the blast-wave.

'Jawid, prep a message drone,' he said quickly. 'Overcook its engines and send it to the *Horton*. If we give Sundeep just a minute's warning on that radiation, it'll be worth it.'

'On it.'

'Wendy, Faisal, I want to know what that cloud is.'

'Whoever they are, they're sending video on tight-beam,' said Faisal. 'We're getting it and so is the colony.'

'Patch it through.'

In the video window that opened before him, Tom saw a grainy picture of a young man lying on a concrete floor. He squirmed backward away from the camera with panic in his eyes. He raised a desperate hand as if to ward off a blow, then nothing. The video reset and started over. Played over the top of it was a track of warbling, poor-quality audio – the sort you might hear from a broken vending machine.

'Trespass detected,' the audio cheerfully informed them. 'Punishment cycle initiated. Damage imminent.'

The message looped over and over in the same flat, chirpy tones.

Tom's skin prickled. Their situation suddenly felt sinister. First a colony that wasn't supposed to exist, and now this? It almost smacked of some kind of prank. But pranks didn't usually start with a near-fatal radiation blast.

'Hold on, everybody. I'm putting some distance between us and whatever *that* is.'

Tom pointed his ship back toward the *Horton* and fired the engines. The thud of warp kicked them into their crash-couches. The slow steady rhythm of gravity bursts picked up tempo, but not nearly fast enough. While the illegal colony shrank, the twinkling cloud kept growing. Whatever it was, it had to be closing on the star incredibly fast.

Tom stared at the cloud anxiously.

'Any guesses, people? What are we looking at?'

'It looks like a munitions burst,' said Wendy. 'SAP analysis suggests a classic drone swarm, but it's way too big for that. I'm seeing warp flashes from more than ten thousand sources and no ship signature behind them. Just empty space.'

'So this is a local phenomenon?' said Tom.

'Unclear,' said Wendy. 'We saw no signs of anything like this from our early system scan. There'd have to be some kind of base for these things to hide in, and we didn't find one. No moon, no engine signature, no comms, nothing. They just sort of... appeared.'

'Could they have come from the Fecund ruins?'

Wendy shook her head. 'Very unlikely. That cloud came in way above the ecliptic. There's nothing up there. We looked.'

'I'm matching the flashes to known drone profiles,' said Faisal. 'They're weird. They don't look like anything in the book. The radiation spikes are too short and bright. Whatever they are, we didn't build them. Sir, do you think this was what the Flags were paranoid about?'

'No idea,' said Tom. 'Wendy, are those things following us? Are we clear?'

'Hard to say. They seem focused on the planet. I'm taking a closer look... They're closing on T-four now, sir. Orbital insertion in five, four, three...' Wendy gripped the edge of her bunk. 'Whoa!' she shouted.

'Share it with us, Ms. Kim,' said Tom sharply. 'Don't make us guess.'

She posted a view to Tom's display. It was a drone cloud alright. A huge one. The space around the planet had been filled with some kind of warp-enabled munitions. Both colony gunships were already balls of slowly blossoming flame. Beams lanced out from the suntap stations, frantically trying to lock onto the blur of targets. Drones exploded everywhere, but there were far too many to fight. Tom watched one station detonate after another, bathing the planet below in scorching light.

'There are over two thousand people down there,' he said. 'Jawid, I want a full record of this event on a secure message drone. Immediate release. Destination: New Panama system, Frontier Fleet HQ.'

'On it.'

'Keep a channel open to it. I want them to see and hear everything.

Faisal, do these profiles match any speculated Fecund drive signatures?'

'Sir?' said Faisal. He sounded confused.

'I want to know who the Flags pissed off. Is it possible that someone was living here already? Someone the original survey flights missed?'

'Sir, the Fecund went extinct ten million years ago.'

'I know that,' Tom snapped. 'Check anyway. And look back over those scans you did. Is it possible that the out-system ruins actually belonged to someone else?'

'N-no, sir. The match was very tight. And no, Fecund warp wasn't that different from ours, sir. If anything, it was messier. Though if they'd somehow survived for ten million years, who knows what they'd have?'

Tom knew he was clutching at straws. 'Maybe another human colony who was here before us, then? One with its own weapons tech?'

Even as he said it, he knew that answer wasn't right either. For a start, colonies with weapons this advanced wouldn't have trouble with Flags. But still, the threat had to be human, didn't it? Otherwise, how had they sent a message in English, no matter how cryptic?

'Give me a matching tight-beam,' said Tom. 'I'm going to talk to them.'

'Sir!' said Wendy. 'I have to point out that we don't even know if there's a pilot on that swarm. It could be autonomous. If it is, you could trigger target awareness.'

'They might not spot us without help, Lieutenant, but they're sure as shit going to notice the *Horton*. That ark lights up like a Christmas tree every time it warps. That means we either assess the threat now, or get ready to defend the *Horton* against whatever those things are.'

He thumbed the comm. 'Unidentified drone swarm, this is Captain Tom Okano-Lark of the *Interstellar Pact Ship Reynard*. We are unaware of the political situation in this system but know that there are civilians on that planet. Please end your assault. If there has been an injustice here, be reassured that the full weight of IPSO law will be applied. We will assist you in making whatever amends are necessary. I repeat: please end your assault.'

He waited for the message to creep at light-speed toward the swarm, his heart in his mouth. Next to him, Wendy shifted uneasily on her bunk. Meanwhile, the message kept repeating.

'Trespass detected. Punishment cycle initiated. Damage imminent.'

'Sir!' said Wendy. 'Some of the drones have changed course. They're headed this way. I recommend immediate retreat.' Her tone said what she didn't need to: *told you so*.

Tom spat curses. 'Hold on, everybody. We're positioning to defend the *Horton*. Wendy, let Sundeep know we're coming. Engaging combat mode.'

The *Reynard* was a small ship, but it was tough. It had been designed for two things: environmental scanning and punching well above its weight when necessary. Changes rippled through the vessel, from the tiny cabin kernel right out to the exohull surface kilometres above them.

Tom's arms went numb as his simulated replacements came on line. His skeletal reinforcements kicked on with a jolt. He felt a sudden flush on his cheeks as the micromesh around his augmented heart started pumping. All around the cabin, his crew sank back into their couches as the same happened to each of them. Machinery buried in every crew member's body woke up and flexed.

Tom boosted the engines. He threw as much power at the drive as he could without giving someone a concussion. It was like piloting a road-driller.

'Deploy countermeasures,' he ordered. 'Disrupters at maximum spread.'

'Already on it,' said Jawid.

'We have company,' Wendy said grimly. 'Sending you the bearing.'

The Casimir buffers snapped like the jaws of dragons.

'Shields at twenty percent, sir,' said Jawid.

'Engaging evasives.' Tom picked a program at random and fired it. Better to live with broken limbs than not at all.

The cabin filled with the clamour of alarms.

'Faisal,' he said. 'I want g-ray scatter. Lots of it. Don't spare the juice.'

'On it.'

Tom grimaced as he watched the horrid blur of action outside his ship. The drones were nearly impossible to hit. They jumped around like crickets.

'Drones headed for the *Horton*, sir,' said Wendy. 'No sign that they've been able to manoeuvre. The radiation wave might have hit them. They're not responding.'

'Shit,' said Tom. 'Diving to intercept.'

His virtual hands flashed over the keyboard, modifying their tumbling flight into one that would head off the threat. He struggled to breathe as gravity pulses hurled him from side to side. Outside, the drones from nowhere flashed ever closer. The growl of the drive became a deafening roar as the ship's autopilot SAP struggled to compensate.

'Deploy everything,' said Tom, his artificial breath labouring. 'Jawid, recondition gravity-shield buoys for self-destruct. Release them all. We're going to buy the *Horton* as much time as we can.'

Tom watched the buoys tear away from his hull in dizzying arcs.

'Fuck you,' he told the drone swarm. 'Leave my colonists alone.'

Space lit up with a cascade of eye-searing nuclear blasts.

The closest drones popped and died like soap bubbles but hundreds more raced up to replace them, apparently undeterred.

They winked and flashed like a cloud of fairy dust closing itself around him. It was the last thing that Captain Tom Lark ever saw.